D0571650

MANHATTAN ON THE ROCKS

MANHATTAN ON THE ROCKS

MICHAEL MUSTO

HENRY HOLT AND COMPANY   NEW YORK

Thanks to my editor, Tracy Bernstein,
and my agent, Jim Stein,
who—even more than deadlines
—were always there.

LIBRARY OF CONGRESS CATALOGING-IN-PUBLICATION DATA
MUSTO, MICHAEL, 1955—
MANHATTAN ON THE ROCKS / MICHAEL MUSTO.—1ST ED.
P. CM.
ISBN 0-8050-1032-7
I. TITLE.
PS3563.U845M36 1989
813'.54—DC19   89-1813
                                                              CIP

HENRY HOLT BOOKS ARE AVAILABLE AT SPECIAL DISCOUNTS
FOR BULK PURCHASES FOR SALES PROMOTIONS, PREMIUMS,
FUND-RAISING, OR EDUCATIONAL USE. SPECIAL EDITIONS
OR BOOK EXCERPTS CAN ALSO BE CREATED TO SPECIFICATION.

FOR DETAILS CONTACT:

SPECIAL SALES DIRECTOR
HENRY HOLT AND COMPANY, INC.
115 WEST 18TH STREET
NEW YORK, NEW YORK 10011

FIRST EDITION

DESIGNED BY KATY RIEGEL
PRINTED IN THE UNITED STATES OF AMERICA
1 3 5 7 9 10 8 6 4 2

TO
MY PARENTS,
CIRO AND ANNA,
WHO WILL NEVER
BE ON THE
ROCKS.

They do, I watch. They dress, scream, carouse, screw, I take notes.

I am the ringleader, the mirror to their marauding, the reflection of their cavalcade. Someone swings from a chandelier, and I muster a wry smile. A woman squirts milk from her breasts at a nightclub audience, and I simply nod knowingly and involuntarily reach for my pen. I am neither over- nor underwhelmed, just whelmed. I don't have sex, I don't drink, I don't do drugs. I don't do. I watch.

As publisher of *Manhattan on the Rocks*—yes, a dread "counterculture magazine"—I've become friend to the zanies, sycophant to the stars, and anathema to anyone wearing Ralph Lauren. Printing my gut reactions to all things bright and beautiful without much regard for advertiser appeasement or social climbing has made me Someone—Someone to distrust, Someone to loathe, Someone for press whores to line up for a visitation with and plead with for a mention, any mention, as long as the proverbial spelling is correct and it's in boldface, preferably 14-point Optima boldface (press whores know these things). These people adore me; a former English lit major, my spelling is as flawless as my way with a new-wave polka at five in the morning for an audience of one. That much I'll do.

Since dropping out of Dartmouth in the second half of my fifth year (still a junior, because of silly things like credits) I've been on a circular party coaster that stops only so I can compile my magazine and occasionally read it, with bodily functions an annoying but only intermittent interruption. Dartmouth was too American provincial, the frat parties I now and then deigned to attend reeked depressingly of impending beer bellies, an English lit degree is ultimately as useful as Mace, and finally I started resenting the mornings I had to race cross-campus to exams without quality time to stop and learn the Oscar nominations and other crucial info that could cement my education. Proust suited me fine, but Robert De Niro's self-imposed weight fluctuations held an even more fascinating fixation. Stendhal was nifty, but more importantly, was Cher really going to wear that hairdo and be a serious actress at the same time?

As someone who studied Simon and Garfunkel lyrics as poetry in the not very esoteric New York City public school system, I was ill-prepared for the required battery of Greek and Roman classics, which most of my blue-eyed classmates could recite with the same élan with which I could list Johnny Depp's film credits (did you know he was in *Platoon?*) and all Hollywood Squares who'd ever had prescription-drug dependencies. *The Enquirer* became my Monarch Notes to a world of glitz and scandal that was so much realer than those in any English lit classic. The Scarlet Letter A was never to be emblazoned across my chest; I was getting C pluses.

So I split. I always suspected the school had only let me in to fulfill their quota of people from Queens (one) anyway. To the chagrin of my family of well-fed Italians—a family that had never been to college, just weddings—I crash-landed back in New York, past Cerberus and into the gates of Kips Bay (Manhattan's forgotten, thank God, neighbor-

2

hood). No one has discovered Kips Bay and no one ever will, so it's a perfect watching ground from which you're under no one else's scrutiny. It's the only audience left in New York—everything else is onstage begging for applause.

My parents didn't want me to leave my liberal arts training, but then they hadn't wanted me to enter my liberal arts training in the first place. My father would have been far happier had I followed his footsteps and joined the DiBlasios' illustrious line of pharmacists—a dynasty of shameless drug dealers (no Squares, but numerous Mafia princesses, served). My mother, meanwhile, wanted me to take *her* lead and become a professional neurotic, wringing hands and biting lips for a living. But since I'd weaseled into one of the top six of the eight Ivy League schools and had already used up so much of their hard-earned money on expenses, it wasn't so perverse of them to want me to follow through with it and be a college-educated pharmacist-slash-neurotic. "My son, the dropout" became my new verbal tattoo, my designation in the Who's Who of bridge-and-tunnel hell.

I was never going to please them, a reality made all the more horrifying because I'm their one and only, and they don't even have pets, just those stickpin rhinos my mother cranked out once in a fit of community-workshop obsession. To a family of failures, I was the biggest failure of all; they weren't even wannabes, just contented cows gleefully chewing their cud in the urban backyard of Astoria, but I—I was a could-have-been. I could have been the best pharmacist they ever produced, I could have been the biggest professional neurotic that ever lived. And here I was, a dropout, a runaway, a party boy with scads of carelessly groomed facial hair. They wanted me to die brutally. How it pained them, then, that their own *Enquirer* worship made me some kind of family prodigy. My mother, the Rupert Pupkin of Astoria, begged me once for Peggy Lee's lipstick imprint or a swatch of Don Ho's hair—"from anywhere," she said, "even his nose." "Fuck you," I shrieked. "I wouldn't go *near* his nose."

To push the folks' heads even deeper into the mud trough, I was going to become the most famous, most compulsive partygoer in the highly competitive world of full-time partygoers. Schmoozing it up with the people who never sleep, I partied with uptowners, I partied with downtowners, I partied with drag queens with bigger pudenda than both my parents had in their prime, I partied with every ounce of that four and a half years' worth of pent-up Ivy League libido until each night's parties seemed to segue seamlessly into the next night's, and there were no exams to grill me on who wore what and whether their shoes matched their colostomy bags. The Spanish Inquisition, WASP version, was over. Unlike *Jeopardy,* where even the answers have to be phrased like questions, I was playing a game where there were only answers—who, what, when, and how they were spelled—and I was drowning in them, eating them up like a social ringworm on an endless sucking-and-gloating mission.

Anxious for something more demanding to do than "working the room"—an art which, once you've mastered it, you can only repeat—I founded *Manhattan on the Rocks,* a publication designed as a shrine to all that information, told my way. I write most of the columns, do the layouts, and even buy copies to inflate sales statistics, relying on others only to take pictures (I can't focus) and sell ads (too tedious for words). For backing, I used money left me by my favorite fat Uncle Vito (out of two fat Uncle Vitos)—the one who got stuck in the closet and had to be crowbarred out by police amid much embarrassment by my family, many of whom are still fuming that I got his entire lump-sum savings and property in Queens, but weren't too mad to ask me for lipstick imprints of *their* favorite stars.

Uncle Vito liked me because I'd sit and watch porno

movies with him and speculate about why the female star had a penis. He liked me because I didn't patronize him, and I only joke about the closet incident now because I know he would have found it amusing had it happened to someone other than himself. If *I* were to get stuck, I'd find it hilarious, because I always feel as if the things happening to me are really happening to someone else and I'm just watching. I feel like I'm a character in a movie I paid to see. If I were to get hit by a car, I'd laugh, because I love action movies.

My favorite fat Uncle Vito is still subsidizing my career down here in Satan's playground, and I just know he's chuckling up in the big, overstuffed closet in the sky, laughing those big, blowsy laughs that could knock you down a flight of stairs. All other expenses are covered by the comp syndrome that goes hand in hand with my entitled way of life. I go to clubs free. I eat at free buffet events and drink rivers of cranberry juice at open bars. Other people pay for my cabs. (That "I only have a twenty" routine works every time.) I buy fashion off the street, and I de-louse it by soaking it in salad dressing, then rinsing clean. The only things I'm not "on the list" for are rent and newspapers, but I've found certain newsstands where you can read the essential columns without them yelling, "Hey, this isn't a library" in five languages. And once *Manhattan on the Rocks* started turning a profit, I convinced myself I'd be living in block-long limos with wet bars and VCRs and maybe even conference call, and not have to worry about rent at all. ("Only in My Dreams," as the very annoying Debbie Gibson sings.)

Meanwhile, I live from hand to mouth, from party to party. Blessed with the social conscience of a flea, I find all the turmoil at my doorstep just a loud and ugly incentive to party harder and throw larger confetti. As more and more crack hotels open two blocks away on fashionable Park Avenue—the kind of residences you can only approach holding an umbrella, because a baby is methodically thrown out of a window about every twenty minutes—I find it a more persuasive argument for staying out till dawn with nary a thought in my mind. As enough homeless people stagger down my street to make it look like a Black Hole of Calcutta version of the set for *Ironweed,* and seemingly costumed-by-Equity extras go so far as to perform intricately thought-out rap songs to ensnare your attention (''I'm not gonna steal— your watch—and hock it/If you would just insert some coins into my pocket. . . .''), I can only long for the party crowd, who could never summon the brainpower to come up with a rap song and are therefore not nearly as intrusive to my own private walls, the tower I'd constructed around myself to ward off anything too ugly or demanding.

As AIDS kept adding to the city's devastation with pain and anger and depression, I wanted to forget, to ignore, to dance—the dance not of a person who didn't care, but who *chose* not to care, because a life of constant caring was draining and demoralizing and ultimately didn't change anything. In the make-believe world of glitter balls and fake celebs, you could change things, turn a mental knob and make it quieter, louder, more intimate, or more frivolous at whim. By magnifying a relatively trivial world and making it earth-shaking, you never had to worry about anything more important than the next outfit, the next invite, the next hangover remedy (two Nuprin and a Vitamin B-complex pill work just fine for me lately—all right, I do occasionally accept substances when forced, but I still consider that a passive activity). You were always OK until the last streamer was tossed and then you just found another party. You were never homeless.

But I'm getting heavy, and that's not what parties are about. They're about whomever you're talking to at the moment, whatever festive mood you can conjure up with the help of the decor, the company, and any other sensory-distracting stimuli at hand. They're about all the things you're escaping to, not the escape itself.

My first big New York party was at Carcinogen, a three-floor shopping mall–style enterprise set in an old car showroom that was now a display case for recalled trendies. If something reminded people of this club, they'd always say "How Carcinogenic!" and think it was so cute. But nothing really reminded anyone of this club, so it was always a bit of a stretch. Besides, my grandmother had died of cancer, and I never felt the name was as appealing a conversation piece as did those who had absolutely no sense of their own, or anyone's, mortality. So maybe I did have some kind of conscience. If I did, that would soon be taken care of.

The more tasteless, I would learn, the better. The more egregiously you grate on someone's nerves, the more of an impression you make. Wear your hair in a genital shape, dress in cacophonous color clashes, make your skin a pallid, vampirelike white (whether via makeup or just bad nutrition), and you are fabulous. Detest all that is bourgeois and love anything of the moment—whatever sundae topping is being subsumed by the fashion victims and perpetrators of that split second—with the fervor of the revelers worshipping false icons in *The Ten Commandments* (I'd quote the book, but I only saw the movie). Hate anything that's become stagnant, or "tired." Worship all that is brand-new and copping the correct attitude. Be exuberant, but don't make too much of a scene at first; newcomers have been laughed out of town for doing less than dancing on a tabletop before they've paid their dues. At everyone else's party, hand out tickets to *your* next party—treat every event as an audition for yours.

Carcinogen embodied all of its own rules like a living guidebook. A raw, warehouselike space decorated at random with shattered mirrors and silver cobwebs, it was maddening, spontaneous, and of the moment, and I was captivated by its raw, dangerous energy—a far cry from my George Romero-ish college experience. The club was infested that night, and as usual, the only one not on public exhibition was the owner, Heinz Proval. No one ever saw the guy—he lurked Phantom-like in his office (or somewhere), lusting after nubile girls from afar while pumping the club with production values that gave us the chance to act out our, and his, recreational fantasies. "He's got to be a real feeb," I overheard someone say on the endless round of Heinz speculation. "A hunched-over troglodyte who trips over his own dick on the way back to his rock."

You couldn't see Heinz—and probably didn't want to—but luckily for voyeurs like me, there was plenty else on parade; the Carcinogen crowd existed to be seen, lived to put on a show. These people hadn't gone to Dartmouth, they hadn't even read Simon and Garfunkel poetry, but they knew exactly how to apply eyeliner. They didn't do *anything* you were supposed to do, and if they ever worked from nine to five, it was nine P.M. to five A.M., in the clubs—their communal offices in which they very professionally networked, soaked in trends, and spit them back out in the form of their latest aberration of style or behavior. They were paid via attention, press, and occasionally, fun. Each had his own fat Uncle Vito story that paid for everything else.

It was a balmy night that made you want to howl, and Carcinogen was thoughtfully playing host to a Vietnam party—were we actually celebrating Vietnam? Some in the new crowd were acting out massacres onstage and looking so chic in combat helmets, you felt bad that they were born too late to participate in the real thing. Their only reference points were really awful movies like *Hamburger Hill,* so they could be forgiven some measure of historical ignorance; most of them probably thought Agent Orange was a shade of makeup. With all the heavy artillery going off, it was hard to talk, but in clubs you learned to say everything, even

"Hi. How are you?" in a piercing scream to rival Marlo Thomas's in *Consenting Adult,* when she learns her son is gay. If you spit all over someone while doing so, it meant you cared enough to send the very best. "Welcome to the trenches," shouted Favio.

He was my safari guide and my roommate, Favio la Ronde (an assumed name; his real one is Charles Speck—I looked at his passport), whom I met over the phone on one of those teen hotlines we both called as a goof. Favio was an obscenely dressed creature of glitz who lived for that crack-of-dawn time most normal people fear more than death itself and saw the world in extremes—everything was either "fabulous" or "tired," worth knowing at any cost or to-be-avoided-like-the-plague, depending on how brightly it was reflected in his *lamé* visor. He came from an uneventful home somewhere on the West Coast, which he never talked about because it wasn't very glamorous. But in the clubs, in his Day-Glo ensembles replete with Christmas ornaments and bagel watches, he was a star and knew everyone from the doormen who escorted you in to the bouncers who threw you out, with all the stops in between (you don't just have to get in, he told me, you have to get into the VIP room and then get not just free drinks, but free champagne—and not any old champagne, but preferably Cristal, even if you don't drink). More importantly, everyone knew *him.*

Favio was twenty-two but felt he was ancient, "a dinosaur," ready for the eternal sleep. He'd already been through a whole other nightclub scene which, at the time, he was convinced was "fabulous" but now thought was "tired," since there were all these fresher, newer people he was suddenly friends with, people who weren't resting as much on their clippings pile or selling out to the *petit bourgeoisie* as anxiously as the last crowd, maybe because they hadn't developed the Machiavellian skills required to do so just yet. "They're the happening people right now. The ones having the most fun," he said, explaining why he had seized onto this crew rather than being loyal to the old one. Not that it was a matter of loyalty. Survival in the club scene by necessity means dropping playmates as regularly as you change shoes.

Alas, the "new" crew was already starting to show early warning signs of that "tired" inevitability—"prechronic fatigue syndrome," he called it with a famous Favio give-me-a-break eye roll. They were talking too much about their press, reminiscing about their past (six months ago) laurels, and even occasionally rhapsodizing over the Pat Buckleys, Nan Kempners, and other uptown society people they openly despised but—Favio suspected—secretly yearned to have high tea with at (Rigor) Mortimer's. Were these new-style bohemians closet climbers after all? I congratulated myself on this quick perception; I was already doing better than a C plus in *this* school.

Favio kept his own uptown fixation tightly under wraps—I never knew about it until I found the drooling scrapbook he'd made of all the society folk and Scotch-taped into an issue of *Blitz*. ("Brooke Astor, goddess," he wrote as a preface to her chapter. "The queen of everything. My new führer.") I always suspected that his compulsive mobility didn't just propel him from the old to the new, but from the down to the up as well. He was chronically transient, a rocket spiraling toward whatever was fresher, bubblier, brighter at the moment, playing hot potato with entire crowds of people whenever their sheen threatened to tarnish. Any idiot could tell he was going to either shoot very high or explode.

The very night I moved in with Favio, before I even had a chance to unpack and argue about certain contact paper choices made ages ago in the communal areas, he swept me out of the house and into the clubs with the urgency of an ambulance worker. His hand gripped my elbow so tightly it was pink for four days, and his mouth never stopped long enough for me to doubt a word he said. Not that you could doubt this man, even if he told you he was Elvis's forgotten love child, conceived in a shopping mall. I believed him, with a voraciousness that may have had something to do with the Ecstasy he forced—yes, forced—me to sample, saying he'd rip my fingernails off one by one if I was rude enough to decline. Why did I do it? I was mortally terrified of the stuff—the only time I'd ever dropped acid I was convinced a toilet bowl was trying to suck me into its evil vortex—but wait, this wasn't like acid at all. It was pathologically pleasant, and suddenly the world became the palest, prettiest shade of green, as I felt the urge to hug everything, to run through fields of Wheat Thins with my thick, black ringlets of hair flapping in the wind and just hug away as pressure hissed out of my every orifice like air escaping from a balloon. Favio's nonstop monologue was the perfect soothing mantra to hug to; if I were with someone prone to long, Pinterian silences, I'd be banging my head against a wall.

And so my new education had begun as he gave me a ten-minute, world's-fastest-talking-man history of nightlife as he knew it and explained that everything in clubland was splintered off into two extremes—there was the boring group with money who wore black and stood around glorified rest homes that catered to their need to flaunt their broken English (no VIP rooms there—*everyone* was a VIP), and then there was the downtown crowd, who spoke English as a first language, weren't boring, never wore black, and outfreaked one another for status. Like society itself, nightlife had become a matter of the rich ten percent against the poor ninety percent, and tonight we were with the majority, the huddled masses yearning to pay the rent by the fifteenth. The Mortimer's group didn't even figure into this scheme; they were in the social stratosphere, the land where you must lip tucks so you can air kiss more attractively, and recharge every two years in Switzerland via monkey-gland injections and salves made from the virgin lamb parts of your choice. When Favio discussed this syndrome, he sounded downright admirational in his disdain.

Clanking up and down the stairs in his ridiculous white orthopedic footwear ("Bend over, I'm an enema nurse," he kept saying), he migrated to the heat of the action on every floor in a matter of seconds. Frantically, he pointed out all the Carcinogen notables and likened them to certain high-TVQ tabloid staples so they'd make sense on my celebrity meter. Most of them had found refuge in the VIP lounge, which was called the Ward. There was paint splattered randomly on the walls and tin foil for carpeting—it hurt your teeth to walk there. The room looked like nothing so much as a big, baked potato. Half-baked, maybe.

"That's Starla Rogers, goddess-woman," he said, pointing to a petite but vavoomy creature holding court in a dress made all of ribbons and bows that she clearly wanted undone. She looked a lot bigger than she really was, thanks somewhat to her heels and tall, brown waterfall of hair, but mostly to a presence you could smell from twenty paces. "Starla's sort of like a young Loni Anderson crossed with that one she did *Partners in Crime* with, you know, Lynda Carter," oozed Favio. "Did you see the rerun of *The Love Goddess* last night with Lynda Carter as Rita Hayworth? Fabulous. One of the best things since Loni did Jayne Mansfield." He meant it. In Favio's frame of reference, Jackie Collins writes better dramas than Shakespeare ever could, and *Like Father, Like Son* was a brilliant auteur masterpiece, better than *Rules of the Game,* which he'd never heard of and therefore didn't exist. Who was I to argue? At Dartmouth, I had to pretend to like *Rules of the Game,* but now I could finally admit—it's boring!

"Angel!" Starla shrieked, wrapping her boa around Favio and getting it tangled in *his* boa. He gave her the chastest possible twenty-second kiss, in the middle of which he noticed someone else, unraveled himself from her with a ten-second goodbye-for-now *air* kiss, and scampered over to tell me. Once bitten, I couldn't notice anyone but the magnetic Starla, though I strained to be polite and at least glance at the other people as Favio pointed them out. Most of them looked like former high-school losers now being celebrated instead of laughed at, for all their deformities.

"Oh, that's Emil Ezterhaus," he gushed. "He throws all the most major parties in the clubs. He knows totally everybody and is real manic because he just got off Xanax and I think onto more energizing stuff you can't get from people like your dad. Everybody says he looks like Judd Nelson, but I told him he looks more like Charlie Sheen, which I think is just a little bit more complimentary, don't you, especially since in his own slightly skewed imagination he's really gorgeous, and he's even trying to get a modeling portfolio together, dream on. Apparently the remark worked, because he's just added me to his permanent guest list, and in a few weeks I'm going to his dinner for Starla's new beauty-product line—as an invitee! I'll see if you can be my plus-one. Emil! You look fabulous!"

"I look like shit. *You* look fabulous," screamed Emil in a high-pitched, neuter voice, grinning so his dimples would show. Unfortunately, his nostrils showed too. He was twenty-fourish, with a dated shoulder-length Sting 'do framing that all-powerful schnoz. He came off like an attention broker—he sucked it in voraciously and meted it back tenfold.

"Did you see my picture in *W*?" Favio asked, desperate to know. Emil had, but Favio handed him two Xeroxes of it anyway. "It's three-quarters of a page. Here, take one, Vinnie." There had already been a pile of them in my bedroom, but I took some more, hoping I'd eventually have enough to make into a piece of cubist furniture. The only press *I'd* ever gotten was a mention in my high-school paper about how, during the senior production of *Twelfth Night,* the guy playing Sir Andrew Aguecheek let go of his fencing sword and it landed in the audience, precariously between my legs.

"Guess who's coming to Starla's dinner?" enthused Emil. "Harvey Keitel! Isn't that fabulous?" Favio was speechless except for that one essential word: "Faaaaaabulous!" Later he confessed, while nervously crumbling one of his press clippings into what he claimed was a ben-wa ball, that he had a raving crush on Harvey Keitel. "He's so goorrrgeeeoussss!" he gushed, making love to every consonant and having every vowel's baby. Oh, God, I was so naive I'd convinced myself the guy was just a little eccentric. The denial phase was over: My Live-in Tour Guide Liked Men!

Oh, well. At least Starla would be at Starla's party too. I'd *better* be Favio's plus-one, or I might risk never seeing her again. She'd swept across the tin-foil carpet as if it were velvet and moved on to another level, no doubt a higher one. The entire room said goodbye.

"Oh, there's Doric," said Favio, pointing at a tall, wimpy guy with a crew cut that made him look like a bean pole. Unlike most of the VIPs, he'd bothered to dress for Nam, in a camouflage jumpsuit and military boots. They'd never let him into any armed service, though—no way. Alas, poor Doric.

What's *his* story? I almost said, but didn't have to.

"He used to write a column, which they actually called Doric column, for *Fabulon*. He was the biggest queen when he first got to town, but now he has a beard—you know, a female front—and I think she has a beard too." Favio laughed uproariously at his own joke. "They're having a baby. He's so young—a baby having a baby. Now he's an artist, only since he's fairly devoid of original ideas, he rips off other artists' work, and when he got caught doing so, said it was an intentional 'collage/*hommage*.' Can you top that? Hi, Doric. Meet my new roommate, Vinnie—Ivy League! Oh, come to my Lust party at Atlantis on Thursday—we're having five hot go-go boys in BVDs." Doric looked intrigued. I took a breath.

I remember being pretty scandalized by all this information steamrollering over my waifish innocence, real dirt about real people (and their germs) standing right in front of me in filthy, dirty flesh and blood. A flaming queen who shacked up with a girl, yaddada-yaddada-ya, and my goddamned roommate throwing a party catering to people like that? The whole concept was so new to my limited sphere of experience that I think at the time I felt emotionally bludgeoned and drained in an alleyway, but, dare I say it, pleasantly so. Maybe it was the Ecstasy. (The lovey-dovey high was wearing off into something else. The green tint was starting to look like mucus.) But whatever it was, something was turning sour, and the real shock was that I didn't mind. My education had finally paid off—all those years of tabloid study had given me a knowledge base from which to appreciate this real-life sleaze, and you can't imagine how fulfilling it is to know that something you'd painstakingly researched actually has practical value. Still, I could easily see how after just a few weeks of this, my relatively benign sense of sarcasm might turn to quarry-size jade.

As armies of overrouged cross-dressers barreled up and down the stairs in lethal high heels, I matured ten emotional years every five minutes. These people had no manners, but they had no shame, either. They flaunted their deficiencies and their faults with equal lack of self-consciousness and got such a kick out of performing their self-styled roles you couldn't help but give them a thumbs-up, if not exactly sweeping them home to meet Mom.

There was no time to absorb anything. As we went in and out, up and down, sometimes even without moving, my senses were pummeled to a throbbing state on the threshold of numbness while Favio kept on keeping on, mentally tallying points for each new person he could schmooze. "Hi, Mary-Ellen!" he screeched—ding-ding-ding, ten points.

"What's *her*—?" I started to say, but he cut in.

"Doric's best friend, Mary-Ellen Meringue, the professional dilettante. A designer—was in a band—had her own club, Delirium, which was raided during a strip-poker party—not because everybody was running around butt-naked, which they were, but because there were a lot of minors drinking without the wristbands that prove you're not a minor. Now everybody thinks she's getting real bed-time-tired. She's extremely geriatric. Older than me. No, seriously, she's like twenty-eight, and has been twenty-eight for at least five years now. She's a broken record when it comes to the word *me*. I'd bet my butthole she's promoting something."

She certainly wasn't promoting style. Mary-Ellen wasn't fat, but she had one of those unformed bodies airtight with more spare tires than you technically need. She had stringy red hair, a multitude of connect-the-dot freckles, and the fashion sense of a bullfrog. "Shit night," she boomed irritably into Favio's ear. She then came up to me, I thought to introduce herself, but as I dumbly stuck out my hand she just repeated "Shit night" and walked away.

I asked Favio for an invite to his Lust party—it did sound vaguely enticing, not that it was really up my alley—but he just laughed. "There isn't going to *be* a Lust party," he admitted. "I made the whole thing up just to give Doric a jolt. Wait till he leaves the wife behind and shows up at Atlantis and there are no naked go-go boys for him to grope—just the usual tired yuppies aching to beat the pants off of him. *That* will be h-o-t hot!" I couldn't believe Favio had taken the time to work up this miniature human drama. His study of the great Jackie Collins had served him well—another educational success story.

"Stop and savor this moment," Favio said suddenly, halfway down the stairway. A shot went off upstairs. I hoped it was part of the theme.

"What?" I said. "Savor which? What? Whom?"

"Savor the moment. This is the best this club has ever been or will ever be. It's peaking. And don't think I'm fooling myself. I know this is the highest I'll ever attain. I'm the ultimate Carcinogen person, so I'm peaking now too." He was *sprech*-screaming this out, in a mocking tone that masked his being dead serious. "Hey, everybody," he announced, "I'm peaking!"

So was I. Green had turned to fuchsia, and I'd started befriending Favio's elbow—the hugging urge had evolved into compulsive grabbing. I was delirious. I wanted to commune with everyone there, to clutch every kitsch ornament that decorated the third floor and take them all home for a talk, to fuck the gossip—literally fuck it as if it were human and had an orifice I could dive into with my entire genital being. Ecstasy doesn't make you less conscious, I learned, it makes you *more* conscious. My mood swings were getting ridiculous. I wasn't even afraid of the toilets. I tried to enjoy this pleasure game while it lasted, since Favio had warned me my head would be explosive the next morning—"the Ecstasy and the agony" is how he referred to this syndrome. People kept thrusting invites and clippings at me, and Favio kept seizing them to use as lip blotters, then tossing them into the bottomless pit of his big Bloomie's shopping bag for future reference. To free myself of his *W* Xeroxes, I flung *them* down there too.

"You've just met *the* crowd," said Favio, as if I'd met anyone—I'd only ogled like a tourist schlepping through the Museum of Nocturnal Oddities. "But there's a whole new— yes, newer—gang of people it's important to be aware of," he added, "and they band together like pigeons, so you've got to be either real sharp or real stupid to break into their ranks. Lord knows I'm still trying." He pulled me down two flights and into a cramped, psychedelic playroom, where hordes of unruly teens were turning cartwheels, throwing paper planes, grabbing one another's privates, and screaming just for the sake of screaming. They didn't bore, but they *were* obnoxious. I left the Ivy League for this?

"And anyway," Favio said as I caught onto his next sentence like a passenger chasing a trolley, "*Fabulon* hasn't written about them yet, but everybody knows they're the next wave, as in tidal. *They* sure know it from the way they carry on. Let me introduce you." As usual, he didn't introduce me—he just pointed. Favio was afraid of my getting too close to any of his human displays. "Let's see, that's Polly Purebred in the Hefty bag, there's José Can-U.C. spitting up in the sandbox—he's the one to watch. Hi, José—looking good. There's Cherries Jubilee, Plum Tart, Polyester Blend, Johnny Come Lately, Jim Nasium, Ivy Druguser, Driven Slush, Madame Ovary, Vanity Unfair. . . ." The names reeled out like when that woman on *Romper Room* gazed into her magical mirror. I closed my eyes and felt like I was on a Tilt-A-Whirl that would never slow down, not in *this* lifetime. Nothing made sense in the present moment, yet I heard every word, laughed until my nipples hurt as each utterance made a booming echo inside my head. After awhile, I couldn't tell if I was laughing like a loon or sobbing or just being quiet with my eyes closed.

"There's Ken Doll," continued Favio, "and Silly Billy and Libby Libby Libby and Sushi Deluxe and Hush, Hush Sweet Charlotte . . ."

Hush, Hush Sweet Charlotte? Were these deranged Lilliputians actually dragging up ludicrous, unwieldy movie titles as names? In that case, could I be Let's Scare Jessica to Death or Bless the Beasts and Children or maybe Who Is Harry Kellerman and Why Is He Saying Those Terrible Things About Me? How about just Gandhi? No, I couldn't live up to such a tag. I needed something simple that wouldn't require me to fast or be relentlessly pleasant. Vincent DiBlasio could become Vinnie Van Go, Vinnie D., or even Vin E., all of which various people had already suggested, at least in my rainbow-colored reveries. But I thought it incredibly daring to stick with Vincent DiBlasio. Any other name would deprive my parents of their full share of Catholic guilt.

Vincent DiBlasio was a shockingly untampered-with label that could dice and slice through everyone else's pretension like a Ginsu; no matter how phony-baloney I got, at least my name would be real. Favio la Ronde was *faux* through and through—a fake name to match the person, however colorful both sounded. Right off, I knew his game. He had about as much depth as a watercress sandwich, and he couldn't talk about anything outside of the club or TV world. (Iran, to him, was an after-hours place that had closed three years ago.) But he was the one who'd allowed me to see these colors and feel these feelings. And there wasn't anything that harmful in his constant quest for the untired. Against my best judgment, I was so intoxicated by his vividness, by the things he said, the people he knew, that *faux* quickly became friend. Fuck my best judgment—where had it ever gotten me? Compared to the old Dartmouth drips— talk about tired—he was blindingly exciting. And I shelved the knowledge that his superficiality could turn on *me* one day, concentrating instead on the ego gratifications of the moment and the voyeuristic possibilities of the millimoment. My mind became muddy anyway with my emerging status as everyone's shiny new plaything, and as Favio continued to ply me with Ecstasy my thoughts were as thick and impenetrable as Tupperware. When word got out that I was Favio's new cohort, I was someone worth saying hello to— fabulousness by association. Once it leaked that I was starting my own scene magazine, I became the most popular new arrival since Absolut.

Emil Ezterhaus offered to throw a party for *Manhattan on the Rocks* before I'd even dreamed up the first cover line. I played hard to get—"Well, maybe," I stammered, arguing that it was kind of premature—but deep down, I knew I'd love a celebration of the future ruling rag that would be the seedpod of the DiBlasio publishing empire. Or at least a decent party with an open bar.

On our first meeting that night at Carcinogen, Emil had been as chilly as sesame noodles, sizing me up and down as if deciding whether I was competition or a total not-happening scene, human caca from the boroughs or someone who might in the long run be able to help his career. Like all the best climbers, he gave me the benefit of the doubt and wooed me with a guest-list seduction, a comp courtship by candlelight. Deep enough to be a model, for sure, this guy was at least entertaining, and having dozed through an entire semester of Wordsworth, I appreciated anyone who could keep me awake.

An afternoon didn't go by that Emil didn't call me to pontificate about this news item or that movie review or to schmooze about the previous night's fracases, all with the same undeniable subtext: "Mention me!" I did—you couldn't not mention him—but if he crumbled I probably wouldn't boycott the party in the wreckage.

On that very virgin night out I came up with the magazine idea, maybe as a high-minded excuse to make myself a party fixture. ("I'm a magazine publisher, after all. I'm merely doing my job!") Just partying for partying's sake would wear thin after a few half hours. But if I were out there on a nightly journalistic expedition of Margaret Mead-like gravity, then every free drink ticket, every socialize-till-you-drop night of debauchery was on-the-job training done only because I *had* to do it out of obligation to the extremely little people, my readers. And the magazine could be a glossy showcase for my two cents—a well-oiled vehicle by which to glorify the stars, denounce the drek, and maybe—all right, I admit it—maybe to move up a notch or two, not so much on the way to Mortimer's, just on the way to some kind of human respectability that didn't involve groveling in a manhole. I had shed all semblance of that urge by dropping out, I know, but you never really lose that sort of thing, just like people who convince themselves they're better off without babies invariably go through their entire lives anguished because they never had one, compensating with potted plants and shelves full of home appliances that they nurture and overprotect. The spawning urge is akin to the climbing one; both breed status. And the second I had shed my respectability, I wanted it back, just like I now wanted my hands on the tasteful, small-collared shirt I'd given to Favio in a Carcinogen-tainted rush of generosity. I wanted my place in the world. But I wasn't that bad—I mean, I never made a scrapbook. I knew my place was one step above the gutter at Chock Full O' Nuts, with deposed Russian royalty waiting on me through three layers of pancake foundation. I knew if I fell through the cracks in the sewer, society would not mourn.

Perversely enough, the *Manhattan on the Rocks* party was the driving force that kept me going, but I played it cool, only talking about it when I had to, not just when I *felt* I had to. I wasn't going to be a Mary-Ellen Meringue, dropping self-promotional hints into every conversation. Besides, first there was Starla's celebration to deal with—a sumptuous dinner at Ne Plus Ultra, one of those chicly minimal French restaurants that look like glorified bomb shelters. Its customers had about a fifty percent food-poisoning survival rate; half the clientele came back for a repeat visit, but no one came back three times. A mild waft of cat pee stained the air—I knew it well from my Astoria days, and here they made the same *gaffe* of trying to camouflage it with Wizard "American Beauty" air freshener, the only smell in the Western world I think is worse than cat piss. What a place. You could almost hear the yaks being slaughtered in the kitchen, wailing as they vainly battled their inevitable transformation into *nouvelle*.

Bad as Ne Plus Ultra was, I guess the collective feeling was that it could have been worse. It had cachet among the Eurotrash crowd, who enjoy the depravity of flaunting their wealth in poverty-stricken surroundings, and the fashion set, who don't care where they go as long as they can pose, and that's all that mattered to Starla. These were the people she needed to court as a beauty icon, putting her name and image on products that she didn't really create but could tirelessly hawk to those with money and connections. (A master self-promoter, she couldn't really do anything, but she didn't need to—self-promotion was now a viable career unto itself.)

Though Harvey Keitel hadn't shown yet, these two crowds were in wicked abundance. And in an act of incredible noblesse, Emil had let in a few pieces of token trash—

namely me and Favio—to prove he still cared about his weeds, I mean roots.

Everyone at the party had the air of someone who had climbed to the top of the beanstalk and was dining just to take a breather. They had made it—they were there and weren't going to budge. We were thrilled to sit there and watch them not budge.

Starla—a bodacious vision with her new brunette hair (the only natural blonde to go brunette in the history of the island because "thanks to Clairol, blondes are a dime a dozen")—was wearing an aqua crinoline dress that billowed out like a Great Lake. She was the quintessential hostess, like Stella Dallas if lots of guests had shown up. Everyone got equal time—from the fashion editor to the fashion editor's friend's accountant, who really wasn't supposed to come. "But hell, I'm glad you did," enthused Starla. "You look fabulous and you certainly liven up this room!"

Those three words—"You look fabulous"—were the cure for any qualms. Say them to Starla and it made her bubble even more, tingle even louder. She didn't seem capable of depression—it wasn't in her Fil-o-Fax. If Starla ever suffered from a hangnail or a bad time of the month, you'd never know it; when she worked a room, that room became her universe, and she concentrated on it with the fierce determination of someone who could single-handedly save it from obsolescence. When it was her own party, she gave even more—her smile was brighter, her breasts stood firmer at attention, as if they knew the seriousness of the task at hand, her air kisses—*mwah*—pause—double-*mwah*—pause— "Hi!"—veered closer and closer to the actual cheek. If there was a disingenuous bone in her body, it didn't matter—it seemed genuine, and what was sincerity anyway except what people took for sincerity? You never doubted for a minute that Starla loved people and wanted to be exactly where she was.

A drab, short, and unhappy Catholic schoolgirl from Ohio, a couple of years ago she had blossomed into this larger-than-life Manhattan star. Like one of those time-release capsules sizzling into efficacy, she had exploded into creation in the isolation booth of the clubs—darkened rooms illuminated only by the flashes of the cameras and the wattage of her smile. Starla Rogers Beauty Products was only the first step in a Hollywood-style legend that was just beginning—I could picture the eyeliners, foundation bottles, and calendar pages flying through the wind in one of those old movie montages that signaled the start of something big. She was going PLACES, and everyone sensed it as they gravitated to her like moths. If she wore a No Pest Strip, she could probably be alone for a few minutes.

The sight of Starla strangely activated the testosterone in me. I should explain that I hadn't had sex since I was seventeen and Melissa Kravitz forced me to mount her, when all I wanted was the chocolate milkshake she promised me. Somehow, there I was on top of her panting, rail-like body, not knowing how to unsnap her bra and not particularly wanting to find out as she urged me inside her and sucked on my tongue as if it were a Tootsie Pop. I've long since rationalized that it was Melissa's animal lust that turned me off sex forever; it was not only unhygienic, it was unsightly. I think I have a pretty decent body—I've been likened to a younger, *Fly*-period Jeff Goldblum—but even the most perfect specimen has knobby knees, and I don't believe you should show your knees to anyone else, not even to a doctor. After Melissa raped me, my role model suddenly became Cary Grant, who actually showered with his clothes on in *Charade*. I watched that film once with my father, who commented that Audrey Hepburn had "no knockers whatsoever"—like Melissa—and all I could think of was that she was considerate enough not to show *them* either. Audrey was a lady, My Fair Lady. I always felt she got that part over

Julie Andrews because they sensed that Julie was the type who one day *would* show her breasts on film.

But I was really only a Puritan when circumstances called for it. I actually considered my asexuality a pretty daring act of libertinism, thinking it made me damned special in my own freaky way. It wasn't always my decision anyway; potential sex partners were terrified of me, Melissa being a rare and demented exception. I always put out a kind of intimidating scent; even when I was being shy, I always came off arrogant, and when I was being arrogant, I came off certifiably insane.

Whatever it was that made me a candidate for monasteria, I found it easier to concentrate on my life's work if there wasn't the distraction of sex involved, because along with sex invariably comes the anchor weight of this other person dragging you down to the level of her petty problems. I had my own petty problems and never bought the myth that being saddled with someone else's too is one of life's beautiful experiences. And sex was embarrassing— every time I saw Melissa Kravitz after that, I had to cross the street, even if it meant dodging Mack trucks. If I'd been suffocating and she had had the only oxygen left on earth, I still wouldn't have said hello.

Naturally, people have wondered about me: Does he like boys? Did he have it cut off to sing in a castrati choir? The speculation always pissed me off—the only time gossip is not my favorite pastime is when I'm the subject of it—but I had nothing to be ashamed of. *I* was the pure one, the one untainted by someone else's deviations—and a far more adept gossip to boot. Without the excess baggage of other people's body fluids, I was an unwitting prototype for the AIDS era, a model of perfectly timed invulnerability. And I was getting a lot done without having to worry about sex—I read about two books and fifteen magazines a week, the ultimate sponge-like activity. Soon I could dry out and become coral reef.

But Starla—what a refreshing Creamsicle cocktail she would be for a thirsty night. The sight of her was the best temptation yet for me to go off my sex-free diet. The first time she said "You look fabulous" to me that night, I got hard. I craved her by entrée time, was insatiable for her by dessert. By the last clink-clink of watery red beverages, I had to have her—needed to sweep her out of that Gallic dive and pump her with a lifetime's worth of male discharge. I'm serious, that was the most romantic thing I'd thought of in a long time.

As Emil made his attention-commanding toast to our guest of honor in that overzealous way of his—"Soon you'll be Super-Starla"—my erection got so big it almost exploded through my pants. Oh, God, was I hot for Emil? No, I was turned on by Starla—aroused by her fame. I hated myself for even feeling a little pre-cum seep out of me as I contemplated the thought of putting her on my first cover.

I sidled up to Starla at her table, which was hardly the glittering assemblage I'd expected; one of the perverse party rules is that the guest of honor has to sit with the worst people there; the VIPs are spread out democratically, the way you'd sprinkle fertilizer on a lawn. If you glanced around your table, you could easily tell who *your* VIPs were, as well as the token trash, the obligations, and the press. If everyone else at the table was a VIP, an obligation, or the press, then *you* were the token trash.

Starla's table ran the gamut from minor fashion editors to downtown drains (one of them had a multicolored mid-seventies Mohawk—was this fabulous again or was everyone too afraid to say how tired it really was?). There was the inevitable Mary-Ellen Meringue, who, in a flogging frenzy, was inviting people to her fashion show at the aptly named Skid Row. And of course there was Doric, that look-ma-no-ideas artist, who'd dragged along his Woman as if she were a canvas or some other piece of irritating but essential baggage. By now I could spot the cruising vibes of both sexes the way most lowland Indians know the mating call of the mongoose, and when Doric suddenly went into a song from *Gypsy* that necessitated putting his arm around one of the busboys for long periods of time, I knew what was happening. As if there could be any doubt about someone who knows a song from *Gypsy* anyway. His wife, Randi—swollen with the proof of their love (and certification that they had consummated at least once)—always glared, Cruella-like, when this happened, but she never got *that* upset; when the baby was born, she'd be home free. Soon it would be suckling at her bosom with sharp, urgent slurps that would let her know she was needed.

Every time Randi trotted off to tinkle, Doric cornered Favio and tried again to find out what had happened to that alleged Lust party, claiming, "I wanted to paint the boys as a comment on exploitation." But then the bearded lady would invariably traipse back, and he never got an answer. Poor Randi. Oh, fuck it—as Danilo Robespierre-Hague, a writer friend of mine at school, always said: *"Sympathy* comes between *shit* and *syphillis* in the dictionary." And she did know exactly what she was getting into when she shacked up with this shmegegie. "Everyone in town knows about *her,"* Favio had told me, meaning Doric. So why did she— I mean Randi—do it? I began to suspect that she hated gays—"Don't mention 'fags' in my house," she always said—and had therefore married one as her punishment against them. More likely, she probably felt that Doric would never cheat on her (with another woman—other *men* were never discussed, and therefore were irrelevant). And she enjoyed being the one to "legitimize" him in the eyes of the art world—even the avant-garde needed to be spoon-fed hetero pablum to appease their queasy stomachs. So, like Trintignant selling out to the fascists, Doric had become one of my twelve favorite movies, *The Conformist.*

"When we both tested negative for AIDS and were able to go ahead and have the baby," Doric told me one night, "it was like the Higher Being was giving us His blessing." Doric had never mentioned religion before, but the social value of his sacred union was a definite cause for hallelujahs. Indeed, He did bless unions like this. They suited Nature's order and fulfilled the eternal guest-list plan. None of this really bothered me, especially since Doric exuded the glow of someone who was about to become very famous.

Whatever, I smiled my jaw-to-the-floor smile of phony exuberance for downtown's resident paparazzo, Delroy Dweeb (he was really Mario DuSemprun, but he thought sounding nerdier would help his career), and forgot about it for the time being, for the sake of the party. The mouth-open stance served not only to cover one's knees, it was one of the two *de rigueur* expressions for posing; the other one was sucking in one's cheeks and going "Ooh." (Two fingers should rest wanly on the chin for that pose; for the first one, both arms should rocket festively into the air in a victory **V**. But by all means, relax and look natural.) As if by some photographic miracle, Starla was assuming the same config-uration next to me—it was the kind of photo that begged to be published.

"You both look incredible," shrieked Delroy, one of those enthusiastic types with a much more youthful person-ality than his graying temples would suggest. (He'd had a near-fatal car crash a few years back and was now terribly, terribly in love with life.) "That's going to make an exciting picture. I can't wait to run it in *Limo.*"

"Don't forget to put that I'm a magazine publisher," I said, pretending to be making a funny while getting the point across. I dropped my mouth open again, so low this time it left skidmarks, and threw my arms so enthusiastically into the air I almost heard my elbows crack, but photo magic doesn't happen twice. He was already shooting Doric and Randi—Doric was doing the sucking-in-cheek movement; Randi was glaring.

"Great party," I said to Starla, thinking that was a stunning witticism for all time.

"It wouldn't have been half as great without Mr. Vinnie here," she bubbled, giving me a knowing rub of the thigh that sent me to the next galaxy. I'd never been called "Mister" before; it was kind of a trip. Starla talked to everyone in the third person; she seemed to be telling the real truth about you, because she wasn't talking about *you;* she was talking about someone else named Mr. Vinnie. This fit in flawlessly with my own scheme of considering myself someone else. The sweet thing about Starla was that, even in her conspiratorial tone, she was always saying something nice. I answered her similarly. "Mr. Vinnie had the best time!"

Was I just the lucky object of her compulsively democratic niceness? Did she really, genuinely like me the way all of Hollywood really, really likes Sally Field? Or because she thought my magazine was going PLACES and could help her, or at least not hurt her? Yeah, dream on—she hardly needed some upstart rag to cement her place in the pantheon. But just in case that was it, I blurted it out: "You know, I want to put you on my first cover—in fact, I wouldn't have anyone but. I already have the layout worked out in my head down to the last caption. If you don't do it, I'll drink cyanide first thing tomorrow morning." I paused, ready to be mowed down by some trendy firing squad.

"Ooooooh," she gurgled, jumping and bouncing and clapping her hands deliriously. "Ooooh. Oooh." It took so little to make this girl happy. "Would you like to blow this chicken coop and go somewhere else?" she said, as I dropped my mouth again, this time not for Delroy. "I think it's time to skip. We can start on the story." She laughed. I was stunned. I knew without a doubt from her tone of voice that "somewhere else" meant her PLACE.

Before I had a chance to answer, Emil just had to trot out one last stunt to guarantee that his party would get press—you can never be too sure. I guess it wasn't his fault that it was timed to screw up my long-awaited voyage out of celibacy. I tried to be nonchalant as my heart raced into overdrive and we all had to watch this last, dubious straw. It was one of those excessively blow-dried, less-endowed-than-Dartmouth male strippers—the hoariest party trick in the book, as even I knew—who performed his deed with a wary self-consciousness, as if he'd looked around the room and realized he'd slept with half the people there. As he read a telegram to Starla, she brilliantly concealed her horror, twisting her grimace into the most lifelike impression of a grin I'd ever seen. It's amazing Starla's cheeks didn't end up in traction. I felt nothing; her hand was on my leg all through it.

"We love your products and adore your beauty," he intoned with all the verve of a third grader playing the Sugar Plum Fairy. "Now I'll strip down until I'm nudie." And to the incredibly original tune of "The Stripper," he bumped his pelvis in her face, removing his glittery briefs only to reveal a G-string, which he made Starla bite off for a photo opportunity. What did this have to do with beauty products? No one could come up with an educated answer, but everyone threw themselves good-naturedly into the ecdysiastic circus anyway, to help the embarrassment go by quicker. Some girl was flailing her arms in the air as her halter top slid lower and lower. Randi was throwing bread rolls at the guy the way you would at a derby horse; I think she sensed he was gay. A middle-aged man was claiming, sure enough, that he'd slept with the guy. Meanwhile, "Princess Tiny Meat"—Favio's expression—didn't seem to notice any of this, intent as he was on bumping and thrusting and collecting his fee. With all the personality of a cold, practiced whore, he kissed Starla smack on the lips and ground his way out of there like a coffee maker. As he did, *The Times*'s Sid Boulle was taking frantic notes—so it worked. By the time two farewell girls came out dressed like Starla Beauty

Products—one was a mascara wand and the other one was a big bottle of either Erace or liquid White-out—I had lost my will to live.

"Mr. Vinnie?" Starla said, to see if I was still there. I dug my nails into my palms until they turned red as I convinced myself that I had to go on, had to believe as devoutly as Doric, because this was only the second of many big parties, and how else would I get through all of them without a belief in something, even if it was just a belief that any day now I'd be an invitee and not just a plus-one. Piously, I prayed to my Uncle Vito in high heaven above not to let Starla come to her senses. Please, Uncle dearest, pull some strings and make her still want worthless-little-piece-of-shit me. I stood in her capacious shadow as she kissed everyone good night with enough *mwahs* to launch a steamship. Favio—who'd left me to my own devices while he worked the room all night ("You're not a virgin anymore")—was now eyeing me, as if to say, What are you doing, and how the hell did you do it? Delroy was taking farewell snaps, and you only had to look bemused to rate one—after dessert, the *de rigueur* poses don't apply, and you simply have to use up film. Doric was spooking down the room out of the corner of his eye one last time, anxious to find young, male prospects to call for the times Randi flies off to visit her folks in Seattle—dream vacations for them both. And a grand old dame—it turned out she was Sylvia Valmouth, the head of the company Starla was merchandising for—looked either mortified or dead as she limped out of the proceedings and into the long, white limousine of my dreams. With a few more runs in her stockings, she'd make a great Miss Havisham in some road company. I think she had one leg—all of New York was at her foot.

"*Ciao,*" said Starla mockingly to *tout le monde,* making that backward hand gesture with the cutest little "Aren't I silly?" giggle. Everyone laughed; it was all in the performance. At the uptown clubs, I would learn, Starla did the *ciao* routine with utter seriousness. She spoke whatever language was spoken in the room she was in. She could probably tell the history of eyeliner to aborigines and make them understand.

"What a bomb party," I laughed to Emil. "You're ruined—Harvey Keitel never showed."

"Fuck you," he laughed back.

Starla was motioning me into the car Emil had procured for her, and suddenly I felt so suave. It wasn't a long, white limousine, but still, it was a car—paid for, free, comp, gratis. Authoritatively, I grabbed Favio and said, "Don't count on my coming home tonight," my voice dripping with the innuendo he'd gotten twenty minutes earlier. "Ouch. I have one word for you," he said, slipping something square and icky into my pocket. Towelette? "Condom." As Starla and I hopped into the car, I took my nails out of my palms and realized I wasn't even remotely nervous anymore. My trauma was so real and immediate that dread had escaped my emotional checklist. I was a man today. "Come to my fashion show," Mary-Ellen screamed out, anxious to shatter any quality moment with her last, tired word. Go to hell, you self-serving hag. "Of course we will," I yelled back. We?

"Oops!" Starla had dropped some of her gifts as we walked into her apartment, one of those high-ceilinged deals on lower Fifth Avenue in a building that looks something like either the Fountainhead or Nell Carter. There were curved, onyx lamps everywhere, crystal globes holding down stacks of papers, and of course, Warhol portraits of Mick Jagger on the walls. Was there a downtown design central that decorated every apartment below Twenty-third Street?

I didn't care about her gifts, and neither did she. Impersonating recklessness, I laughed, "To hell with them," trying to sound like Clark Gable but coming off more like Harvey Korman. I jumped on her, tackling her halfway to the floor with a move any linebacker would have been proud of. I figured if she thought I was serious, we could just fuck all the preliminaries and get on with the act, and if she thought I was joking, I would just laugh it off with a carefree flick of my pouff bangs and pick up the gifts. She knew I was serious. "Vinnie! My hair!" She'd dropped the "Mister." Her hair? There weren't any cameras in here. Ah— but the mental pictures. She knew I'd be telling all the Occidental world about this the second I left her apartment, and she had to look flawless. I might even write about it.

"You have to take things one step at a time," she said instructively, getting out of her shoes and motioning for me to unzip her dress with a devastating seductress's half-smile. "Sex is work, after all," she continued. "It must be done professionally."

Sex is work? As I toyed with her zipper in stuttering motions, I felt my huge erection wilt so far down someone should have yelled, "Timber." I'd worked enough at that dinner party—just getting to this point was highly skilled labor I should be getting magnificent wages for. My whole life had been work-obsessed in anticipation of this one genuine party moment. I'd worked my ass off at school (to no avail) and even did part-time grocery packing in the summers for extra cash because my mother insisted it would build character. I'd worked on the apartment, networked at Carcinogen, slaved on a journalistic *raison d'être*. But at this particular moment in time, at five in the morning with my hand fondling the crack of the ass I'd been contemplating all night while drooling for the entire Condé Nast organization to see, I did not particularly want to work. I wanted to get down with my bad self and never come back up again. I wanted to dip into her without a life preserver, to devour her without utensils. At least that's what I *had* wanted, something I only allowed to happen about once every six years. Lunar eclipses happened more often. Margaux Hemingway winning Oscars happened *much* more often. But it was going to be another six-year wait before the next earth-shaking bout of foreplay interruptus. Now my limp dick was pointing in the direction of the exit. I couldn't go through with this. I couldn't afford it.

"Look, Starla, I really like you and all," I stammered, "but I don't think we have to jump into this just yet." I was half-zipping her back up with all the intimacy of a stage door dresser. "I mean I barely know you and hell, I don't even have a condom. . . ." She flung open a desk drawer that was like a treasure chest of condoms. I've never seen so many inanimate objects in my life.

"*Voilà*," she exclaimed. Was that like *ciao*?

"Great," I shrieked, horrified. "But still . . . I . . ."

"*Caro mio*," she said, caressing my temple and affecting a gurgle that was the most flesh-crawling thing I'd ever heard, "I understand performance anxiety. I mean, I get nervous sometimes before I have a big meeting or anything where I have to be 'on' and fabulous. Even tonight before I walked into my party I was a teensy bit shaky, I really was. So believe me—I know what it means to"—mentally, she reached down to my crotch; I could feel it—"not get it up. No problem. We'll just book it in another time." She winked to let me know this rescheduling concept was all in fun, but you shouldn't shit a shitter. I knew she meant it, and would wait for her people to call my people.

As I stumbled down her stairway—why do things like this always happen in walk-ups?—I was so mad I wanted to slam my hand against the wall until it bled, as I had done during a sense-memory exercise in acting class one summer at NYU. (The teacher had said it was a breakthrough.) But I just kept on running, pissed that I'd let myself be the latest fly in Starla's web simply because I was new and she'd probably already demolished everyone else from here to Intercourse, Pennsylvania. How could I have been such a chump and three-quarters? Then again my own motives probably hadn't been all that farm-fresh. I admit that a portion of her allure was the fact that she was a Somebody-in-training, a definite riser, but what's the harm in that? I liked her, and an intrinsic part of who she was was a Somebody—there was no way around that. I'd be attracted to a nobody if they looked like they could be a Somebody someday. Or if they treated *me* like a Somebody and at least a little of that Somebodiness rubbed off on them. Shit, why did I tell her about the cover?—Now I was stuck with her castrating face on the debut of my big-city shame.

Rather than skulk home and be greeted by Favio's inquisitive smirks, I stalked the streets for hours, pacing, reforming my ideas, getting furious, then ultimately convincing myself it didn't matter and I'd have to roll with it. I'm Italian. If the ravioli burns a little, you just pour extra sauce on it. My calves throbbing, my ears aching from all the crackpots analyzing the pros and cons of NutraSweet at the twenty-four-hour diner, I finally stumbled home at nine A.M. and found Favio wide awake and ferociously washing dishes, targeting a lifetime's worth of anxiety against poor, defenseless Melmac. He'd never dirtied any dishes—*not* being Italian, he doesn't cook—but he'd done so much coke in the ladies' room at Ne Plus Ultra, he was buzzing with activity-compulsion and had to do something. One dish was getting so shiny it looked like he'd been washing it for four hours. "I've been washing this dish for four hours," he said, eerily, and as the *Twilight Zone* theme ran through my head, I wondered what *I* was on. Certainly not Ecstasy— that was three weeks ago, wasn't it?

"So come on, come on, come on," he said, scrubbing faster and faster, harder and harder. "How big's her dick?" This was his pre-scripted first question about any sex experience, regardless of gender.

"Umm," I said, not knowing how much to tell, if anything.

"Was she good in bed—a real ultravixen?" he twittered. "I hear she's a real gorgon. When Doric screwed her, he said it was like Godzilla versus King Kong."

"Doric screwed her?" I blurted. So other women *were* a threat to Randi. But how could Starla let that dinky artist-by-proxy worm his way on top of her? Did she only screw gay boys? Did she think I was one?

"Yeah, he screwed her, so what, come on," said Favio, looking ready to design the plate into my lip in some Nigerian beauty-makeover rite if he didn't get an answer. "Tell-tell-tell-tell-tell."

"Oh, nothing," I said with assumed bashfulness. "I mean not nothing." Even though Favio had recently been parroting that Starla was "over," I knew that was his insecure way of saying she was getting so big she was out of his hands now. She was far from over. In fact, every time her name came up, he still misted over with obvious obsession. I felt my status would plummet in his eyes if I admitted I hadn't gotten the whole enchilada. "It was incredible," I said, transforming my utter humiliation into exuberance the way I'd learned in that acting class. (They taught us to transfer one emotion into another—any horrible feeling could become glorious, at least for a few seconds.)

"It was?" he pulsed. He turned off the water and clanked down the dish, and it smashed—a clean, smashed dish. I could finally hear myself think, but I didn't want to hear these thoughts.

The phone in my room rang and sounded like a screaming baby. Who the hell would call at this hour? This was supposed to be Kips Bay, the forgotten neighborhood. It was probably Mary-Ellen reminding us to come to her fashion show.

"Oh, God," said Favio. "That's probably Starla. She's been calling like every twenty minutes for the last few hours."

"You've been answering my phone?"

"No," he said, "but I could hear her leaving messages on your machine, even with the water running. Of course it helped that I turned up the volume," he laughed. I wasn't worried; I knew Starla wouldn't have said anything too incriminating on tape. "Why did you leave her house so early anyway?"

"Oh," I gulped. "I didn't leave *that* early. But staying the whole night was pointless when we'd peaked so soon—quit while you're ahead and all that." That was the fastest improv I'd ever concocted—I was proud. I let out a nervous chuckle and grabbed the phone like I was slamming a bug.

"Hello? Oh, hi." It was her. I suddenly felt the urge to run back to my campus of yesteryear; school wasn't that bad.

"Hi, honey," she said, cheerily. She was assuming that comforting tone that made you feel about five years old and ready for your first notebook. It was just what the doctor ordered. "I don't want you to feel bad about what happened," she said. "You ran out so abruptly, I thought maybe you were mad at me. I want to try again with you. I think you're special, not just out for yourself like everyone else." She sounded so kind I didn't hate her anymore. I worshipped her like I had earlier, between the yak and the stripper. I could almost feel aroused again—God, one New York night is like a year anywhere else. But I knew I didn't want to be penciled in for yet another anxiety-filled performance. Ever since a teacher dragged us to see that thing with Julie Harris, I've found one-woman shows really stultifying.

Hunched Quasimodo-like in a corner of my shoebox-size room, drowning in Favio's press clippings, I became seized by an epileptic fit of honesty. "Starla," I whimpered, "I don't know what came over me, but I just told—well, implied to Favio that you and I did it and it was incredible—"

"We *did* do it," she interrupted, "and it *was* incredible. So tell me something I don't already know, kiddo." My jaw dropped and my heart rose. This could be the girlfriend I always dreamed of—one who didn't drag me down to her own petty needs, et cetera. She didn't *have* needs in that department—sex was just another job to her, and if she didn't have to do it, it was like a day off, a paid vacation. We were made for each other. Never would I have to suffer embarrassment between the sheets, and I still had the prize— to the world at large, Starla Rogers could be my girlfriend.

"It was good for me, was it good for you?" I laughed, getting into this ruse.

"Cigarette?" she giggled, as we both broke into hysterics. I found myself talking baby talk and blowing kisses into the phone as I gently hung up, as dreamily romantic as any dim-witted Partridge Family member. The second Favio heard the phone hang up, he barreled into my room and started in again: "Well-well-well-well-well?" He was still so high from his powdery binge he was practically scraping the ceiling with his spiked hair. His lips were a mess—he'd chewed on them one night when he did too much Ecstasy.

"I think I'm in love," I cooed.

"Shit," he said. "*I* was going to seduce you tonight." He went back to the dishes.

3

One night in the throes of the mind-numbing starvation that comes after a night of relentless clubbing, we were all forced to eat at a brutally lit diner on Canal Street—the only place open for miles or we would have skipped the humiliation, for sure. When I say brutally lit, I mean it was like an FBI interrogation room, but brighter, indescribably brighter, as if designed by a sadist. Each pore of everyone's face took on a life of its own, and we all talked with hands casually draped across our flaws to hide the destruction as much as possible. After five minutes of this, I was ready to confess.

Going there was so antichic, so unfabulous, it was almost fabulous, and I think the communal, unspoken feeling was that we were the coolest thing ever to hit that dive. The novelty of it all almost made the lighting worth risking, and the brightness at least gave Delroy a chance to take some very sharp pictures for a change.

I sat next to Starla and played footsie, handsie, and kissy-kissy with her all through the meal—we weren't going to do much together, but such as it was, it would be done in public. Doric sat entrenched with Randi like a Claymation slab, and Favio, Emil, Delroy, and Mary-Ellen squeezed in where they could, huddled in various states of emotional disarray around the breadsticks. I didn't talk much—I never did—but it wasn't out of disinterest, it was for the chance to get an intoxicating earful. I was fulfilling my perennial role as the observer. Besides, if you talked, people looked at you, not advisable in this lighting.

As my eyes teared from the light, my ears burned from the talk. It was the freakiest thing—the conversation went democratically around the table like a minute hand, and each person seized the chance to change the subject of the moment, with the most finely honed manipulative skills, to himself or herself. I always thought the *seventies* were the "Me Generation." This must be the "Me-Me-Me Generation"—a new breed idealistically striving to make their portfolios a better place. Under these bohemians' flamboyant, carefree exteriors and excessive layers of not-ready-for-prime-time clothing was a yuppie mentality, a climber/achiever/self-gratifier yearning to crawl out like an alien. Being the reigning Peeping Tom of ego, I loved it.

"I got recognized so much at Atlantis tonight," beamed Mary-Ellen.

"Someone recognized me on the street the other day and wanted to take me home to kiss their baby. Can you believe it?" said Favio, wearing three hats—he subscribed to the theory "more is more."

"*Our* baby's going to be the most famous art baby since Paloma Picasso," said Doric, unable to hear the word *baby* without relating it to his own imminent progeny from hell.

"Can I see one of those menus?" I said.

Still in the collegiate frame of mind, my analytical thought processes immediately went to work on this scenario. Easy—without the pleasure of sex available anymore, these guys needed to find other forms of ego gratification, to supply their own pats on the back that would spell fulfillment of self. All that frustrated energy has to be sublimated into something else, which is probably why Delroy was nervously doodling on the tablecloth; Emil was tapping the rhythm of "Something's Gotta Give" on the wall with his knuckles; I was now giving Starla a neck massage that was making her *more* tense; and Mary-Ellen was telling us about her new designs, not conscious of whether anyone could hear her over the doodling-tapping-massaging din or wanted to. Maybe they did have sex but were still frustrated. Maybe they weren't having *good* sex. As someone who could only get it up for himself, I belonged in this group.

"They're angry, but not intimidating," Mary-Ellen said, giving us a live commercial for her clothing line. "Tailor-made for people who want a taste of avant-garde, but not really."

"Sounds a little like my paintings," said Doric, trying to veer the conversation his way.

"Sounds like that Ave campaign," muttered Favio.

"Oh, yeah, let's hear about *that* again!" whined Emil, tapping like thunder.

We heard it again. Favio was a prime contender for that beer's ad campaign using supposedly cutting-edge people, until they came across a picture of him in a dress in *Fabulon*. I guess they didn't want to be *that* avant-garde.

"I wasn't getting erotic thrills out of wearing the dress or anything," Favio moaned. "It was a joke. And it was just the underground stuff they said they wanted. What was so wrong about it when it's OK for them to use that guy who writhes around onstage playing with himself?"

"That's satire," said Randi, delicately. "You're *sick.*"

"You've got to get some three-piece suits, Favio," said Doric, nibbling on Randi's ear until the food arrived. "That's how I got that vodka ad."

"You did?" oozed Emil, tapping twice as fast now.

"Oh, just be yourself, Favio," said Starla, the only one with the nerve to be phony enough to talk about someone other than herself. "Another break will come along. They sound pretty screwy and hypocritical to me—you're too good for them. Alcohol's not healthy anyway—people get drunk and drive and kill people. You don't want to sell that stuff.''

''Yes I do,'' he said.

''Well, at least this way you can sleep at night,'' smirked Doric. ''You have your integrity.''

''Fuck that. I'd rather be famous.''

''We have so many gifts for the baby already,'' said Randi, on her own tangent. ''It's going to be the most pampered human who ever lived.''

''If it's human,'' laughed Mary-Ellen.

''If I hadn't posed in the dress, I would have gotten the goddamned ad,'' said Favio, and everyone groaned.

''But you did, Blanche,'' said Doric, doing Bette Davis. ''You did.''

The waiter looked horrified as he slammed down the food and ran—I'm not sure which of the freak shows going on at the table scared him, or maybe it was the collective performance. We all dug into the living grease festival except Starla, who pretended to have a sudden interest in talking about the good times at Carcinogen, just so she wouldn't have to take in any calories. Everyone else went along with the conversation switch; it was more interesting than rehashing Favio's dress again. Favio was right: if the gang was already waxing nostalgic about it, Carcinogen *must* be postpeak.

''My favorite time,'' said Starla, ''was when that crack addict chased me down four flights of stairs holding a gun, ha-ha, under his jacket. He demanded I take him home and sign an entire checkbook of blank checks, and I almost did it, out of sheer terror. 'I need my next fix,' he kept saying. 'If I don't get it, you're a dead bitch.' I kept screaming all the way down the stairs of the club, but everyone assumed it was just part of the usual fun and games. They all winked at me as they passed me, like, 'Wow, *you're* having a great time.'

''Eventually, I figured he was probably bluffing, and I

finally got up the nerve to grab his gun—the scariest moment of my entire life, I swear. Well, it was a cucumber. I took a big bite and spit it in his face."

Everyone laughed. Delroy put his arm around Mary-Ellen in a brotherly way, and she got all dewy-eyed as if this was an advance she'd been waiting for since birth. She petted his knee and nestled her head into his chest, causing him to flinch a little and pull off, not interested in *that* kind of communion. Her eyes sank with rejection. They could now join the ranks of all the other coitus-interruptus couples at the table. It's lonely being part of the Me-Me-Me Generation.

Doric chimed in with his story: "I couldn't believe the night that bartender, Joachim, peed into the champagne and didn't tell everybody until afterward."

"And once we found out," said Randi, "we sent a shitload of it over to that big producer's table."

"I hate that stupid place," said Mary-Ellen, bitterly. "Piss is more expensive than their champagne anyway." Randi started laughing, and everyone but Mary-Ellen joined in, more because it let off libidinal steam than because anything in particular was all that funny. I felt really out of it. While they were busy laughing, Mary-Ellen started unknotting her fire-engine red hair in annoyance—it had to be done eventually, so why not now. I snuck extra fries onto my plate.

"Poor Vinnie," said Delroy. "You missed out on so many of these scenes. Thank God you hooked up with Favio—the best tour guide there is."

"That was decades ago," I said, emphatically. "I'm one of you now." I didn't want to feel like a tourist, even if I was.

"Our first Ivy League man," said Favio. "And I met you on a hotline!"

"You did?" said Doric. "I never met anyone on one of those."

"What, you geek!" exclaimed Randi. "You call those sleazy things behind my back?" She was so livid she stopped for a second eating grease for two, but Doric appeased her by nibbling on her neck and saying, "Dummy! Why would I call a hotline when I've got you?" Emil was pulling Starla's fingers out of my hand and kissing them one by one in an act of bizarre public worship. Mary-Ellen was inching away from Delroy, a little too eagerly trying to send the message that she was alone and liked it that way—tonight's incident would never come up again. I, meanwhile, was avoiding Favio's eyes, not about to encourage the dress story—or anything else—again.

"You missed so much," repeated Delroy.

I'd make up for lost time.

"Dessert?" asked the waiter from a mile away, and Doric said, "Yes. I know what I want." That offhand statement sent chills down my spine, because I knew his ambition didn't just extend to the menu, not by a long shot. This was just like the end of freshman year, when I realized everyone was already convinced of what type of pre—law-med-engineering—they were going to study and what they were going to do with it, while I was blindly pursuing an English lit major for lack of anything else—a gut subject that I somehow found staggeringly difficult because there was no sense of purpose behind it. Once again, everyone knew exactly what they wanted—fame—and exactly what kind, and how to get it, as I sat there trying to decide between rice pudding and cheesecake.

The magazine took up every waking hour that I wasn't primping or schmoozing, which wasn't a lot of time, because I had to primp and schmooze so much more now that I was on a dire quest for copy. I was alphabetically correct on a lot of the lists—my fantasy come true—so along with all the health club fliers inviting you to kill yourself while striving for the biceps that will make you truly complete, every day's mail brought a treasure trove of glossy cards and foldouts beckoning me to celebrate basically anyone willing to put a blender on his head and call it a fashion statement. I remember an invite for the opening of a new club called Zymurgy, which said it would be "the last word in nightlife." After a few days, Favio finally figured out the gimmick: *zymurgy* is the very last word in *Webster's*. It was going to be the absolute end.

Even Odile, that glorified icebox where anyone who has a good time is shot, got into the rampant mailing mania, sending invites to fetes for the very well-bred celebrity juniors—show-biz biggies' kids who were born with silver spoons up their noses, which may explain why they always talked so nasally. I had a sneaky feeling that even with an invite, you still couldn't get into Odile, but who wanted to? On a good day, Frank E. Campbell's Funeral Home was a much nuttier good time.

Having the club scene covered, I started calling publicists (from a list Emil had "borrowed" from Heinz's office) to weasel into celebrity events, thinking with unrealistic grandeur that they'd all gang-rush me into Lauren Bacall's place at the Dakota for a mimosa brunch that very day. Unfortunately, the guy who used to handle all the big movie stars said he was now handling the Care Bears. And the rest wanted tear sheets, references, practically a pap smear— even for B parties. All I managed to get into at first was something at the Javits Center celebrating Gloria Vanderbilt's salad dressing and a party at the Hard Rock for Holly Farms chicken—slim pickings, but not compared to Champale-punch dorm parties where the chips run out after twenty minutes, but the dips stay all night.

The salad dressing tasted better than Gloria's jeans though it wasn't the best brand for thriftware cooties. The chicken was delish—Dinah Shore was there ramming every part of it down people's faces as she blew those sweet ole kisses and smiled warmly. She certainly knows about chicken, having dabbled in it in the form of almost-half-her-age Burt Reynolds. And when a platoon of paparazzi let off an artillery of flashes on this perverse spectacle, it did seem terribly exciting, even if it was just for poultry. Dinah—no chicken herself—was so nice, but I couldn't tell my mother about this. She'd think I was impressed.

As my rep grew, there'd be bigger parties to attend, more important photographers to dodge. One day I woke up with a jolt, having dreamed that Greta Garbo and J. D. Salinger were camping out in my apartment and talking effusively over a six-course buffet they'd brought. They were saying the most amazing things—Greta in particular revealed some mind-boggling secrets about her sexual proclivities—and as we were finishing up our delicious pumpkin-mousse dessert, they both chimed in, without having been asked, that this was all *on* the record, by the way. I woke up sweating boulders—I think the waking state protects you from anything too horrible. And for someone with a deep-down fear of real success, that dream was terrifying.

The magazine had to be ready in time for the party, and that was incentive enough for me to meet those dread dead-lines. So I set to work writing up the cover interview with Starla in which she told me all the same things she'd already told me in private. Was she so full of defenses that there was no difference between her personality while being inter-viewed and while being almost-fucked? She said she didn't want to be just a party star, she wanted to be a star who went to parties. She said the new beauty line was designed to transform "any domestic beast into a dazzling beauty of the night." And she concluded the interview with: "I'm going to keep on rising till I'm A–number one and the top of the heap." I laughed, assuming she was quoting "New York, New York," but as she didn't laugh back, I'm not sure.

Delroy and I had the idea of photographing her in a terry-cloth robe on a chaise longue, with her feet in a basin of cold water and her hands in Madge-the-manicurist–like bowls of goo. ("I dig rock, Madge." "Your hands *look* like you've been digging rocks.") But her face would be dazzlingly made-up with Starla beauty products, and her hair would be funky-fresh—Favio's latest expression now that he'd decided black was cool. It would have been a cute juxtaposition of the ordinary and the glamorous, but Starla thought the idea demystified her too much. She was so uptight about ever being caught without blinders on, without those two smallish but personable heat-seeking missiles giving a standing ovation. We ended up with the generic shot of her throwing her arms in the air and opening her mouth real wide. As she cranked open that air-kiss canyon, I saw my first Pulitzer walk out the door, thank you.

The rest of the mag consisted of my critiques of anything that consumed the mind of any conscious New Yorker, or at least myself. Though typical of absolutely no subgenre or special interest group in the entire city, I was at the age where you figure that any take you have on anything—dog glaucoma, *anything*—is so terribly fascinating it's worth imparting to the masses at any cost. To farm out the ego, I did give Delroy his own page, Star Wars, which featured nothing but people having fights, an even more common party occurrence than people saying hello. (In fact, some of the fights were because someone *hadn't* said hello, and one, between gossip columnist Horton Shreibel and a certain Countess Dina de Maupassant, erupted because he'd said, "Hello, Dina," instead of the more respectful "Hi, fake Countess.") But everything in the magazine sprang from the splinters in the windmills of my mind, and mine alone.

I did a column called Breakfast in Bed, in which I actually had breakfast in bed with someone—a brilliant case of concept imitating title. The virgin subject was Pat, who was a guy named Pat, then a girl named Pat, and then a few months later had his fake breasts removed and became a guy again. Still named Pat. First you cry.

Pat had suffered a traumatic case of boy-gets-girl, boy-loses-girl, and his favorite song, I wonder why, was "A Man and a Woman." As that lyric-free ditty droned in the background, we devoured cream-cheese omelettes and discussed what it's like to have memories of one's mammaries. Pat said he'd "milked" the transsexual routine for glitter and photo opportunities long enough; now that he'd done his color charts and rotated a few crystals, he felt he was centered enough to face up to his natural-born gender. ("Thank God I never cut my pinga off," he added, spiritually. "There's a reason they make those operations so expensive.") As a man, Pat felt he had a better chance of being an incast instead of an outcast. "I want to be an innie," he shrieked, still sounding pretty womanly. "I don't want to be Pearl Chavez!" That remark said it all; anyone who went around quoting *Duel in the Sun* as a change-of-life inspiration was doomed to outiehood forever.

To appease the newies, who were already planning their own magazines to compensate for their lack of press in *Fabulon,* I decided to give them a page a month, but it wasn't the most flattering showcase for their awesome talent void. It was a quiz wherein I'd ask them *College Bowl*–style questions and get hilariously retarded responses that sprang from their having been clubbed to death at such a young age. The inevitable first subject was José Can-U.C., Favio's current fixation, who was particularly priceless. Like most of the newies, José's every bleet and whine was subsidized by his parents, and so he couldn't exactly live a life of punk rebellion. Not being against anything, he wasn't really *for* anything either, which is why he spent his life in a hedonistic limbo designed mainly to pass the time. He reminded me of myself a little, only younger (he admitted to sweet sixteen, but legend had him at fifteen), Puerto Rican, ruder, not possessing half of a diploma, and more impractically dressed. I wouldn't be caught dead in the see-through vinyl hot pants he sometimes wore as though they were painted on, replete with a flawless view of his manhood, a view that made it very hard for most people to describe what his face looked like. I ran just a head shot.

José's quiz answers were as magnificently redolent of a schooling-by-boob-tube as I'd hoped. He guessed that *Crime and Punishment* was a porno magazine, Kierkegaard was a character on *Star Trek,* and *The Magnificent Ambersons* had to be a Voguing house. He was made a laughingstock in at least a ten-block radius, but thanked me profusely with a box of chocolates and a Hallmark card he said he got in the section marked Grovel. The box turned out to be empty— asshole—but I knew he loved the story, and so did everyone else. *Spy* had made it cool to be smartass.

I also included a write-up on a big, splashy party for Faye Dunaway at Mortimer's—top of the world, Ma! All right, I crashed it after reading a notice of the event in the *Post,* but they didn't give me such a hard time at the door, so obviously I looked like I *could* have been invited. (I said I was from *New York* magazine, and when they couldn't find me on the list, I made the biggest scene since Tallulah Bankhead didn't get to do the movie of *The Litte Foxes.*) Nobody there seemed to know exactly what the event was for—it was just for Faye, and that was good enough. But Fayeness was not the order of the day, the place not serving as its usual high-society version of the Russian Tea Room, where you can only try to imagine why the almost-Someones and used-to-be-Someones have been placed in which Siberian regions. This night it had sold out to glitz, giving way to a media zoo where there was little society or decorum at all—the whole place was Siberia and everyone was out for a piece of Faye, whatever she was there for.

After an hour of something wrapped in bacon, our hostess arrived and was the most entertainingly affected creature I'd ever seen. She wore jet-black sunglasses and was whisking herself with a big *lamé* fan—to assure that there'd be at least one fan in the room? I found her mesmerizing—a real movie star who was somehow lost without a camera to snag her mannerisms. She seemed to have escaped off celluloid and to be looking for her way back.

Emil helped me piece the magazine together, I guess so he'd have a stake in it from the ground floor. I mercilessly let him do all the slaving he wanted, but promised nothing—this operation was going to wheeze from day to day, without obligations or regrets. And we did have fun as he raced around to typesetters, printers, and potential advertisers while I sat back in my Tennessee Williams–style wicker chair and tickled the ivories of a computer I can thank fat Uncle Vito for. Blessed with that delightfully overbearing mother who dressed me until college in brain-damage-inducing polyester oddities and zippered turtlenecks and to this day offers—no, begs—to come over weekly to vacuum my bed, I never trusted anyone else to so much as point me toward the nearest public phone. But now I trusted Emil deeply; I knew he wouldn't fail this potential ego-stroking gold mine. To thank him, I titled him Creative Director. Favio was Consultant, saying things like, "Tired as she is, you have to mention Mary-Ellen just because she's there"—a remark that was unusually considerate of him and got him reduced to Contributor. Starla and I were the board of directors, and at least we knew that sex would never interfere with our many meetings.

One night Emil and I were planning our party and deciding stuff, like only Manhattans should be served at the bar, place mats should be made of our first back cover (a picture of Starla's back), and all the other nitpicky things you have to do to contrive an event and not just another oh-you-again kind of deal. Emil had arranged to have it at Zymurgy because it was so new—we'd have the first stab at the last word. And the word—I looked it up—did have something to do with winemaking and brewing, so the vibes were already decent, no matter what was going to be served at the bar.

Just as we were discussing the entertainment—I wanted a man I saw on public access who played spoons on a prosthesis; Emil wanted a tango band—Favio, his larynx panting, called from the street. I thought his mother had died, or worse, Brooks Astor. "You guys," he screeched, "you've got to sputnik over to Carcinogen immediately. I was right—not only has it peaked, but it's closed! They were raided and shut down and it's over—I can't believe it's over. That place was so startling, wasn't it? Quick—we're having a funeral party outside. I'm drug-free—I swear. Wear black." He sounded half devastated about the club's demise and half thrilled over this impromptu happening. He'd often told me that funerals were the parties of the eighties.

"We'll be there," I said, definitively. Emil was already wearing black—his badge, I always thought, that said he wasn't a bona fide one of them, just someone looking to get his rocks off. The same applied to me, but my camouflage was always more convincing, my armor more humorously impenetrable. In a desperate rush, I threw on a Banquo's ghost–type shroud from Favio's closet and the big, black, three-years-*passé* gaucho hat I'd gotten for fifty cents on the street, and said, "God, we look ready for Odile." We were half out the door when Emil suggested we do some "schnitzie" first, because "we're gonna need it for this."

"Sure thing," I said, not willing to confess that I had no idea in hell what schnitzie was. I thought it was probably some kind of German sausage. He produced it from his back pocket and made lines of it on his hand. So he *did* do coke. I could handle that. The one time I did it—having been forced—I felt so sexual I never wanted to get off; the feeling itself was like intercourse minus all the things that bothered me about it. I prepared for a night of washing dishes.

We couldn't believe the throng outside Carcinogen—it was a funeral to rival Princess Grace's, but ten times more dramatic because the characters looking undone under their black veils were the ones who usually wore multicolors and made like banshees. Favio had somehow gotten hold of a black Body Glove he must have run out and bought on a moment's notice. God knows where he found a store that sold them at one in the morning; I don't think those all-night Korean fruit stands carry Body Glove. He looked heartbroken, not so much because he was going to miss Carcinogen, but because now he had to come up with his next move. "I'm Exing, I'm Exing," he said, meaning on Ecstasy—a man of his word—but didn't *seem* Exing. Even Starla wore a black ensemble and tried to look dour, not one of her better emotions. "Hiiii!" she screamed, grabbing me by my negligible love handles and giving me a big, sloppy kiss that I swear only involved tongue when she was sure someone was looking (and everyone was looking; Starla's downtown appearances were becoming so noticeably less frequent this could have been a funeral for her career as underground star). I slipped her the tongue back and grabbed her by the buttocks in a way that announced, I own you; if we were going to "beard" for each other, then we were going to have to do it well. Soon I was lifting her up and spinning her around as Delroy and two other photographers used up their flashes like it was the photo of the decade so far that night.

Was this a funeral for the whole scene, or maybe the whole depraved, fucking universe? Who cared, as Doric took Starla from me and started twirling her around, and Emil clutched onto her ankles like a human barnacle and dervished with them; the schnitzie had kicked in already. Starla unleashed him with a giggle—she didn't want a run in her nylons—and he looked privileged to have merited even a shove.

She had the right idea—to work the funeral for one more good time. I mean, it was a great crowd—maybe the best the club had ever drawn—so why waste it on sorrow when you could just kiss the boo-boo away? Starla's spirits were infectious. Even for the most devoted Carcinogen regulars who were counting on this cry-in to use up all their maudlin emotions for the year, the solemn mood was much harder to keep up than Starla's gemlike breasts in her support-free blouson. All the Carcinogen regulars had been walking with their heads bowed, holding lit candles, and chanting some kind of sick, Latin incantation, but it was just a matter of minutes before they snapped out of their Bergmanesque personas and into their real, certifiable Cyndi Lauper ones again. The candles were summarily tossed to the wind, and as if by divine will, Favio led them all in a conga line into the street, using the cab drivers' honking horns as a rhythm track.

"So," said Mary-Ellen, "the piece ran." I had no idea what on earth she was talking about. "The piece in *Fashion News*—I told you they were doing a story on me. It ran today." Yeah, she had told me, but that must have been at least two weeks ago—a whole lifetime had passed for me. Did she really think my every waking thought was about her piece in some obscure Seventh Avenue newsletter I'd never even lined bird cages with?

"That's great," I said.

"Fabulous," oozed Emil. "I knew you'd get written up in there—it only makes sense." Even on schnitzie, Emil was Mr. Diplomacy. There were limits, though. She was piercing us with her raccoon eyes, and the clear undertone was that she wanted us to ask her something, anything, about the clipping so she could pull it out of her beaded bag and ram our faces in it. But we refused even to say, How did it come out? We just grinned silently, which was especially evil of Emil, who knew firsthand how strong the urge to flaunt one's press can be. But would one drug addict give another drug addict his last vial of crack? No, and neither could these press whores give each other the satisfaction they craved in order to go on living.

"I hear your magazine's coming along quite spectacularly," said Mary-Ellen, plowing on. This was her subtle-as-a-wrecking-ball way of finding out if she was in the first issue or not. I just kept on smiling my best, cryptic smile and nodded my head without a hint of information exuding from any part of my face—another cruel blow. She wasn't a bad person, probably just a neglected child who was now trying to compensate for parents who went bowling a lot. She did have a brain, unlike some of the party people, and when she relaxed and didn't think of her press, she could actually be pleasant and funny. Unfortunately, that only happened when she was in severe pain.

"It's sad about Carcinogen," I said, stating the obvious without much conviction; I don't do regretful well either. She made a face and put two fingers down her throat in a gagging gesture.

"Good riddance," she screamed. Oh, right, she hated Carcinogen; Heinz had stopped booking her fashion shows because her draw was diminishing, yet with each career slippage, she was becoming more demanding than Coco Chanel. That's why she'd ended up at Skid Row, the club, and skid row, the place. And that's why she was shamelessly exulting at the funeral, perfectly in sync with the general mood by now. A couple of beehived drag queens were acting obscene on car hoods by having beer bottles gush out of their bras; how they'd opened the bottles I didn't even want to know. Everyone else was dancing up and down the narrow street on one another's shoulders and singing old Sister Sledge songs. (With the death of this club, and all that was present, it was pretty inevitable that the seventies would come back like a bad Mexican dinner.)

Emil was having a blast-off too, having reached his wired-for-sound maintenance level. I saw him trying to sneak some more coke into his highly talented nostril, but when the conga line started dancing his way—these people can smell anything white for miles—he tucked it back into his pocket and acted painfully nonchalant. "They should hire these people as detective dogs," he said, annoyed.

"Or truffle pigs," remarked Mary-Ellen.

"That's not nice," said Delroy, the one who loved life so much he made everyone else want to murder him. One night when José Can-U.C. had his hair sticking up like a boner a foot and a half into the air and Favio remarked that he wanted him to "fuck me, fuck me, fuck me with your hair," Delroy actually said, "No you don't. You just like him as a person." I liked Delroy as a person. At least you could count on him for favors.

By now I liked everything. The shnitzie had given me a buzz that felt like I was being gently electrocuted, fried in an easy chair one tiny, delicious volt at a time. It relaxed my natural anxiety and transformed it into an enjoyable sense of danger—a low, ringing sound in my ears that said anything might happen. Starla wouldn't go near the stuff— she already *had* a low ringing in her ears, and being the type that even bathed in Evian water, she wasn't about to pollute her temple with grease, magazine-publisher semen, or drugs of any kind. Mary-Ellen and Delroy were also good about abstaining—Mary-Ellen because she didn't want bags, and Delroy, of course, because it was the nerdy thing to do. They were the new age of innocence you read about so much. Favio, meanwhile, was avoiding coke for different reasons. "It kills the Ecstasy high," he informed. "Never mix, never worry."

The whole gang was going off to Dramamine, the after-hours club by the river, but Starla wouldn't be caught dead at such a dive. It was a noxious meat-packing warehouse where they left the sawdust on the floor and called it "atmosphere," and you could light a match and call it gone. Everyone there was on major drugs and desperately needed to get a life. When they played Sid Vicious's "My Way" and turned up the lights at nine A.M., it was the most depressing moment since the Challenger blew up. I wanted to go, but Starla said no way, and we were a team now—the board of directors, chairmen of the bored. As we all waited for cabs Favio threw his arms around me and half kiddingly said, "Why don't you sleep with me tonight?" It was the other half that bothered me.

"But I do sleep with you," I said, laughing much too hard to sound natural. I was shaking a little bit; I'd been propositioned by guys before, but never by one I'd have to eventually come home to the same night. Someone had pulled a switch, and all the volts were on now. Favio's arms darted off me like they'd been struck by lightning. I decided to spend the night at Starla's, where I was safe.

4

We didn't even have foreplay-as-a-main-course that night. We could barely get to the bed, now that her room was strewn with products and promo materials, real romantic stuff. (I'm serious—all that merch did turn me on, but this time in a more cerebral way. The coke had worn off and I enjoyed feeling my mind race around this glamorous maze of beauty paraphernalia.) It was a twisted kind of kick to realize that Favio was probably home jerking off right now and thinking about me. But it was an eerie, chilly feeling for sure—what the hell would I say to him when I finally got home? Or would I never summon the nerve to crawl back, just send my mother over to pick up my stuff and then move to a faraway, mountainous island to live platonically with the goats?

At eight in the morning, schmutz in the corners of my eyes instead of beauty products, I dragged myself out of bed and decided to deal with this live–action bad dream. Wending through the mascara wands with enough finesse not to wake Starla, I made it to the glaring outdoors (who lit *this* place?), where I stood on a corner for a good twenty minutes before a cab would stop for me. They probably assumed that anyone in a black shroud and gaucho hat at this hour was not responsible enough to pay the fare. I hate when they make assumptions like that. I do not usually dress this way. And I could not only pay them, I could give them an invitation to Zymurgy.

While waiting, I spotted Vogel Johns on the other side of the street. He was a stuck-up writer who'd just put me on the "Out" list in *Limo*. A few minutes on the scene, and I was already over. Actually, I loved the mention—it meant I was worth judging in the first place. And as my first real press, it baptised me by fire into the world of fame orgasms—an intoxicating state, as I should have gathered from all my friends' religiosity about it. Your eyes dart to your name like magnets, your head gets woozy, and you almost black out from the sense of importance: what you do *matters*. By the tenth time you've read it, your lips are chapping, but you barely notice; press—even bad press—makes you drunk against discomfort.

He spotted me, but I kept my eyes focused on a nearby license plate and acted like I didn't see him; that one acting class had served me so well in so many situations. There must be a God, because Vogel kept on walking with increasing briskness until fully out of view. One great thing about New York is that everyone's so vain; no one will stop you on the street at eight A.M. and see how horrible you look because they'd rather die than have you see how horrible *they* look.

I finally got a cab, and naturally the driver was one of those scarifying types out of central casting who had all the mannerisms of Tony Perkins trapped in the body of Rod Steiger. Who else would be driving a cab at this hour? "The Yanks are having a great year, aren't they?" he said, before I even closed the door. He had a beard soaking with what seemed to be clam sauce and smelled like he had rubbed Mitchum antiperspirant on his face. "Yeah," I said, just to shut him up.

"You asshole," he countered, wittily. "They're having a horrible year. I just said that to test you." I wanted the schweinhund to die. I wanted his dick to fall off from dry rot. I wanted him to get nothing but the cast of *Eight Is Enough* as his fares from now until doomsday. Still, the verbal abuse wasn't half as bad as the thought of having to go back onto the pavement and keep hailing. I might run into Vogel again.

"I'm sorry," I said and played an internal game—trying to think up a hundred ways to pronounce Dusan Makavejev—to avoid catching any more of his rantings. By the sixteenth one—Dus-*onn* Makave-*yev*—I was home free.

When I walked into the apartment, I had to let out a little gasp. Favio was wide awake, if mentally sleepy, lying seductively on the couch in a slinky, vulnerable position that fully complemented his zebra-print peignoir and fuck-me pumps. I contemplated making a run for my cell and locking the door for life.

"Now do you want me, sailor? Hmm?" he purred, throwing his legs back behind his ears. "Face it. I'm more man than you'll ever be and more woman than you'll ever get."

I started laughing uncontrollably, and so did he, rubbing his butt with satirical lust. Thank God he'd decided to make light of this nerve-wracking situation or we'd never have cleared the air. I couldn't be sure whether Wizard air freshener works on cat pee, but it definitely doesn't work on homosexual tension.

"I don't care if you're a fag and you don't know it," he said, jumping up and turning on the light. "Someday you'll know it and you'll want me. Only then you'll have to pay."

"I'm not a fag," I said, smiling but with great gravity. I had to drive that point home. I was so sick of everyone just assuming things.

"I can't believe Carcinogen is over," he said. Finally, we were back on a real subject. "Over, over, over." He was repeating it like a mantra. Without that playpen to frolic in, Favio was lost—a party boy without a runway, Telly Savalas with hair. The money would still keep coming in from his mystery parents, but what good were all the outfits without a public showroom in which to display them? Oh sure, there was still Atlantis, but that was to Carcinogen as Tuna Helper was to beluga. And no one even mentioned the after-hours clubs as a consolation—they never lasted more than three weeks, usually ending in some kind of horrible violence you were upset if you missed.

"All the rules will be different now," I said, incensed that I'd learned them so quickly and so well.

"Something will happen," said Favio, convincing himself. "The newies will do something." He flipped wanly through the tattered *Vanity Fair* he'd committed to memory by now.

"And there's always Zymurgy," I said.

"Yeah!" he exclaimed, and ran into his room to start piecing his outfit together for my party there. It was six weeks away.

Zymurgy turned out to be not so much the last word as the last straw. Judging from the advance publicity and the opening itself, it wasn't going to be a wild and woolly petting zoo for the young at heart. It was another glorified funeral parlor, a second-rate Odile, just as Atlantis was a cheap knockoff of Carcinogen and Michael J. Fox was a bad version of Mickey Rooney. This place promised all the pretensions of haute culture with none of the dazzle, and, to paraphrase my new bible, *Fabulon,* there's nothing more offensive than pretension without justification, attitude without backup. Atlantis wasn't stuck-up, just second-rate.

Zymurgy was both. Maybe I was just being pessimistic. But isn't pessimism known in many circles as common sense?

The decor included a ticker that rattled off all the newest developments on Wall Street—not just cute, but practical— a poster for a TV movie about Klaus Barbie, and an open casket filled with dollar bills everyone was too cool to clutch for, though you know they wanted to. "It's fabulous," said Emil, unpredictably. OK, so it's fabulous.

There was a basement of coldly calculated environmental rooms, where, after having checked your fur, you could sit around and mourn the depletion of our natural resources. But everyone was packed, anchovylike, into the main floor, which was replete with conceptual art banging you from the eight-foot ceiling and a metal stairway out of a maximum security prison, that was icy to the touch. The place had been a drug-rehabilitation center and was now a kind of Betty Ford clinic for those who didn't want to be strapped down overnight. Before it was a rehab center, it was a treasury department office building.

Only because it was owned by Garth Free, who was part of the woodwork at the ultimate downtown club, Love Kills, a few years back (the only place, aside from Carcinogen, that you were allowed to reminisce about without seeming tired), everyone assumed Zymurgy was going to be creatively insane, a merry-go-round of uncontrollable fun swarming with all the struggling, artistic types and professional partiers that made mornings worth staying up for. We were counting on it to revive everything that had been buried with the Carcinogen funeral, but that was an impossible dream; since that club first made it chic to be a starving artist the struggling folk had either made it in a big way or been frozen out by the new financial crunch, and as a crowd, didn't exist anymore.

Zymurgy was tailor-made to suit the new times— conservative, money-grubbing, elitist, colorphobic. "Greed is good," these people had come to believe without any sense of satire, *buying* the artists as investments, not becoming them. Making it the same way everyone else was making it was the name of the game, only you had to make it bigger and fiercer and with less distracting individual style. Everyone had woken up one day as Kafkaesque cockroaches and weren't questioning it, just forging ahead according to the cockroach rules as aggressively as possible while convincing themselves that their new pustulence looked *faaaaabulous*. Most disconcerting was that, in the course of this one night, the very downtown folk who'd expected a lot more from Zymurgy took one look around, decided that good or bad, this was what would be happening, and adapted to it on the spot, pausing only to make sure their hair was on straight. They'd managed to resist Odile's dubious charms for a while, but now that Zymurgy had come along to cement the repressive trend, everyone recognized that to keep bucking it would be poisonous; in they marched.

Like Joan Crawford, who wasn't mad at her maid but "mad at the dirt," you couldn't really be mad at the place so much as at the times it was symptomatic of. But what were you supposed to do—go scream at an almanac? I was mad at Zymurgy. I was mad at all the constrictions I'd been running from and had now met full circle. And I was mad at Emil, who I suspected knew all along what kind of place we were dealing with but led me on to think differently so he wouldn't lose the party.

"What's your problem?" he said manically, adding one more time for effect, "It's fabulous." Oh, really? I guess he had a selective sense memory that could extend only as far back as the last spoonful of schnitzie. When all the nut jobs were dancing on tables, he had practically drooled on their outfits in delirious appreciation. Now that everyone was sitting around looking like they'd just smelled a fart, *that* was the happening deal, and he loved that, too. "What the fuck is going on here?" I moaned, jealous that he could adapt so well, furious that he really *did* seem to love this place. If a waiter served you a rotten piece of fish, would you refuse to send it back simply because no one else had? There was room for enough self-exclusive circles in New York that no one had to conform if they didn't want to. But they wanted to. Suddenly they *wanted* to sit around and emulate the grandparents they'd always made fun of in all their inert boredom. Nightlife was now about acting old instead of young. Thank God circles were gradually coming in under my eyes.

Without any alternative, I prepared to march into the Roach Motel with the best of them and take up residence in the slimy chameleon guest room. Face it: I'd have to adapt before it was too late or risk being left behind like an empty beer can. I glanced around desperately and tried to enjoy the multisensual constipation. It wasn't easy.

Forty-threeish Garth was the severest-looking thing I'd ever seen, a spindly cross between Dorian Gray and the star of *Glen or Glenda?*. He scurried around the place, making things happen with a minimum of fuss; a major control freak, he didn't talk much, he just *did*. All the help— attractive in that anemic, WASPy way these places die for—had bamboo shoots under their fingernails and poles up their asses, their occasional hatchet-toothed smiles perfectly accessorized with linguini-thin lips (but I don't mean to be nasty).

"Someone should break the news to Favio that he has to tone down his act," Emil told me as we were preparing for the party. "He's getting out of hand." He wasn't getting out of hand—he was doing the same act he'd been doing for years, only suddenly it wasn't popular anymore. I wanted to scream so loud Garth would try to bury me alive in that coffin, but we were laying out the place mats and there was no time for big scenes right now. My stomach had been tied up in dozens of tiny Boy Scout knots, but now I was suffering from that sunken feeling you get in the cheeks after you've done badly at something—all your facial muscles drop to the ground and you see stars as if you've been hit. I couldn't believe I'd valiantly met my deadline and dragged over hundreds of copies of *Manhattan on the Rocks* just for this journey into Maalox. Instead of preperformance jitters, I suddenly felt premature postperformance depression.

Chill, I told myself, digging my nails into my palms as I was wont to do in moments of desperation. At least our guest list might lend some dazzle to this place—we could make our own fun. And it was new, new, new, and anything new was innately exciting until it turned into just another harbinger of stultification. Tonight it might be, would *have* to be, a sparkly good time, for the sake of my own newborn self-aggrandizement. A *constipated,* sparkly good time, but maybe not the total abortion it looked like.

Miraculously enough, as the guests started schlepping in—not until a full ninety minutes into the announced time (everyone has a dread terror of being the first one there)— the place did vivify a bit under pressure, like one of those sea monkeys that almost comes alive in water. Hold on, Mr. Vinnie, I thought. This could work, in its own oppressive way. In New York, triumph can turn to suicide and back again in a matter of minutes.

Of course, it started agonizingly, but that was fine— things could only get better. The first one to arrive was Mary-Ellen—"Shit, I'm always the first!" she barked—and I tried to convince myself it wasn't because she had something to promote, but because she was really being a friend. I went to greet her and felt my heart sink as she handed me a flier announcing her rummage sale. I laughed—this girl was such a riot. Not since Kent State had there been such a riot.

But the occasion started rising to *us* as photographer Stanislaw Lavelieri sauntered in with Rima, a really hot designer (I'd never heard of her, but Emil assured me she was a really hot designer), followed by the trendy triumvirate of *Fabulon* editor Jonathan Formento, his star columnist, Sean Valve, and a model, Dovima Powell-Lyng, all in deep conversation over the decline of mousse as a popular art form. And a slew of impeccably dressed people were making it past the ropes like cattle in a John Ford movie, among them Colette Joie, a well-known PWM (Person with Money), and Taormina Strayhorn, a reliably entertaining lush who had beamed onto earth from another planet decades ago and claimed to be thirtysomething—in dog years, no doubt.

"That's Drindl," said Emil, ready to wet himself as he spotted a tall, tan vision in a Dorothy Hamill wedge cut. "She's going to be a big star." He ran over to literally kiss her tuckus. This was getting pretty upscale.

Doric and the pregnant accessory showed up, and they were in a foul mood, having fought the whole day about whether or not Doric was going to "settle down" in some eight million different ways once the baby was born. Randi was pouting so hard her face looked as swollen as her abdomen. Doric reeked of gin as he leaned over into my ear—all the way in—and said something cryptic about his "inner demons." If this guy had any inner demons, they were running around with their arms in the air acting out Judy Garland movies. Fortunately, they both lightened up after a few seconds and prepared to gin-soak their troubles away some more.

On their heels like a scuff mark was Vogel Johns, whom I'd invited just to show I was better than he was. I gave him a big hello—"You look incredible!"—to let him know just how *much* better I was. He looked unremarkable. Soon, I bet myself, he'd be asking to work for my magazine.

José Can-U.C. was the only newie we'd invited, and I had to insist on it; Emil, who was usually so taken by the up-and-coming, had wrongly assumed this Zymurgy stuff was the only game in town now and nothing the least bit imperfect could ever matter again. I was surprised at his tunnel vision and made an ugly scene demanding we let José in as a token exemplar of the new. "He's a really good friend," I whined, lying through my gingivitis. Emil, while striking from the list other possibilities who weren't fabulous enough (like anyone from Dartmouth—"boring"—and my cousin Valeria from Queens—"*tacky* boring"), finally conceded to José, only because "He's in the magazine, though God knows why, and we should have people there who have something to do with the magazine." Everyone else there had something to do with the magazine, but unfortunately the magazine was *Fabulon*.

José, doll that he is, came with five other newies—not the usual plus-one—all wearing Fabrice tutus they'd obviously bought on a group discount. They were blowing bubbles, lighting up sparklers, and generally wreaking unsightly havoc that belonged in a sideshow for mutants, not at the very tasteful Zymurgy. I loved it, but Emil quickly escorted them to a corner table with a phony "Fabulous," not realizing that these kids couldn't be contained as easily as fungus. When José got up and commandeered a more central table, turning the place cards into confetti, all the tutu people followed suit. He was developing a hypnotic power over them, half Dr. Dolittle, half Manson. "They're just tu-tu," I said to Emil, but he didn't laugh. "Rim shot," I added, and he still didn't laugh.

Diane Plewge was there in her famous bubble glasses, urging everyone to come to her next benefit or go to hell, an interesting variant on "Be there or be square." She was a pushy AIDS promoter—she didn't promote AIDS; she promoted events that supposedly *fought* AIDS, but Favio told me she was more likely promoting herself. Without AIDS, after all, she'd be a nobody. If they ever found the cure Diane Plewge was supposedly fighting for, it would also be the cure for Diane Plewge.

And, as much as he may have disapproved, Favio was on her arm and dressed in an elegant black leather suit—it looked hotter than hell, tempwise, but one suffers for one's fashion when one's spent that much money for the privilege of suffering in it. The suit's only idiosyncracy was that the shoulders bagged out a little, like beanbags. Had Emil talked to him? He didn't even have makeup on, thus depriving himself of his favorite leisure-time activity—blotting his lipstick on invites. Everyone was oohing and ahing over how "masculine" he looked, and Sandahl DeVol, a sixty-fiveish Riverdale socialite who had just done a home-accounting video, the proceeds of which, if any, were going toward AIDS research, was inviting him to her house in Maine for the weekend. She'd never even said hello to him before.

To round out the circus, Emil had invited puffy-faced Fred Geze (it was almost part of his name), who'd written a semibest-seller in '81 and spent the subsequent years drinking away his semicelebrity and having trouble coming up with a second book. Fred never left the bar, and wasn't about to until dinner was called, but he didn't have to worry; dinner wouldn't be called until Starla made her entrance, even if she didn't show up until Wednesday. Like every party she went to, this was going to be her event.

Too bad the Manhattans-only-bar idea was going from a cute gimmick to a major nightmare as Fred started screaming at the bartender that he wanted a J&B straight up or he'd base a character on him. The bartender seemed thrilled by the prospect but obliged anyway. Face it—you can't drink a gimmick.

The room had started to buzz, and it wasn't as eerie a sound as in those killer-bee movies; it was the sound of success. Everyone was talking, chattering, clattering, balking, and making a big noise. Loudest of all was José, leading the tutu people in a round robin of "Chitty Chitty Bang Bang"—it was a deafening exercise in psychotic sweetness. Delroy, who'd snuck in when nobody noticed, was trying to join in with them, and they were reluctantly letting him, even though they were all too disdainfully aware that he was old guard. Even a relative newcomer like me could remember back far enough to when he was new guard.

Finally, the moment that happens at every party came, when all the hubbub suddenly quiets down, and, struck by a mysterious sense of foreboding, everyone knows it's best to sit back and watch. It was just at that moment, as if she'd been waiting outside for hours for it, that Starla made her entrance—though not blessed with the best business acumen in the world, she did have an uncanny sense of timing that should be captured by the Japanese for some kind of digital-watch advance. She was wearing dozens of extensions that would have been tired on anyone else and jewel-encrusted flats that were an incredibly daring choice for someone of her height. It made us respect her more.

With her windswept visuality and dynamite line reading of ''Hiii!'', Starla could turn even a low moment into a peak, but this time she was right on the button as she grinned at her own brilliance and just stood there causing an impressive commotion. The newies, who knew she was someone but weren't sure exactly who, were dumbstruck. The Carcinogen crowd was electrically charged—they'd yet to begin really dishing her—and Favio in particular did not look like he was gasping over someone who was ''over.'' The few socialites Emil had managed to drag down there, assuring them that it would be ''cool'' for them to go slumming for a change, were horrified; this girl was clearly nothing but white trash. Dinner was served.

The first course was some bizarre cross between moussaka and slab marble. It turned out that though nothing else about the club was ancient Greek, their cuisine was—one of the warning signs that Garth Free was truly losing it. The food had the texture of grit and tasted like it was probably found in an excavation in Athens and then microwaved by a blind person. If you asked for some seasonings to make it taste like it had once been alive, the waitresses informed you that they didn't have those spices in ancient Greece. They didn't have waitresses either.

As everyone dug in (with twentieth-century utensils, thank God) I tried to ignore the thought that just a few breakdowns ago I'd been studying *The Odyssey,* and now my closest connection with ancient history was this hunk of runny, red, seasoning-free, *faux* mountain-goat diarrhea. Fortunately, no one eats at their own party. You're too nervous and much too preoccupied as you hippity-hop from table to table with effortless charm and make sure no one's going to murder anyone, or if they do, that they'll clean up the mess. Of course, Emil fancied himself the host of this one, but I knew whose ass was really on the line.

The party talk had middle-grounded to a nice, chirpy level—people of different cliques had sandblasted through one another's walls and were actually not passing out from culture shock—and the deejay, crinoline-clad Valerie Rapchuck, was spinning just the right esoteric blend of music to underscore it—everything from They Might Be Giants to the soundtrack from *Carousel.* At least the music wasn't Greek or we might have to listen to quaint folk songs about buttfucking. Whenever Valerie took a break, the tango band went on. (Yes, Emil had won out—the amputee spoon player was not going to be. Maybe Sylvia could drop by and do a one-legged soft shoe.)

"This is the rulingest party," enthused Favio. "I really mean it—the best!" If this were a game show, an alarm would be ringing as confetti flew and a blond woman massaged some prize, because it was jackpot time, one of those rare instances when Favio was saying the same thing he was thinking. He was being staggeringly sincere—to him at that particular point in time, I was the It boy, the ruler of his world, the Frankenstein-monster-turned-fabulous. I paused for a second, breathed in deeply, and (as he'd taught me) absorbed the moment. I was on top—of a very small dungheap, but so what, I'd conquered it. For years I'd been sick of being the only one on the food chain who never got fed. Well, now I was eating it up to beat the band, joining the ego parade instead of just watching it from the peanut gallery. We'd done the impossible and not only transcended the club's attitude, we'd used its newness and curiosity value to our advantage and made a hot mix of place and personnel, of affect and effect. And it was for me—vanity had won me over to Zymurgy. People were saying "Vinnie" as if it were "Serge" or "Raoul." My name had a whole new cachet. Only in New York.

The party was so undreadful that people were getting on the public phone and urging their friends to "crash like a Delta pilot." Halfway through the appetizer, three drag queens from a gay bar, Manstench, barged halfway through the entrance in full regalia, one as Vivien Leigh, another as Barbara Stanwyck, and the third as, of all people, Anna May Wong. They were all wearing glittery lipstick, pendulous drop earrings, and platforms that could kill a New York rat—I'd never seen Barbara Stanwyck in platforms before. These were probably the shoes they'd hunted the appetizer with.

The girls commanded so much attention, however dubious, that Favio couldn't help looking a little jealous while trying to do excited. Emil, on the other hand, looked totally appalled while trying to do excited, and Garth showed no emotion whatsoever—he never did—as he instructed the doorman, Vlad, not to let them get *all* the way in under any circumstances. This was right before Vivien Leigh lifted up her dress to show everyone the glitter on her crotch and said, "Look what Anna May's been eating!" That did it—they were on the list. I personally pulled them in as some people in the room, the ones who wanted to get mentioned, applauded. Anyone who wanted to get mentioned in *Manhattan on the Rocks* at this point was a dubious human, but it was still a small, brilliant victory for *moi*. Garth just started talking about something else—his difficult childhood in Nantucket—not about to admit defeat on his home turf.

The magazines were everywhere. We'd lined the entire place, including the bathrooms, with them so there was no escape—you couldn't even puke without seeing them and you couldn't see them without puking. Everyone was buzzing about it—if they didn't, they were wasted or maybe just petty, envious, or dyslexic. Delroy gushed that it was incredible, the freshest thing he'd seen in ages, and Garth cornered me to say he really thought the publication had potential. (Fuck you, too.) The only blatant dissent came from Rima, who said it was several months behind, stylewise, and Vogel, who didn't say anything but purposely put on a sour face while flipping through the magazine just so I'd know. I did know—it meant he liked it. The coke Emil had just slipped me—by force—in the men's room was helping eliminate any insecurity. (A little coke makes you very sure of yourself; a lot of it makes you a paranoid mess.) "I'm so glad you all like it," I screamed, doing a tipsy performance out of *The Carpetbaggers,* replete with a little two-step and half a cartwheel. If there were a chandelier, I would have swung from it, but there were only a few candelabras, the Barbie poster, and the coffin, and I couldn't think of any tasteful performance that would incorporate those three themes. Emil laughed and gave me a "shut up" look. I forgot; you can only get away with stuff like that if you're a bosomy girl.

"I love your magazine. So wacky and irreverent," said pinched-mouthed Colette Joie, who looked bulimic in her Chanel but still rich and therefore pretty gorgeous. I couldn't believe someone this socially advanced was at my party and not being sadistic. I looked at her head-on and tried an acting exercise: not saying a word, but making my eyes say, Back me, back me, goddamn you! while my nostrils said, Or at least advertise! Just a game—we played a lot of them in that acting class. I hoped when my nostrils were trying to talk, there wasn't any white powder left in them. "Thank you," I said, articulately, with my mouth.

The main course was truly a Greek tragedy, some kind of fish with green sauce. The fish wasn't deboned because—everybody now—they didn't debone fish in ancient Greece. It was at this moment that, with typically revisionist timing, Doric decided to present me with one of his new paintings. How silly—everyone was too busy pulling fish vertebrae from their gums to pay much attention, and Delroy didn't get to shoot the presentation, not even with a gun. If I was going to have to deal with this framed anxiety, I would at least have liked to get a photo opportunity out of it. Before Doric even unveiled it, I had thought of at least four practical things to do with it around the house—shuffleboard, anyone?

The piece was Doric's most disturbed ever—an Edvard Munch–like scream, except instead of skin, the guy screaming had oozy, pustulent pulp, like a peeled peach, and it looked as if his tongue had been cut out, because his mouth was all bumpy with blackish, dried blood. What a charming gift for a dinner party. I guess those inner demons weren't so inner anymore, especially now that this kind of gratuitous angst had become commercial. Of course, Doric didn't even do his own work—the artists he pilfered from did, and then he fixed it up to look original. It was they who must have been tormented, maybe because they involuntarily worked for him. "Thank you," I murmured, simply, then raised my voice to a delicate boom and said, "Look, everybody—Doric gave me a painting." Everyone turned around. Colette Joie spit out her fish, but Taormina liked it. "You are so talented," she told Doric, "and so are the people you pillage. You're my four hundred favorite artists." Doric winced; he didn't like people being reminded that he didn't always come up with his own ideas. It was one of those privileged secrets that Favio had shared with half the modern world as we know it. Doric just flung the swizzle stick to the floor and guzzled a non-Manhattan.

Randi looked unenchanted, but it wasn't her usual malaise, it seemed to be something baby-related. "If she miscarries," said Diane Plewge with that between-you-and-me voice, "that'll be some party." This was the caring soul who devotes all her life to AIDS? I loved it. Taormina, who in her backless dress looked like a road map of her hometown on Mars, was now saying something about how they should all go home and try to suction the baby out already. It would have been fine with me, but they decided to stay—the reason she was having this creature in the first place was so they could go to parties like this. They were going to enjoy it.

"This baby," said Randi, "feels like it probably has three sixes tatooed on its scalp." Damien—such a nice name.

José, meanwhile, was selectively handing out invites to a party—something in a subway station. It was totally illegal, so he was urging everyone to come at the crack of eleven because it would surely be raided by eleven-thirty. This could be a history-making do: the first one where everyone would show up on time. He handed one of the invites to Taormina and several to Drindl, but I saw him conscientiously skip Diane Plewge and Sandahl DeVol, who wouldn't be caught dead in a subway station, or maybe would *only* be caught dead there. The invite was shaped like a subway token and had about fifty hosts' names on it, but Favio—a staple on every invite—wasn't one of them, not even as a token, as it were, of the established crew. By now my eyes were trained, like German shepherds, to spot names, or the lack thereof, and the absence of Favio's was the loudest exclamation on the entire thing. In the tiny fishbowl we happened to be in, this was as shocking an omission as Dustin Hoffman not being nominated for the Tony.

I asked Favio about it, of course, to semirub it in. "I didn't want to host that tired party," he rationalized, as if hosting were really a chore and not just an ego fluff that meant you didn't even have to be there—only lend your stellar name.

"He begged me like, forget it," José later confided in me, "but we only wanted the newies. I like Favio all right, but . . . you know. . . ." Ouch. I knew too well. Like Delroy, Favio had become old guard in a few short weeks. His own damnation of everyone else—"tired"—was now boomeranging in his face like a big, ugly mudpie. I used this piece of info not so much to turn on Favio but to pivot slightly away, which I now feel may have been a little selfish.

Emil was becoming a dusty slice of history too, but he was still in the denial phase—"I'm so sure that little twit José is a threat to me," he smirked whenever I rubbed in his rising status. "He's not competition any more than my dead grandmother is." Later, he'd be in the bargaining phase—"Please, God, I'll do anything if you make him go away." And finally, acceptance—"What can you do?" Mary-Ellen wasn't phased by any of this—she'd been through so many scenes, she was her own scene, a dinosaur for all seasons. I was so lucky I'd entered the picture between eras and so didn't have to carry any unwanted associations with something that had died not through my own fault. I wasn't condemned forever to wear a label that said Carcinogen, and even though I was helping launch the place, I wasn't going to be labeled a Zymurgy person either. I was *Manhattan on the Rocks,* and as long as I could keep that fabulous, I'd be fabulous too.

"Such a success, Mr. Vinnie," said Starla, and for the first time that night I noticed that *her* style had been considerably streamlined too. She still looked spectacular, but in between the extensions and the flats it was a more designery look, without any noticeable flounce or side effects, without the doodads some dresses feature to distract from their not being expensive. This dress was pricey and screamed it. It was as if, by her incredible nightlife intuition, she knew exactly what kind of club Zymurgy was going to be and had dressed accordingly, out of an instinctive, new, tasteful-era wardrobe. She couldn't fully pull it off quite yet—there was still a slight suggestion of a hooker-y quality, a caricature of femininity that made those uptown folks queasy—but come on, Robocop wasn't built in a day.

We'd been playing games with each other all night—only when you know somebody that well can you get away with not even saying hello for hours. But now this was our moment together, and the whole room was watching as if they were trench coat wearers in a porno theater. We gave them the show they wanted. Starla bit me on the ear like it was a radish, and I glided my hand along her torso as she pretended to slap me. The slap turned into a clutch of the neck that guided my mouth to her cleavage. "Hello," I yelled down there, waiting for an echo. Then we drowned each other in dozens of miniature kisses that led to a big, saliva-y one that seemed to go on so long I wondered if my next deadline was coming up. Open-mouthed kisses provide quality thinking time, and I spent this one musing about whether or not Starla was getting some real action on the side, and if she was, whether or not she was enjoying it, and if she was enjoying it, whether or not she'd go public with the guy and humiliate the shit out of my pants. This kiss was about as erotic as a live sex show, except I was enjoying the forced intimacy; in a room of air kissers, it was kind of perverse. Doing it with the premiere air kisser of them all was outright scandalous.

The second no one was looking at us anymore, she brushed her hand against my crotch in a pseudocasual way that I knew was actually prerehearsed, to see if my pepperoni was happy. "It's limp," she said into my ear as if it were a joke. "Awwww. Poor Mr. Vinnie."

Dessert was served, and the Greek theme had obviously run out because we had a choice between crème brulée and passion-fruit tart. "What's new?" I said to Starla as if I hadn't talked to her on the phone three times that day; I just wanted to take her mind off my lack of erect membrane.

"Well," she said, affecting a Southern drawl, "I just touched a limp dick. What's new with you?" She thought this little shtick was hilarious, but I wanted to wring her neck and say, Go to hell. If it *wasn't* limp, you'd be running like an extra in a Japanese horror film.

"Did I just hear something about a big dick?" said Emil, wasted and bouncing his head like those Buddha dolls in the rear windows of cars. "What would Vinnie know about a big dick?"

"She said *'limp* dick,' silly," I chimed in. "We were talking about *you."* Soon everyone in the place had heard their own version of the "dick" story, and by the time it got to Colette Joie, she was spitting out her crême brulée. I figured the woman always pretended to be appalled just so she could remain thin.

"Apologize or die," I said to Starla, acting more casual about this than I really felt.

"I'm sorry," she whispered, sincerely. "But you know it's really an insult to me. Your not getting it up is a reflection of *me*. How do you think that makes Starla feel?" I couldn't deal with this right now, especially since she was talking about even *herself* in the third person. I went back to the original question: "What's new?"

"Great stuff," she said. "I'm shooting the magazine ads tomorrow, and Monday I'm being interviewed by Sid Boulle of the *Times*. I'm also going to do a video about the products and try to get it on HBO—kind of a different approach to promo." Sylvia Valmouth was sure getting her money's worth—when it came to promo, Starla's mind was like a one-person William Morris Agency.

"The magazine will be on some newsstands starting Monday," I said, fading out toward the end of that tidbit as I realized I couldn't begin to compete with Starla's career excitement. "A video!" I exclaimed, changing course before she could respond. "How great." We'd already discussed her video on the phone that day, but we could discuss it again.

As people started to leave, Emil was handing out slices of some mystery cake with great determination and trying to scream a toast to *Manhattan on the Rocks* "and more importantly, to Garth Free and his fabulous new club. And let's hear it," he added, "for Sean Valve, whose book, *Island of Glossed Souls,* makes Brentano's best-seller list as of next week." Everyone cheered, and suddenly it was a party for Sean Valve. I'd been crowned and dethroned, all within an hour—suicide again. Favio gasped and jumped on Sean; he'd been looking for an excuse to anyway.

"By the way," said Favio as he flitted out with Diane Plewge to hit three more clubs, "José is totally asexual. He can only get it up for himself. *Ciao, bella!*" If Favio thought this newsflash (a lie, it turned out) was going to antagonize me against José, he was wrong; it only made me relate to him better. Still, I wondered how long it would be before even José got tired—not from jerking himself off but from going around the block enough times that someone else comes along who can walk it faster and fresher. In his constant quest for thrills, he was an irritating motherfucker, and as long as he was still new, the rudeness could work in his favor. But I could see karma someday slapping him back even harder than Favio. Favio was just thoughtless, but José was a brat with a chip on his shoulder everyone around him had to pay for. He'd better watch it—while no one ever got anywhere being nice, no one not-nice ever went downhill without being spat on. It was one of those catch-22's—either you make it as a schmuck and pay for it later, or you're a mensch and never make it at all. This was good, developing a case against the Josés—the Zymurgy frame of mind was setting in.

As the last dribs and drabs dawdled out, there was still a real-person side of me that wished I could turn on a "good vibes'' button so they'd all leave happy and remember my party well. The last impression of any event is usually how it stays in the memory. That's why I stood grinning by the exit—"like a Cheshire rat," Doric said—as they filled out.

"My compliments to the chef . . . Boyardee," was Vogel's last quote as he joined the exiting swells. The guy could bring a junkie down.

"Don't forget," I said to Starla, "three weeks from Sunday we're going to visit my parents for a drop-dead Italian dinner."

"Another party!" she enthused, clapping her hands and giggling like a windup doll.

5

Starla and I had attacked some challenging fetes together—
the odd fashion dinner or marketing reception that she was
expected to go to (black tie or die), and the occasional Cath-
erine Deneuve promo party ("Eet eez more than a scent.
Eet eez perfume.") or Diana Ross record-release affair we
occasionally throttled our way into. "Hi, I'm Diana Ross,"
she said, coming up to us with a warm smile. "Yes, we
know," we replied, and almost fainted. They were draining—even harder work than sex must be, a major effort,
from the mock-enthusiastic entrance to the slapstick stumble
out the door, with the rewards buried like favors under shit-
loads of pretense.

The fun starts when you have to convince the hench-
men—usually moustache-twirling types who look like Gale
Sondergaard—that you really do belong there, even though
they can't find your name on the list (it *should* be there—or
will be someday, as God is your witness). If you're lucky
enough to make it through, you're in for a jousting competition with men with the world's smallest dicks for a buffet
of the world's smallest vegetables. Twelve of these cauliflowers make a real cauliflower, but the Munchkinland plates

they give you only allow for three of them. Take four plates and keep calling out to imaginary people that you'll be right back with their food.

The exception that proves the rule being Diana Ross, the star is usually too overwhelmed by camera crews posing questions like "Your son died in a motorcycle accident; how has this affected your fashion sense?" to greet the hoi polloi. By Channel J News time, he or she is ready to beat a hasty retreat out the back door and head for the nearest retirement home. Meanwhile, you've schmoozed with the star's brother's groupie's hairdresser's ghostwriter until your ears are burning with revelations of those who might almost have touched near-fame. You've devoured enough miniature cauliflowers to line the inside of your stomach with the state of Iowa. You've been ogled at, bumped into, poured on, and sneered at. All in the name of a good time.

Fortunately, I happen to enjoy all this.

Fear of being alone combined with a complete distrust of people have put me in a strange, confused predicament, but as the fear of being alone (monophobia—the opposite of agoraphobia) tends to dominate, I need to be in a room—even an emergency room—with a lot of people at any cost. Maybe I'm compensating for being so lonely as a child (of course I've felt lonely many times since in crowded rooms, but without the edge of panic). Maybe I'm trying to forget things by always running toward the next schmooze target and finding a new spectacle to crowd into my consciousness at the expense of some other, more vaguely important idea. I'm not sure, since I never think about it and only go to parties so I won't *have* to.

In any case, I was blessed to have Starla as a partner—the ultimate party person, able to transform the worst public disgrace into a personal triumph. I never could be sure what she saw in me as a date—maybe just someone reasonably attractive who wasn't going to press her into sex acts she'd rather not mess her makeup by doing. I even started thinking she'd dragged me home from her party that time so we could get the ineffectual sex attempt over with and never have to deal with it again. Whatever twisted psychodrama we may have been acting out, it was clicking, and together we were learning to work the room with the best of them. We were a team, bulleting together with a combination of looks, sheer gall, and a scientific understanding of party rules.

Starla always said hello first—rule number one—and she never left me hanging in the lurch or introduced me as just "my friend Vinnie." It was always "Vincent DiBlasio, publisher and editor of *Manhattan on the Rocks,* a terrific new magazine." This way, when I introduced her to people, she was always "Starla Rogers, as in the beauty products." A lot of times they already knew who she was, but if they didn't, now they would. She wasn't something that easily slipped through the colander of one's mind, and I'm sure she could become the Uta Hagen of the eye-communication game— "beauty products, beauty products"—without even trying.

With Starla, you were guaranteed to end up as close to the storm center of any party as was humanly possible. You had to make all the polite, obligatory stops on the way there, but you always ended up almost dangerously in the heat of the action. She was even able to wrest some camera crews away from waiting for the guests of honor and was just starting to make the crucial leap from Fox to network and CNN. Her rule of thumb was never to say anything negative on the record, always to come off like a nice guy. As we left the premiere of the big bomb action-adventure flick of that fall— I think it was called *Ramona!*—she looked straight into a camera and remarked, "It made me glad to be alive!" It was something about an extraterrestrial cow coming to earth to teach the homeless how to fly.

The best party, Andy Warhol said, was one where you were the most boring person there, but that always struck me as a nightmare. My idea of the ultimate party is one where I'm the *least* boring person there, and everyone else just revels in my fabulousness. While working toward this dream, Starla and I were becoming popular.

Our goal was to make it so big we could start going only to parties without camera crews at all. A crewless party was a truly private gathering of Someones, not just a publicity stunt for pretenders. You couldn't barge into it with a press card and a loud voice; if you weren't on the list, you might as well hail a subway.

"We should stop going to things below Fourteenth Street too," Starla said one night, after a few drinks. She said it with a seriousness that sent chills down my spine, especially since I'd been thinking the same thing. Admit it: nothing was happening downtown, it was beat. To be even indirectly associated with it was admitting you were yesterday's hash browns, that you'd learned nothing and gone nowhere, only gotten soggier as you flogged away at that decomposing horse, which could be far more productive turned into glue.

Unfortunately, there were only two alternatives: the Odile/Zymurgy scene—i.e., uptown goes slumming, downtown stays home—and the real, big-time, lip-tuck, uptown scene, and they wouldn't have you if you were the last-climber on earth. I tried to trash these forbiddingly alien worlds to Starla a few times, but she wasn't buying it.

"Odile and Zymurgy are just glorified rest homes," I said once at a party. "And the really uptown crowd is so boring. Mercedes Kellogg, Pat Kennedy—who cares? I really don't think their having money makes them intrinsically interesting." I paused for approbation, but she made a face. "It's fabulous," she said as I searched the room to see if there was a hidden camera crew somewhere. *"They're* fabulous."

After a while, if enough people start telling you something's fabulous, it does become fabulous for you. Horrid as these clubs were, they at least had the glow of freshness. "I mean, who would you rather read about right now?" Favio said one night between E-tabs (the shop term for Ecstasy). "Frank Sinatra or Terence Trent D'Arby?" It was his curious way of saying people always have more immediate fascination for what's hot at the moment. And to think I used to read Homer, who was even more historically significant than Sinatra.

It was all so calculated, and I was suddenly spending more time analyzing nightlife than actually enjoying it. Fun didn't have a whole lot to do with anything anymore, but as I was just a reflector of all the activity, I was not meant to have fun anyway—merely to absorb and spew back to make room for more absorption. How could anyone have a good time with homeless crack addicts with AIDS running around announcing a depression, anyway? The best you could do was escape the horrors by sitting around in over-upholstered chairs and acting as if you didn't know any better. By putting on a *blasé* air that read not as ignorant, but as adult.

The biggest casualty in all this transition was Favio, who wanted more than life itself to be accepted by the grown-up crowd but felt a sociopathic need to keep his finger in with the newies too, in case they started to break out beyond bargain tutus. He suddenly had two separate wardrobes— one for uptown, in his room, and one for downtown, in our communal closet (which I never needed—I only have six outfits). In a precarious social limbo, he never seemed sure what to wear when and how to behave to suit the sartorial choice.

With Starla, at least, I had someone who was mobile in the right direction. There was no dichotomy about *her* image anymore; she'd consolidated all her wardrobes into one— sexy yet elegant, eye-catching yet well-made. Her trashy appearances of the old days were over (Favio told me she once wrestled with a female bodybuilder in chocolate pudding for the title of Miss Carcinogen), and if she did happen by a place like Dramamine and people tried to drag her onstage or make her do Lola Heatherton–type things, she left. No one was getting Starla for free anymore, especially not the "over" downtown crowd.

Why had I started a magazine about the scene when it was kaput? Because there are always a million scenes happening, and you just have to find the right one. That's what Emil told me anyway—"New York is loaded with scenes. They all have different cast lists but basically the same stage directions. If one dies, just look for another one that's still breathing."

Zymurgy was on Fifteenth Street, so it qualified for Starla's new regulations. We went back there a few times after my party, and Garth treated us so gingerly, it didn't offend me as much. I mean, it's all perspective anyway—if you're in a mood to like a place, it's quaint; if you're on the rag, it's boring. And there's the matter of adaptation: if you were thrown into a tub of lye fifty times in a row, you'd probably start minding it less each time.

And people aren't evil just because they dress in black. They aren't brain dead just because they speak with a foreign accent. I met some interesting models there—yes, interesting models—and if they didn't rule in sandboxes, at least you could be reasonably assured that if you asked them for a cigarette, they wouldn't put one out in your face. They would sit down and have a conversation with you—in French, albeit, but a conversation—and had a worldly knowingness that offset the smarm inherent in their misguided pretensions to high class. I put them in my second issue as the Moi-Moi-Moi Generation. I didn't think they were as fabulous as Starla did—she segged seamlessly into this crowd as if this was always all there was—but I could fathom them, in a bizarre way. I even had a regular table (I never believed in "no pain, no gain") and was beginning to feel the place was less constipated than before, as if a giant enema had cleansed it out and enabled me to penetrate.

"You're changing," Favio told me one night as we

watched *The Matchmaker* (the game show, not the Thornton Wilder play). "Definitely moving up in the world. Great!"

"Are you selling out?" Delroy said another night as we worked on the new issue. "Vincent, don't fail us now." I wasn't selling out. I'm a journalist, and I have to cover what's happening, not what happened. If I were a war correspondent, I wouldn't still be writing about Vietnam, I'd be finding new wars and skirmishes. Shit, I'd even start one if I had to.

Starla and I never talked about ourselves much at these things, just about what was immediately on our minds—the buffet, the guest list, our next act of career advancement. We'd discuss D'Arby, not Sinatra. Both forward-looking people, we weren't about to drag up old inadequacies when we could be holding court for our present-day miracles. Former nerds, now wreaking our revenge, we went crazy when our past lives were belched back at us via bad societal plumbing, like when someone we'd de-Rolodexed ages ago suddenly jumped out of a time warp and wanted to be friends again. History belongs in books, not in my face. I didn't want to see those old college drips anymore—I couldn't believe I'd almost invited some of them to my party—and Starla hated it when old friends from Ohio waltzed into town and expected her to give them a big, down-home kiss and a grand tour. The Starla they knew was as different from the one they were talking to now as a burn victim is after reconstructive surgery. Just *how* different became clearer when one of them kept calling her "Chris" one night. Was that her real name? Was she a sex change *à la* Pat? If so, couldn't she have kept "Chris"?

The only people from my past I kept in touch with were my parents because, being Catholic, I had to. There's a certain blood knot etched in pasta that defies weather or second thoughts. And my mother has always been world famous for cooking sumptuous meals—no minivegetables served here, only watermelon-size mutations that could have stopped up the well and saved Baby Jessica. I brought Starla home to show her off like a new Rolex and to see if she'd still like me after glimpsing this overbearing domestic smorgasbord out of *Come Back, Little Moonstruck,* a frightmare of relentless motherlove that would have plunged me back into my breeder's womb if I could fit. It might help explain the "flaccid membrane" phenomenon—how could I love any woman but Mom?

This was a realistic test. I mean, would we have liked Diana Ross if we had gone back to the Brewster Projects in Detroit and sat in the rubble while she sang gospel tunes? Would I still find Starla captivating if we went back to visit the land where she's known as "Chris"? Questions, questions. Most of all, I wondered if the same rules that governed all parties would apply here. Would this be just another room for me and Starla to work?

My mother had laid out a spread big enough to feed everyone at the Live Aid concert and some of the countries the concert was for. Two boat-size trays of lasagna were merely appetizers—she might as well have served them on a cracker. The tray of meatballs and sausages that landed next was not the main course either—just a warm-up, a figurative piece of watercress to nibble while waiting for the entrée. The tow-truckful of sauce and Parmesan they were drenched in was akin to a frothy little *garniture,* a maraschino cherry, something ever so quaint and disposable. And the entrée turned out to be three entrées—half a ham, a whole chicken, and a turkey and a half, all with the requisite juices, stuffings, and side dishes (three kinds of potatoes—sweet, baked, and candied yams; two salads—lettuce and three-bean; two quiches—plain and zucchini; plus a bowl of pitted black olives, some corn on the cob, peas, and, of course, plain bread, garlic bread, breadsticks, and rolls). "I hope I have enough," said my mother, who could have invited the cast of one of those Sid and Marty Krofft ice spectaculars and still had leftovers. To drink, enough Mountain Dew to irrigate Wyoming for a year, plus a bottle of that exquisite brew, cherry khiafa. Harvey's Bristol Cream was placed downright upright in the liquor cabinet for the truly daring and sophisticated.

"Can't you dress respectable?" my mother said as we sat down to dinner, slapping me on the head for effect. Already this was like a Three Stooges act, the early show. Though I'd shaved clean, my hair was going in three hundred directions, and my shirt was ready for a men's shelter, with three fewer buttons than it was supposed to have and a huge stain of something I couldn't remember. (Except for that desperate shroud, this was as far as I'd go in the fashion field; generally I was content to reflect the daring of everyone else's clothes.) "Aw, stop," I said, reduced to monosyllables. The second I walked into that house I became a tricyclist again.

Starla had dressed down for the occasion, her idea of down being a pink-and-fuchsia-print ensemble replete with matching headwrap. She looked like Ann Sothern as Panama Hattie and was well on her way toward her apparent dream of becoming Joan Collins. With the most considerate manners possible, she treated the incredible spread as if it were a totally darling nuisance. She pushed half of her lasagna portion back into the tray. She declined any meatballs or sausages. She said she'd try two kinds of potatoes, but she actually only nibbled on one reluctantly. This kind of behavior does not go over well in my mother's house, and when my mom just started forcing things on her plate— "Eat. Don't be shy."—I could see Starla scanning the room for a potted plant; she'd obviously seen the same *I Love Lucy* episode I had. Soon my mother would be skipping the plate motif and ramming the stuff right down her throat by force.

We don't keep potted plants in that house anyway. We

keep those pushpin rhinos, as well as 3-D Jesus portraits, two-headed Mexican dolls, and a long giraffe's leg that had been converted into a lamp. (Our neighbor's daughter is a missionary in Zimbabwe and brings us home lots of these very practical converted animal parts.) Ingenuity definitely prevails over expense. When a clock stops working, it gets covered with a psychedelic print or a doily rather than thrown out; it becomes an art piece.

My old room was particularly art laden. Meticulously preserved as a shrine to me, not a hair of it had been changed since the day I moved out. *Quel hommage.* The electric kitty-cat with the wagging tail, the throw-the-hoops-on-the-poodle game, and the Keane paintings of dewy-eyed children you want to gouge, adorned with African rosary beads (giraffes' toenails?) were all intact and even cleaner and fresher-looking than when I left. To anyone who understands kitsch, this house is a finer showplace than the Louvre.

"So what's new? Talk to me," my mother said. "He never talks to me." I hadn't brought the magazine home, because I just didn't feel they'd get it. Maybe next time. Meanwhile, I was a complete wastrel with nothing to show but some finely honed attitude—exactly the humiliating creature I wanted to shame them with. "I don't know," I said. "I've just been—"

"Going to a lot of parties," my father chimed in, spitting out the skin of a chicken breast. I hadn't noticed he was there until that point. I wasn't sure whether or not I'd introduced him to Starla.

How could I turn this around in my favor? "We met Diana Ross," I said, all twinkly-eyed.

"You did?" This inspired my mother to get up and fill Starla's plate with about three sties' worth of ham, drowning everything on the plate with pineapple sauce. It was like a three-ring pineapple circus, with meat of all nations and mutant veggies that were starting to look like ax murderers. Starla looked sick.

"Yes, we did," Starla said. "She was so nice. Genuine. Not a bitch . . . um, *b*-word." Dad made some remark about how she should be sent back to Africa where that giraffe's leg came from, and we all let it pass, Starla kicking me under the table with much embarrassment.

"Stop," I said, to my father, but aimed at Starla as well.

"More turkey?" said my mother to no one—meaning everyone—in particular. "Come on, don't be shy. I slaved all week over this in the sweltering heat—now you better eat it. I've got stuffing and cranberry sauce." She had an entire Thanksgiving Day dinner as one of three full options, and it was June. Starla didn't say anything in response, so my mother took it as a yes.

"My niece Valeria likes Diana Ross," my mother said. She was getting comfortable, a sign that she was going into a monologue.

"Is this going to be a long story?" I asked, and she slapped me on the head again. My father was communing with the turkey by now.

"Valeria was born with a clubfoot," my mother continued, pleased to have, in Starla, a new audience. "She was always a little bit of an outcast, but lately she's been beyond the pale. She shoplifted marinara sauce—as if anyone in this family would be caught dead eating that stuff from a jar. I said to her, 'If you want marinara sauce so bad, just ask me—I'll make it for you fresh. Or if you have to have it out of a jar, I'll give you the two dollars as a birthday gift, even if it's not your birthday.' Then she gets a job at that fast-food place and she gets fired for giving free ALF puppets to all her friends. A generous girl—she's got a good heart. But it pains me, it pains me right here." My mother was getting teary-eyed—crying over ALF puppets.

Starla tried to say something—about the turkey?—but didn't have the minutest chance. Mom continued: "My nephew Angelo is another stunato. When my brother-in-law Vito—not my brother-in-law Vito who lives upstairs, but my other brother-in-law Vito who passed away, may he rest in peace—anyway, when he was stuck in the closet, Angelo tried to get him to tell him his life story so he could write a book and cash in; what a dodo he is. As if he had such an interesting story to tell, God rest his soul. And as if he's going to think of playing *This Is Your Life* in such a condition. He couldn't move—that's why he was stuck. What a shame! Because of this, Angelo wasn't invited to my niece Gloria's wedding, not that that stopped him from showing up outside the church that day with such a foul temper you never saw, so help me God, may I die a thousand times for invoking the Lord's name in vain. He smashed in Gloria's wedding-car window—a limousine—and he blackmailed Valeria to go running after them, with her clubfoot, mind you, and try to crack eggs all over them—on their wedding day! The window of that expensive limousine—and to this day Gloria's picking shards of glass off her wedding dress, the dress I helped her pick out, not that she'll ever need it again, I don't hope. Things were already bad enough because a grain of rice had landed right smack in poor Gloria's eye, and she looked like she had a thyroid condition all through her honeymoon.''

Starla fidgeted as if she wanted to die, probably from uneasiness more than any empathy for Gloria. She started playing with a sausage.

''Anyway,'' continued Mom, ''my sister Jo Butch grabbed Angelo by the neck when she ran into him at Big Bella's discount store, and pushed him against the wall and said, 'Look, you piece of so-and-so,' pardon my French, 'you go near my Gloria again and I'll throw you into a meat grinder and make you into tiny balls'—Some more meatballs, Starla?—and this in the middle of a store full of people looking for bargains, including my neighbor Nina-Joanne, whose daughter is a nun in Africa and had never heard such language so foul; she hasn't left the house or the convent since. The nun is in town right now, as we speak, in fact she's right next door, but she's not leaving the house, I swear to you, until my niece Michelle's wedding; I hope nothing goes wrong at that one. She gave us that giraffe lamp—the nun, that is, not my niece Michelle. Say a prayer for that poor giraffe that had to be turned into a piece of everyday furniture. Well, anyway, Angelo's a boxer—he was once engaged to a lady midget one, wrestler, that is—so he threw Jo Butch a few clenched fists and was making her scream with agony you wouldn't believe. Screaming like a stuck pig, in public yet—my poor sister, what she went through. Oh, my God—I forgot something.'' She bolted out of her seat and ran to the kitchen, coming back wearing a fashionable oven mitt and holding another big tray as she smiled deviously. "Mashed potatoes!" she exclaimed. The fourth kind.

"Anyway," she continued without missing a beat, "he had slipped some tape cassettes into her pocket when she wasn't looking, because he's a professional thief himself, and now he's screaming, 'Help! Help! I've got a shoplifter here,' that tricky little bast—devil. I swear he's gotta have some Sicilian blood in his stunato veins. Well, the scene, as Jo Butch desribes it, was quite possibly the biggest one to hit Big Bella's since my cousin Lydia-Marie slipped on bubble bath in there and knocked over a whole counter of Summer's Eve. I'll never forget the sight of her drowning in all that dou—um, stuff—forgive me God for laughing a little. But anyway, it was all settled because she gave him the evil eye, and it turned out Angelo had given Bella herself a violation when he worked for Consumers Affairs before he got thrown off for—no, I can't even go into that one—no, you're new here and I'll start crying like Vinnie here did when he was a little baby; he used to cry so much and keep me up at night—he was colic—and the sixteen hours of labor he put me through almost tore me apart.'' My mother, by the way, still referred to my conception as "the time your father hurt me."

She went on: "So they believed Jo Butch and they even gave her a gift certificate to make up for her troubles. This oven mitt was one of the things she bought with it— serviceable, no, if a little too green-colored? She gave it to me for doing all her shopping when she had sciatica, oh, she was limping around something terrible, the pain she grieved."

"So what's the point?" said my father, the only one to strike up a relationship with the mashed potatoes.

"The point is that Vincent is the great hope of this family, and what does he do—goes to parties!" I knew the monologue would somehow wend its way back to their favorite subject, me. What my partygoing had to do with douche and sciatica was anyone's guess, but I didn't mind this so much as their talking about me as if I weren't there. Had the entire world gone mad with third-person frenzy? "Why couldn't he have finished school?" my mother said, for the eighth time that day alone.

"But he's doing so well, Mrs. DiBlasio," Starla chimed in, persuasively. "He's getting up there." If not getting it up.

"*You're* doing well," said my mother. "I know that much. I see your name in the papers and I've even seen your products."

"They've made it to Queens!" said Starla, half to herself, implying that if they'd made it to this planet, then they must be everywhere. "I hope not in the bargain bins." We all laughed, a little phonily, hoping to clear out any residue of tension. It would have taken a crane. Starla looked semidazed from the monologue and the meal, but that meant they were both filling. She didn't look like she'd cut me out of her will.

We collapsed on the couch, never wanting to hear the word *food* again. Starla let out a contented bleat. No, she hadn't really enjoyed herself, but at least she hadn't bolted for the door. She wasn't so caught up in everything shiny and fabulous that she couldn't, without blatant expressions of disdain, spend time with some real people. And she'd managed to maintain her waistline while not offending my mother too much. I was starting to feel the experiment was worthwhile—the peculiar dementia of people who care about you is so much more affecting than that of those who don't. The day had worked. They believed she was my girlfriend. She believed they were my parents.

At this point, my mother brought out a tray of her very own specialty dessert. Not crème brulée or passion-fruit tarts, but jelly donuts cut in half and packed with more jelly donuts. They were so obscene we couldn't even look at them. "If I eat one of those, I'll have to buy a whole new wardrobe," said Starla, making the sound of a helium balloon bursting—intentionally, I think. And she'd just *bought* a whole new wardrobe. My mother packed them for us to take home.

"Become respectable," my father said as we left, saddled with CARE packages that also consisted of milk cartons and dozens of eggs—to throw at newlyweds?—plus endless supplies of dishwashing liquid, paper towels, Combat, and Brillo. We'd never have to shop again.

Become respectable—the two words a Japanese man had written to his son while crashing in that doomed airliner a couple of years back. I remember reading about it and thinking they were the most horrible, damning last words a father could impart to his son. But my father didn't talk much, and when he did, it was with a certain earnestness. I was as tired of trying to spite them as he was. If only I could be a party rebel and be respectable too, then everyone would be happy, at every stop of the Lazy Susan. That's what I'd been working at all along.

The two words stung me like a sharp twist of the balls, and I wasn't sure if it was because I resented them or believed in them.

6

When I got back home, there was such a ruckus going on in Favio's room I thought I was at Big Bella's. This wasn't what I'd had in mind. I wanted to drop dead from the food binge for at least forty-five minutes and eventually get it together to start working on my next cover story—Colette Joie. (She hadn't agreed to an interview, but hell, I had great pictures of her from the party and could write something reasonably factual based on rumors.)

I turned off the music I always left on to keep the burglars away (although it usually served to attract them, if they wanted stereo equipment), put a Styrofoam cup to the wall, and prepared for an earful.

Fortunately, the walls were much thinner than the ham slices that were clogging up my system. Every word rang as clearly as if it were happening, docudramalike, right in front of me, as palpable as Favio's clipping pile. I gathered that these were his parents, who'd come to town for some business reason—a convention or something—and dropped in by surprise to see if Favio was living up to everything his letters and calls said he was. Favio must have lied and said he was leading a life without eyeliner, but now he was caught and squirming loudly. I knew what that sounded like. Just the other day I'd woken up to the sound of a mouse struggling in a glue trap, which must have been a sign from God, because my alarm hadn't gone off.

It seems Mr. la Ronde (Mr. Speck, actually) had run across some of Favio's copious press and figured that this painted harridan dancing in miniskirts and climbing up potted palms was his boy. Favio was throwing open his closet—the uptown wardrobe—and showing them that this was his new persona, very respectable stuff, and everything else was buried behind some other door that would never be opened again. Unfortunately, the uptown wardrobe was not Favio's best defense; he'd left a pair of ruby slippers and some fishnets in there too, and they screamed even louder than his father. I could hear his dad flinging the slippers against the wall and shouting, "All the money I send you has come to this! Money you bamboozled from my pocket and wrenched from my soul. I'm cutting you off, you worthless piece of shit." And he stormed out, pulling along his wife—who I don't think was his wife at all but some trollopy thing who didn't say a word, no doubt from a lack of the thought process required to articulate something. He slammed the door shut behind him, and that slam still resonates in my cavity like a car crash.

I was half-shaking, half-enthralled when Favio came out of his room crying. I wanted to applaud, to boo, to laugh, but kept quiet, a good audience technique. Finally, I tried to talk to him—morbid curiosity and all that—but he locked himself in the bathroom and just sobbed away, short, piercing sobs that he never used to emit when he wore makeup. I'd hear him say occasionally between sobs, "I have to purge this out of my system." When he finally came out, he had circles under his eyes the size of saucers and was whiting them out with Erace. After what seemed an eternity, he spoke. "My father caught me," he said, "the filthy, amoeba-ridden asshole."

"What do you mean?" I said, trying not to push too hard or act too interested, which made me sound like a real jerk.

"He found out I haven't been going to school with his money. I never even went to orientation. I've spent every penny he's given me on flouncing around and just surviving and I've got nothing to show for it except my fucking microscopic fame, and he hates that stuff anyway. He wants me to be a dentist. The fuckface is cutting me off." Become respectable, in other words.

I started scrutinizing posters on the walls, which I already knew intimately, just to avert my gaze from Favio and try to wend my way inconspicuously back to my room. I knew what was coming.

"Vinnie," he said, sure enough, sobbing again, between syllables even, "would you mind putting up my half of the rent just for the next month or two? I swear on my mailing list I'll get a job or get money somehow and pay you back, no matter what it takes." Pause—sob—pause—Dondi-like pleading look. Dondi should have been shot.

"Sure," I said as I kicked myself inside and thought, Moron of the year! But he was such a pathetic figure standing there in a torn T-shirt and acid-washed jeans (which he was now wearing as a joke—"a revival," he said), and he was the one who'd introduced me to all this, after all. Wait a minute—should I pay his share of the rent or slap him? "Don't worry about it, Favio," I said, doing the sincere voice I'd learned from *All My Children* (which I'd missed Friday because the alarm didn't work *and* there was no trapped mouse to wake me up). "Everything will be all right."

"Oh, I know," he said. Suddenly he was smiling and self-satisfied, as if nothing had happened. He had a scary way of letting everything roll off his back, at least for show.

"Did you hear about Randi?" he said with that insinuating tone that came so naturally to him. He could make items like this sound so *faux*-nonchalant that you'd kill to know what it was.

"What?" I said, my curiosity piqued. "What? What? She had the baby?" He paused for a good ten seconds; his family feud hadn't diminished his sense of timing one bit.

"Miscarriage," he said, dropping the word like a bomb. This was good. If we focused on Randi's life traumas, maybe we could forget Favio's.

"She must be . . ."

"Devastated," he chimed in. "Absolutely devastated." He was clucking his tongue like one of those Tupperware junkies who visit my mother regularly to commiserate on the tragic ailments of everyone else on the block. She *must* be devastated. That baby was their ticket to stardom, her passage to better guest lists and higher social circles. Everyone was having babies nowadays. They had become the new status symbol, a chic new plaything you furnished the house with to complement the velveteen couch and shag carpet. Even people who didn't want one wanted one. Nowhere else among human relationships could you feel the same sense of dependency as with a baby squealing for your attention, clutching hungrily for the sustenance only you can offer. At least Randi would never have to know the sense of betrayal that inevitably follows; when the baby grows up, it turns into a walking bundle of spite.

"She's still in the hospital," he said as an afterthought.

"And you didn't visit her?" I screamed. As a hardcore Italian, I was taught visiting as a way of life.

"Well, I'm sorry," he said, "but I didn't exactly plan on my father blowing into town with that call girl and turning my life upside down. Believe me, I'd much rather be spending quality time in a hospital."

The next day we traipsed over to Mother Mary Agnes's, and I was hoping this wasn't the place where they'd hooked the kidney patient up by mistake to an air conditioner instead of dialysis. What a chilly way to die. As we walked into the lobby, Diane Plewge was leaving with Vivien Dietrich—a.k.a. Cha Cha—who, Favio quickly explained, was a major downtown party girl who'd totally dropped off the face of the scene to devote herself to AIDS protests. This was a rarity; once you got swept into the party cycle, few had the audacity to stop and try to achieve something worth celebrating. My most political act so far was deciding to put Colette Joie on the cover.

I wondered if Diane was attracted to Vivien because Vivien used to be a party star or because she was now dedicated to a serious issue. Probably both, plus her being coolly sure of herself and obviously having the guts to match her external assets. Why Vivien kept Diane around was another matter that seemed to be based on sheer tolerance, the way you don't swat a fly sometimes because there are other priorities. For all her anger, Vivien seemed incapable of rejecting even a fly. "She used to be fabulous," said Favio, providing a verbal flash card. "Now she's tired."

Diane spotted us through those obnoxious bubble glasses and came running over. How curious—the woman who'd joked about Randi miscarrying was now showing up to console her. She probably was a combination comic-witch, with powers to turn her evil jokes into reality. I hoped she'd never make a ha-ha about me. "You guys look so normal," she said. I always look normal. And Favio wasn't exactly going to wear a Day-Glo Sprouse ensemble to a place called Mother Mary Agnes's, especially after his altercation with his dad.

"She's doing fine," said Vivien, sweetly. "They say she'll probably be out by tomorrow." As if by reflex, she then handed us fliers about a demonstration that was going to happen when the President was in town, an unfurling of the names of all the people who'd died of AIDS, to protest his not doing anything about it. Favio looked so bored, he couldn't wait to get up to the party in Randi's room. I was mildly intrigued, only because this was a little less boring than my usual boredom.

Whether we were interested or not, Vivien was going to talk about AIDS. There were all these drugs that could help AIDS patients, she explained, in the incongruous tones of a flight attendant telling you how to use your seat cushion for flotation. But because of red tape, they were all sitting untested on a shelf as people died by the tens of thousands. She said people weren't going to "sit back and accept this inhuman reaction anymore"—heavy stuff for so early in the day without drink tickets—they were going to take to the streets, just like blacks had to do in the sixties to get what they needed. "AIDS protests are not going to be polite pleas for attention anymore," she said. "They're going to get goddamned bloody angry." To hear this good-natured, pretty, former party girl say this was absolutely spine-tingling. I hoped bonfires wouldn't start replacing parties as the thing to do. Like capuchin monkeys, I have an innate fear of flames.

"Emil told me you were coming to the benefit tonight at Mise en Scène," Vivien said as I nodded, hoping Favio wouldn't screech, What benefit? He just put on his quizzical "Why wasn't *I* invited?" face and all I could say was, "Well, Emil said only press." Favio's new masculine look had gotten him an initial flurry of social bonuses, but that proved short-lived as they realized "you can take the man out of the dress" is not a vice versa–type concept.

"Only press, and he invited Vivien Dietrich!" he exclaimed in utter disbelief after they'd walked away.

"Well," I lied, "it's a benefit for AIDS and she's directly involved in the cause." It was actually a benefit for the homeless, and I hoped to God he wouldn't find that out.

"She's soooo tired," said Favio one more time for effect as they got well out of his finely calculated hearing distance.

We picked up our visitors' passes, and as we worked our way to Randi's room, on the seventh floor, we saw a variety of horror shows they really should shield you from with big, protective goggles like Diane's, or maybe opaque plastic domes that roll toward their destination via radar. I almost puked as an intern tried to stick an IV in a guy's arm by hammering the needle into it a dozen times in search of a vein. A few days of this and your arm could strain spaghetti. We saw a kid who had that aging disease and looked like a shriveled-up, horribly sad little George Burns. And I swear I peeked into one room and saw Pat lying there anesthetized, probably having the tits put back in so he could become Pat again. Had he gotten flack from my article? What kind of hospital was this anyway? Would we all leave looking like George Burns with holes in our arms and big breasts? "I hope they make mine firm," said Favio, with a mirthless laugh.

Randi looked like she'd been beaten up, probably more from the downtrodden emotional state she was projecting than from anything physical. For the first time, I felt for her. It wasn't monsterly of her to want to procreate; after all, it was probably the most productive thing she could do— or try to do. Maybe she did want the baby for some human reasons. I was the ultimate journalist—I could see anything from both sides.

"Hiii, Randi," I said.

"You look great!" bellowed Favio. We were resorting to the same icebreakers we used at any party.

Doric was hanging his newest portrait on the wall—a snake devouring a rat, this time with real blood squirting out of the snake's mouth, all against a photo of the set for *The Donna Reed Show* (gratuitous angst mixed with gratuitous kitsch was one step better). If it were a movie, it would star James Woods.

"Where's Heinz?" I said, and even Randi mustered a little laugh. It was the running joke of all time—this guy made the invisible man look high-profile. Starla wasn't there and neither was Emil, who was working on the benefit (I hoped he'd snuck in some errands for the magazine in between his inevitable schnitzie-mountain climbing).

But of course Mary-Ellen was loudly, polka-dottedly, in attendance, not about to miss this chance to see and be seen. And Taormina had shown up, drunk to her nipples and tipsying around with even less finesse than that intern. I could just picture her running giddily down the hallways, accidentally pulling out everyone's IV and rerouting them like a soused switchboard operator. This woman was amusing in a disturbing way, but needed more attention than Randi did, and no one should be allowed to upstage the patient of honor. Fortuitously enough, it was change-of-guest-list time, and Taormina had to leave so the next person could come up—the model, Dovima Powell-Lyng, whom I had seen at Zymurgy on twelve of the last thirteen nights; I think you could safely say she was a regular. She used to be part of the decor at Odile, but since O'Dette, the aging studpuppet-owner, was off romancing some Spanish vixen on Ibiza, Odile's moment of glory had given way to the perverse rise of Zymurgy. Zymurgy was now not only the last word in nightlife, it was the only word.

"*Bientôt*," said Taormina as she sailed off into the sunset to try and find her face.

The second she left, we wanted her back. At least she was lively and distracting and never shut up. The ghastly silence—punctuated by other patients' moans and sickly demands—was getting on my nerves. We were used to working rooms where, if a certain situation bored you, you just excused yourself to get a drink or go to the bathroom and moved on to the next social setup. No one had to talk to anyone for more than five minutes; an instinctive socializing timer was built into everyone's mouths. But here you couldn't exactly say, Excuse me Randi, there's a much more fascinating miscarriage down the hall. It's been nice chatting with you. We had to put in our time, which Favio and I decided was twenty minutes minimum, thirty-five tops. We fidgeted a bit, pretended to be interested in Doric's painting, and told Randi how sorry we were four times.

"Where's Starla?" she asked, conscious enough to know which invited guest hadn't shown.

"She's not feeling well," I said, lying nimbly. "We went to my mother's house in Queens and had the usual feast— you've heard about my mother—and Starla ate a little too much, which she's really regretting right now. She's in meatball shock—maybe downstairs in intensive care, ha-ha. Of course she sends her best." I'd have to remember to tell Starla this alibi, and looked forward to it. I actually don't mind covering for people, because so many skills are required from so many actors, it becomes an ensemble piece akin to the Moscow Art Theater's productions of Chekhov. Randi, for example, was giving her very best impression of someone who believed what I said.

The word *baby* kept tastelessly running through my mind, and I had to work overtime to avoid slipping—So how you doing, Randi baby? or What you need right now is some babying. I hoped I wouldn't start humming "Baby Love" or "There Goes My Baby." Mary-Ellen broke the silence. "I'm having an art show at the Artillery Space," she said. No one had even an inkling that she was launching a new life as an artist, and no one dared ask if this sudden career move was precipitated by her failure as a performer, entrepreneur, designer, or human being.

"Great," said Randi, feebly.

"You're kidding?" said Doric, nearly letting his own work fall to the floor. What a time to drop the bombshell that she was going to compete for this poor couple's livelihood (not that she'd be much competition). Favio didn't even have to do his "Can you believe this?" look—I could smell it. Suddenly I had this vision that Diane Plewge was joking somewhere about me being in a car accident, and not only would it come true, but Mary-Ellen would visit me in my coma with some cheap flowers and the news that she was starting her own magazine. I glanced at my watch—just five to go.

Dovima slinked in with her Dianne Wiest cut and Modigliani features and looked so exquisite in her black Azzedine there should have been a commentator describing her every strut. She'd brought not only a bouquet of two dozen long-stemmed roses but also every Sade CD in existence. Doric and Randi loved Sade—most angst-filled people do— and had just gotten the most state-of-the-art CD player there was. See: models wearing black are not all evil people. Tedious, but not evil.

"Darling," said Dovima, swinging my way with one fluid body movement, "people are still talking about your party. It was so special. And so's your magazine." She'd told me this twelve of the last thirteen nights, but club conversations don't count. "I loved the thing you did on that two-time sex change," she added.

"He's down the hall," I said, "going for a third," and we all laughed. Dovima may be the most boring person on earth, but she never rocks the boat and has a surface style that camouflages any lack of depth. Naturally she was one of the most popular people at Zymurgy. Who wants depth anyway? She and her friends—Mimsy Maumstein, loudmouth daughter of Fred Maumstein, the Gordon Gekko of the minute; and Daisy Penhaligon, the colorfully unreal spawn of expatriate British publicist Maurice Penhaligon— were the new ruling class, the expense account–bred, supercoiffed, VISA-for-brains darlings who could charm you one minute and club you like a ton of bricks the next. Dovima was the most likable of the bunch, but I found them all pretty compelling; it's exciting to be sitting every night with people from elaborate dynasties, any member of which could significantly alter your career. You could forgive their glamour-length nails.

I looked over at Randi and saw that she wasn't laughing along with us; she was crying uncontrollably. I think the gifts had reminded her of why she was there in the first place. Doric asked to be alone with her, and we split. I looked down at my watch—thirty-five minutes, exactly.

Favio went off to meet some homeboys he'd become friends with—as all the other groups phased him out, the street kids were finding him fascinating enough to keep around as a curio. If only he'd spend the day looking for a job.

Starla and I were set to go to that homeless event at Mise en Scène, a tacky but revered haunt of the rich, near Sixtieth and Park. Emil had helped organize the thing with Colette Joie, and all sorts of debs with hyphenated names were expected, as well as a few dribbles of the downtown crowd, comped with Colette's approval to add some token local color (though Emil had specifically stated "No Favio"). Even if it was awful, it would be a fascinating journey to awfulness.

I called Starla from the street to arrange our entrance. "Hi, baby," I said, finally able to use the word in peace.

"How's Randi?" she said, without wasting a beat. She sounded so concerned. If she was so concerned, why didn't she visit?

"I told her you were in meatball shock," I related, not bothering to answer her question.

"I'm sending her over some flowers," she said. "I wish I could have come by the hospital, but . . ." But there weren't any photographers. But it was too much fuss on a day when you could be hawking beauty products. But you never liked Randi that much anyway. "But I sort of have hospitalphobia, and I just got so caught up in all these ad campaign meetings and stuff today. I haven't even had time to look at all that food your mother gave me. It's all clumped together in the fridge."

"It'll keep," I said, from experience. "Italian food never dies."

Starla's career-advancement news digests always struck me in two ways. They made me drool with lust for her burgeoning fame—An ad campaign meeting? Ooh, tell me some more sweet nothings, babe—but I would always read an unspoken "*I* had meetings and you didn't" inflection into them too. Maybe it was my own chronic insecurity—I didn't even have a magazine at this point, being eons beyond the monthly deadline I'd ingenuously set for myself. But there was no party for the rag this month, so there was no motivation to do the rag. And since issue one was out— Emil had hooked us up with a distribution company that got it on seventeen newsstands in New York, a few in L.A., and even one in Texas—it was my time to just bask. Maybe the magazine could come out every decade—I could do the next one as a retrospective of the twentieth century and then retire. Who was I kidding? I wanted more issues, more glory, more work. I just didn't feel like doing it.

I wished I could advance in my career and social networking without a whole lot of effort, but an Italian from downtown-via-Queens has three balls-and-chains to drag, and unfortunately a magazine requires painstaking labor, no matter where you come from. Though I'd convinced myself I never set out to climb, that was ages ago, when it wasn't even a possibility in my limited sphere. Now that it was an option being dangled in front of me like bait, I wanted to bite. A mere whiff of it proved addicting; once you moved up a step, you never wanted to stop until you could look down and really have a view.

Peer pressure made it even harder to swear off the urge. Doric was selling to biggies, Delroy was kissing famous ass, and Starla was actually looking at the rich crowd from eye level. Though *New York* magazine had just done a big piece on the new downtown crowd, Starla confided in me one night, "It's beat, trust me. Here's a little trick: if you don't even look at it, it doesn't exist. I'm not even going to look at that article."

"Doesn't downtown mean anything anymore?" I asked, truly confused.

"Not at the moment," she said. "You can't just be famous for the sake of being famous anymore. You have to have substance—or money. In fact, it really irks me that downtown's taking up a whole cell of my brain that could be used on something else. Get out," she said, banging her head to release the misguided gray matter. "Leave my body now!" I'll never get over how impressed I was that she could organize her brain so that every component of it was harmoniously at work on her cause. Any traitorous cells were promptly excised.

And here she was, delivering sweet little career-advancement news digests into the phone. I had to do a career-related remark just for symmetry's sake. "I finished my cover story on Colette Joie," I said, brightly.

"Great! We're going to see her tonight, aren't we?" she countered. Back to her business. I wondered if I should tell Colette that night about the cover story, or let it be a surprise to her. Either way, I couldn't imagine it would mean much to a woman of her stature and jewelry collection. "Honey," added Starla, "would you mind . . . Wait, let me lower the TV." She was watching *Dodge City;* she loved those old period pieces in which Errol Flynn saved Olivia de Havilland from the bad guys. "Hi," she came back. "Would you mind a whole lot if I brought Sylvia Valmouth along? Things were a little tense today, and maybe a night out could win me some brownie points." It was fine with me. Sylvia Valmouth was someone to reckon with, even if she did hobble. And though I was only down plus-one, Emil would love for us to shatter the rules this time. Brilliant—already this was shaping up as a much better guest list than the hospital.

There were enough limos outside Mise en Scène to perform a Grand Prix of limos. In one of them were the three of us— Starla, myself, and Sylvia, who looked like Broomhilda on Bromo and exuded an aura of regal importance from every artificially tanned pore. The way she kept her pinkies always half-cocked suggested she was at a perpetual tea. She had enough perfume on to napalm a horse and didn't talk much, breaking her vow of silence only to regale us with one-liners about her late husband, Maurice. "Maurice would have despised Mise en Scène," she said, without any further explanation, as I kicked Starla secretively. She kicked me back even harder. This was the Boss Lady, Big Mama, and we were not even to kid in front of her. Much currency rested on her every whim. Thank God we didn't accidentally kick *Sylvia's* leg, or it might have fallen off and rolled into a sewer. "Maurice had a little wiener," Sylvia added cryptically.

I couldn't believe I was riding in that awesome dream machine with two real sort-of-Someones. Midterms and tiny marshmallows in the cafeteria cole slaw and notes from my dad's doctor friend exaggerating my allergies so I could get out of phys ed were all in the past now, so remote it was as if it had all happened to another person, someone not worth knowing. I felt like I'd just been born and this was the very beginning of my life—not a new beginning, but *the* beginning. I felt so young—a babe trapped in a twenty-three-year-old's body, like a character in one of those body-switching movies. (Somewhere, a baby was now stuck with *my* personality.) We were all clinking Evian cocktails and toasting one another's successes—a far cry from cherry khia-faville. The *Jeffersons'* theme—"Movin' on up to the East Side"—was becoming *my* song.

A battery of photographers stood outside like predators, jostling one another for better views of no one in particular.

As we got out of the car—and it took Sylvia so long I thought she'd gotten stuck and was going to murder my chances right there—the photogs started snapping with a why-not-they-look-like-Someone half-interest. Sylvia knew the flashes were for her and barely unclenched her face to register approval. Starla assumed they were for her and did the suck-in-the-cheekbones, hand-under-the-chin number. I imagined it was all for me and realized this could be addictive.

With awe-inspiring grandeur—heel-ball-hobble, heel-ball-hobble—we walked into the blindingly ornate interior: the Belle Epoque meets early Reign of Terror by way of the Harmonia Gardens in *Hello, Dolly!*. I looked around and spotted not a single camera crew—success! Thanks to Starla's uncanny timing, we'd hit the place at just the correct moment. The invite was for cocktails at seven-thirty and dinner at eight-thirty, but no one ever pays attention to those suggested guidelines. It was eight-forty-five and peak schmooze and guzzle period, with no dinner in sight, just rows of merry widows like Sylvia, all lined up like bowling pins and drinking their mandatory eight-forty-five curve-balls. The median age in there was about sixty, and it wasn't hard to detect the Depend products under the Lacroix gowns—some of the ladies had diaper line. These women were professional shoppers and drinkers who only inter-rupted those processes for occasional facials, nail wraps, tummy tucks, and charity events like this, at which they spent money for a Good Cause so they could be seen doing so. I'm sure most of them didn't think there really was a homeless problem in New York—it was just a clever fabri-cation, a festive excuse for another dinner party—but as long as everyone else believed it, it was worthy of a place on their checkbooks' calendars. Sylvia was different—she didn't care about nail wrappings, except to sell them. And she did seem to have a brain. The only people in the party scene who seemed to have a brain were the ones who didn't talk much.

"Don't say hello like that to me," said Emil, more paranoid than usual. Like what? I hadn't said anything to him.

"Did you meet with the printer?" I said, thinking it best to get my petty business out of the way as soon as possible and move on to bigger things.

"Don't talk about your stupid stuff here," he snapped. "I've got a party to throw!" I should have known. In Emil's scheme of things, I was a mere speck of lint next to the awesome dustball known as Colette Joie. He looked annoyed that he'd even invited me.

But I was forgotten quickly enough as he glided over to Starla to gush, "This new look is the most amazing thing I've ever seen. You're like the Eighth Wonder." And then he tap-danced over to Sylvia to drool so copiously he should have had a bucket hanging from his mouth.

"I like that Eighth Wonder idea," Sylvia said, in a rare moment of verbal communication. Emil looked about to explode with excitement.

"You do? Feel free to use it," he enthused. "I give it to you carte blanche. But if you *do* do an Eighth Wonder line of cosmetics, make sure you let me throw the party. It could be so major. We could have big mock-ups of the seven wonders, and a huge lipstick—bigger than the things at Starla's party, bigger than the Eiffel Tower—that says 'Sylvia Valmouth's Eighth Wonder.' " He was jumping the gun a tad, and Sylvia resented that this guy would throw a party for any stray word that tumbled out of her mouth. "Blech," she said, half to herself.

Vivien was there with Diane, and both had changed outfits—Where do these people find the time?—almost looking as if they weren't from the 'burbs. Vivien was in a form-fitting, coral-colored Ungaro. Diane was in a beaded St. Laurent grape-cluster ensemble, which screamed the fact that her selfless work on AIDS benefits actually pays very well. "Adapt or die," she laughed, giving me a wicked pinch.

Vivien looked upset. "Emil didn't tell me Colette Joie

was involved in this," she said, munching nervously on the remains of an ice cube.

"What's wrong with Colette Joie?" I asked, shooting over a look at the woman. I couldn't believe there could be anything wrong with Colette Joie. She was in a red Chanel suit—very smart, very trim, and pert in a manner that said, I know where I'm going. Now watch me. She looked aggressive but not obnoxious, friendly but only if all the elements called for it. A true party pro, she'd probably rubbed Preparation H under her eyes to remove bags—a common trick—but tomorrow they'd swell up twice as big. Her earrings were brighter than the decor—she must have had ear implants to be able to hold those things up, or maybe she rubbed Preparation H on them too, and *they* had swelled up twice as big. I wondered if she was one of the professional shoppers and figured yes, she must be trash who married into money and became Someone. She became Colette Joie. It turned out she did do Something—she had a lace-doily franchise—but that didn't detract from her being Someone. Neither did the fact that the money she married into had died. Uptown, widows are the happening deal.

"Don't you know about her? Don't you read the news?" said Vivien, outraged. I felt she was mad at me more than she'd be at most people because she sensed I had some potential.

'Yeah, I read the news," I said. "I read Liz Smith, Page Six, Billy Norwich, and *The Enquirer*. What important thing could possibly be happening that wouldn't be in those columns?" I was about thirty percent kidding.

"It was a big news story about a month ago," she said, trying to regain her composure, "that Colette Joie's son, Herve, advocates quarantining anyone with the HIV virus, the pig. He's a fucking Nazi; I don't care how rich they are. Not only that, he refers to the disease as 'God's revenge on homosexuals, prostitutes, drug addicts, and all other sinners.' It wouldn't have been such a blow if he were just another crackpot from the Moral Majority shooting his mouth off, but he's a pretty respected professor who writes books.''

"And is very influential to the government," added Diane, well rehearsed.

"Ooh," she said, losing it. "I just want to strangle that bitch."

"Go for it," said Diane. "Think of all the press it'll get." Diane could never help but think of all the press things would get; it was an involuntary spasm.

"I'm so surprised," I said. "She looks so, I don't know, winning and kind of, you know . . ."

"Fresh?" said Diane.

"Fresh as a daisy," snapped Vivien. "The daisies she's gonna be pushing up any day now."

The photographers had moved inside *en masse* now that the arrivals were over. Once dinner started, they'd be cleared out like so much chattel.

Vivien was seething and urging me to do an article attacking Colette. I couldn't work up the nerve to tell her that my cover story extolling the woman as an icon for all time was ready for typesetting.

"But what's wrong with Colette? She just spawned the guy," I said, clutching at any straw whereby I could like Colette and still have Vivien approve of me.

"Yeah," she said, "and that alone condones his mental midgetness. She certainly hasn't come out against him. In fact, they're oedipally inseparable; he's forty-five and still lives with Mommy. It's insane for her to be giving him such credibility. So many of her friends are gay."

"And prostitutes and IV drug–users," laughed Diane. Most of the gay ones, I learned, were trapped in the closet even more than my Uncle Vito ever was. Some were even closet Jews.

Herve, alas, wasn't there, or I'm sure Vivien would have gouged his eyes out with Colette's earrings. *That* would have been some party, but he was off on some incendiary tour, spreading the word, not the virus.

"So you made it uptown without a nosebleed? Well, what do you think?" said Colette, taking me by surprise, as she looked me up and down like I was a mackerel.

"You look incred—" I started to say, but before I had a chance, a noisy scene at the door interrupted us like a Bastille Day parade. Everyone, already bored to tears by this event—Was dinner being mailed in third class?—raced to the door to get a load of it. It couldn't be any less interesting than the sight of seventy-five merry widows scrutinizing one another like proctologists.

"Oh, God," shrieked Emil. It was José—wearing a pail on his head and a poncho made out of a plaid tablecloth that covered his crotch, at least—and his posse of overdone, overwrought looney tunes. He was demanding to get in—for free, of course—and kept insisting that Emil had invited him. "We have a gentleman's agreement that we can go to any of each other's parties," he lied, "benefit or no." The doorman said he'd be glad to admit them for a total of two thousand dollars. That was being kind. I'm sure there wasn't enough money in the world to get these people into Mise en Scène.

Starla backed off about half a mile; if she'd let José say hello to her, and anyone saw, it could be career suicide. Sylvia didn't seem to know anything was going on at all, as she downed yet one more what-the-heck cocktail. Colette, meanwhile, tried to nip the problem firmly, threatening, without raising her voice, to call security if they didn't "vanish." But nothing was going to reduce this swelling.

"I swear I didn't invite them, Colette," Emil was saying. "I hardly even know these people."

"Call security," screamed José, shooting crepe-paper streamers and leading the newies in a chant of "Call security, call security." The din obscured anything else that was being said for miles. "I was invited!" he added, barking out those words like the bad seed on the rag. One of the idiot photographers was taking the newies' picture as they tried to form a human pyramid. They'd never leave if there were photo opportunities available.

"It's so weird," said Vivien. "My whole life is spent trying to get arrested while I'm protesting, and theirs is spent trying to get arrested while crashing parties. I'm so glad I dropped out of all that." Without my having asked, she explained that her protest organization, SCREAM (The Society to Combat Right-wing Efforts at AIDS Moralizing), *wants* its members to get locked up because that makes for a stronger show of support and a better story for the papers. They even train them in civil disobedience, teaching them how to handle the arrests with the least possible fuss. SCREAM members who haven't been arrested are considered black sheep.

José wasn't asking for an arrest by this point; he was pleading for a grisly death by gunshot with his every irritating whine. He knew there was no chance in hell of getting in; it was just a matter of creating the biggest scene imaginable so they could feel they'd made an impression while being rejected. Everyone inside worked on the opposite principle—If I'm not unduly noticed and haven't offended anyone, then I've had a successful evening.

José wanted to ruffle feathers—not as an act of principle, just as an act. He wanted to make these people sick to their stomachs for the same reason dogs lick their own balls— because they can. He was finally about to give up, but not before taking one last shot at a collective migraine. "You're all invited to come to our 'Just say yes' party," he shouted, throwing dozens of invites, which were shaped like little vials of crack, at the poor, rich widows. "You see," he said, *"I'm a gentleman."* Before the newies even got five feet onto the pavement, a tuxedoed man without a green card was sweeping up the vials for disposal, and Colette and Emil shared the unenviable task of emotionally hosing down the victim-

113

ized women and apologizing. It was Emil's chance to meet them, though at this point he wished he hadn't been born. "I've never seen those people in my life" was his new agenda.

"How dare she?" said Vivien, as we sat down to dinner. The José incident had barely scraped her consciousness; she was still fixated on getting back at Colette.

"How dare who what?" said Starla, realizing in mid-question that this could be potentially thorny stuff that might upset Sylvia. "Look, Sylvia," she said, pointing at the pre-placed appetizer. "Salmon, honey. You love salmon."

"Maurice hated salmon," Sylvia said spacily and started digging in.

"Randi's getting out of the hospital tomorrow," Diane announced to the table.

"Great," said Starla, sensing another potential jackpot subject. "Salmon, Sylvia," she repeated. "Mmm-mm." She was always protecting Sylvia from things that wouldn't necessarily disturb her at all. The woman was old, but not totally unhappening. It was possible to be ancient and not tired, just like you can be fifteen and completely over. Look at Diana Vreeland. Look at Gary Coleman.

The dinner was so ritzy, in that inedible but extravagantly laid-out fashion, that I had to wonder if sitting here stuffing our faces was really helping the homeless in any practical way. By the main course—some kind of veal with some kind of green vegetable with some kind of mushy potato—Vivien was shaking so hard she looked like the queen of the San Andreas ballroom. I guess the dinner wasn't helping people with AIDS either. Everyone watched her go up to Stanislaw Lavelieri—the only photographer allowed into the dinner—and buzz something into his ear that had him picking up his camera with a demonic grin. Stanislaw was a fashion photographer, not a paparazzo, but Vivien had clearly come up with the photo op that could launch a whole new career for him, albeit a far less distinguished one. Not trembling anymore, with an awesome sense of purpose, she storm-trooped back to the table to pick up her plate of brown and green and beige charity food. "Watch this," she said, as if there was anything better going on.

What happened after that I felt I'd already seen in my mind's viewfinder, so it was with a spooky sense of *déjà vu* that I saw it unreel in actuality. Vivien went over to Colette Joie's table with a very well-performed offhand air and pretended to be saying hello. So Colette had a big, phony smile on her face, with laugh lines in full bloom, as Vivien covered her with oozy, drippy veal and trimmings—the legendary Sylvia Miles trick—all to help the homeless. As the plate crashed to the floor, the food thickened to a standstill on Colette's face, which was frozen into a very convincing impersonation of horror. The brown stuff wrapped around her hairdo, the green stuff congealed on the slope of her nose, the beige stuff made her lips into stalactites. She looked pretty fierce, actually. Stanislaw got a full roll out of it and shrugged his shoulders at Colette as if to say, Well, I'm a photographer, and if something happens, it's my moral obligation to shoot it.

"That's for your fascist baby boy," said Vivien, taking a bread roll and mushing it into her face for final effect. Just doing *her* job, too.

The room was so scandalized you'd think Vivien had thrown acid in Colette's face instead of just veal. I think everyone was acting a lot more upset than they really were; this was by far the most enjoyable thing so far.

"Right on," said Diane to Vivien as they prepared to escape like thieves. "The food was caca anyway."

"Catch you on the flip side," Vivien said to me with a victorious smile, and they left. A vein in Emil's neck was throbbing as if it was going to burst and splash Colette with one more mushy substance. He looked like a trapped ferret and was beginning to defy that one crucial rule—never let them see you sweat.

"I can't believe it," he was saying to Starla and anyone who'd listen. "First José and now this. Colette's going to have me strung up like a deli window display. It's over." Emil might finally be able to begin his long-delayed modeling career.

Without a moment's pause, he and several of the tuxedoed penguins were wiping Colette off while vowing to rinse Vivien with hot oil next time. Not that there'd be a next time. Emil could wipe as hard as he wanted, but he couldn't erase his dire failure. Colette knew Vivien's presence there had been his doing; new-fixated though he tried to be, Emil was still a year and a half behind in pegging Vivien as a glamorous, harmless party girl.

Stanislaw was racing out, having decided it was worth antagonizing a sinking shipload of ladies at death's door to rush-develop the photo of the year.

"We can't leave now," Starla said, "or we'll seem like traitors." And so we stayed to the bitter end, knowing that nothing else would come close to that special moment. Colette's face remained fixed in a Tussaud version of shock all the way through dessert. As we approached her to say good night, she flinched as if we were going to throw scalding coffee on her. "I'm putting you on my next cover," I said like an asshole, and she didn't respond.

Starla sprang the next stop on me without warning: we had to drop by Spermicidal Foam because *NewsPrime* was doing a piece on her there, in her own milieu, as it were. Starla had never been to this relatively new, every-other-night club, but we weren't going to tell *them* that.

We had some time to kill while Sylvia went to the bathroom, so I called my machine for messages, which I would neurotically have done even if there weren't time. Remote message retrieval was one of those inventions it was hard to imagine how I'd lived without before it invaluably enriched my life.

This time the messages ranged from the ridiculous to the subliminal. There was the thrice-weekly call from Mom— "Did you eat all the food? Don't eat too fast or you'll choke. What size pants are you? I saw some nice polyester slacks on the avenue. Have you made any headway? My neck is killing me. Your father wants to say hello." (Background mumble resembling "Hello.") Then a call from Mary-Ellen—"Don't forget about my opening." (The one between her legs?) A rant from Mimsy, calling from the Zymurgy pay phone (50 cents for the first five minutes) to say she was becoming allergic to her own body. And a frightening monologue from Favio, the only person in New York who needed so desperately to communicate he'd call his own roommate. He sounded gone on something and was calling from God knows what dazzling gutter. Police-car sirens, ambulances, and screaming junkies provided a rhythmic backdrop against which he could do his disturbed rap.

"It's your roommate," he said. "I almost just got killed by some gang right out of *Mad Max,* but fortunately they were afraid of *me* when they got a closer look. It's so noisy out here. Was the party fabulous? First off," he continued, "I want to say I love you, I really love you." Okay, so he was on Ecstasy. He was crying uncontrollably, but I couldn't really sympathize with him. Maybe he desired me, but loved?

"I'm probably not going to come home for a few nights," he went on. "I've got to find myself." Oh, God, had he gone California on me? "I'm at wit's end; I don't know what to do. I can't believe Emil didn't invite me to that benefit, and he invited Cha Cha. You don't know how that hurts." My mother cries about ALF puppets; Favio cries about dinner parties.

"I didn't want to tell you this, but I went to Zymurgy

the other night, and they wanted me to pay! Can you believe that? Me—me who's been in *Fabulon* only thirty-five times. And it's not even because they don't like me. That I could take. It was because the new doorman had never *heard of me* and wouldn't even budge to get Garth and ask him who I was." Yeah—was.

"My father keeps calling to harass me—Oh, Vinnie, I love you. You are the coolest person in New York right now. I have to get a job. I never worked a day in my life. What can I do? I don't want to wait tables. I certainly don't want to *bus* tables. If I were more what the chicken hawks wanted, I could at least sell myself on Fifty-third and Third, but they're afraid of me too. Maybe I'll go pimp some of the crack kids in the salt mines, I'm serious.

"I was with some friends—the homeboys—but they went off to some Vogueing ball and they said it wasn't a good idea for a white boy to come along." The machine hadn't beeped yet. Favio had some psychic connection with it whereby the usual twenty-two seconds could stretch into eternity. "God, my head is spinning. All I can see is a pukey shade of orange. I did some green Ecstasy from Australia and a lot of other crap. I didn't even ask what it was. I think it was Special K—the stuff they used as a painkiller in Vietnam. Well, it doesn't work. Anyway, I've got to run around and look for myself, look for something. Don't worry about me." Translation: worry about me.

"Any calls?" said Starla, who'd been entertaining Sylvia in the car. "No," I said and blithely hopped in with them.

We dropped Sylvia off, and she let us take the car to Spermicidal Foam, which was truly in rarefied form, throbbing with the last gasp of Carcinogen's exhaust. Any off-the-beaten-track, fashion-crazed demento left in town was there because you *had* to be there or wait a whole day for it to happen again. Besides, there was nowhere else to go. This was the last stomping ground for all of them—a giant trash-bin filled with victims of time and fashion who had to party very hard to forget that they were doomed. No one here had his hair parted and combed on the side, and there was nary a button-down shirt or sensible shoe in sight. Being poised on the dynamite fuse, they were dressed for a big bang, having assaulted themselves with every accessory they could get away with and still walk. They seemed desperate.

A six-foot bald woman with hoop earrings was dancing on a speaker as a two hundred–pound (I'm being kind) drag queen flounced a boa between her legs. Couples of all genders were dry humping on the dance floor, and the air was so thick with libido a girl could get pregnant just standing still. Yet the atmosphere was frighteningly wholesome. This was the AIDS generation. They pretended to do It, talked about It, almost did It, and watched It, but they never actually did It.

Favio always said it was the freaky dressers who were actually the most moral people; it was the ones who wore funeral black and snuck through dark alleyways looking to cop feels and drugs who were the real sleazes. I was never sure if that was a justification for his own excesses. But whether it was a medal of honor or of shame, no one here was the least bit coy about their fashion outrage, wearing either nothing at all or totally too much. In all their finery, they were the most extreme reaction to all that Zymurgy stuff imaginable. Tucked away by a Republican society that considers *fringe* an even dirtier word than *liberal,* they'd popped back in full force, looking and acting ten times weirder, looking and acting like *this.* I wasn't worried—this was a countertrend, and I was more interested in following the trend itself.

Presiding over the madness were Arianne and Marianne Ding, nineteen-year-old twins who were in matching Shirley Temple/dominatrix outfits and never talked except to scream—the only rational response to all this. The Dings weren't even up to the legal drinking age, but go figure; they were the booze ringleaders of New York. They had the

119

last stranglehold on weirdness, and as such were the high priestesses of something, I guess. Like Lana Turner in *The Prodigal,* they'd decided that a high priestess cries once when she is born, and never again. After that, she screams.

I searched the high-energy dance floor and saw both regulars and oddities, about eighty-five percent of whom were wearing the same exact Sprouse camouflage jumpsuit. There was Mary-Ellen making one last stab at promoting her art show; Dovima, Mimsy, and Daisy, slumming and looking like they'd been buried alive; Marla Hotchner, the original Starla, who'd failed to make it in uptown society and was now crash-landing back downtown, where no one would have her (or even knew who she was); José and company showing no sign that they'd caused the mental collapse of at least forty people that evening; and Doric—*Doric?*—who was probably getting in his last cruising rites as Randi finished up her hospital stay. Starla gave him a bear hug that could have proved deadly if it had lasted one more second. She was probably scanning the room for that camera crew as she did it. Unlike certain presidents, she could do two things at once.

They were interrupted by a lackluster girl with too many moles on her upper lip, tits that were pigeon-toed, and static cling that gave her dress an obscene formation. "Hi," she said to Starla with an overenthusiasm befitting the Cleaver clan. "I think you're the best. In fact, my goal in this lifetime is to become you." Oh, really? Better luck next lifetime, girl. This drab troglodyte looked like she might be able to pass for a Catholic schoolgirl from Ohio named Chris, but wasn't fit to trim the toenails of beauty maven Starla Rogers from New York. I couldn't believe it—between Marla and Starla and the pretendress, there were three generations of Starlas. This topped any Kennedy reunion.

"That's nice," said Starla without a trace of sarcasm. She had the best approach to everything and must have taught the little tramp a lesson in dignity that night. I don't know; the girl was never heard from again.

Onstage, the bald woman, now practically naked, was massaging herself with a vibrator, and the audience was cheering as if this were the height of erotic entertainment. "Read my lips," she said, and made her vagina speak volumes. Her lips were bigger than Barbara Hershey's. The fat drag queen with the boa was now in s&m leathergear with the black mesh on her face that Sigue Sigue Sputnik made so popular for two weeks. She (He? Hesh? It?) had gone from simply lewd to outright menacing in a matter of minutes, I guess because lewd doesn't pay as well. This blimpazoid was applying clothespins to the breasts of the baldie with the vibrator, as if they were laying out her nipples to dry. Then fatso lit a candle, dropping hot wax on baldie's inner thighs, and everyone screamed except them, the Dings louder than anyone in their flawless, screaming harmony. A camera crew was shooting all this with bright, scrutinizing lights—as background to the Starla piece, I guessed. The camera crew! "Don't worry," I said to Starla. "They won't be able to use any of this footage." She didn't buy that.

"Dilemma," she said, fixing her eyes into a think-clench. "If my face appears in this setting, it won't be what's generally known as a good move. But if I leave them in the lurch, *NewsPrime* will never do me again." She had crystallized the situation as she spoke, in a matter of seconds. Rather than panic, she was going to analyze and act.

"Say you're sick," I suggested. "It got me out of gym. It's gotten me out of a lot of things. Can you do sick?" I knew she could do sick. It was one of the few emotions she excelled at with a minimum of exertion.

"I feel cerebrally sick right now," she said, "but I can't do physically."

"Just think of Colette's face," I said, inspirationally,

"dripping with all that veal. Sense memory." She looked intrigued and mulled it over for a few seconds.

"And vegetables. And potatoes. And blech. That's good!" she said and shot over to the camera crew with a queasy look reeking of cookies about to be tossed. They rescheduled and shot the next week at Mise en Scène.

On our way out, Vogel Johns oozed into the club, wearing a Sprouse camouflage jumpsuit, took one perfunctory look around, and said, "Isn't this incredible?"

"I guess," I answered, noncommittally. "Sorry, gotta run."

He grabbed me by the neck and said, "Wait." His breath smelled like peanut butter. "The island was really great this year."

"What island? Greenland?" I said. I didn't care what island; I knew this was just a setup for something else.

"*Fire* Island," he whined, as if it were as natural a word association as *drink* and *ticket*. What was he talking about? Fire Island hasn't been fabulous since disco glitter balls went public domain.

"You're not going to believe this," he continued, on another tangent already, "but last night Arianne and Marianne called me, and then Doric beeped in on the other line. I had three semilegends on the phone at the same time."

"Wow," I said, rolling my eyes. "Well, I just came from Mise en Scène, so get over yourself. *Ciao.*"

"Wait," he said again, spewing peanut butter fumes into all my mucous membranes. "Maybe you'd want a story on this place for your magazine?" Jackpot. He was groveling.

"Maybe I would," I said, and walked out. Maybe I wouldn't.

7

A couple of weeks passed before I saw Favio again. They seemed like years, not because I missed him—in fact, it was great having the apartment to myself, especially since I was paying for it alone anyway—but because so much happened. The picture of Vivien slapping Colette with the meat hit page three of several major papers—this plate was the biggest dish in town. I watched Starla shoot her video amid more smoke machines than MTV ever dreamed of. (I wondered if everyone involved would die of cancer in seven years like after that John Wayne movie about Genghis Khan—but it was totally glamorous, like something out of *Valley of the Dolls,* before the part where they wait for the rush of exhilaration and it doesn't come.) I got out the second issue, with only about a thousand and a half hitches. And I almost went to that AIDS bonfire, only it was too early and I couldn't get anyone else to go with me, since there wasn't enough press yet on this sort of thing to be really gala. Whatever press there was, it seemed, Vivien was getting, probably because, unlike most activists, she didn't make a point of being unkempt and intimidating. She was the girl next door, who happened to be SCREAMing all the time.

Hot off her veal write-ups, she was now splashed all over the papers again, being arrested. When it was all over, she called to tell me *I* should get arrested for my cover story on Colette. We made a date for lunch.

Emil was conspicuously doing less coke, and I wrongly assumed it was because he was weaning off it. Actually, he was doing more, just privately. After a while, I guess, it becomes part of your system, and though you get increasingly desperate for the stuff, you're more accustomed to the desperation and are able to treat it more casually in public, though in private you're as tormented as any needy person and start doubling your doses. If that sounds confused, you can imagine what a blur it is if you're on coke. He stopped offering me any, which was fine; I was as hookable as a rug and always felt obliged to consume what was laid out in front of me out of sheer politeness. If forced, that is. Being cheap, lazy, and slovenly, I wasn't about to go out of my way for drugs, and now that Emil was hoarding the crystals and Favio was broke and absent, they weren't in my lexicon, period. It was probably for the best, though there were nights I tried to recreate that soaring Superman sensation in a drug-free state, only to end up feeling like Don Knotts.

Emil loved my cover story on Colette, especially since I left out the veal incident and out of respect didn't even include it in the Star Wars column, though it was easily the ultimate star war. He did a sidebar for me on the haunts of the upper class, which he said was what people wanted to read. I hoped that didn't mean what people wanted to read a year and a half ago, but being a blank blackboard waiting for anyone to scribble on, I went along with it. The subject of wealth and all its trappings became my new drug. We ran all sorts of charts detailing the Trumps' yachts and the Helmsleys' baubles, and I tried to keep any trace of sarcasm out of it all so no one would laugh when we referred to the "radiant and tasteful Ivana."

"What is this?" said Delroy one night, flipping through the magazine. "Is this a *National Lampoon* parody?" I didn't know what he meant. Wasn't it what people wanted to read? Besides, there was lots of nutty, iconoclastic stuff in that issue too. I tried to show him that, but he flung it against the wall and looked dumbfounded.

"If he wants to be like that, let him be like that," said Emil. "He's just a gaping asshole." Still, it disturbed us that this gung-ho goonie was mad for the first time we'd ever seen. It was typical of just about everyone; be super friendly and supportive at first, then lay on your dark side with a roller.

"Is this going to be a different kind of publication every issue?" Garth Free asked me another night, at a really terrible fashion show at the Almanac boutique in SoHo. (I only went because they sold the magazine there.) "What can we expect next month—*Popular Mechanics* or *Honcho?*" I merely grinned and pointed to the counter, where someone was buying it.

One bitterly cold September night, Emil and I went to see *Bambi* just for a hoot, and I found I couldn't really mock it out, but I couldn't get that worked up over it either. Bambi's mother getting killed had been the traumatic low point of my entire childhood. On seeing it again, that scene was the dramatic high point. Had I become jaded?

On the way home from the movie, we were accosted by one of those drunken homeless people who should be force-retired to a show-biz rest home, or at least have a drummer following him at all times to do a rim shot after every line. He was so persistent and annoying—Why can't these people take the first ten nos for an answer?—I fantasized that he'd bludgeon us just to end the pain. If they were heckling this guy off the Carnegie Hall stage with bad tomatoes, he'd be coming back for encores. But, in this grungy alleyway, you couldn't boo anything away.

"Yo," he said, "excuse me." He was in tar-stained overalls and smelled like the lobby at the Heritage U.S.A. Hotel.

"You're excused," said Emil, and we walked on. But that's not enough to get rid of a show-biz bum. If anything, the response was an encouragement for him to invade our world with even more determination. He grabbed me by the neck and started singing "Mona Lisa" as I tried to untangle myself and resolved to shower as soon as possible. He spun *jetés* around Emil a few times with a demented flourish and imitated Madonna saying, "Come on, come on"—the sickest thing I'd seen in New York so far. Then he got on his knees and did an insane version of "Swanee" that had a cur chorus in nearby alleyways wailing in appreciation. I hoped he'd take it up an octave so the dogs would be the only ones who could hear it.

This guy was the Antichrist of taste. He was Sammy Davis, Don Rickles, and Tina Turner all rolled into one, and he wouldn't leave until we gave him "anything you can spare—twenties and up." Ba-dum-pum. We turned the corner at a clip and were sure we'd finally gotten away from the schmoe when he startled us by jumping out from under a car. This guy was everywhere, faster than the rodents that were charmingly running their very own Hialeah all around us. Maybe he was something Diane Plewge had conjured up with an evil spell.

Now he was singing "Alexander's Ragtime Band" and flailing his arms as if a six hundred–piece marching band was behind him. There probably *were* six hundred of his friends waiting under cars with brass instruments and complete musical arrangements. I relented and cracked a half-smile, but Emil was starting to lose it.

"Where you from?" the bum said, to either one of us.

"Shut up," said Emil, furious.

"Shut up?" the bum said. "What kind of place is that?"

"Queens," I mumbled.

"You're from Queens?" he said, grinning. "I'm from straight parents myself." With that he let out a raucous, self-satisfied laugh that ended as suddenly as it had started when Emil turned burnt orange and kicked him viciously in the balls. I thought this was pretty excessive; the line wasn't *that* bad, even if I'd already heard it in every club in town. But Emil was not amused. He was going beyond the breaking point, his face throbbing like a cartoon of a faucet about to split open—it was a scary side to him I'd never seen. After having Delroy throw my magazine against the wall, I'd had enough of people's ugly sides. It got uglier, and I think the bum became the punching bag proxy for all of Emil's anxieties. He became Vivien and José and Favio and anyone who hadn't given Emil a break.

As the guy doubled over, Emil grabbed him by the neck with both hands and squeezed it like a lemon, pulling him over to the nearest wall and throttling his head against it a few times. "Shut up, shut up, shut up," Emil was screaming, banging the guy's head harder and angrier each time until blood started to gush. The poor bum was bleeding buckets and whimpering, "You motherfuckers," as all the dog-wailing came to a deafeningly silent halt. "Emil, stop that," I said and pulled him off. "You just threw a benefit for these people." We ran to the corner of Third and got into the first cab.

We never talked about that incident. It was a dark underpinning to every conversation we had, just like every time I see my ex-neighbor Tony all I can think of is how, when he and I were ten and seven, respectively, he tried to get me to "kiss" his dick. No matter what we're talking about—international politics, computer software, movies—all I can picture is that nauseating exhortation to make love to his thing. And now I was stuck eternally with the goods on Emil, the bumbasher, but could only keep carrying on as if the la-

127

de-da stuff we'd done together, the tinsel and champagne, was all there was. I chalked it up to the coke. It possesses people, makes them not themselves. The coke had beaten up the homeless man. Arrest that spoon immediately.

Just a few months on the social-go-round and I was torn between so many conflicting subgroups and stratagems that I felt like a cultural wishbone. I wanted to party like a loon and felt no need to excuse myself for it; frivolousness— reckless, light-hearted triviality—must never be underestimated as a way of life, an antidote to all the middle-class bullshit that threatens to destroy you with predictability. All these political causes were starting to become like a religion, piously above mockery with their high-minded sincerity. Fuck them. I wanted to laugh my head off, dance my ass off, erase every debilitating thought with one more mindless event.

This would have been the clear-cut route to go if parties were still the way they were. But even Emil admitted once in a moment of weakness that "parties aren't parties the way they were when parties were parties." A truer word was never said. They'd become work, and this new surge toward respectability had swept me along like boot camp. After twenty-five years of this, you get baggier, saggier, tireder, wireder, and no gold watch.

Unfortunately, Vivien elicited a similar shoulder shrug. All that sincerity made her staggeringly novel, for sure, but when she aggressively bid for martyrdom, it made her about as appetizing as a Drear Garson movie. Was there a gold watch for mixed feelings? Just like I had found the handful of badly dressed, superaggressive radicals on campus a fascinating drain, so were these new activists compelling, attention-getting, and totally unnerving. "Anger only begets anger," I heard Quentin Crisp say at a dinner one night. He felt political movements were a waste, that the best way to get action is simply to wait for it. Was he right? I'm sure SCREAM didn't think so, and whether they'd accomplished anything solid or not, they (meaning Vivien) had at least succeeded in awakening my consciousness a little, to the point where I knew that a crisis was happening. But I didn't want to know that it was happening. I wanted them to stop screaming and go away. But Vivien was so nice. But, but, but.

I don't know why I stayed with the party people. I guess because they were transparent, but not boringly so, not the way a simple piece of cellophane would be. Their transparency had shades and textures to it, like stained glass that's see-through when you put it up to the light but looks dazzling from any distance. They were so *entertainingly* silly, and when you analyzed them, no sillier than people who devote their lives to memos and data and survival rites that are too tiresome even to describe. At least these people sparkled in their tedium. They all played back-stabby games, but amusing ones, and nothing anybody said was really that offensive, because it had been written into the rules that anything goes. If Emil dished Favio to me, it was OK, because Favio had probably just dished Emil to me, no doubt just before dishing me to Emil. Once you accepted the guidelines, the game was a kick—a career and an industry unto itself—and these people were the best players in town. If Emil were a surgeon and I had to get cut open, I'd demand him because he'd be the best, most intense and dedicated surgeon there was. If he had to, he'd screw a thousand other people to be sure my operation would be perfect. That's the kind of person I want to be around.

I got a few messages from Favio at odd hours, always telling me he was still searching and I shouldn't worry, even though panic-stricken screams invariably wailed up in the background. He probably had made an ambient tape of these sounds and played it for effect.

Starla went away for a weekend in Newport, which she said she couldn't take me to—it must have been really A—and when she came back, we had some long, if not exactly in-depth, talks like we'd never really had; our whole relationship had consisted of thrashing about each other's places getting ready and then having those club conversations that were always mercifully interrupted by a procession of third wheels. Our sex fiasco always kept us from total intimacy, hovering over even our smallest talk, just like my goods on Emil and my ex-neighbor Tony made sure those relationships would never be relaxed again. But with Starla it was doubly embarrassing; we had the goods on each other.

So we never really cut through that wall—we buried the mess so far into our minds' embarrassment tanks it would have taken a robot society's worth of electrodes to yank it to the surface. And then what could we really learn from it? Screw it, we would be politely intimate. Publicly private.

"What do you want from life?" she asked me one night as I munched furiously on Cracker Jacks and she sipped fancy French water on the rocks. Her apartment was in disarray because she was getting ready to move to a place she'd just bought farther uptown. There were boxes of press clippings everywhere, some of which were starting to turn yellow. Not to worry—there'd be newer, whiter ones through eternity. I stammered an answer. "I guess everything I have now, but more of it. More fun people . . . more glory . . . success . . . approval."

"Hmm-mmm," she said, appreciatively. "I want there to be a Starla style that's so deep-set into the consciousness that people just have to say 'Starla' and everyone will know what they mean. A way of doing things that just spells out my name."

"*C-h-r-i-s?*" I grinned. She didn't laugh.

"*S-t-a-r-l-a,*" she said, dryly. "And I'm not stepping down until I get there." You couldn't not believe her. Clearly her current title was just a rung on the way to the nationals and then, of course, Miss Universe. She'd already copped the congeniality prize.

"Were you a lonely child?" she asked. This was so college: pretending to be deep while really digging for dish.

"Yeah. I was almost catatonic for years at a time," I confessed. "In fact, I don't remember much of anything about my childhood except for a few landmark events that unfortunately traumatized me for life. Basically I'm ashamed of it all, that nothing was handed to me on a silver platter except for my total anonymity. I had to work and drudge every step of the way just to get over that bridge—it's a longer trip than you think, you know."

"But you come from such good people," she said. "You have nothing to be ashamed of."

"I know," I said. "I don't mean them. I mean I was ashamed of myself—for being nothing, a big, wussy zero who had to force my way into any privileged situation rather than be welcomed into it. You can't help your birthright, but you can hate yourself for it anyway, just like I hate the fact that my hair is black and curly instead of silky blond."

"I had the opposite problem," she laughed, carressing the locks she had perversely changed from blonde to brunette.

"But you know," I continued. "I never had anything paid for by any kind of corporate expense account until recently—and even that was *your* expense account. Do you know I've never even been out of the country? 'I'm deprived onna cowna I'm depraved.' "

"Such a babe," she tsk-tsked. "You have so much of life ahead of you." She was sounding like a Carpenters song, and that always made me ill. She sipped, I crunched, and we just sat there in one of those cavernous silences in which the minutes pass like hours. Morrissey droned on in the background about some love obsession; I'd rather hear the Carpenters.

"What about you?" I said, trying not to seem too pushy. "Were you ashamed?"

She paused for an eternity, then said, "You don't know what shame is. You don't know what it's like to be the ugliest girl in a Catholic school full of ugly girls with glasses that look like the back of a Plymouth. The one the nuns used to beat for chewing gum, for not keeping up with my Bible studies, for not understanding why all the sins were bad."

"I can't believe you were ugly," I said, sincerely. I was convinced she'd made this up, just like Paulina chronically moans about how average she looks. I always felt Starla should do those Kelly LeBrock "Don't hate me because I'm beautiful" commercials. Whatever flaws she had in looks somehow all jigsawed together into perfect beauty.

"I kid you not, kiddo," she said. "Dogsville. Kennel time. A walking short joke. And much worse was that I *felt* ugly. They treated me like a loser, a worthless, drek-for-brains piece of nothing. They didn't beat me in private either—it was done as a Passion Play for the whole class to see. 'I'll show you, bitches,' I used to think with every crack of that whip."

"And now you're selling beauty products," I said, astutely. Another dead silence, and the subject was not to be touched again. We went to Zymurgy.

A few days later, Starla called to say she hoped I understood that everything she'd told me about her childhood was OTR (off the record). At first I resented that she trusted me so little she thought she had to say that. But I was probably even more irked because now I couldn't print all that juicy stuff.

Still, I guess I could understand her reticence. New York is such a small town it only takes twenty minutes for one tiny piece of gossip to hit the far reaches of all five boroughs. To any truly professional public figure, "This is off the record" is the most practical everyday phrase, as in: "This is off the record, but hi, how are you?'' or "This is off the record, but could you pass the salt?'' It was totally apt that we *faux* lovers were exchanging it as a term of endearment.

We tried to reach Colette a few times via lilac-scented notes and insidiously friendly calls, because Starla thought it would be a good idea to live down that evening, for our futures' sake. But Colette wanted none of it—to her, everyone associated with that night was a potential veal-thrower, a mass murderer of class. Vivien had not only ruined herself with her dish-flinging, she'd ruined every name on that guest list. But I guess she'd made herself at the same time, having been nothing much before that. If you can't get in through the door, throw things at the window.

I missed Colette. Her appearance at my Zymurgy party had rubber-stamped it with instant chic, but that was as remote a safari as she was ever going to take. She'd been cajoled into mixing with "bad people," given it a whirl a few times, and was now going to retreat back into her ivory tower, where there were no weirdies, only maid service, room service, postal service, and round-the-clock tower guards on a constant veal watch. We had gone back at least three giant steps by losing our connection with her. Do not pass go, do not collect two hundred dollars.

I prepared a chart for the magazine detailing who'd gotten how far socially and how (forget why—there really was no why). I had Starla on a perpetually upward curve—if I didn't, she'd kill me. Emil I had drooping after the Colette incident—by now I could risk mentioning it and admit that the plate had figuratively rocketed into his face too. Vivien went from pretty near the top, to nadaville, and back to the middle again—it's a quicker climb to the middle the second time around. And Mary-Ellen I put on a constant low burn, a perpetual buzz of nonactivity. I knew I could use her as the joke because she'd pretend to be mad but would actually be thrilled to be mentioned.

Most people never comment on their mentions anyway,

which is why you can get away with so much. They think it would be uncool to say anything; it would make them seem too appreciative or grovelly or petty, which they are, but don't want to broadcast it. So they keep their orgiastic bold-face worship to themselves. This mindset, of course, doesn't stop them from flailing all their *other* press at me as a subtle reminder that they're still eminently newsworthy. And they can flaunt their mentions in my magazine at everyone else—just not at me.

My only outwardly appreciative subjects were the drag queens, so it was too bad I'd stopped writing about them. What can you say about a drag queen after you've described the curve of her pumps? Rhapsodize about the way her arms shoot into the air like drumsticks halfway through Diana Ross's "Love Hangover"? Or how her mascara involuntarily gives in to lachrymose gland trauma by the time Liza sings, "When I go, I'm going like Elsie"? (A few years ago, Miss Minnelli changed this defiant statement to "I'm *not* going like Elsie," but I don't buy that, and how dare she tamper with my favorite line from a classic song anyway? Drag queens, though, fall for it either way.)

One of the local drag stars, Tess Tosterone (the one who liked to do herself up as a *Superfly* version of Stanwyck) had this habit of calling me at odd hours with items—complete with exposition, climax, and denouement—disguised as off-hand conversation. It was thanks to people like Tess that I learned how to screen calls, the second-greatest modern luxury after remote message retrieval.

One day she left me a long-winded message about her having gone to the Gaiety male burlesque theater the night before, and how she fell in love with the very first dancer—"Usually a troll, but this time they saved the best for first—a real dreamboat. I still wake up screaming over him, then realize I wasn't even asleep." What the hell did I want to hear this for? She sounded like she'd scripted out the message and was reading it, with all the dramatic intonation of a carefully rehearsed drag queen–slash–S.H.I.T. (drag shorthand for Susan Hayward in Training). She'd been smoking too much, however, and with her car exhaust-drenched voice sounded like Colleen Dewhurst doing an O'Neill monologue for some acting studio comprised of re-formed alcoholics.

"He was magnificent," she said, "the king of his craft. He didn't come off like a hustler or a cheap piece of termi-nally blown-dried trade like they usually do. He had dark, tousled hair and big, saucerlike eyes and looked as if he'd just stepped off a Greyhound bus from somewhere that stopped existing the second he left. He didn't have to act the part of innocence, because he exuded it down to his soul and announced it with every ingenuous move of his torso. He stripped to 'Angie,' and by the part with the violins, he'd mesmerized the entire audience of geezery men and placed them so delicately in the palm of his hand that they were all young and idealistic again, not jaded voyeurs sitting in pools of sticky substances. These old guys usually look like demented Pekinese—or you know how those lapdogs get that look in their eyes when they get older? But for this brief moment they were knights in shining armor, Lancelots of the Gaiety. He transported them.

"There was nothing filthy in his eyes, just sweetness, as he looked us over and drew us into his beautiful mind, stalk-ing the stage like a fawn learning how to hunt for food and just keeping us hypnotized with that untarnished face I wanted to dive into with both arms out. He kept looking at us, then looking at himself, then looking at us again as if to say, You like my body. *Why* do you like my body? He didn't even seem to know he was hot—that was the sweetest ges-ture of all. All the way home, every time I passed a manhole cover with steam spewing out of it, I felt it was Brigadoon."

At the point of almost being touched, I slammed off the machine, which had once again allowed a nightmare message to drone on well past twenty-two seconds. I unplugged it for safety, but it was too late; I think that was the end of his story. Later, Tess crowned herself *Madame* Tess and was starting to believe her own delusions of grandeur. I was polite next time I saw her but decided not to bring up the phone message, or it would encourage more of the same.

Favio finally came home after two weeks, and I felt like Roddy McDowall welcoming back Lassie. He seemed like a different person, with half-moon-shaped circles under his eyes and a tattered ragamuffin look that I don't think was another intentional act of fashion victimization. This was the kind of person Emil beat up on the street.

After hearing about that sensitive Gaiety boy, it was a rude shock to come face-to-face with his antithesis—Orca the killer clubbie. The "I love you" motif was over; the drugs must have run out. He was gruff, irritable, and mad at the world—all the symptoms experienced by people on aspirin commercials. "I see you found yourself," I said, trying to lighten things up.

"Fuck you," he said. Fine—fuck you, too. I'd been watching *Talk of the Town* to see if I was going to make it into their segment on Zymurgy, for which I was filmed offering the revisionist theory that the place is fabulously exciting and excitingly fabulous, et cetera, et cetera (the Starla rule: If you can't say something nice . . .). It was sort of going to be my television debut, except for having been in the background of Starla's *NewsPrime* piece, and I was all sweaty-palmed, knowing this could make me Zymurgy king for at least one more week. I would have been far happier collating myself with the tube than dealing with Favio's constipation of the month, but the VCR was taping anyway, and this was the most fascinating scenario Favio had brought home yet. I'd sat through worse.

"I missed you," I said, eyes darting between him and the set. "I'm going to be on *Talk of the Town* any minute.

They shot me at Zymurgy the other night." It was weird having him in the house again—he already qualified as someone from my past, and I hated return engagements. I realized that though everyone had asked for Favio the first few days he was on the lam, no one had brought him up at all lately.

"You are so tired," he said, annoyed. "Look at this." He picked up the issue and made a puking noise. "Colette Joie—blech. I can't believe I actually am cognizant of someone who would waste typeface on that name." Little did he know that I was half the readership of his scrapbook and had seen the major chapter he had on Colette. She was to him as Don Ho was to my mother.

So now I was tired. Could it possibly be because I'd gotten somewhere while he was sliding down that ladder with the greatest of ease? In just a few short months, he'd gone from my mentor to my biggest fan to my lowly detractor, all because I'd learned his lessons all too well and not taken him along with me for the final exam. Not that I didn't try, but he'd stopped fulfilling his Contributor title, just like he'd stopped paying the rent and stopped being a human being with any realistic concerns that didn't involve a crimping iron. He couldn't bear to be part of my success when he had none of his own left. Now *I* was the one who could introduce *him* to people, but he'd never deep-six his pride to let me.

The fact that I was getting along with Vivien was the real killer, though. Once he decided someone was "over," he hated having to reevaluate them and decide maybe they were still conscious after all. Most of all, he couldn't stand having his friends do the evaluating. It reminded him that he wasn't a leader anymore, he was a follower. I guess he always had been.

"I'm on the way out," he said, sullenly.

"I know," I smirked.

"I mean out of *here*. I got word from my brother that our

137

mutual asshole progenitor's going to be stampeding back to town to look for me and try to, quote-unquote, straighten me out. I'd rather have my contacts replaced by quartz paperweights while Nana Mouskouri records played. So I'm going undercover for a while. I found a place on the Bowery that's real reasonable, and I think I got a part-time job at a fab store.''

"What kind of store?" I wanted to know. He said it was a boutique, but I figured it must be a laundromat. "You don't need to pack your uptown wardrobe for the Bowery," I said, smugly.

"Fuck you," he said again. This had *definitely* replaced "I love you" as the motif. "Things are coming together again for me. I'm well on my way to being fabulous again."

"Shut up, shut up, shut up," I interrupted, as the segment on Zymurgy came on. I couldn't miss this for anything, and I just knew all of New York was anxiously watching along with me, at any cost. There were shots of the crowd outside demanding to be comped—but where was I? There was Garth looking pasty and coughing up more phlegm than Frank Carvel—very attractive—saying how he wanted the club to be a living tableau, the spacial equivalent of performance art. He rarely allowed camera crews in the club, but here they were, zooming around capturing all the posturing and Gauloise smoke and French people trying to sound Italian and Japanese people trying to sound French in the most brutal of glorification lighting. But where was I? No one seemed to be talking English except for those witches of East Hampton, Dovima, Mimsy, and Daisy, who were prominently comparing nails in the foreground—great, but where was I?

As the narrator droned endlessly about how chic-chic-chic, trendy-trendy-trendy this "new conservatism" and "new sobriety" were, I was sure my chances were shot to hell, but then suddenly there I was, talking and looking almost handsome—well, at least not wrecked—for someone compulsively out every night. It's the weirdest feeling watching yourself on television. Since I already feel like everything happening to me's happening to someone else, this time I felt like someone else watching yet another person—glory twice removed. It was a person I could like, especially since they identified me as "Vincent DiBlasio, magazine publisher"—so miracles do happen. I felt a huge, throbbing hard-on erupt under my pants for the first time in a week. My stint only lasted a few seconds, but a few television seconds are like an earth decade. "Can you believe it?" I said ecstatically to Favio, but he was already in his room, packing.

I turned off the answering machine the second the segment was over, convinced the phone would be ringing off the hook with congratulations. This was one time I wouldn't want to screen calls. Fifteen minutes after staring despondently at the phone, I learned one thing: no one calls you about *your* press either. My mother was the only one who finally called, but it was her thrice-weekly phone day anyway, and she wanted to remind me about my cousin Michelle's wedding in two weeks. "I already RSVP'd for you, plus a guest. Are you going to come to the actual ceremony this time, or just the free food after, like you always do?"

"Ma," I moaned, "I told you I can't make the ceremony. I have to interview Lena Horne that afternoon." It was a blatant lie, but a choice one; who wouldn't rather be with Lena than at a wedding you can't do anything about?

"Interview her at the ceremony," said Mom. "Oh, all right, just come for the food. I'll make up something—a hemorrhoid attack—and don't contradict me. Who are you bringing to the free food? Bring that Starva girl." She always mispronounced things on purpose; her malapropisms were carefully rehearsed. "But I hope she's not bulimic or anything. Is that why they call her Starva? She didn't eat much. And I don't think it would look good for her to be throwing up all over a wedding. Bad enough there was the eggs at your cousin Gloria's wedding and the rice got in her eye and—"

"Ma," I said, not about to endurance-test through that one again. "She's not bulimic. She's healthy and fine and everyone will love her, OK?" I was more irate over no one calling about *Talk of the Town* than anything else. My mother was proud, though, "even if it did look like a sleazy dive."

Favio emerged from his room with a few boxes and a brave smile, not to say goodbye, but, "Did you go to Mary-Ellen's art show?" Shit, shit, shit, it had totally slipped through the Disco Donut holes in my mind, just like Mary-Ellen's fashion show had. Starla never even brought it up, and without Favio around to remind me of the scheduled events, I'd been totally without a social conscience. "No," I said, ashamed; tired as it was, it was an event. I'd have to make it up to Mary-Ellen in some other blood-curdling way. Meanwhile, I could save face by telling her my grandmother died. She did—five years ago.

"How about José's birthday party?" he asked. "I heard it ruled."

"Yeah," I said, "but I got there five minutes after the cops raided it. It looked like it was fun, though." I remembered that Favio had been frozen out of José's invitations. "But not that much fun," I added. I am such a noble soul, up there with Eleanor Roosevelt and Dr. Schweitzer maybe. That "Gandhi" tag might work after all.

"Has José been asking for me?" he asked, without warning.

"No, um—I guess, yeah," I muttered, unconvincingly. "What is this, an inquisition?"

"Oh, well," he said, brightening up in that weird way he had, "I just came to get a few essentials. I'll be back for the rest of the shit, but if you have to start throwing things out, toss away—just don't hit any homeless with it. Listen, thanks for laying out my rent money. I'll make it up to you." And I won't come in your mouth. And I'll always be there for you when you need me. And if you bend down and look between your legs and the sun is over the trees, it's time to milk the cows.

"One last chance to get it on?" I laughed, thrusting my pelvis at him in a mambo move. He gave one of his mirthless laughs, one that made me very depressed. "Fuck you," he smiled, twirling off as if he were setting out on the most glamorous expedition. He came back to take a copy of the magazine, made a gagging noise, then scooted away, saying, "Love you, lunch." I could always add the two dollars to his bill.

8

Starla had all sorts of excuses why she couldn't go with me to my cousin Michelle's wedding, and that's how I knew she was lying. If she had one solid alibi—"I have to go out of town," let's say—I might have bought it, but a million of them—"I have to have dinner with Sylvia," "I have to do an in-store appearance," "I don't have anything to wear"— cemented the notion that she was grabbing for any half-truth that would get her out of the obligation. I doubted that she was having dinner with Sylvia, who she'd just told me was home sick with some kind of stomach virus. What would they be dining on—pasta with Pepto sauce? More likely, Starla felt she'd already paid her dues by going to my house in Queens; suggesting she take that voyage into kitsch once again was pushing it. *Quel fromage,* as Favio always said. I thought she'd enjoy the bad taste, the endless food, and the forced joviality. Besides, my mother had told everyone about her, and they were expecting to meet her and indulge in a communal cosmetics fest—a veritable seminar on blush. What was I going to do now—saddle myself with Mary-Ellen? I did owe her a favor for not going to her art show, but after this, I might owe her two favors.

One day Vivien called to ask me to come to a SCREAM event the next week—they were going to roll up to Mayor Koch in beds and throw condoms at him in response to the little they felt he'd done in the way of providing AIDS education and hospital space. In the Starla mode, I had a million excuses why I couldn't go, but while I had Vivien on the phone I decided to ask her to be my "semidate" for the wedding. She was attractive enough to impress the whole family, and as long as she didn't start a bonfire at the catering hall, would probably be decent enough company. And we *were* supposed to have lunch; this would be a year's supply of lunches rolled into one. "Sounds insane," she said, and we made a semidate.

We hired a car service—I don't sun, swim, or drive, making me a perfect candidate for New York life—and the whole way there, talked about AIDS. She talked, I listened. Favio would have died if he knew I was going on a semidate with Vivien and actually sponging in her "tired" ramblings. Starla would have too, but I didn't tell her—I was keeping one fake girlfriend a secret from the other, an impressive feat of juggling invisible balls. I'd told her I was going alone and was starting to think maybe I should have, as Vivien exercised her gums in the car.

She was wearing blond extensions to add to her already flowing blondness, and a kelly green gown by some schizophrenic Filipino guy, which was sequiny on top and chiffony on the bottom. Style is not like bike-riding; once you stop doing it, you do forget. The combination of the blond and the green, the sequins and the chiffon, was hideous—perfect for an Italian wedding—but she looked amazing in it anyway. She should have just posed and let the sunlight catch her lush, trampolinelike lips, but she ranted on, about how the government was treating the AIDS crisis as if it were a hangnail, and it needed a big slap that only SCREAM had the nerve to deliver right now. "Naturally," she said, "the government's being so irresponsible because deep down they agree with the Herve Joies. They feel it's only affecting 'un-desirables';—negligible people who are social lepers any-way. It's so unbelievably infuriating. Not only are these people dropping dead, but they have to deal with society feeling they deserve it, too. God, it's a human disease—it can strike practically anyone.''

Gimme a break. I felt like I was on a semidate with a Sally Struthers telethon. Hand over the collection box and I'll be glad to toss in a quarter if you'd simply shut—the—fuck—up. ''Look, Vivien,'' I said, ''I agree with what you're saying, I guess, but please lighten up a little. My family's not going to want to hear about this.''

''Neither does the government,'' she snapped, then laughed. ''Oh, all right, I'm sorry. Let's just have a good time.''

''That's what today's about,'' I underlined. ''A silly, crazy, food-filled good time. You're going to eat like there's no proverbial tomorrow. Be prepared to leave feeling sepa-rated at birth from Pizza the Hut.'' I touched her tummy in the most uncarnal way possible; I didn't want her getting ideas.

''So what have you been up to?'' she said. I hated that well-meaning but by far most boring question in the world. If people want to know what I've been up to, why don't they read my magazine? Or why don't I just hand them my calendar with all the appointments and activities scribbled in and little evaluations in the margins—''Tuesday night watched *Cagney and Lacey* rerun. Sharon superb, but Tyne a little off.'' I didn't remember what I'd been up to because my life is so nonstop and full, even if it's just full of emptiness. You can't explain a New York month to someone who hasn't lived the same month. It's hard enough even to live it.

''I don't know,'' I said. ''I went to Zymurgy last night.'' That much I could remember. ''It lacked a certain some-thing. Garth hasn't been there lately. I wonder why.''

She narrowed her eyes and exuded significance all of a sudden, giving a Maria Ouspenskaya "Don't go near the hills. Something terrible is going to happen" look. She clearly wanted me to figure something out before she had to say it and was pretty good at the silent-communication-via-pupils game, I must say. I remembered how terrible Garth looked on TV when he was coughing up his guts. He'd looked terrible as long as I'd known him, actually, but I assumed that was to keep in step with the vampirish aura that was so cool in anemic clubland. The grayer your skin was, the more natural you looked in club light. "What?" I said, panicky. "What? What?"

"I thought you didn't want to talk about that subject," she said.

"Oh, no," I moaned.

"It's just an unconfirmed rumor at this point, and I don't like to deal in unconfirmed rumors," she said.

"But . . . ," I prodded.

"But Garth is in the AIDS ward of Bethune Hospital." Damn it. I'd heard talk of AIDS till my ears were blue. I'd seen the posters and the commercials and the AfterSchool Specials, even rented the Morgan Fairchild safe-sex video on a two-for-one with Donna Mills's *The Eyes Have It,* an eye makeup how-to that was Starla's favorite—to watch, not take advice from. I'd heard of this person's brother getting AIDS, and that person's stylist's assistant. But no one I knew, really knew, had any actual encounter with the disease beyond shooting their mouth off about it constantly to win high-minded approbation. Now it had a reality to it I didn't want to deal with. I was assaulted by damned questions—them again—instead of the answers I'd gotten used to reveling in. It was midterm time again: How long did he have to go? Would Zymurgy go down the drain? Did Garth get It from doing It or shooting It? And how the hell did Miss High and Mighty find out all this before *I* did, anyway? I guess the AIDS hotline was starting to scoop clubland on the *real* life-and-death dish.

"I always assumed Garth was straight," I said, genuinely confused.

"Didn't I just tell you?" she said. "It's a human disease." Yes, Sally. "How he got it," she continued, "is not the issue. We just all have to take care of him."

One look at the sumptuous Majestic Terrace in Corona, Queens, and our mood perked up considerably. That sounds callous, but the place did allow us to put our gnarly feelings on the back burner for a few hours—when you're at the Majestic Terrace, all you can think about is the Majestic Terrace. Like a long, narrow totem pole for weddings, it featured room after relentless room packed with Yankee Stadium–size meatballs, women with whiskers, and bands playing "Feelings" with a frightening ease that could only be Pavlovian.

The place was a blinding cacophony of styles—a Loretta Young stairway next to Corinthian pillars next to paisley walls offsetting Anna Magnani posters and LeRoy Neiman paintings, with some very curious Bauhaus lounge furniture to rest on between weddings. It had more conflicting motifs than Zymurgy and therefore was probably more fabulous, boasting a higher level of aggressive self-confidence in its schizophrenia. Everything in it screamed grandeur and excitement in a no-taste manner that canceled out any possible grandeur and excitement. The excess was there to commemorate this very special day so garishly you'd never forget it. The fact that there were eight couples celebrating their own very special day in various rooms—well, that you weren't supposed to notice. *Your* room was the entire Majestic Terrace as far as you were concerned, and you were trapped in it, as the seasons changed, until you forked over your generous wedding gift (see, it wasn't really "free" food) and returned to life.

Our room was the Crystal Room, and you could see why. The chandelier—far more precarious than anything in *Phantom of the Opera*—looked like it could slash you if it jiggled, and it jiggled a lot from the heavy-duty stomping around the buffet trays going on in the other seven weddings. The fine crystal on the table looked like stuff you collect from repeat visits to certain gas stations, but hey, if they said it was crystal, it was crystal, even if just by the Queens guidebook. Everyone was deep into the cocktail hour, standing at the buffet table like it was a trough. These people don't need plates.

Aunt Jo Butch was making a particular spectacle of herself with the chow mein. An obscenely large woman, she suffered from the opposite of anorexia, meaning that whenever she looked in the mirror she mysteriously saw a twig who needed to eat more. I always told her she had aixerona, which is anorexia spelled backwards.

My mother came running up to me with a napkin, smushing it against my face as I tried unsuccessfully to flee from her. "Your nose looks like it's running," she said. "You didn't take your allergy pills."

"Ma, please!" I said. This was not the glamorous introduction into the Majestic Terrace I'd hoped for. For Vivien's sake, I wanted to be treated at least like I was out of toilet training. Mom placed some money into my pocket surreptitiously and said, "Don't tell your father." Hush money, huh? Well, that'll cost you more, babe. "Use it in good health," she said. I'll use it on the illest thing of all— my magazine, woman.

"Thanks, Mom," I said.

I introduced her to Vivien, explaining that Starla absolutely couldn't make it, though she'd desperately wanted to, more than gloss itself. Mom was crushed, but covered it up professionally, stamping her foot and exclaiming, "Shit—excuse my French."

Recovering well, she said to Vivien, "You look familiar," and I hoped to God she hadn't seen any of her AIDS press.

"Maybe you saw my picture—" said Vivien.

"In *Fabulon,*" I interjected. This was going to be a long night.

They were all there, and I could just see Army Archerd standing like death at the end of the tunnel, announcing the stars in that way he has at the Oscars. What an array! Aunt Jo Butch and her husband, Cosmo, were in matching Korvettes classics from the early seventies. And there was my other Uncle Vito (Vito II—This Time It's Personal), a widower, who's Michelle's father; our neighbor, the heavily corsaged Nina-Joanne and her daughter the missionary, rosary-accessorized Sister Crucifix; evil-eyed cousin Angelo; clubfooted cousin Valeria; my ex-neighbor Tony (a must-avoid); and the groom's side of the family. By the end of the night, we still knew these people only as "the groom's side of the family." That was fine—like the club scene, the wedding circuit is not about meeting new people, it's about reinforcing your ties with who you know.

"Hey, *paisan,*" said Aunt Jo Butch, grabbing me into a clutch and kissing me a dozen times on the face so hard I almost got bruised. She tasted like chow mein. "We saw you on TV, you famous thing." She slipped a twenty into my pocket and said, "Don't mention this to your mother." I could get used to all this secrecy.

Aunt Jo Butch then went back to the buffet as if by radar and started sucking in eggplant parmigiana as if it were oxygen. Angelo had spotted me from there, but being mid-meatball, wasn't going to acknowledge me yet. Sister Crucifix, though, had been to enough of these to know that the good eats come with the actual dinner; this was quality schmooze time.

"Hello, Vincent," she said, warmly. "You look wonderful. I've heard lots of wonderful things about you."

"Thank you," I said. She looked so serene, especially as she said the word "Vincent," two syllables I'd heard so infrequently lately they almost sounded like a new word. *Vincent*—say it soft and it's almost like praying. I hoped Vivien wouldn't spoil all this serenity by railing against the Catholic church.

"Nice to meet you," said Vivien, succinctly. Phew.

Michelle looked spring-fresh in all her assumed whiteness, but being the most Caucasian woman in the world, you couldn't tell where the dress ended and her flesh began. I hoped Vivien wouldn't start throwing condoms at her. With Starla, there wouldn't have been any of these worries.

Michelle sat with her hubby, Frank, on the dais, where the majordomos of the event get to recuperate from the eight months of planning. Everything—from the choice of room to the seating plan to the memorial *tchotchke* everyone would earn—had been meticulously thought out, though like I said, the band plays "Feelings" whether you want them to or not. I'm sure there had even been a summit meeting about whether to serve Italian or Swedish meatballs in the cocktail hour (as if that's ever really an issue). If this was what it meant to be respectable in the world, I wanted no part of it. I didn't have the time.

With all the planning, the Italian Big Day never gets to have any personality of its own. Though there are tiny discrepancies from wedding to wedding, there's always basically the egg rolls, the bouquet, and the cake. There's also always going to be some crusty-smarmy, Gig Young–like emcee getting the bride's name wrong as he announces the bouquet-throwing event. And without fail, a married woman will try to sneak in and catch the damned thing. At least club parties had different guest lists and a slightly new frisson from night to night. Didn't they?

Michelle's egg rolls had just been unveiled, and the band

149

was playing "Color My World" (the second-most obligatory song) as a soothing counterpart to the conspicuous consumption going on at the buffet. Contrary to the self-deprivation popular on the other side of the bridge, the more you eat at an Italian wedding, the more fabulous you are. With sauce dripping from her mouth, Aunt Jo Butch was the queen of the scene.

By the time the pigs-in-blankets came out, the band was playing "The Rhythm's Gonna Get You" as their entry into the hot-new-sounds-of-today sweepstakes, and the lead singer, a squat girl in purple spandex pants, who looked like an eggplant, was doing the most obscene conga by herself. There's nothing more depressing than a one-person conga line. Besides, we'd already had eggplant. As the buffet trays were rolled away, with Aunt Jo Butch's hand in one of them, we were asked to sit down to dinner.

You'd think we were at Mise en Scène the way everyone made such a fuss over the seating arrangements. Aunt Jo Butch, returning with nothing better to do between courses, cornered Uncle Vito II and loudly let him know that he had a lot of nerve seating Angelo with her daughter Gloria after the way Angelo had "shot Gloria's wedding day right smack into the toilet." The fact that this new tragedy was happening to ruin another wedding rang all the wrong bells in Aunt Jo Butch's head, and she looked on the verge of delirium tremens as she started screaming, "Get my daughter out of that table or I'll call the police!" (You're under arrest, Uncle Vito, for illegal seating?) Unc, who'd paid for the whole shebang and was a mess over it—we called him "Tranky" because tranquilizers were his life—wanted everything to go smoothly more than he had ever wanted anything. "I hope everyone's happy," he had said a million times during the cocktail hour. "This is my last chance to give a nice family party. I wanted to throw something your Aunt Margie, may she rest, would have been proud of." Sensibly enough, he'd assumed that the family could put their squabbles on the back burner for one day and stuff their faces together in peace before dragging them up again. Not even Custer had ever been so wrong.

Aunt Jo Butch was crying against the wailing wall of Uncle Cosmo, and Uncle Vito was in a corner banging his head against the real wall. He didn't have any padding except for a cheap toupee, and I wondered how long it would take for his head to explode like a Scanner, cannonballing the wig into someone's face. Angelo stood in the middle of the floor with his arms crossed, huffing and puffing and clearly dreaming up his next obnoxious strategy. Finally, he grabbed the microphone from the singer—in the middle of her rousing rendition of "We Are the World"(she was just at the part where Kim Carnes does that two-word solo)— and announced to the crowd that he wouldn't sit at that table if it were the last one on earth. "In fact," he screamed over the bone-chilling reverb, "I'm not going to sit at any table. Goodbye, you motherfuckers. Have a nice time in hell." And he stormed out. The singer, shaken up, but being paid by the hour, resumed singing about the great big family we are all a part of.

"This is even better than the veal incident, but it probably won't get as much press," I said to Vivien, hoping to lighten the mood. She laughed, and I wondered if she'd toss some meatballs on Uncle Vito.

"Is it always like this?" she said.

"Yes," I answered, sagely. "When Italian people love, they love with a vengeance, stopping only within the bounds of reason. But when they hold a grudge, they will stop at nothing. Don't take it seriously—just enjoy."

"I guess," she said, and dug into her—oh, God, veal.

None of this stuff really fazed Vivien, who was used to staging much bigger fracases. I knew she could handle it if I explained the closet and the crowbar and the will, not to mention the douche and the sciatica, and how they all formed a dramatic backdrop for this current scenario, but I was too tired to go into it; digesting the cocktail hour had taken everything out of me. At least all this drama had taken our minds off Garth. Tomorrow I'd have to visit—Did the obligations never cease?

Sister Crucifix was trying to comfort Uncle Vito, but she was still in pretty bad shape herself over Angelo's X-rated verbiage. Valeria, meanwhile, was limping over to try to comfort Sister Crucifix and tell Uncle Vito she didn't care where she sat, as long as she could sit somewhere. Nina-Joanne was telling the other side of the family that it was just as well that Angelo was gone—"good riddance to bad prosciutto" is how she put it in her Shavian way. And just when we all thought wedding reality was setting in again, Angelo stormed back in and went right up to the dais, smoke practically steaming out of his ears. I ran up there too, not about to miss this, but Vivien stayed seated and nursed the veal—the veal she hadn't gotten to at Mise en Scène.

Our entire side of the family gasped, and I'm sure I heard my mother say, "Dear God, I hope he doesn't have a gun." He reached into his pocket, and my mother screamed a scream worthy of middle-period Jamie Lee Curtis. "Here," he said, holding out a bill to Michelle. "I did partake of the cocktail hour, so I feel I owe you part of my gift. I was going to give you fifty. Here's twenty."

"Don't be silly," said Michelle, trying against all the odds to keep her cool on this very special day. "That's OK."

"No, I insist," said Angelo. "Otherwise, I'll have to stick two fingers down my throat and give you all those meatballs back."

"Take it and let him go," ordered Aunt Jo Butch to Michelle. Suddenly this was *her* affair, and this time she was going to take control. She was so persuasive she could probably start a new career as a wedding counselor. Michelle finally said she'd take the twenty only if Angelo went home with the souvenir—a porcelain floral bowl that looked like it should be pumped out with Sani-Flush. He took it as a memento of the nightmare and left. For him, of course, it wasn't such a nightmare; he and his family could talk about this for months. A big part of making trouble at weddings was how much mileage you could get out of it later on. Vivien knew about *that* syndrome.

Once all that excitement wound down, time seemed to run out of gas, and since we'd pretty much agreed not to talk about the A-acronym, Vivien and I sat in uneasy silence most of the time. Vivien could only talk about that one dreary subject. If they ever found a cure, she'd have to become a mime. "A plague on both your houses," I said, casting a mock spell on the room, but she didn't laugh.

Our table was ghastly—a lot of death's door types and even some of the groom's side of the family (another mistake, but I wasn't going to bust Uncle Vito's chops over it at *this* point)—so Vivien and I went on an impromptu tour, finding that everyone looked like they'd just had electroshock therapy. The bride is actually supposed to come over to you and make sure everything's OK, but I didn't fault Michelle for retreating to the dais in a semicoma brought on by a combination of the meatballs and Angelo (the Queens answer to José Can-U.C.). I noticed Uncle Vito handing her a few of his famous tranks.

We hit all the major tables—the Someones, Wannabes, Used-To-Bes, and Never-Wills, Neapolitan-style. After we got the large and leisure-suited subject of Angelo out of the way, everyone we went up to had pretty much the same comments: (1) When was I going to settle down and do something? (2) Vivien looked familiar; and (3) You're next—the two most frightening words you can hear at a wedding. But to fulfill everyone's sense of symmetry and justice, you can't just go to weddings, you have to throw them—once, or twice, or three times. If everyone went to weddings and nobody threw them, then nobody could go to them anymore.

"Is this the lucky girl?" said Nina-Joanne, and Vivien

nicely said, "You never know." I wanted to hand her all the hush money as a payoff.

"What do you do?" asked Sister Crucifix. "You're so pretty."

"I'm an AIDS activist," blurted Vivien, and Sister Crucifix suddenly made the sign of the cross and ran off to talk to someone else, probably her Saviour.

"Is it running?" my mother said, dabbing my nose with the napkin. No, but she was dabbing it so hard she'd reactivated the tender spots from where Aunt Jo Butch had kissed it, and it started bleeding. I hadn't even said hello to my father yet, though I did notice him characteristically undressing Vivien with his eyes. I should have brought Madame Tess Tosterone and seen if *that* turned Dad on.

The band was playing "Feelings" again—Do they get improved pension plans every time they play that song?—and the emcee was announcing that we should get ready for the throwing of the bouquet and garter belt, as if there's any way to prepare for those two horrors. But first there was another *de rigueur* ceremony to be done; we all barbarically clanked our forks against the water glasses, a signal that meant the bride and groom should make out for our voyeuristic pleasure. My father always started this, and everyone else followed like Huns, performing a veritable chorale of clank. Starla and I could have put on quite a show, even without anyone banging silverware for it. But Frank and Michelle weren't natural performers. As the clanking din rose to fascinating heights, they merely pecked each other gently on the lips and held up their glasses in a toast. "Ripoff," my father murmured.

All the single girls got up there for the catching—Valeria, Nina-Joanne (a widow), poor Vivien—and (didn't I say so?) my mother tried to join in as a joke until everyone pushed her back into her seat and replaced her with Sister Crucifix, who looked twenty Hail, Marys' worth of embarrassed. "Now let's have our lovely bride, Marie," said the emcee.

"Michelle," screamed half the congregation.

"All right, sue me—Michelle," he said. "Can I have a drumroll, please?" He got a drumroll, the same one from "Color My World." "Ready," he said, "set—and throw." Michelle tossed the bouquet way back, as if it were a grenade she were hurling at the departed Angelo, and it found a home in the unsuspecting hands of Sister Crucifix. It was the last thing she wanted, so she pretended to fumble with it a little and tossed it onto Valeria, who unwittingly became nubile-person-of-the-minute. So Valeria was "next"— funny, she hadn't even had a date yet.

The horrifying inevitability of the garter belt finals came next, and as I tried to sneak off to the men's room, I felt my mother's paw encircle my waist as Aunt Jo Butch's arm wrapped around my neck so tightly I was gasping for air. They were pulling me irrevocably toward the fray and had me in such a stranglehold I couldn't even shoot over a "Why me?" look at Vivien.

The emcee got the groom's name right, at least, and as I jockeyed for position with dozens of bachelors with gold chains and (I'm sure) embossed business cards that said, "Silent, but deadly," I determined not to catch the thing even if it fell into my sweaty hands. I stood right up front because I knew that would be the last place the garter would go. I didn't want to be a star here—this wasn't Zymurgy.

Frank shot it right at me like a dart. Everyone cheered, but I fumbled it, figuring if it's good enough for a nun, it's got to be the virtuous thing to do. The garter landed on the floor, which was eerily speckled with stardust, like a haunted-house re-creation of the yellow brick road. As balls—the Italian answer to fate—would have it, my mother dove on the thing before any of the other bachelors could make a go for it and jabbed it into my hands, where it's now become an integral part of my corporeal makeup. Aunt Jo Butch mounted me and said, "I told you you were next," then I did the spotlight dance with my cousin Valeria. Fred and

Ginger we weren't. Gabby Hayes and ZaSu Pitts are more like it. I kept tripping embarrassingly over Valeria's spastic legs and eventually thought it would be cute to avoid this by lifting her by her armpits and spinning her around for a few seconds. Sadly enough, this didn't really complement the beat of the song ("Sometimes When We Touch"), and when I accidentally let go, Valeria landed in a mangled mess under the saxophonist's music stand.

The dance floor was then cleared for one of the most climactic minirites of all the minirites that add up to an Italian wedding: the bride cuts the cake, the bride cuts the cake.

And that she did, stuffing a big, heaping piece down the new hubby's throat—the first of many times he'd be gagging in a long and happy relationship. It wasn't pretty when Frank started coughing up bits of cake, but no one commented on it, and we succeeded in not drawing undue attention to something better left unnoticed.

My mother picked the sugar flowers off the cake by hand and was forcing them on the nun, who was insisting that sugar is the devil incarnate as the flowers were smushed all around her mouth. Aunt Jo Butch was slipping me another ten dollars and saying, "This is from Uncle Cosmo. Don't tell your mother." And then—oh, more minirites I'd forgotten—the groom danced with his mother (to "For All We Know"), the bride danced with her dad, Uncle Vito (to that very Italian song, "Sunrise, Sunset") and—this sort of made sense—the bride danced with the groom (to their song of choice, "Lady"; I would have hoped more for something by the Sex Pistols). All three couples tried avoiding the coughed-up cake, but unfortunately, footsteps had brought the mush to every part of the room, and Michelle slipped on it and rocketed toward the band, who grabbed their music and ran for the exit.

Once they came back, everyone was asked to do the

hokeypokey, which the over-ninety crowd obediently performed as we younger guys danced onto that duty-free gift line (you give cash, you get a porcelain toilet bowl). Vivien and I lucked out and got a bowl for each of us—souvenirs down which we could flush the memories of this wedding for a whole lifetime.

Finally, it was over—but not really, not at all. The good nights take about forty minutes because each relative has to hold you so long and hard you start picking up their congenital bone ailments, and if one aunt sees another one hugging you longer and harder than they did, they have to wrestle you again for equal time. My mother held onto me so long I was dragging her along like a clutch bag as I finally decided to wend my way toward the door. "Take care of him," she said to Vivien. "He's potentially in trouble at all times." What a thing to say. So's everyone, but what's a person to do—never leave the house because someone could drop a penny from the top of a building and pierce your skull? Most accidents happen in the home anyway—should you not risk being there either but maybe stay out in the dark, dank hallway all the time, dodging rats and neighbors? There's only one answer—to stay with Mom forever, and if possible try to crawl back into the welcoming sanctum of the womb itself. It's free rent, open bar, and endlessly inviting, pleading with you to return to where you started it all and can retire at any time in supreme comfort. That's the DiBlasio philosophy—don't dare, don't travel, just stay—making sure, at the same time, that you accomplish enough while standing in place to make them terribly proud. I had to leave.

"Wait," Mom screamed, not releasing her hold on me. "Did Aunt Jo Butch give you money?"

"Yes," I muttered, ashamed at having been forced to betray my aunt.

"How much?"

"Twenty," I said, feebly. "And then another ten."
Armed with this knowledge, my mother ran over to Gloria
and gave her thirty dollars—and she was even.

"Good night," yelled my ex-neighbor Tony, his first
word to me all night. Not exactly clever, but probably a step
up from "kiss my dick."

9

"I feel like Margaret Mead leaving an aboriginal culture to head back to civilization," cracked Vivien. I wanted to *enter* an aboriginal culture; after a day of suffocating emotionalism, I had the urge to howl with my true native species of sensitivity-free clubgoers.

Vivien felt it too. She'd been away from the scene for so long, a night out held both nostalgia value and novelty appeal for her. The Garth hospital visit was growing more and more ominously imminent, and I knew a primal release beforehand would be refreshingly cleansing. It would take her mind off the endless dramatics of fighting against the administration and the FDA, and would take mine off the trauma of Angelo battling Aunt Jo Butch.

"Listen," I said to her in the dire car-service wreck, a beat-up old station wagon that was light years from the white limo I'd ridden in with Starla and Sylvia, "if by some chance we run into Starla at some point tonight, let's not tell her I took you to the wedding, OK?" The confidence game again—what fun.

"But you told me she couldn't go, didn't you?"

"Yeah," I stumbled, "but it just wouldn't seem right to rub it in her face that I took you. You know?"

"You mean this is a *date*-date? I thought it was just a semidate. You *have* a girlfriend." I sensed from the way the driver was craning his neck that he might be listening in. His radio was on awfully low.

"It *is* just a semidate," I said. "I just like you as a friend. We both already have attachments. I have a girlfriend, and you have—AIDS." I didn't mean it like *that,* but the driver's jaw dropped, his eyes bulged, and he careened a little out of the lane, into suicide territory. We would have been killed, but there were no other cars riding in Corona, Queens, on a Sunday night. He turned up the music and stopped listening.

At least we'd gotten that over with without Vivien having to grab my dick and comment on its petite inattentiveness. We were just going to be friends and now could relax and enjoy the rest of the evening, and relationship. The Angelo of our mind had stormed out, and now it was funtime.

The second we made it to the city, I called my machine and found a message from—God, she works fast—Mom, saying don't forget to take the allergy pills; something from Emil saying he was going somewhere out on Long Island for an afternoon spin on Sandahl DeVol's yacht and did I want to come along (funny, he knew I was going to be busy all day with the wedding); an anonymous heavy breather ("Write about me. I'll spread for a spread. You can plug me for a plug."); and another twisted scenario from Madame Tess, this time about how she'd experienced the height of aesthetic beauty on the third floor of Bergdorf's. "You are a vicious, self-serving asswipe," she added. "Oh, come see me perform at Manstench tonight." Someday they'll invent remote fast forward. Maybe they already had, and I was falling behind.

There were no calls from Starla, but then why would she call when she knew I was tied up all day? And she did have those eight thousand things to do. After a day of Queens realism, I ached for a long, drooling look at her.

Vivien and I didn't hit just a few clubs that night, we hit them all, in a brazen attempt to stop time with compulsive, reckless partying. We both had so much pent-up energy to burn, and since we weren't going to expend it on copulation, we might as well party it off and just fuck everything. Her idea of partying was telling everyone about AIDS—the subject taboo was lifted like a cage door. My idea of partying was to watch throngs of people meet, dance, drink, and go home as my mind became exhausted and my body slowly rotted in the pleasant knowledge that others were being fulfilled. I was the human sponge; she was the human squirt gun.

For a freezing October Sunday, there was such a scarifying amount of activity it was as if everyone in town, even invalids, had been possessed by the same subliminal werewolflike calling to stalk the streets. "Must be a full moon," I said, the rote thing to say in a situation like this.

"No, look," said Vivien. "It's a strawberry moon. That means the moon is at its closest ever to the earth." So she was into that stuff, too. Maybe she *would* get along with Favio now.

"Cool," I said, ready to scream.

We started at Odile, where they swept us in with a swift crack-open of the gate that looked like it could have given the doorman whiplash of the wrist. I would have liked to chalk up this reception to my burgeoning fame, but I knew it was just that the club had gone incredibly downhill. And any delusion of grandeur was quickly shattered by our having to pay fifteen dollars admission—the only comps at Odile were young girls O'Dette wanted to sleep with.

Everything inside corroborated that they still were going to act like the ruling place, even though everyone knew they were moldy mustard. The waiters all had that Uriah Heep look they were legendary for, and O'Dette—who had come running back, in an attempt to flounce this dead horse into life again with his annoying circa-'79 cornrows—was still pleasantly aloof in that mock cordial way of his. If only the salmon appetizer he served was as cold a fish as he was, it would be edible.

Fiftyish and demented, O'Dette talked with a bizarre Eurasian accent whereby almost all his vowels came out like i's, even though he was reputedly from da Bronx. But he didn't say a word to me that, or any, night, just smiling that half-smile that meant Fick you. Except for cradle robbing, O'Dette was never known to be tied in directly with pleasure of any kind. He had kind of a punk relationship with it.

I looked around and suffered that ultimate nightlife nightmare. It was fairly crowded, but I didn't know a soul, not even the help. The prevailing crowd consisted of girls in scanty *lamé* dresses looking like they thought models should look—from that very reliable source, *Model* magazine—and their dates, paunchy Arabs who smelled of patchouli and had gold chains in the shape of dollar signs. There were also a few bridge-and-tunnel people of the "I can't believe we got in" variety (I am technically bridge-and-tunnel myself, but it's more a state of mind than a location) and several tables of Eurotrash, but they weren't the higher class of Eurotrash I was accustomed to. They were fakers—deep down, they probably spoke English and had taste.

"I've been away so long," said Vivien. "I don't know anybody."

"Neither do I," I confessed and suggested that we move on rather than encourage the place with our presence. On the way out, some middle-aged Italian man insisted on talking to us, so we succumbed to his gregarious dictatorship and tried to communicate. It turned out he was Fellini's casting director, and when I clapped my hands excitedly and said, "I want to be in a Fellini movie! I want to be in a Fellini movie! I'd be perfect—I already feel like I'm in one. Don't even give me lines—I'll just stand in a corner of the frame, a bemused bystander," he just bored through me with a blank look that made my spirits crumble.

"You're too *bruto,*" he said, bluntly. *Bruto?* Too *bruto* to be *in a Fellini movie?*

"You're a disgrace to my race," I snapped and pulled Vivien out of there. You could tell O'Dette wanted me to leave anyway because I'd been clapping my hands— outward displays of emotion were not welcome there.

Odile's second-rateness was especially depressing since I'd read an article a few days before describing how New York had become a second-rate city. (I only started reading it because it caught my eye next to something about serial murderers' astrological signs, but once I started, it became an obsession.) It said that as the cost of living skyrocketed and bohemia was pushed closer to the edge of the map, there was no room for a creative element anymore, only for ex- tremely wealthy people who got where they were by con- forming and being ruthless. Because of the AIDS scare, thousands of couples were getting married very young and moving off to the suburbs—so those hideous Ziploc-bag ha- vens were going to become hot again, no longer a subject of ridicule as the city itself eroded into a rich-versus-poor bat- tlefront/ghost town. L.A., which was also a cultural waste- land but at least didn't have Broadway, offered a much higher quality of life and might even surpass crack- and homeless-ridden New York in various qualitative ways by the midnineties.

What's worse, America as a whole had long been losing technological steam to Japan, resting on its postwar laurels as the Japanese continually forged ahead with more state- of-the-art brilliance. Japan is easily the most advanced com- munity on earth, wiping us farther off the map every time they politely shove us down a technological flight of stairs. Odile was now a second-rate club in a second-rate city in a second-rate country—on an off night yet. I wanted to die.

If we were going to go to a bad-genre club, it might as

well be the best bad-genre club there was, so we scurried over to Zymurgy, figuring Garth would want us to keep patronizing his place, now more than ever. That was quite a stroke of genius, convincing ourselves that we had to party as a favor to Garth. Unfortunately, Zymurgy was even more funereal than usual, the staff shuffling about with hangdog looks and all the clientele buzzing about the new scandal in hushed, highly charged tones. A lot of it had the sound of sleazy sensationalism sugar-coated with feigned concern, but I'm sure some of it was real.

"Did you hear about Garth?" everyone was saying in a Meryl Streep repertoire of accents. Doric was there, still without Randi, but everyone was too preoccupied with the current buzz to murmur about whether *her* hot gossip had broken them up; they were last month's fabulous tragedy. Their falling-out fascinated *me,* though, and I could only figure that Doric, a true woman-hating man, had probably taken the miscarriage out on Randi. He'd gone to the trouble of penetrating her, after all—an act he found distasteful, but useful—and she hadn't come through with her half of the deal. Drop the bitch!

Delroy was there *sans* camera, claiming, "I'm not taking any pictures tonight, out of respect for Garth. I think it would cheapen the mood." He then showed me the scars from his car accident, a display he must have felt elevated the mood. Delroy knew what it was like to have a brush with death, he said, but was lucky enough to have beaten the odds. "No one beats AIDS," he added dramatically, and we all went, "Oooh!"

Mary-Ellen was there, getting to the heart of the matter as usual: "How did he get it? Is he Haitian?" she grinned. Emil wasn't there—I guess his yacht jaunt had turned into an overnighter. Starla was absent too, but the second biggest buzz of the night was that she was coming with Tracy Neuwirth, only one of ten or twelve totally top debutantes in the world. That would be quite a coup, especially compared to my schlepping in from a wedding in Queens with a glamour girl from a year and a half ago.

Spartacus, the six-foot-six manager of the club and a major hamsterbrain, took our drink orders personally. I needed two stiff cranberry juices on the rocks, but Vivien settled for a Long Island iced tea. "I haven't seen you in ages," he said to her. "What have you been up to?" That question again.

"I've been doing a lot of work to fight AIDS," she said, and his face went empty, much as Sister Crucifix's had, but comparing Spartacus to a nun was like calling *TV Guide* literature.

"Oh, yeah, that's right," he said. "I read about that." Spartacus reading—now that was news. He wasn't the most enlightened person in the world, always having made a living off his brawny way with the babes, not his deft handling of Wilde. To him, Garth's illness was just a temporary disruption during which he would obediently hold the fort. "He'll be fine," he told me repeatedly, not faking his brain damage in the least.

The real dish, I found out, was that Garth had been sick for a long time, but rather than confront it, didn't confess his symptoms to anybody, not even a doctor. He chalked up his coughing fits to having stopped smoking a while ago. "It releases all the mucous in your system and makes you cough harder than when you smoked," he told people. "If you're a smoker, stick to it." His increasing thinness, accompanied by that ravaged facial expression, was actually taken by the trendies to be a step in the right direction; they all told him he looked better than ever. Most of them, of course, looked like death already.

Without Garth, the club seemed more lifeless than usual. It was packed but without a focal point, so all the conflicting motifs really grated. After the Majestic Terrace, I knew how conflicting motifs should be done. "I'm dying to take your picture," said Delroy. "Vinnie and Vivien—what a couple of the month if I ever saw one. If I had my camera, I'd use up the whole roll." He always knew the right thing to say, though he did flinch a little on the word *dying.*

"Where were you at my art-show opening?" said Mary-Ellen. She always knew the wrong thing to say.

"Um," I said, brilliantly. In situations like this, I could do a symphony of "Ums."

"He was out of town," Vivien chimed in.

"Oh, really?" said Mary-Ellen. "Where?"

Vivien and I looked at each other and then both answered at the same time. This was beautiful coordination in action, except we gave different answers (I said "the Hamptons"; she said "D.C.").

"Well, anyway," said Mary-Ellen, "it was really special. *Art Life*'s doing a piece on it."

"Front of the book or a full feature?" Vivien asked, learning to play the game again.

"Full feature," said Mary-Ellen, after pausing a little too long. "But even if it's front of the book, that would be nice, too."

"It really was a good show," enthused Delroy.

"Is a good show," said Mary-Ellen. "It's on through the twenty-third."

"Are you snubbing me?" asked a husky-voiced woman, who was supremely tasteful in a simple, pleated, black Mary MacFadden dress adorned only by a string of pearls. Why would I snub someone who could save me from a conversation with Mary-Ellen? I scanned the scrapbook of my brain for any clue as to who this elegantly de-debauched creature could be. Someone I'd met on the party caravan? An advertiser wanting to pay up? Melissa Kravitz all grown up and hoping for a reinsertion?

"Of course I'm not snubbing you, hon," I said. (The way to deal with a predicament like this is never to admit ignorance, just ask generic questions and wait for that mental cloud to lift). "How are things?" Offensive as that question was, it was generic enough.

"Flawless beyond belief!" she said. "Better than ever. I really feel at peace, and that's not just hype."

Something in the intonation, especially on the words "at peace" struck a chord, but I still couldn't place her, not without a clue. "Did I see you running down the hall at Mother Mary Agnes's Hospital by any chance?" she said. "I hope it wasn't anything terminal."

Bingo—it was Pat. She'd gone from male to female back to male again, and now she was back in her original female aberration. Three operations to get once-removed from one's natural gender seemed like a roundabout way to get across a dangerous street.

"You look great!" I said. She really did. There were no hairs on her face—electrolysis takes care of that for good—and the breasts she'd had removed were back with a vengeance, appearing more succulent than many biologically correct ones I'd seen. The surgery had taken better this time, and her look was so refined you never would have guessed she was a man-woman-times-two. She was more convincing than most of the real women there. But then what is real anyway in a world of fabulous artifice, tra la?

"I *feel* great," she said, explaining that she'd eaten a lot of brown rice and located her aura. "This time's for keeps."

We were interrupted by a bustle at the door as Starla walked in with, 100 points, Tracy Neuwirth, both looking ravishing in that dress-up-the-crack-of-the-ass designery way—these were what real *real* women looked like. Everyone was dying to gape at them in lust-confusion-curiosity-awe, but you have to keep up your facade in these places, so most people only half-gaped, casually swerving their eyes back and forth à la Benny Hill. Delroy ran up to them and said he would love to take their picture if only he'd brought his camera (was this going to be the new photo op—someone saying he *would* have taken your picture?), and Doric snagged them on the rebound to say he'd be glad to do an impromptu portrait. Tracy didn't look about to go for it; to a woman used to Avedon, a painting of her spewing lizard guts probably wasn't an appealing concept. Besides, Doric didn't paint. Amid the imaginary flashbulbs, they walked arm in arm, grinning from Starla's right ear to Tracy's left one. They looked like Siamese twins, as styled by *Elle*.

This time, there wasn't going to be any game playing; maybe because she was plus-the-fabulous-Tracy Neuwirth, Starla shot right over to me like a bullet. This was good. People were starting to think of us less as a couple lately, and we needed some public reinforcement that we really were. We gave each other one of those Ripley's Believe It or Not kisses where both your mouths are open, but no tongue is exchanged. I would have slipped tongue if she had, and vice versa, but neither of us did, so it remained chaste, yet provocative enough. If people started clanking, we could really French.

"Tracy," she said, "this is Vinnie DeBlasio, magazine publisher. Vinnie DiBlasio, Tracy." I guess the one-name effect was to emphasize how close they were, a tendency that always made me think Starla would be a great sidekick to stars like Cher, Madonna, Prince, and even Tiffany. The sick thing was they *did* seem really close, in that very superficial way party friends are close. Tracy obviously worshipped her, but more as a downtown novelty act to slum with than a peer. Starla was like a wacky, shimmery toy of the stars, a piece of costume jewelry they accessorized themselves with before rudely dropping her for some real gems.

"Hi, Vivien," said Starla. "You're out again—what a treat. Tracy, Cha Cha, Cha Cha, Tracy." That was a real low blow, using the name Vivien went by when she was a party bimbette.

"Is your name really Cha Cha?" giggled Tracy, redefining bimbette. A nuclear physicist she wasn't.

Vivien slyly answered, "Never mind my name. Let's talk about you. I really admire your work. I think you've done so much to advance the women's movement. *Tout le monde* drools over your body, but as a fellow feminist, it's your mind that turns me on."

"Thank you," giggled Tracy, jiggling out of control. "I'm so glad you said that because I do consider myself kind of a new-style feminist." Vivien and I rolled our eyes in concentric circles; the girl was *serious*. I'd always thought dum-dum debutantes were a stereotype; this girl was shooting all my deb-awareness training back to preschool.

Starla just let all this pass; we could mock Tracy Neuwirth all we wanted, but she was still *her* famous appendage, not ours. A closer look at Tracy showed her looks to be as deep as her psyche. Puffy skin under the eyes betrayed too many late nights with the booze and the boys. Her smile was so tight—how tight was it?—a percussionist could do rim shots on it. And except for the bags, every inch of her looked like it had been liposuctioned out with straws, leaving only the foamy residue that's left when you finish a milkshake. She was all foam—something you could blow away if you thought it was worth the effort. What put her over was a fresh, little-girl quality that high society was going for at the moment. I must have been the only one who could see that it was as real as the Barnum and Bailey unicorn.

"So you two went to the wedding?" Starla said, taking me by surprise. How did these things leak out? Is there no privacy left, even in the second-rate, crumbling society of New York? I tried to act like I didn't mind that she knew, especially since I *didn't* mind that she knew (well, not that much), and the information didn't seem to really bother her anyway. Playing it cool was a better idea than screaming, Who the fuck told you?

"Yeah," I said. "It was OK."

"Especially the fight over the seating arrangements. It

was like something out of *The Godfather*," said Vivien, knowing you had to be there but giving it the college try. Tracy's eyes were wandering in opposite directions, and Starla was waving to Mary-Ellen and mouthing Tracy's name while pointing at her famous friend. It was so gross—a "Look, I'm with somebody" routine. If the somebody was Mother Teresa, you might understand all the fuss. But Tracy Neuwirth?

Delroy grabbed Starla and pulled her aside for a second. Not invited, I followed anyway, and Vivien came along as my plus-one. "Did you hear about Garth?" he asked Starla, with great portentousness.

"I sent flowers," she said, as if by reflex.

"Flowers conquer all," Vivien muttered to me. "Give the lady her Nobel."

"Great," Delroy said, "but we have to do something. A floral arrangement is nice and all—"

"I didn't know Garth that well," Starla interrupted. She was already talking about him in the past tense and had probably written her speech for the memorial service. "He was so quiet and hard to get to know. I mean, I liked him. He was a nice guy. And I like his club. But what can you do anyway? You can't do anything about AIDS."

"We're his friends," Delroy argued, not about to let the ball drop. "We all party together night after night, and this small circle of people has become like his family. He doesn't have much real family—we're it. Shouldn't we try to do *something?*"

"Look, I'm going through a very trying period in my career," said Starla in a no-bullshit tone that was pretty scary. "Maybe not trying, but challenging. It's make-or-break time. I have to be 'on' at every moment, on constant 'up' call. You know what I mean? If Sylvia calls me to do something at five in the morning, boom, I have to be up-up-up for it, and frankly, anything too depressing clogs it for me. It weighs me down. Lately, when I hear 'AIDS,' I want to bolt out of the room. I feel for Garth, but my watching him suffer is not really going to improve either of our lives. I sent him flowers—something bright and flourishing to perk him up. And I still patronize his club—I even brought Tracy.''

Tracy heard her name and thought Starla was calling her. "What, honey?" she giggled, toppling our way. "Did you say something about my *Vogue* article?" Starla just pushed her down into the nearest thing resembling a chair.

Vivien told Starla she couldn't help overhearing some of what she'd been saying. "What we can do for Garth," she said, "and for everyone else who has or will get AIDS, is demand that the government wake up already. They're not doing shit for us, and if we don't start knocking down some doors, we're not going to have *any* friends left. Someone of your name and stature would add so much to the cause. You can make a difference.''

It was commercial time again. Starla looked like she was either going to strangle Vivien on the spot or sign up to tear down the White House first thing. She decided to handle it diplomatically, as usual. "That's not my style," she said, "sweetie." "Sweetie" carried daggers.

I sensed a potential contretemps in the fetal stage, and much as I needed another Star Wars for the next issue, I preferred to plea-bargain for my throbbing head.

"The newies are having a party on a pier," I said, brimming over with fake enthusiasm. "Wanna go?"

It was "Let's put on a show" time, and even if it had been a *book-burning* on a pier, I would have been willing to round everyone up for it, just to avert an ugly scene. I mean, if Starla and Vivien were going to fight over anything, I'd rather it be me, not AIDS. I pulled out the invite and everybody passed it around as if they were surveying a decaying rodent. It was called the "We are the champions" party, and addressed the earth-shaking issue: "Are we the champions? A jury of our piers will decide."

"Get it?" I laughed, "Piers—peers." I knew it was the lamest-sounding thing in the world, but I didn't want to go home yet. I figured if I said "piers—peers" with twenty different intonations, maybe one of them would hit. Finally, intonation number four worked on some of my more vulnerable subjects. With a little prompting, Vivien and Delroy said yes, but Doric and Mary-Ellen claimed they needed to sit alone and talk somewhere, probably to figure out ways that Randi's miscarriage could help both of their careers. Starla said she had to pack it in early. I suspected she wanted to work Zymurgy with Tracy some more and wouldn't dare bring her somewhere as undistinguished as a pier—a stenchy wooden thing overhanging water that didn't emanate from some high-priced French spring. My going was breaking our downtown taboo, but not really; that only applied to our joint exploits. Solo, I was free to disgrace.

"How could you take *her* to the wedding?" Starla whispered in my ear as I prepared to leave. So it did bother her. Of course—after the Colette incident, Vivien was the veal-wielding enemy.

"I was desperate," I said. "And I had to take someone where sex wouldn't be an issue at all. She's so sexless, a total droid."

"Tell me about it," Starla said.

We made our *ciao-ciaos* and hopped a cab over to the pier, a rickety cesspool on the Hudson, where there was nothing left but dozens of used Styrofoam cups, a Himalaya's worth of rubble, and a sixteen-year-old newie named Johnny Come Lately looking for the watch that had fallen off his wrist at some point in the ritualized madness. Maybe Starla had the right idea.

"It's shaped like a dick," he explained, which gave Delroy a pretty good clue as he helped the guy search for it in all the festive muck and slime.

"How was the party?" I asked. I hated asking obvious questions, but no one else was going to.

"It was the best," said Johnny. "We all played a big game of Twister—the world's biggest ever—and Driven Slush won a whole case of Grand Marnier. That was the prize—José stole it a long time ago from Carcinogen the night they closed. We had a live band—the Yeast Infections—and stuff, and everybody was dancing, like hundreds of people, and some girl almost got raped. I don't know where they all came from, but they were carrying on as if this rank smell was, like, Bill Blass–brand perfume. Then the police came and everybody ran. I have to find my watch and get home or my parents will kill me."

"Is this a sanitation pier by any chance?" asked Vivien, plugging up her nose with both hands. It did smell pretty foul, but then most party spots do. Zymurgy to me always reeked of yogurt gone bad.

"You got it," said Johnny. "You can rinse yourself off in the river, but that's probably not very hygienic either."

He stayed to keep looking for his missing penis, and we all went on to Velveeta, which had replaced Dramamine at least a whole week ago as the reigning after-hours place. Johnny said everyone had gone there, and I pretended it was the most inevitable thing in the world, even though I'd never heard of the place. I didn't want to admit I was losing my touch, especially after showing up too late for the pier party thanks to the absence of my own penis watch, Favio.

Velveeta was beyond *outré*. An abandoned warehouse in the West Village without any ventilation whatsoever, it was a fire trap, a hellhole, and a health hazard posing as a palace of beauty. Strewn all over the dance floor, which was still under construction, were pieces of plywood with nails sticking up, anxious to give you free, impromptu rearrange-your-face treatments. About a third of the stairway was missing, so you could easily touch down on a fashion victim on the lower level. The air was pure sawdust, and it was so hot your sweat could start forming a separate person replete with its own credit cards and psychological disorders.

There wasn't a single person in there besides our group who wasn't on some kind of mind-bending drug, but they were all copping attitudes anyway—at us, at least. At three-thirty it was still pretty early; as the night wore on, the drugs would rain more heavily, and the attitudes would provide a fiercer umbrella. In the meantime, everyone was getting pretty wild among themselves, providing a floorshow of either entertainment or depravity, depending on the strength of your stomach muscles. A manic-looking guy with bulging frog eyes and nothing on but BVDs was hosing a big-chested girl's cleavage down with a squirt gun. A pathological liar was traipsing around—not imitating the Jon Lovitz character but really living it—telling various people that he was a porn star, a gynecologist, a Rhodes Scholar, and Howard Hughes's grandson. A blitzed girl, who was leaving a trail of drool everywhere she went, was offering to lick people's balls for a bag of heroin. And another mistake of femininity was being chased by a forty-fiveish–looking man who looked even more out of place than we did, so we loved him— saying she'd give him "boom-boom" if he sent her to Martinique for two weeks.

These newies clearly hadn't gone through the homogenization process that turns party debaucheries into quarts of consumable respectability, but give them time. Right now they were more like the missing kids on the sides of those quarts. Most of them had probably told their parents they were staying over at friends' houses as they guzzled Ecstasy and let off libidinal steam, dancing for hours to mind-crunchingly repetitive songs that to them were the height of sensory stimulation and screaming "Look at me" as if their seminude bodies and grinning pelvises didn't make that phrase redundant. A few months ago, I could have watched them endlessly, but after riding in a car with Sylvia Valmouth and dining with Colette Joie, I had whole new aesthetic values. Starla *was* right about the rules—I didn't belong here anymore.

A few people smiled hello, and José, who was dancing on top of a speaker, threw a beer bottle at me—some kind of greeting, I guess. No one acknowledged Delroy, noticing as they did that he'd left his tool of fabulousness home. And only one person remembered Vivien, stumbling up to her and saying, "Didn't you used to be Cha Cha?"

We were only being paid homage to by the nightmares—the sociopaths who invade every new place in droves because that's their profession—and they were assaulting us with drug-induced witticisms like "The moon is in the seventh house," "Words are just clothes for ideas," or "I drilled my dentist today." To be on the outs at something as low as this was depressing; better to be an outie with the uppies. Now I knew how Favio felt.

Johnny Come Lately raced in holding the schlong watch that was covered with 57 varieties of sanitation. It dropped ooze that went right through the holes in the floor and down to the basement level. The trendies down there probably thought it was mousse from the gods. "I wonder where I can wash this off?" he said.

"There's a guy with a squirt gun," I offered, but nobody listened.

'Right here," said José, pouring a bottle's worth of Heineken over it. It worked—that Heineken is pretty amazing stuff. José flung the empty bottle halfway across the room and hit someone deliriously dancing with himself, then went behind the bar and took a fresh one. The guy who'd been hit never screamed or even so much as blinked. What does it take to get a reaction out of these people?

"So you found it?" I shouted over the din. Again, the

obvious—I needed a new writer. Johnny just nodded his head and walked away. On the pier, postparty, I was the only thing happening, but at Velveeta, midparty, I was over.

"Wanna split?" said Vivien, reading my mind.

"But this is great," said Delroy. He wanted to stay, probably to frame some more imaginary shots and show the new people his scars. Vivien and I were out of there.

10

The scene at Garth's bed at Bethune Hospital wasn't as colorful as Randi's cursed event, I guess because we all sensed this was going to be a more tragic loss. I went with Emil, who didn't look any calmer from his day of nautical splendor. In fact, he was shaky and kind of sallow, but I couldn't tell him that. Vivien would have been a more attractive date, but was way too busy for sympathy trips.

"You look great," I said, pandering to his modeling wannabe tendencies. "All refreshed and healthy." Well, at least he didn't have white, oozy stuff coming out of his mouth like Robert Downey, Jr., did in *Less Than Zero*.

They were only letting people up two at a time because Garth was in such frail condition he wasn't exactly in a housewarming mood. He shouldn't have been seeing anyone at all but was so determined to announce his good health to the world in a big way that he would have turned the hospital into a twenty-one-floor Zymurgy if he could have. Dovima and Mimsy finally came down from their visit—we were becoming hospital buddies—and we went up to a floor that no articles, photos, or talk of bonfires had prepared me for. The moans in the hallway were a dozen times louder than at Mother Mary Agnes's and every bit as startling. It turns out no movie moan has ever come close to capturing what it really sounds like to be in pain. You want to clutch your ears and say, Make it stop, but you're there to encourage these people, not let them know they disturb you, and it's the nonchalance with which you have to deal with the moans that's really chilling. Every pained wail reminds you not only of your own mortality, but of how horrible it is to get there. It pierces through every jaded thought in your head and reminds you that without your health, nothing else matters; *nothing*. My father always said, "Your health should be concern number one at all times," and I always laughed it off—when you feel well, it's the *least* important thing in the world. But here in hospital hell I was reminded of what he meant. AIDS tended to put Zymurgy in perspective.

A guy who looked thirty going on ninety rolled by in a wheelchair, so skeletal I let out a selfish little shriek and couldn't stop staring. One man in a room we passed was on a respirator, his eyes wide open as if he were vividly experiencing every moment of it. I glanced into another room, where a woman sat immobile, dotted with purple sores that made her look as if she'd been horribly beaten up. A middle-aged couple—decent-looking people who must have been her parents—sat across from her, shuffling their feet and vainly trying to pull words out of the silence. The father wore a protective mask; the mother just had a lot of makeup on.

"Be upbeat," said Emil before we went into the actual room. No, dork, I'm gonna walk in and scream, Garth! I can't believe you have AIDS. You look horrible. And then start crying. Though not a hospital tenant since birth, I'd visited people in them for everything from hysterectomies to radiation and knew the rules of the game. This was the land of the sick, a separate subculture with precepts and bylaws all unto itself.

I put on a brave smile—not too vigorous, you're not

supposed to look like you're happy about this—and waded in through a rain forest of potted plants, bouquets, and centerpieces. I immediately knew which one was Starla's—the gaudy one with birds of paradise and big, pink bows all over it. I flipped open the card and it said, "Get well, you poop, and let's have lunch."

"I'm gonna beat this," Garth said before he even said hello. Well, at least he was past denial and had accepted the challenge. This combative attitude was encouraging. If he put every ounce of energy he'd put toward making Zymurgy exclusive into roping off his illness, he *could* beat it—or at least, maybe extend his life by another year or two. Unfortunately, he'd run away from his sickness for so long that he was already pretty far gone. His usual Munsterish skin tone had darkened into the ominous gray of a sky about to erupt into storms. I could see the tail end of a big scar where they'd cut open his chest and taken out part of his lungs. He was breathing heavily and had trouble getting his words out, especially since all the drugs they'd put him on made him woozy. When he wasn't breathing heavily, he was coughing a dry, heaving cough that it hurt just to listen to. Each round was so intense it sounded like it might never stop. "I'm—gonna—beat—this," he kept saying between wheezes.

This couldn't be God's punishment on Garth for making that remark about my magazine having "promise," could it? Of course not. Only people like Herve Joie could think such thoughts. You see, Vivien's commercials were starting to sink in; after two thousand viewings of June Allyson's diaper ad, even *that* made its mark on my TV-compatible psyche.

"Of course you're going to beat it," Emil said, nudging me.

"Yeah, of course," I added. "They pumped you up with lots of drugs, and you'll be fine. It's just pneumonia."

"No, it's not," Garth said, suddenly letting out a long

whine that reminded me of Stan Laurel, though far less comic. "It's AIDS." As he coughed and cried, cried and coughed, Emil and I looked uncomfortably at each other, then pretended to examine the different floral arrangements. I was sort of glad when Garth launched into a major coughing fit, because it forced him to stop crying for a minute. But as the coughing hacked on into what seemed an eternity, I started to long for the crying. I wanted glamour, not this.

I stared the arrangements down until I memorized them all, and can still see the orange tulips laced with blood-red roses in my dreams sometimes. I hardly knew this guy. I should be home working on the magazine and getting a list of important people to start mailing it to for free. Without Favio here to time me, I could be stuck beyond the thirty-five-minute limit and stay all week. No, we'd have to vacate eventually to make room for the next lucky couple.

The air smelled so clinical and medicinal, even worse than that sanitation pier. The pier smelled like rotting sewage, but this place reeked of death itself. Garth had been lucky enough to get his own room, but that was a mysterious quirk of fate that would prove transitory. They were going to transfer him to a double, and I hoped it wasn't going to be with someone who was in the final stages. Health depends so much on your emotional state, and having a roommate at death's door would tend to wear your spirits down just a little.

"Delroy's been so great," Garth said, trying to accentuate the positive in a sadly desperate way. Delroy *was* a devoted friend. After his smash-up five years back, his old boss—an advertising biggie named Dennis Carbonell—refused to rehire him, saying he couldn't possibly be capable of handling his job anymore. Delroy vowed to spite Carbonell by making a name for himself in the field he always wanted to pursue—photography—and reveal himself not just capable, but a major prodigy. He also vowed never to betray anyone he knew who was ever hospitalized, even for a tonsilectomy—he'd be the defender of the sick, the Marvin Mitchelson of the infectious. Favio told me all this one night, and though I took everything Favio said with a large grain of salt, that was one scenario of his that had panned out.

Lately, Delroy was spending all his time in hospitals because so many people he knew were sick, and he couldn't betray any of them. He'd just been to visit Garth, but went out for a bite before coming back. During the food break, he probably visited other sickies.

"He made this collage of pictures of me," said Garth, pointing to a visual jumble on the wall behind a coleus. "It's a good inspiration—to remind me of how I could look." It was a well-meaning pastiche of pictures: Garth with Spartacus, Garth with Bianca, Garth with me, even. He looked awful in most of the pictures, but at least he was standing. If an artsy-craftsy collage was going to make him feel better, then fine. Maybe I could whip him up a mobile or some macramé plant holders.

Garth started coughing again, and a nurse came in to give him his four-times-daily dosage of pills. She was either terribly busy or just terrified, banging the plastic pill cup down on his tray and scurrying out like a scared squirrel. She should have worn a full-figure Hefty bag for protection, I thought, remembering Polly Purebred, one of the newies, on my first night at Carcinogen. With all this safe-sex mania going on, Polly looked in retrospect like a very practical-minded, condom-wearing human penis, not an attention-starved ditz.

I was getting strange new perspectives on things that once seemed perverse. Fucking a grapefruit—a feat one of my college roommates used to perform quite dextrously—was actually a clever form of safe sex. Kissing a prison inmate from the other side of a bullet-proof glass window was also very realistic. And a full-figure Hefty bag was the ultimate —in fact, it was the only logical thing to wear in a world where germ-infected hypodermics and vials of HIV-positive blood were washing up on the beach and landing on the streets and probably coursing through every liquid short of those very refined waters that Starla intelligently chose to ingest.

It was weird living in the middle of the kind of crisis you usually only read about in history books—strangely charged and horrible at the same time, and all too immediate. All the worry eras from the past held very little meaning for me, I'm sorry to say. The Holocaust was inconceivable, the McCarthy thing was something staged for PBS documentaries, and I remembered Vietnam much better from the Carcinogen party than from the actual event. But AIDS was palpable in every word that was spoken now, in every gesture, and even in the silences. It was everywhere—you couldn't see it, but you could. Its awesomeness drove us to greater heights of escapism, but AIDS was stronger than our party drive. It kept knocking down the walls of our forced festivity, heating up our fun in a pressure cooker of fear and anxiety.

AIDS was wiping people out with a devastating three-strike count. First was the constant sense of mourning—dour-faced people were always talking about this memorial service or that person they missed so much, looking slightly more debased with each death notch. Second was the imposed celibacy that robs you of carefree hedonism in your youth—you had to cut off your impulses constantly, deny yourself things your body naturally craved. And strike three was the panic, the terrorist approach to life that makes you wonder if you're a walking time bomb who'll be the next one they plunge a respirator into. For Vivien, anger was an added, fourth dimension. I didn't suffer from these syndromes—as a watcher, participatory fears were alien to me—but was starting to feel some anxiety anyway, maybe because it was the thing to do.

One day I was walking up Fourteenth Street when I noticed I'd stepped in some gooey substance that could only have been semen, probably the semen of some HIV-infected junkie hemophiliac prostitute. Just my luck, I was wearing my new bought-on-the-street, cloth-soled shoes that were so thin I might as well have been barefoot. I jumped into a cab, keeping my knees up in the air so my feet wouldn't push into the semeny soles, and raced home, frantically walking up the stairs on the sides of my shoes. Once inside, I gingerly pulled off the shoes and socks, threw them in the garbage pail, and ran into the shower to scrub myself down à la Karen Silkwood. Would I become a victim—sorry, patient—6.8 years from now as a result of that incredibly fulfilling sexual experience? I could just see myself explaining to everyone, But I never even touched anyone. I just stepped in some junkie semen! Shit, why couldn't I be as unenlightened as the people like Spartacus, who didn't even know AIDS when it boogered them in the face? This dizzy brigade was so blissfully ignorant they didn't suffer from any of the anxiety or the self-denial traumas, and certainly none of the anger—just the mourning, and not much of that, either.

"I have some great ideas for parties," Emil told Garth chirpily, then shrugged his shoulders at me as if to say, Well, it was worth a try. I don't think he was really trying to talk business, just making a feeble stab at taking Garth's mind off the surroundings. Or maybe he was really trying to talk business.

"Yeah, some great parties," I echoed brilliantly—hospitals always inspired me to new heights of raconteurism.

"Is there an echo in here?" said Emil. We laughed, but Garth didn't join in. He started involuntarily rotating his head from side to side like he was possessed by some Satanic demon and needed an exorcist. Not about to wait for the split-pea soup, I said, "Maybe we should move on and let the next people come up."

"Good idea," said Emil uncomfortably, and we said "so long," not "goodbye"—as my mother had always instructed me when visiting my grandmother—and fumbled an awkward handshake with one hand combined with a fake-jaunty wave bye-bye with the other. We'd never make it as synchronized swimmers.

As we stumbled away Garth did manage to croak out a few parting words. "I had a blood transfusion a few years ago," he gagged. "I want you to know that's why this happened." No one remembered Garth ever having any illness that required a blood transfusion, but you don't stand there and yell "liar" at a sick person.

"Sure thing," we said, giving him a bizarre thumbs-up and taking off. The next twosome—Sean Valve and Valerie Rapchuck—were waiting downstairs with Delroy, who'd bought Garth three of those little plastic containers of watermelon the Korean fruit vendors thoughtfully prepare. He must have known something about the therapeutic value of watermelon that no one else did. Valerie was all over Sean, nuzzling his neck while bobbing up and down on his crotch like a very trashy four-year-old, but there was no sense taking it seriously; we all knew at least seven reasons why they couldn't possibly be doing It.

"You want to take a walk?" Emil asked Sean, which translated to "Do you want to go somewhere semiprivate and toot up?" Sean declined, which worked out fine, because I honestly don't think Emil had any to offer.

"Your book's doing so well," I said to Sean, and he looked up and said, "I know." *Island of Glossed Souls* was the biggest underground hype of the year, though "underground hype" seemed as much an oxymoron as that show I liked to catch sometimes on WOR, *Newark and Reality*. But now that all the mass media wanted to know about every breath taken by the people who dared to be different, there *was* no underground. It had been subsumed by the mainstream like everything else that starts out bubbling under the surface and becomes Cheez Whiz. Sean Valve had given these people credence and was now making a big success off them, a success that discovered them, glorified them, and killed them all at once. Though one of the reviews called the book "the literary equivalent of the Ramada Inn," I liked it. Everyone was talking about it, and even if you couldn't get past the first page, it was beyond being a book anyway. When you talked about *Island of Glossed Souls,* you weren't talking about something that was actually meant to be read, you were talking about a phenomenon.

"It really is doing galactically," said Emil. "We should discuss doing a party for it real soon before you get scooped up by Hollywood and all that." He'd already left this exact message on Sean's machine three times, but Sean never returned calls.

"Not only have we *had* a party," said Sean, "we're already planning another one. And I *have* been scooped up by Hollywood." I'd been to the first party—something pretty small and informal at Taker's Choice when the book came out. Sean had begged me not to invite Emil, whom he despised, and I remembered admiring his inability to mince words.

"Come on, you piece of shit," I said to Emil, taking Sean's lead. "Let's go." Before we left, I leaned over to Sean and told him I was putting him on the cover of my next issue. It hadn't dawned on me before, but standing there in his megawatt glow, it seemed so inspired. He was the hottest, the most luminescent property right now, and much more feasible than the other cover idea I'd entertained— Garth. Garth was perversely cool because he represented all three worlds tugging at everyone right then—uptown, downtown, and AIDS. But I couldn't mention the AIDS thing, and the piece would end up reading like a puffed-up sympathy card without any of the details. Meanwhile, Sean was zooming so loud it hurt your eardrums, and there weren't that many things about him that you couldn't mention. He'd already been accepted into all kinds of society cliques it takes decades to break into, and now he was going Hollywood—probably with a movie version of his book. (You couldn't exactly ask—prying questions were one sure route to his hating you.)

"I hope I don't have to do an interview or shooting for this," he said, gruffly. "I'm promoed out." Delroy was hand-feeding Valerie from one of the watermelon containers, and I knew he'd neurotically go out and replace it so Garth could have a full three. No, I assured Sean, he wouldn't have to lift a finger. "You ass kisser," said Emil as we walked out.

"You taught me everything I know," I grinned.

It's amazing I got the magazine out at all that month. Paying for the whole apartment was starting to drain my living-expense quotient. And the complimentary life-style was getting more and more expensive. There were more people to tip, more cabs to take, higher-priced meals to eat while striving for the ultimate high. My only remaining income was the rent I was getting from a family of four my father had arranged to move into Uncle Vito I's place. It wasn't a lot—no one pays *that* much to live in Queens—and I lived in constant terror that they might call on me for something important or really feel the need to treat me like a landlord. I'd rather starve in the gutter. But, God, I wanted that money. I wanted not to have to worry whether five dollars I impulsively tipped some coat-check martyr meant dinner at Wendy's the next three nights. The horrible thing about sneak-eating at Wendy's was that other important people were doing the same, and this was one place where you didn't want to see and be seen. Getting caught there was like being found in the hermaphrodite section of a pornographic bookstore. My technique—taught me by Favio— was always to shift the embarrassment around right at the top: "What are *you* doing at Wendy's?"

I felt really isolated for the first time since my party jaunt had started, because everybody wasn't on the same jaunt anymore. It had splintered off into a dozen different sub-stratospheres, and I wanted to be part of all of them, or maybe none of them. Suddenly I was like a visitor to twelve small, tightly knit towns, a perpetual tourist without so much as a toilet bowl to take home as a memento. And my companions were all suffering from some kind of life crisis or other that suddenly made them habitually absent. Favio was off finding himself and/or the money he owed me. Emil was strangely aloof, trying to live down a million embarrassments and piece his career back together again, I guess. Starla was hanging out more and more with Tracy Neuwirth at the kinds of parties world-famous debs get to go to. Delroy was spending every day at the hospital as Garth's liaison to the watermelon world. And Doric and Randi had indeed split up, though the word-of-mouth information service assured me that he was determined to court her back and had only taken up with a seventeen-year-old Hispanic hustler to ease his mind of the pain. Vivien, of course, was out destroying buildings.

Only out of dire necessity, I started spending dread quality time with myself—the agoraphobia was catching up with the monophobia, or maybe I was just burning out. Defying the reality that I needed every remaining penny for the survival of me and my magazine, I bought a membership to a video club and started renting everything from A (*Anastasia*) to Z (*Zabriskie Point*), seeking solace in the remote people and high-toned dramatics of screen fiction boiled down to tube size. I knew practically everybody in New York already—movie characters were the only fresh faces left. So the escape I'd found in parties I would now look for in screenplays—flights of fancy that could transport me to cheerier times, or even drearier times, as long as they took me somewhere out of my lonely cell in Kips Bay.

It was hard to find movies bizarre enough to qualify as really escapist, considering that the life I was living was already a finely crafted piece of fiction penned by some external force that refused to take credit for it. But I was willing to try all of them, any of them, even ones with subtitles, as long as they had something in them that wasn't Zymurgy. Glued to my set, I reveled in the antics of Hayley Mills holding prisms up to the light and playing "the glad game" in *Pollyanna,* of Rex Harrison singing a love song to a seal in *Dr. Dolittle,* of Sophia Loren saying, "I spit on charming" in *Houseboat* and "I spit on all your little birds" in *Man of La Mancha* (spitting has been a major motif in her career, for sure), astutely announcing in the same film that "The world's a dungheap and we are maggots that crawl on it." Sophia quickly replaced Nietzsche as my fave philosopher.

I'd already seen so many of the classic movies, but what the hell, I saw them again. There were none that didn't have some obscure reason that was begging for me to rent and embrace them for two hours. If it was nominated for the best sound Oscar in 1942, I had to see it. If it was deemed one of the worst movies of all time, then I definitely had to see it—it was those movies that usually turned out to be the most worthwhile. The cinematic version of *Portnoy's Complaint*—considered a worthless vulgarization when it came out—I found mesmerizingly funny and real. *What's So Bad About Feeling Good?,* a whimsical hippie-era fantasy clobbered by the critics, turned out to be fucking brilliant!

I couldn't bear the thought of sitting in a theater and sharing movies with plastic-crinkling, annoying people anymore, which was a shame, because I was starting to get on the list for an occasional screening notice. The tube was my friend as I solemnly sat and devoured the history of trash cinema. Like a drug addict waiting for a new shipment, I lived for the new releases that would come every two weeks. I rented everything but *Willy Wonka and the Chocolate Factory* and *War and Peace*—double trouble to look forward to.

I knew my mind had turned to Grey Poupon when I rented *The Oscar* and actually rewound three times through the part where Milton Berle says to Stephen Boyd, "You ever see a moth smashed against a window? It leaves the dust of its wings. You're like that, Frankie. You leave a trail of dirt everywhere you go." If I could have thought of stuff like that to say to Starla, maybe I could have kept her.

I still went to parties, anxious to unearth some new excitement, but more often than not, I went alone. I went to something for Judith Krantz at Scarlatti's, where she told me she was tired of everyone thinking all the sex in her books was the product of a feverish imagination—she'd done it all herself (with her husband, of course) and wanted credit for every orgasm. I went to something for Liza Minnelli, where Miss Diva herself held my hand for a good twenty seconds and thanked me, thanked me, thanked me, for telling her how great her voice sounded lately. Why was I complimenting Liza Minnelli so effusively, even though she'd changed that line in "Cabaret"? Because I knew she'd hold my hand and be really, really grateful? Had it come to this?

I went to something at the Public Theater where Jackie Kennedy (screw the Onassis—she was still Jackie Kennedy to me) munched on a big cookie and walked around looking pleasantly unselfconscious with her escort, incredibly wealthy gem dealer Maurice Tempelsman. This was the tops! The next day I rented *The Greek Tycoon* with Jacqueline Bisset— second best to being there.

Zymurgy was going further and further downhill without Garth's creative guidance to keep its carefully contrived boredom exciting. He'd been let out of the hospital and was mostly resting at home, not able to exert himself all that much, though he pathetically tried to do all the things he used to and more, just to assure everyone that he wasn't really sick. It was very sad one night to see him hosting a party for some French ballet troupe, trying to make the rounds of all the tables and be effortlessly scintillating even though he could barely move without a big production.

"You shouldn't be doing this," Delroy kept saying.

"You shouldn't be exerting yourself, especially in a smoky room with all these people's germs."

"Fuck you," Garth answered bitterly.

Spartacus finally got him to sit down in a corner of the room and, an hour later, drove him home.

Another night, Garth dragged himself to the club, only to hear a fake duchess murmuring to her Euro-model friend, "Did you hear? Garth is dead." "Oh, really?" smirked Garth, lurching toward her with a sinister grin. She didn't have to be bounced out of the place—she ran.

When Garth couldn't make it to the club—which was often—Spartacus was in charge, and his egregious bad taste ruled the day. I always thought Garth had chosen this brawny, if not brainy, guy because he was no threat to him, just like in the first Broadway play I'd ever seen—*A Matter of Gravity*—Katharine Hepburn surrounded herself, I could only assume on purpose, with a cast of the most amateur players east of a high-school varsity show. The always magnificent Hepburn shone even brighter that way. And, in a similar coup, Bush was starting to look blindingly brilliant next to his egg-laying V.P.

But no one could have anticipated the turn of events that would put Spartacus in charge of the whole show. The first one to deny Garth's illness, he was now leaping to accept it, because it meant a whole new power play for him and added some sinew to his Jheri-curled, swelled head in a big way. (A white male with Jheri curls—you can see what we were dealing with.) A minor presence, he suddenly became tyrannical and overbearing, carrying himself with the hauteur I'd seen so many club doormen and managers assume once possessed by their thimbleful of power. (Only Vlad, who'd long since quit the club's too-barbaric door and gone off to become a singing minstrel with some theater troupe, was above this syndrome. He wasn't really nice—just affably impartial.)

Spartacus started giving all his tacky friends free dinners

as if they were business cards and letting them throw truly B parties with Cimino-ish expense budgets for whatever event they felt like (saints' birthdays suddenly became of utmost importance to this crowd). And he froze out anybody from the old Zymurgy gang that he didn't care for, like Emil, who was persona non grata because Spartacus always found him too "aggressive" (translation: too much of a threat). Other regulars took the hint, like Dovima, Mimsy, and Daisy, who went cold turkey on the place and must have ended up in some Zymurgy detox center. Even if you despised these three, you had to admit they knew where it was happening. Their absence spoke volumes.

"Will you ever bury the hatchet with him?" I asked the spurned Mimsy one night at Ne Plus Ultra.

"Bury the hatchet where?" she screeched. "He's fucking spineless. The man's a walking sphincter muscle."

Everyone had pretty much agreed that when sphincter muscles learned to walk, it would be the beginning of the end of New York society as we knew it. That rainy day was here.

Emil started calling me again when he lost his star on this piddling walkway of fame. "How's the issue coming?" he asked one time, and I said, "It *came* along fine. I finished it—myself." Rub it in, rub it in, guilt, guilt, guilt. Though not Jewish, I'd learned how to do it many guilt-years ago. The ways of Jews and Italians in New York are exactly the same, ploy by ploy.

"I'm sorry," he said. "I've been going through rough times."

"So have we all," I said. I was in the middle of watching *They Were Expendable* and resented the interruption, though the movie was boring and it was nice to know I still counted, even with someone who didn't. I needed Emil's energy, however unnatural. Schmuck though he may have been, I craved his approval.

"I don't know what to do," he said. "Maybe I'll start getting my modeling portfolio together." Suitably enough for someone who liked coke, Emil's nostrils were big enough to inhale Jayne Mansfield. I couldn't imagine him becoming a model for anything but gas masks. Now that I thought about it, coke was so seventies anyway; why was he still indulging in that tired, rock star way of life? If you've got to be stuck on a drug, at least find one that's current. I wondered if heroin was part of Emil's daily diet too. No way—that always inspired drastic weight changes, so if you started out as a hump-backed whale, you became a strung-out bag of bones, and vice versa. Emil was always plainly, drably in the middle weight-wise, probably because whatever calories he burned off on the stuff, he took back in on that endless carousel of dinners. Crack couldn't figure into his scheme either—it was too common a fix, a cheap high any street urchin could cop. He was on the breakfast of champions, the snuff of the elite, and nothing else would be good enough.

"Not that my party biz isn't booming," he added, too insistently. That didn't fool me; I knew he didn't have a single party lined up, either to throw or to go to. "But I can't wait till Heinz opens his new club," he continued. "That ought to perk everything up even more."

"Heinz is opening a new club?" I said, then mentally kicked myself; you're not supposed to admit to not knowing things.

"You didn't know?" he said, pleased to have the upper hand this time. "That's the rumor, though of course no one can reach Heinz to find out. I've left him a million and a half messages."

"What's with this Heinz?" I wanted to know. "What does he look like—Anne Ramsey? Or maybe he's so special-looking he doesn't see fit to share his beauty with the rest of the world. He's got to be a very extreme case, either way."

"Only a few people have even seen him," said Emil, "and they say he's plain as pound cake, just painfully shy, to the point of terror. He gets off on people having fun, but doesn't seem capable of it himself, so he just immerses himself in his work, slaving away far from the madding crowd. They even built a secret elevator and back door for Heinz at Carcinogen so he could come and go in peace. I did all my business with him on the phone, and he never said more than five words at a time. There are rumors that Vivien knows him, but she won't deny or confirm.''

''Heinz works in mysterious ways,'' I said. ''If his new club is anything like Carcinogen, it'll be the best.''

''No,'' he snapped, ''you can't go back in time. Carcinogen was last year. This would have to be something new, to suit the times. Like Zymurgy, but one step newer and better.''

''Heinz wouldn't do that,'' I said. ''He wouldn't adapt so blatantly. That would be a sellout.''

''Realism is not a sellout,'' said Emil, quite seriously. Throughout this—and every—conversation with him, all I could think of was: this is the guy who beat up a homeless vaudevillian.

Heinz never opened his new club; at least not in our lifetime. This phantom nonhappening started making the rounds of everyone's lips as a fervent buzz of anticipation (''I can't wait for Heinz's new club''), then mounted into a frenzy of desperate need (''When's it opening? When's Heinz's club opening? What should I wear?'') and finally petered out into a defeated, running joke (''When's Heinz's club opening, ha-ha?''); all this within a couple of weeks. At one point, the news even got around that Heinz had named the place Vloolv, which was supposedly a word he'd picked up on his travels to some primitive culture in the very far reaches of the Pacific. The word had the incredible distinction of being a palindrome, meaning it's spelled the same backward and forward, so you could scrawl it on your forehead and look in a mirror and it would still spell Vloolv—a big advantage for a place where people would be looking in mirrors a lot. It was probably an acronym for ''I am the walrus'' or maybe ''Roman Castavet,'' the name of the devil-worshipper that Mia Farrow unravels via Scrabble tiles in *Rosemary's Baby*. Reports had it that Vloolv either meant *soul* or *rent*. Who cared? Whether this place was going to be a salvation or a sellout, it wasn't meant to be at all.

When we all finally accepted this, we started going back to the old haunts and doing our best to make them work again. There was no other choice short of getting backers together and opening our own clubs, and that was too draining; there were enough logistical annoyances in just going to a club to have to worry about running the place too. So we went back to Zymurgy and even Odile, with greater determination; we followed the newies on their endless rule-breaking caravan and tried harder to find something in them to relate to; and we had long drawn-out meals in restaurants like Ne Plus Ultra, Mise en Scène (on the rare occasions I could get a reservation there; even on a Monday once, they told me it was booked), and Hudson Street (which was actually on Varick, but what's in a name?), finally giving in to the by-now-ingrained-in-the-collective-consciousness trend of eateries as nightlife.

No one went to restaurants anymore to eat; they went to display their newest outfit, to wait an hour to get served by surly actresses who've just come from doing Lady Macbeth in scene-study class and have yet to break character, and to nibble on garnishes as a main course while chatting up fur designers who still believe that Ingrid Bergman shouldn't have left her husband for Rossellini. What do you say to a fur designer? "Skinned any good sable lately?" It was a moot point as long as your accent was suitably bizarre and you had as much respect for food as you had for fur-bearing animals.

Restaurants had for a while been parading grounds of the terminally chic, and you didn't have to throw those comp dinner parties anymore to get the right crowd—people would pay unrealistic amounts to be there on any night of the week just because the posing disease had hit even the most basic bodily function, eating. People couldn't wait until club time to start striking those poses; now they could begin at nine, looking fabulous as they toyed with their $11.50 arugula salad with a mere hint of goat cheese. That's why Zymurgy and Odile had incorporated restaurants into their premises: to let people act out their "Darling!" compulsions for longer chunks of time. As someone used to meteor-size meatballs served with lots of cheese and no pretension, this trend didn't sit well with me at all, but I went along with it. At least I might run into Starla more often.

One night, Emil got Sandahl DeVol—his last, faulty link to society—to take us to Mise en Scène for dinner, her treat. When it's their treat, you have to play by their rules, so as you sit there cowering from their flaws and feeling your flesh crawl over their failures, you bite your tongue and toast to their success. Picking up the check gives someone despotic power until that meal is over. Someday I'd be able to pay for dinner for three at Mise en Scène without thinking twice, and would know what it's like to rule two living organisms.

It turned out Sandahl wasn't as big a deal as I'd originally thought, yacht or no yacht. She had money from her absentee husband (one of the restaurant's original investor's—the only reason they reluctantly booked her a table) but no class and having failed uptown, she desperately wanted to hobnob with the downtown crowd and be accepted by people a third her age. There was something pathetic about her, but she was wealthy and personable enough in a brash, everything's-coming-up-roses kind of way. I especially admired that she didn't seem to realize the downtown crowd had also failed uptown and were meeting her at some societal limbo for bad people, Pleasure Island in *Pinocchio,* where the naughty boys were taken to be turned into donkeys. I loved that she took this all so seriously and had no idea we were all donkeys trying to be fab.

Sandahl didn't camouflage her motivations in the slightest; everything about her was on the table, like her tacky, ball-fringed handbag. She was hoping we'd be her entrée into the lower rungs, which at least were more interesting than the middle ones. I just wanted an entrée, period—anything but veal. Her main value to me tonight was that she'd gotten us the reservation, even though we were seated in the back room and might as well have been across the street, we were so far from the action. Emil liked the idea of returning here inconspicuously through the "Siberia" section and worming his way back to the A-room in due time. He was praying very hard that they wouldn't remember he was the specter of the veal, and from the way they ushered us in—quickly and with pathological efficiency—they *didn't* remember, or maybe didn't care.

The second we sat down, Emil went off to the men's room, where he stayed an inordinate amount of time. Either he was writing "Vloolv" on his forehead and looking at it in the mirror, or he was doing his white-powder trick. When he came back, he insisted on talking about his day on Sandahl's yacht all those lifetimes ago, probably to rub in one more time my not being there. It was the last thing he'd done that he could rub in, and he hadn't rubbed it in in a while. "It's so beautiful," he kept saying. "The sleekest, most amazing thing. Better than the Trump *Princess,*" he laughed.

Sandahl mercifully let it drop. She wanted to talk about Starla's party at Ne Plus Ultra, which she insisted had been the high point of *her* life thus far. I didn't remember her being at that party, but that was even more lifetimes ago; I'd give her the benefit of the doubt. Like I said, despotic power.

"She's your girlfriend, isn't she?" she asked me. I rolled my eyes and said, "It's a long story"—a good, generic answer.

"Oh, please," Emil protested—no one was buying that anything was going on between Starla and me anymore, and I don't know if anyone ever believed it in the first place.

"She's so terrific," said Sandahl. "I'd love to get to know her better." So would I.

I glanced over to the next room—the A-room—and flinched as I spotted Colette—the designered diva, the emblem of the rich bitches, the human money tree. She was in a silvery, aluminum foil-like ensemble that made her look like a big, expensive capon. The man she was with—no doubt her son, the pig, Herve—was in a classic Italian suit and was quite dashing for an older man—a pig—with cheekbones that gave him a Continental elegance his beady eyes didn't deserve. Even if you had no idea who they were, they were unquestionably Someones.

I didn't realize it then, but now I think Emil somehow knew that Colette was going to be there and had scrupulously planned this as his chance to reconcile with her—or at least catch a furtive glimpse. That could explain why he was so insistent that we go to Mise en Scène that night, dragging Sandahl on God knows how many guilt trips to get us there. After some pretend resisting, Sandahl gave in, seeing this as a chance to impress us on what she'd pass off as her home turf. She probably hadn't figured on us being seated right next to the kitchen.

Table hopping at Mise en Scène was a no-no—fasten your seatbelts—but that wouldn't stop Emil. His eyes had been rolling like marbles into the other room ever since we got there, and when he saw me locate Colette with my line of vision, he followed as if scouting for Nazis through a periscope. Sandahl was going on and on about her home-accounting video that was going to help AIDS ("You really should write about it") and about how she was thinking just the other day maybe she should do a signed version for the hearing impaired. I was just nodding and saying, "Yes, whatever," hoping against hope that she'd run out and do the signed version right then. I was only half listening, actually, fantasizing that Colette would spot us and, through some act of icy benevolence, crawl toward our labor camp to say hello. This *was* hard labor—listening to Sandahl talk about herself was the most strenuous drudgery on earth. I'm sure Emil wasn't listening at all as he sat there sweating and bug-eyed, looking like a murderer who'd just decided to go for the kill. There was a sick mixture of triumph and terror on his face as he excused himself and robotically got up from the table. If the mountain wasn't going to come to Mohammed, Emil was going to go to Colette.

We watched as he took that long journey into the other room—well, *I* watched. Sandahl just kept on talking about how she wanted to throw a party at Zymurgy, but Spartacus was being so weird, and she'd invited him on the yacht, but he probably hadn't gotten the message because he hadn't returned her call, and by the way, I could come on the yacht when it got warm again (a brilliant catch—once that happened, the offer would have been long forgotten). The yacht was Sandahl's big draw. Without it, she couldn't even offer you seasickness.

As Emil barreled along on his own rough-water cruise, a waiter tried to point him the other way, assuming he was looking for the men's room again. Emil brushed him off like he was swatting Mothra and kept walking. When he got to Colette's table, I turned off Sandahl and flicked the channel to this new show.

A cold scene transpired that sent icicles down my appetizer. I expected Colette to at least put up the pretense of politeness, but these people hold grudges that make my family's look like minor snubs. Emil's approaching her—or even being seated under the same roof—was as ghastly a *faux pas* as my cousin Angelo's being seated at Gloria's table at the Majestic Terrace, except that this place reeked of real money. Real money begets real grudges. You can't buy your way out of these predicaments, because there's nothing you have that they need.

She didn't look like she was chewing Emil out, but then she wasn't exactly introducing him to her son and handing him blank checks. She just looked as forbidding as a metal detector; she emitted a few curt words, and he dejectedly skulked away, knowing the situation could only get worse if he held out for applause. The maitre d' finally decided to go over to the table and ask Colette if anything was wrong, but Emil had already crawled back and was plastering a presto-chango phony look of exuberance on his face to convince us his audience with the queen was a big hit.

The rest of the dinner was draggy and uneventful. My chicken gai yung was drowning is so much sauce I needed a fishing rod, and why were they serving Chinese dishes, however pretentiously, in this place anyway? Didn't anybody believe in sticking to themes anymore? What was the theme of Mise en Scène anyway—money? At these prices, they should serve gold, not beef, bouillon. I'd only ordered the chicken because it was the fourth most expensive entrée on the menu (except for the specials, which I can never remember), and I think when someone else is treating, ordering one of the top three things on the menu is taking advantage. It was so vile I wanted to make it fly again, but Mise en Scène wasn't about the food, so like everyone else, I grinned and made poultry Etch-a-Sketches with it. Hell, we were at Mise en Scène—that was fulfilling enough.

Sandahl kept on yammering away, and I tried to at least feign diplomacy and appear to be listening—a technique I'd learned with Favio when he went off on one of his tangential dissertations you knew you were better off not hearing. What you do is plaster a half-smile across your face, make eye semicontact (look at the bridge of their nose, imagining there's a dot on each side of it, like they used to put on Norma Shearer's to make her look not cross-eyed), and pack up your mind and take it on a frequent fliers'-club journey. With enough practice, you can transport your thoughts a million miles away and still have the immediacy of mind to be able to snap back into the situation when the other person says, "Are you listening?" When this happens, a sharp "Of course" saves it for you. Act insulted. Make *them* feel like shit for doubting you.

Emil couldn't even play the half-listening game; he was so gone he might as well have been in Kamchatka. He wasn't even touching his food, and Sandahl was starting to feel cheated.

"Should we send that to the Coalition for the Homeless?" I grinned at Emil, pointing to his steak, which looked so much more appealing than my chicken ever did. You never had to deal with the homeless problem here. Though some of them were right outside, you couldn't see them, thanks to the frosted windows that protected you from any ugly reality that might stroll by. In here, everything was hand-picked and beautiful, sparkly and sugar-coated. I wondered how much of the money made by that benefit had actually gone to the homeless, once all the expenses were paid for. Did some street derelicts get to sit down to a meal like the one we were eating? (I hoped not; I hoped they got something decent.) Was Favio now one of them, stalking the streets in search of a handout, chasing respectable people down dark alleyways to treat them to *his* version of "Swanee"? I was thinking of Favio an awful lot. Irritating as he was, I missed him. Not as he was now. I missed Favio when Favio was really Favio.

"So Colette looks pretty incredible, no? What did she have to say for herself?" Sandahl asked, practically foaming from the corners of her mouth, I'm sure not over her lamb. (There was no veal on the menu, by the way; like Joan Crawford cutting her exes out of all her photos, this restaurant was going to erase any reminder of that incident, as if it was the veal's fault. How ironic that Emil, the Goebbels of that event, was here, and they didn't have any recollection of him at all. Thank God for turnover.)

"Oh," said Emil, making this up as he went along, "she said she'd been to a few fashion shows today, and she's been throwing so many parties lately she was enjoying just sitting down with her son and catching up. Herve said he's been touring a lot and working on another book, and it was really nice to meet me, he'd heard a lot about me."

"You talked to Herve?" said Sandahl. "Maybe you can introduce me to them later. I've always wanted to get to know them."

I didn't say anything about Herve's remarks regarding the disease Sandahl was supposedly so dedicated to fighting. She was treating.

"I don't know," said Emil. "I think it would be rude to interrupt them again. I'll gladly introduce you some other time. They're all over the place." Emil hadn't seen them since the homeless benefit, though Lord knows it wasn't for lack of trying. Absence had turned his Colette fascination into an obsession, and he was furious—at himself and at the world—that his one awesome connection had slipped out of his hands. He likened it to getting to the foreign country of your dreams, only to find you'd forgotten your passport and have to go back. Emil didn't even *have* a passport—he was faking it all along.

"I know them already anyway," said Sandahl, faking it too. "What's wrong, Emil? You look distracted."

That was the understatement of the century so far. He looked as if his brain had snapped like a breadstick, that's all. He was panting like a dog and sweating all over his steak. I monitored his eyes and saw him fixate on Colette and Herve—leaving. Leaving Mise en Scène. Leaving his life and going back to their ivory tower, slamming the door shut with a loud, exclusive bang only he could hear. He bolted up.

"Colette, don't go," he screamed, as everyone craned their necks in horror/delight. Was this place never going to see an end to its distracting scenes? The maitre d' fumed, looking like he'd toss Emil out on the pavement by his nostrils if the guy took one more liberty, but it was OK—

Colette and Herve were out now, and so was Emil, chasing them and screaming after them with painful desperation. Whatever happened outside the restaurant was not the restaurant's business; they were only responsible for what transpired within those frosted windows.

I know they were outside because I was outside too—I'd excused myself from Sandahl for a minute and explained to the maitre d' that I would go out and take control of the situation. Actually, I just wanted to watch.

"Colette, come back," he begged, chasing them as they walked toward their car, then circling them to get their attention like a crazed, wild bird of prey. He was serious, not even having stopped to get his coat on the way out, though it was the kind of nippy night that could drive you into bed for a month. I—impulsive, yet neurotic—*had* gotten mine, so I could be comfy while getting my kicks.

Herve turned around and barked, "You get away from us right now or I'll have you taken care of in a very unpleasant way." Emil hardly heard this—though everyone on the street did—and just kept following them and screaming, "Colette, I love you. Colette, come back, I love you." He grabbed her by her ankles and almost succeeded in tackling her, and I shuddered to think this might become a replay of the homeless vaudevillian incident, this time done with love. But she managed to kick him off with her deadly heels as Herve pitched in by slamming him a few times with his valise. They jumped into the car, and as they made their getaway Colette was still muttering very unladylike expletives. Emil was on the ground, shaking, and crying, "I love you" as the car pulled off.

We never went back inside to Sandahl—there'd be too much explaining to do, and she was so bloody boring. We just left her there with the check. That was definitely going to be the last Emil saw of Sandahl—the final link of the chain had been broken.

I'd now seen the polar opposite of the Vivien approach; when *she* ran after Colette, it was to throw something, not to scream "I love you." But both scenes, *all* scenes, were welcome in my world; in addition to being deliriously entertaining while they transpired, they gave me fodder for phone calls for months to come. I sometimes wondered if New York Telephone staged these things just to perk up those failing message units. Whenever life threatened to get terminally dull, stuff always happened, as if by divine intervention, to restore our faith in the delightful evilness of the human race and give us something to talk about. It was too bad that they always happened at Colette's expense. But not that bad.

The magazine's sales were not exactly taking off; in fact, they were down a little from the previous month, down to an embarrassing figure not even worth mentioning. I think it was because Sean Valve had already been more oversaturated than high-fat milk; it was kind of a joke for a supposedly cutting-edge magazine to put him on the cover when the guy had already co-hosted Regis. Besides, I'd lost the gay audience by glorifying Colette, and I'd lost the newies, who were now much more interested in their own publications, which gave them the kind of glory press they wanted. The Starla crowd—I now pictured her surrounded by thousands at all times—had graduated to *WWD* and *Vanity Fair* and couldn't be bothered with two-bit shit. That left *Manhattan on the Rocks* in some uneasy middle ground where there was no particular readership that needed it, and for any magazine to make it, it has to be a need—veritable oxygen on the printed page—and not just a baubly whim to entertain between career moves. No one needed *Manhattan on the Rocks* except me.

Of course, it's my awesome hindsight that allows me to see these things now. At the time, I only let the magazine serve whatever I was thinking at the moment I sent it to be typeset, and it always seemed the right move to me. But I could see it wasn't right to everyone else. Even Delroy was getting less enthusiastic as the momentum pooped out of it. He was far more excited about working for *Fabulon* and *Limo,* which were growth organizations, glamorously spoon-feeding the underground to the masses. He still delivered the goods, though, maybe because I'd just gotten over a cold.

I used all my wiles to try to make Delroy think the magazine was a lot more happening than it was, just because I liked having him around. He was spirit-lifting, even though lately he always had some progress (or decay) report on Garth to foist on me.

One day I took Delroy to lunch at Hudson Street (How was I ever going to save a penny with gratuitous meals oozing out of control from my pocket?), trying to stay in his good graces with all of the five food groups. The lunch turned inevitably into a seminar on Garth. Delroy complained that Garth had been put on AZT, and it had helped him at first, but now he was suffering from violent side effects—apparently it's a very toxic drug that can sometimes be more lethal than the disease itself. Unfortunately, as Vivien had repeatedly droned, a lot of other possible drugs used against AIDS are still in the experimental stage because of all that hierarchical bullshit. You have to be a private detective to even find them, and a kamikaze pilot to risk your life on them. It was distressing when I related all this to my own situation (and face it, anyone's reaction to a mass disaster is simply a function of how it relates to *them*—"I was almost on that plane that crashed"), but I calmed myself down with some highly educated, Jeanne Dixon–type predicting. I figured the semen I'd stepped in was probably coursing through my body right now like a bandit. By the time it manifested itself, there'd be a cure or at least some valid treatment that would help me get through.

I know there'd have to be a cut on my foot for the stuff to have entered my bloodstream, but how could there not have been a cut after schlepping around in those paper-thin shoes? Besides, Vivien told me about macrophages, these new scavenger cells that didn't necessarily register in the blood but hung out in mucous membranes and maybe the skin, then *carried* the virus to the blood. They weren't really new, they'd been around forever, but they were just starting to attract publicity and get really famous. Had scavenger cells suddenly acquired a publicist? Were there going to be ads for night sweats, promotional departments set up to give swollen lymph nodes a higher profile? And lesions could certainly use a better TVQ.

Anyway, whether my foot had macrophages or not, I might as well assume it did. And I might as well assume the future would eventually bring comforting answers to all this anxiety, or I could go certifiable. "Dream on," said Vivien, when I told her of this, my very own glad game. "Very little is being done, and there may never be a cure, especially at the pitiful rate the government's progressing. AIDS isn't a medical issue anymore—it's a political issue. That's why we have to kick ass." I was doomed—a walking, rotten-magazine-publishing time bomb. And I still had to listen to Vivien.

Starla and I hadn't communicated in a while, and I was stunned at how quickly she had gone from being so territorial with me to totally laissez-faire and so fucking pleasant about it. I missed her sparkle and got tired of running into her only at parties and being treated like just another schmooze target, a twenty-second "Hi-hi." I guess Tracy Neuwirth was a more glittering partner in crime than I ever was. I was starting to be overtaken by the urge to brutally maim Tracy's face so her debutante career would crumble and, for lack of an attractive curtsy, she could return to her true forte, neurosurgery. Maybe I should run after Starla screaming, I love you—no, that didn't work very well for

Emil, so scratch that idea. Or start nasty rumors that Starla and Tracy were having a madcap lesbian affair. No, those rumors had already surfaced (the gossip mill is the fastest-working industry in New York) and Starla handled them with a giddy laugh and a giggly, "Yeah, right!"—the best way to confront any lie.

I didn't want to hurt Starla anyway. I just wanted her back and chastised myself for not having strapped her demonically into my possession in the first place. When you're in the thrall of an intoxicating relationship like that, you tend to be so dubious of your luck, you start to nag yourself with negatives—she doesn't really like me, she's not the most fascinating company, things could be better. When it's over, you realize that the relationship was the best thing that ever happened to anyone in the history of human interchange. Suddenly, you have all the time in the world to reflect back on The Way You Were, and as I rented the fifteen-and-a-half-hour *Berlin Alexanderplatz*—desperate—I had fifteen and a half hours to let horrible regret gnaw away at what was left of my brain.

Delroy felt she wasn't really mad about the Vivien-wedding thing, she was just using that as an excuse to dump me and remain mobile. I convinced myself that she was still insanely in love with me and was passionately, derangedly jealous of Vivien. She wanted me to crawl, but I knew she'd be the one to get down on her knees first.

Favio called, and the second I heard his voice, I started rummaging through my mental calendar for some info he'd doubtless demand. Um, Spermicidal Foam was probably the same as it was last time, Zymurgy was sliding, Velveeta closed, Starla was in *Vogue, Bazaar,* and on the cover of *Fabulon*—again. I was shooting (I hoped he wouldn't ask, up or down?).

But shockingly enough, he didn't bring up any of that. In very sober tones, like an alky determined to prove he can walk a straight line, he dispensed with all the "Hi, what's been going on?" formalities and dropped the bombshell— was this a bad connection?—he had my money.

"When can I get it?" I said with great compassion. I was trembling and suddenly believed in every religious icon my mother had ever wrapped in plastic.

I met him the next day on his lunch hour on a bench at Broadway and West Fourth. He said it was close to his work, and it would be better than my dropping by "the store," where it was too "crazy" to deal with these things. He offered no more details about this capitalistic temple of doom, and I didn't push it either, though when I got there, I did make a point of scanning the other side of the street for spots that could fit the bill. There was one of those rinky-dink boutiques filled with the tackiest aberrations of fashion, which cater to women who think that its French name (Voulez-Vous) makes it the absolute lap of elegance; there was a Make-Your-Own-Frame store; a sushi restaurant (the last of a dying breed, the Mary-Ellen Meringue of eateries); a trendy-schmendy makeup shop populated with spiky-haired Vulcans with black lips and no eyeballs; and a Burger King.

I figured it had to be the makeup shop—Shazork—and though Favio was dressed a little colorlessly for that, they must have seen some of his past glory in his eager eyes and/or press clippings. He hadn't even dressed out of his uptown wardrobe—it was from his new closet of middle-class, middle-rung desperation. It was the first time I'd ever seen him in a button-down shirt.

"Has Attila the Dad been around looking for me?" he said, with forced casualness.

"I don't think so," I said, honestly. "Somebody's been calling me at five in the morning and hanging up, and some-one—maybe the same person—has been buzzing me at odd hours, but if it were your father, I think he'd say some-thing."

"He'll come by," he said. "It's as inevitable as PMS. Just tell him I died."

"No," I said. "Why should I make that asshole so happy?"

"True," he said. "Tell him I've become the world's tallest drag queen and I've shacked up with a rich, pot-bellied old sugar daddy and will never need him again. Tell him I've become incredibly famous."

Famous at Shazork? Not bloody likely.

It was chilly—this bench idea was a lame one—but the thought of the money was keeping me warm and cozy. There's nothing more comforting than some rightly deserved income.

Favio looked beaten—not into a bruised and humiliating submission, but worse, into a cheerful acceptance of failure. He was energetic and pleasant and frighteningly well adjusted to his new Bowery/boutique low-glamour life-style. Had he adapted again, as his chameleon instincts always enabled him to do? Maybe it was just a performance and I was being had one more time.

"Pull the plug on your magazine," he said suddenly. "It's tired. No—sleepy." How typical: now that I was writing about some people he *really* worshipped, he was proclaiming it tired—a projection, by any chance? Even that bitter remark was said with a perkiness that could drive you insane. I wanted my old Favio back—the one who could be enthusiastic for real because he had something he could be enthusiastic about. But—I'm a journalist, remember—I felt for him in a way. It *was* kind of sad that he'd been victimized at his own game. "Yeah, right," I said, "and you're not tired?" I didn't want to say anything *too* horrible until I got the money.

"Case closed," he said, snapping his fingers. At least when you pulled a bigger number on Favio than he had on you, he chilled out.

We sat in silence for a while, taking in the street parade of every type the stores catered to—the dumpy women who need to seek romance in clothes because they can't get it from their husbands; the vampire trendies with complexions like peanut brittle; the grease and cholesterol addicts; and the people no stores cater to—the bums, druggies, and derelicts.

"So what's new?" he said, inventively.

I felt like Vanessa Redgrave in *Julia*: "Lost a leg, had a baby—I named the baby after you." I could do a pretty comparable routine: Went out with Vivien, watched Emil pounce on a bum, visited Garth in the AIDS ward, watched Emil pounce on Colette. "Oh, nothing," I said.

"Are you out of the closet yet?"

"Fuck you!" I bolted up and started shrieking, for the entire parade of street freaks to watch. "We don't have anything to talk about if that's going to be the level of the conversation. We're not friends anymore, so you have no right. Just hand me the money and get out of my life."

A policeman sauntered over and asked Favio if everything was all right. Where are they when you need them? Favio assured him it was a personal dispute and no men in uniform were on the guest list, and the guy moved along with a sour expression. "Look for some important crimes, like littering," I muttered, more for Favio's sake.

"Sorry," said Favio, facetiously. He reached into the Banana Republic bag he used to wear as a joke and pulled out a crinkled, white envelope with the goods. "Count it," he said.

"I trust you," I said, desperately wanting to rip it open and tally it all, bill by bill. Hell, even if it wasn't the full amount, it was money—currency of some kind that could be exchanged for another reprieve from real work. His volunteering it was the greatest act of misguided noblesse since Ford pardoned Nixon. But behind every act of misguided noblesse is some self-serving smarm. I suspected he was doing this so I'd relay to everyone how he'd gotten his act together, was solvent again and on the way up. Unfortunately, everyone else was slobbering in some gutter or other and needed emergency resuscitation just to be conscious enough for me to tell them this good news.

"So what's new with *you*, Favio?" I said, folding the envelope into my pocket. Already, three street people were eyeing it anxiously.

"Charles," he corrected me, dramatically. "Charles Speck. I never told you, but that's my real name."

You don't have to tell a reporter. "Oh. So how are you, *Charles?*"

"Great!" he said. "But enough about me. Have you gotten a new roommate yet?"

"No," I said. "No offense, but I'm sort of enjoying having the place alone. Having it all—money, fame, success, and loneliness—I mean, privacy. And let's face it—you're irreplaceable."

"Is there anything else?" he said, in a cheerfully businesslike way, as if this were a power lunch coming to a fruitful finish. He got up and dusted off his pants. Poly blend.

"No. I'll take responsibility for the full rent from now on—somehow. Don't worry, you don't owe me another dime."

He started laughing uproariously. The street people were giggling along with him—had he hired them as background? "Of course I don't owe you another dime. *You* owe *me,*" he smirked.

"What?"

"You owe *me.* For . . . for everything."

"Say again?"

"You're boring—a college student from Queens is boring, real boring deep down, no matter how hard he tries. And you didn't even graduate!" He wasn't smirking anymore—Dr. Favio and Mr. Speck. "You're so smug with your two-bit success, and you don't know shit. I bet you don't even know what acid house is. Why did I even bother with a fucking dropout! What a waste of time I could have used for myself and my own causes."

"But *listen* . . ." I vainly tried to interrupt.

"I led you along to be nice and show you how not to be boring," he kept plowing on, "and some people fell for you for a while. You weren't bad company, though you did siphon off me like a fucking lamprey eel sucking out the guts of a fish. But you're over. You and Starla and Doric and Emil and that whole group are all over, everyone says so. Time's up, kid. There's a whole new crowd coming up. If you hadn't been so pleased with yourself, you might have seen them barking at your heels. And now it's too late. As the board game says, 'Sorry!'" He just had to say all that before he split. I wonder how long he'd rehearsed it. Two street people were applauding. He'd probably get the street-theater award for the year.

You don't belong to anything anymore, Fav . . . Charles Speck, and the best punishment of all is you have to live with your miserable, rotten self. That's what I wished I had said, two days later, but all I could think up at the time was, "Too bad you're not fabulous Favio anymore. You're a blah person with a blah name, and no one wants it." Not bad, actually.

"*I* want it," he said, impressively. The words echoed all the way up to Broadway, and I expected a disco orchestra to suddenly rise out of a manhole and start playing "I Will Survive." "Take care," he added, as if nothing had happened, and walked away. At least he'd learned to keep them succinct.

He loitered for a while in front of Voulez-Vous and kept looking over to see if I'd left. I knew he wasn't really interested in Voulez-Vous—he didn't have *that* bad taste—he just didn't want me to see the workplace he'd finally have to crawl back to on bended knee. I played along and walked around the corner, pretending to be far gone—the cue for him to go back to his factory of necessity. Then I darted back just in time to catch him oozing into Burger King, where I guess he slipped into his outfit and sold some fabulous fries.

12

The next day, I was awakened by a call from, of all people, Emil. It was a jolt that stung me back into reality—my reality. This was becoming old home week for fallen meteors of nightlife, and I was starting to feel like a derangement counselor.

"Fabulous," he said, instead of "hello." The "shalom" of the eighties, the word had come to mean anything you wanted it to—hello, goodbye, I love you, fuck off, probably even vloolv.

"Fabulous," I answered back. "You sound weird." Even on that one word, he'd been slurring, and the *f* was as saliva-filled a consonant as any by Daffy Duck. "I hope you have a prescription for whatever you're on." At least in all his slurring there wasn't a trace of embarrassment over the "I love you, Colette" affair, just to pick one incident out of many.

"I'm not on anything," he insisted. "I'm high on life, okay? Look, do you want me to hang up and not tell you the fabulous thing I've done for your magazine?" Magazine? Oh, right, I published a magazine. "I met with that printer you wanted me to meet with," he continued, "and negotiated some very agreeable rates with him. I have it all typed out for you." It was four months since he was supposed to meet with that printer, but at least he'd gotten the deed done. Emil always came through—you just had to hope you were still alive when he did.

"Great," I said. Shit—now I had to come out with another issue. At least I could save a few pennies on the printing—that is, if he'd really had that meeting and not hallucinated it in some substance-induced delirium. (Emil may not have had much substance, but he was boffo with substance*s*.) Any devious way of cutting corners was as warmly welcome as a plane flying overhead during an outdoor Whitney Houston concert. If all the advertisers paid their bills on time, I'd really be set. Instead, most of them responded to my feeble attempts at collection with that oldest line in debit history: "The check is in the mail." The chilling thing about clichés is that people really *do* say them. "Let's have lunch," "Let me let you go," and "We were just talking about you—nice things, of course" are actual, daily conversational occurrences. If all those checks were in the mail that were supposed to be, my box would explode one day in Sensurround and kill at least seven people.

But they'd never come, and no advertiser would ever meet me on a bench with a white envelope and a bitter tirade. (Favio's envelope, by the way, contained not only the full amount owed, but an extra two dollars—for the magazine he took, or maybe for emotional damages.) My biggest creditor—Zymurgy—owed me a small fortune, but what was I supposed to do, insist Garth spend his money on my vanity project instead of AZT? AZT was toxic, but then so was my vanity project.

"So when do you want to get together?" Emil said. "You've got to get the next issue out—maybe this will be the incentive. I haven't talked to you in ages. I don't feel like we're friends anymore. What happened?"

"Nothing," I said. "My VCR keeps spitting out tapes. It's bulimic. And my phone hasn't been working."

"For a whole month?"

"No, no, no," I said, covering one bad excuse with another. "I've just been busy. Really Bellevue-ready."

"With what? There isn't a new issue. I looked at the stands and there was no new issue."

"No," I said. "Not with the magazine. Just busy with myself. There are other things besides the magazine, you know." I almost said something about "finding myself," but stopped short when I remembered how Favio's rendition of that phrase sent me into shell shock. I certainly didn't want to tell him that I'd joined a gym real cheap and then quit in humiliation when, after three and a half weeks of misusing the machines, an instructor wanted to know if it was my first day there.

"Have you been to a lot of parties? You never invite me."

"Well, you haven't exactly been brimming over with invitations either. Haven't you thrown any parties lately?" There was no harm in asking.

"I'm planning some big things," he said. "They're going to be really special. The earth's going to quake with what I've got up my sleeve."

"Ooh, I'm scared," I said.

"And I'm still working on my modeling portfolio," he said. By the time that thing was ready, he could model orthopedic shoes.

"You wanna get together tomorrow night?" I said, nobly. "Spartacus is debuting his nightclub act—can you believe it? It's bound to be the biggest hoot since the birth of Mary-Ellen Meringue."

Emil started to say "Blecchhh," but changed it in midsyllable to—that word—"fabulous." The way he said it made it clear that he meant "blecchhh," but he wasn't all that nauseated by the idea. This event could be his re-entry into some kind of civilization, however declining.

We arranged to meet at his place just as a novelty; Emil usually never let people penetrate his inner sanctum and was finally letting me do so out of a new insecurity bred from disgrace. As the walls around him came tumbling down, it became open-house time.

Like Garth, he was a "neb"—nebulous about all things personal. In our many conversations, he'd never told me anything too deep about himself—I never even heard him say whether he liked boys, girls, or barnyard animals— mainly because his line of work called for him to like every- one of a certain stratum, without preference for gender or species. Now, I thought, maybe he'd let down his defenses a little, wash out the gel, and get real.

But this best-case scenario was not meant to be. I was lucky I even got there, because it was pouring and you had to murder people on street corners just to get a cab. I ended up walking all the way over there, to the West Village—talk about seventies—with one of those three-dollar umbrellas that turn into weather vanes with the slightest wind. How apt that I was on my way to see the human weather vane, who turned whichever way the wind blew, and he was in shambles too. (Such poetry, for someone who got a C in that subject!)

Emil's building was harder to get into than Odile ever was. I buzzed and got no answer, buzzed again and got no answer, and then sadistically leaned against the buzzer long enough that I knew Emil would finally respond just to make it stop. After what seemed like ten solid minutes, he said something incomprehensible over the speaker and buzzed me in. It sounded like "Klaatu barada nikto," I swear.

As I walked to the fifth floor—walk-ups are even more irritating than buzzers—I was assaulted by a World's Fair of smells, from curry to Lysol to tomato sauce to curry again to gas. It was a big building for Indians and suicides.

No smell at all emanated from Emil's apartment, which assured me that everything was probably OK. But the buzzing routine had been a joyride next to the desperate knocking shtick that now awaited me. His bell didn't work, so I had to bang the hell out of the door until I got a spasm in my forearm and still couldn't get a response. My fist was starting to look like a beet salad, and the only answer I got was the anguished Talking Heads song playing in the background like a low, injured-mouse whine. "Emil," I screamed. "Emil, let me in." He slobbered a few words in response and thoughtfully welcomed me by thrashing around what sounded like a toaster, but still didn't open the door. After another five minutes of loud pleading that had a few of his neighbors swinging open *their* doors and demanding I put a lid on it, I decided to go look for the super—definitely a last-ditch effort.

In a curry haze, I found the buzzer that said the guy, Mr. Minadeo, was in 1A, so I banged raucously on his door—this was now my instinctive approach to getting into anyone's apartment—only to hear a wild dog barking out of control. Minadeo opened the door and irritably slammed off a tape—it must have been from an old *Benji* movie and was much more convenient than a real dog because it didn't need feeding, cleaning, or humoring, only rewinding. If I were a tenant here, I don't know if I could really entrust my safety to this man, whose main weapon against intruders was a three-minute cassette. But since I was an intruder, he was my only hope.

"What do you want?" he barked, louder than the tape. "It's way past working hours. Give me a break."

I gave him a five-dollar tip—advance tipping is the key to conditioning supers. "Can I help you?" he said, suddenly perking up. He was fiftyish and wearing a too-small white T-shirt that carressed his every love handle and made him look not unlike Tweedle-Dee, West Village version. He was drinking Rolling Rock—the C&C of beers—and watching a rerun of *Three's Company,* the one where everyone else toasts to "good times" and "happy days," and Chrissy raises her glass to *"Little House on the Prairie."*

I explained my predicament and said I was really worried about Emil, for once not having to call on the usual repertoire of acting skills—I really *was* sorta-kinda worried. He paused for about two milliseconds, then went into the other room and promptly came back with Emil's key. Now that's a good super—one who'll give entrée to a tenant's apartment to anyone who has a convincing enough explanation for wanting it, plus five bucks. This could be a new game show—Name That Reason You Want Emil's Key.

My super, thank God, didn't keep a copy of *my* key, and he actually had some real guard dogs, not just the Cassingles version. I vowed to give him a gratuitous gratuity next time I saw him. "Bring it back," Minadeo said with great concern, returning to the show with obvious annoyance that he may have missed a turn in the plot.

I schlepped back up the stairs, and by now curry seemed as natural a gaseous substance as the air itself. I convinced myself that it was a good smell, so I wouldn't have to dry-clean everything I had on—another spurious expense. I knocked again, just to give Emil the chance to let me in by choice. Hearing nothing but that same Talking Heads ditty drone on in continual repeat, I let myself in. Just the chance to turn off the record alone would be enough of a mercy mission to warrant this intrusion.

Emil was lying on his living-room floor in a pool of something brownish-beige, his hand outstretched and pointing to a picture in a magazine. "Oh, hi," he gurgled. "Look— I'm in *Fabulon.*"

I'd never seen anything so pathetic in my life. Even in a puddle of puke, a shattered toaster by his elbow, he was pointing at his press. I glanced at the picture (not a flattering one) and read the caption—something vicious about how Emil would indubitably end up at Skid Row, the club, and skid row, the place. But hey, it was a mention. The smell of vomit was really annoying—now there'd be no way around that dry-cleaning expenditure. I flipped through the pages of the magazine to see if there was a picture of me, but my radarvision couldn't locate any. Fine—whenever my picture was in, I always felt slightly doomed, as if the month was ticking off and soon it, and I, would be over. This month I was nothing. Next month I could be something.

"Are you all right?" I said, wiping off his mouth with a paper towel I found and helping him to stand up. "What are you on? Do you want me to call an ambulance?"

"No, no," he slurred, "I'll be fine. I just had a stomach ache and really had a hard time getting up when I heard you buzzing. Just give me a minute."

I dragged Emil into the shower and turned on the cold water, not bothering to take his clothes off—they needed washing too. This was the Cary Grant scene from *Charade* happening right in front of me, but with considerably less panache. The water braced him into some kind of consciousness, and he was starting to return from his out-of-body experience. "I just took too much," he said.

"Too much what?"

"Too much—much," he answered. "I'll be OK. I want to go to Zymurgy."

Whatever the too much-much was, I found myself leaning my wrist against my pocket in sudden wallet-possessiveness. While Emil used to be able to appease his dealer by throwing occasional parties for him (not *billed* as parties for a coke dealer, of course), the guy probably wanted to be paid in bills now that Emil wasn't able to offer him fame anymore. I couldn't imagine how Emil was coming up with the money, though I must say his place looked pretty bare bones. He must have been paying the guy off in furniture.

"Are you sure you don't want to see a doctor or something?" I asked him. "We don't have to go to Zymurgy." I wanted to go to Zymurgy more than life itself. Being seen with this, though, was not exactly going to up my social standing.

"I'm fine," he said, changing into new clothes so slowly I wanted to either fast forward or stop. At any moment you looked at him, he looked like he was in freeze frame. What could I do with this guy? An emergency room could take six or seven hours. A detox center could take six or seven years. And Spartacus was going on in half an hour.

"There—all ready to go," he said, putting on his second shoe, which didn't match but at least fit. I could have pried for more information and maybe pushed him to some other form of action, but I'm not a persuasive enough person to change someone's entire life. Just wiping up the puke was a major effort for someone who could barely make his own bed.

As someone pathologically obsessed with the best cosmetic result with the least effort, my way of dealing with a zit is to cover it up with foundation or a Band-Aid. If I could, I'd just have thrown Emil into bed and tossed some blankets on him, but there he was, almost standing, and even spraying Paco Rabanne all over himself with the indiscretion of someone who needed to be forced out of his house and into a club. Though my darker instincts said, Leave him behind, my Catholic conscience knew that getting him to Zymurgy would be the honorable thing to do.

"Easy with that Rabanne," I warned, "or no one will go near you all night."

"I think I'm losing my mind," he said.

"Not a great loss," I said, and we were off. I didn't pause to ask about the printer information that I'd come there for in the first place. It might have seemed cold-hearted, and besides, any delay in my having to address the life-threatening pressure of the next issue was very welcome.

On the way out, we dropped the key off at Mr. Minadeo's, for the hell of it. As I knocked on his door I figured
the *Three's Company* episode was ending, because he was applauding like a maniac and cheering as if he'd just seen a
live presentation of a fine dramatic play. Maybe it was a
tape of a super applauding that he played at the end of every
show. I banged and screamed, "Hello, it's me. I want to
return the key to you," and he screamed back, "Hold your
horses. Let me see the end of my show." He actually sat
there and waited until the very last credit rolled off the
screen, and when it finally went to commercial, he opened
the door.

"Yeah?" he said, seeming to have no recollection of who
I was.

"Here you go," I said, holding out the key, and he simply took it and banged the door shut. No "Is everything all
right?" or any other silly little formality like that troubled
his oral cavity. For all he knew, I was a terrorist-burglar
who had cleaned out Emil's apartment and was now taking
him hostage. It was nice to be trusted.

Zymurgy was really primo that night, due to a bizarre mixture of circumstances that had to do mostly with morbid
interest in Spartacus's debut. People of all sorts had come
out in their finest spirit in order to mock this priceless occasion—every type from debs to dregs, with each step of the
social (and cash) register represented in between. Some people were cracking smiles, and a few actually seemed to be
dancing for fun, without any neurotic motivation to impress. I even heard a few American accents in the air, the
most shocking turn of events since Zymurgy printed up its
first comp invitation.

Some girl in a diaphanous pink bodysuit had broken
down her defenses to the point where she was pulling the
dollar bills, one by one, out of the display coffin, the first

Zymurgette ever to be so bold. When she noticed that a crowd of fifty had gathered to watch her, she self-consciously stopped, only to receive a wild round of applause for her nerve. Honored, she was inspired to pull twenty or so more bills out of the coffin and toss them our way. Generosity at Zymurgy? What was going on? I managed to grab seven bucks as a satire on the greed of our capitalist society—plus I needed the dough.

Since we all knew this fun stuff was a fluke that wouldn't revive the place for more than those few hours, we enjoyed it a hundred times more tenaciously. Delroy said he was savoring every minute of it as if we were all stranded on a tropical island with one can of tuna—tuna never tasted so good. It was just one of those things—a combustible night where the novelty of the event or some stupid configuration of the stars not only brought everyone out, but brought them out in style. Even Mary-Ellen was kind of carefree, throwing everyone knowing grins as she tossed her hair back and forth and dirty-danced with herself. What did she want?

Doric and Randi had come separately (Doric with Mary-Ellen, and Randi with a group of giddy career girls—the first nonclubbies I'd seen here in ages. God—fresh faces!) and actually said hello to each other. Delroy, meanwhile, was even bushier-tailed than usual, trying to repress a smirk as he told us how Dennis Carbonell, the old boss who had ditched him, just had a stroke. This had to be the first time Delroy didn't have a breakdown over someone who was sick, though I bet the guy would end up visiting Carbonell with flowers and a photo montage anyway.

Starla and Tracy hadn't arrived yet—no matter how late I was, I couldn't ever outlate her entrance. Garth was home sick, and Dovima, Mimsy, and Daisy were elsewhere, boycotting the perverse rise of Spartacus the Dork. But there were some other stars to ponder while waiting, like Terence Floss, the blond, hulking British movie rebel who hated being out in public but went out every night anyway (always

to spots frequented by photographers, even though he considered them "lower than Hitler"), and Angela Burdine,
the latest in a long line of "new Sandra Dees"—a breed
outnumbered only by the new Marilyns and the new Mar-
lon Brandos (of which Terence Floss was originally touted
as one, before becoming famous enough to spawn a breed
of new Terence Flosses). Angela had the doe eyes, baby
voice, and minimal talent to fit the mold. *Them* magazine
had already put her on the "What's Not" list in their
"What's Hot, What's Not" issue, which was *Them*'s way of
saying: "We've exploited you to death on our covers, and
now that we've overexposed you, you're not selling magazines anymore, so we'll declare you over"—but she was still
the hottest thing we'd seen in a long time. Just to get to the
"What's Not" level at nineteen was a major feat.

Not until later did I realize that Terence wasn't her
date, but a third wheel; she was really with stringy-haired
spandex-worshipper Lance Marano, a supernasty music
rebel and the lead singer of the extraordinarily annoying but
internationally known metal group, Hemlock Headlock. Two
stars together were four times as exciting as just one of them
alone. *Three* supernasty rebels made for a staggering amount
of glittering antiglitter and glamorous antiglamour. Face
it—we weren't going to get Jessica Lange and Cybill Shep-
herd in here, so we had to settle for leather-clad antiheroes.
Fortunately, they were the best and brightest of the leather-
clad antiheroes, antimatter that mattered. Shit, they were
famous—the most famous people Zymurgy had ever had.
(Except for Margo Fain, whom they absurdly turned away
one night when Vlad was out of town and no one knew what
they were doing. Garth later ran into her at a horse show in
the Hamptons and begged her to come back, whereupon
she belted him in the face.) Sure, they were roped off within
a roped-off section—the first time Zymurgy had ever set up
a VIP room, let alone a VI-VIP room—but they were there
as plain as waxworks.

Delroy had the field all to himself, since the club had no idea these three were coming and so hadn't notified any photogs. Spartacus had probably never heard of them anyway. But by being everywhere at all times, Delroy had lucked out and gotten the chance to an exclusive shot, which I was sure could land him a credit in some supermarket rags that paid. *Them* could probably use it in a few weeks when Angela would be "What's Hot" again.

Spartacus looked as polished and preening as a dog-show contestant, his skin more tanned (from expense-account jaunts to Rio) than fine Corinthian leather, his hair displaying all the versatility of Tahnee Welch. Hovering by the impromptu stage as his band arrived in dribs and drabs and assembled their instruments, he looked nervous enough to shit a brick, but so excited he couldn't wait to do it in public. "It's gonna rock the house," he said, believing his own hype. "My life will never be the same after tonight." Probably true. He carried on about how he'd been rehearsing this act for two whole weeks, and how the club had even rented a sound system for the event. I wondered, just for a laugh, how many AIDS drugs the sound system was equivalent to.

"How's Garth?" I said, to work his nerves.

"Oh, Garth?" he said.

"Yeah, you know—the owner of this place," I smirked.

"The guy's sliding, man. It's real sad. Wait till you hear my opening number—'Born to Run.' "

"I see you're real broken up about it," I said.

"No—it's phenomenal, totally awesome. Wait till you hear it."

"Forget it," I said, irritated. I turned around and saw that Starla and Tracy had arrived. They were in identical black, two-shoulder-converted-into-one-shoulder dresses like Bette Davis's famous one—God, they were even dressing alike now, and out of drag-queen closets. Starla waved hello at me with a broad smile that suggested maybe tonight I'd be more than a don't-blink-or-you'll-miss-it "Hi. How are you?". I blew her a kiss, and for symmetry's sake blew another one to Tracy, who didn't respond, either because she didn't see me, didn't remember me, or thought I was overstepping my boundaries by presuming to be on a blow-kissy basis with one of the world's top ten or twelve debs. It wasn't until Starla pointed at me and whispered something in her ear that Tracy half-heartedly nodded and smiled a hello with all the spontaneity of a Pee-Wee Herman doll. If Starla had told her to spin on her head and whistle "Dixie" while doing obscene things with a baseball bat, she would willingly have obliged.

Tracy should get together with Spartacus, I thought, playing the matchmaker game that always overtook me whenever I was standing idly as everyone else talked to one another with that impenetrable *entre-nous* look in their eyes. All people who deserved one another should get together and deserve one another at closer range. Maybe even Doric and Randi should reunite and rent some war orphan to be their baby—they could toilet train it on a canvas and sell the art piece for five figures. And while we were at it, if only Delroy could get over his revulsion for Mary-Ellen, *they* could settle down together, as Mary-Ellen had often dreamed. He could cater to her personality ills by medicating her with hourly photo ops. And if she were ever hospitalized for these imbalances, Delroy would be the perfect compulsive visitor—one more bedpan to pay hommage to. Pre-op, Mary-Ellen definitely needed help.

Emil had plopped down woozily at one of the lesser tables after trying unsuccessfully to strike up a conversation with Spartacus. As he weaved in his seat a little, rubbing his eyes and trying to become conscious, I brought him three glasses of water to do with as he liked. He drank them and seemed to feel better, if just from the psychosomatic influence of the liquid. "Water cures everything," my father always said, and I never reminded him that if that were true there'd be no need for his profession at all. Besides, certain accredited people were building a much stronger case for urine therapy lately. Maybe I should pee on Emil.

"Angela Burdine is here," I said to him with the barest hint of a nyah-nyah, "I saw her first," intonation.

"And Lance Marano and Terence Floss," he interrupted. No amount of delirium could interfere with this guy's celebrity-spotting acumen.

"But no Harvey Keitel," I said, giving the bratty tone full rein. "We're still waiting." I'd learned to say just the thing that could drive everyone crazy—not a long drive in most cases.

Nobody was going to come up to me as long as I was attached to Emil, so I had to start mobilizing like a demon to work the room—it was charley-horse time. I stopped at Randi's table and said hello to prove I hadn't been friends with her just because she was an extension of Doric. (Though why *had* I been friends with her? Anyone who spells Randi with an *i* has to be suspect.) Randi looked pretty but vanilla-plain, as if she'd give anything not to be noticed. She had bare, Ingrid Bergmanesque makeup on, and her hair was close-cropped like some kind of Christian martyr's. Randi of Arc.

"It took a lot to get me to come here," she said. "It's my first time out since before the, you know. We all went out drinking and ended up here like iron filings."

She introduced me to "everyone" at the table—thank God she didn't go into individual names, since those always go right out the window anyway—and said, "Can you believe Angela Burdine is here?"

"And Lance Marano and Terence Floss," I grinned.

"But no Heinz," she laughed. We might as well stop actually going to parties and just discuss the guest list the next day.

I wended my way over to Doric and made very sure to spend equal time with him—no favorite-playing here. He was talking to some important-looking art world people, and this time I hoped for the individual name bit, but he did the "Vinnie, meet everyone" routine. I could always get the names later.

Doric exuded a special glow lately. The bitterness he supposedly seethed with when he wrote a column had been excised out of him by success. Now a mass media phenomenon in the making (though an art industry joke), he exuded pride and security—in everything except Randi.

The bastard had made it uptown, even though he didn't have any particular looks or talent that made him stand out from the pack. Maybe it was *because* he didn't have any particular looks or talent, and also that he pillaged other people's ideas, so they were already vaguely familiar, and therefore less threatening, to his weak-stomached patrons. No one of money and stature wants to be disrupted by some upstart with an intimidating gift that doesn't cater to their need to preserve the status quo. They'd rather be cajoled gently into a fake sense of danger, wooed by complacent plagiarism posing as avant-garde (and it helped that he had that Robo-wife for a while too). Doric's pseudo angst, trapped on a canvas, was as far as the uptown folk would go in the world of ugliness. It made them feel hip and daring while not really saying anything that would upset their glass-enclosed world. *My* creative ugliness, on the other hand, had disturbing qualities. I was going to have to keep toning down to move up.

"You talked to Randi. What did she say?" He pumped me, right off.

"Nothing," I said. " 'Hi, how are you?'—deep stuff like that."

"But what did she say about me?"

"It may shock you to hear this, Doric, but she didn't even mention your name once. There *are* other things on her mind. And other people on her face."

"You don't have to lie to protect me," he said. "Even if she said something horrible, you can tell me."

"What she said was the most horrible thing of all—nada." It got on my nerves that Doric had dumped Randi and now seemed to be waiting for *her* to apologize. You don't shoot a dog in the leg and then expect it to send you a Hallmark card. I didn't want to talk to Doric anymore. I'd given him his equal time, and Starla was looming so-near-and-yet-so-far, like the Emerald City itself. This time, instead of yellow bricks, there were dozens of fashiony, *moi-moi-moi* Europeans in the way. I excused myself from Doric in midreality therapy and pushed over them like a steamroller with that clubby smile that says, "Welcome to America. I'm not bruising you for life; I'm just trying to get by." As I got within reaching distance of Starla, she extended her arm and yanked me into her sphere. "Angela Burdine is here, Mr. Vinnie," she exclaimed. So it was Mr. Vinnie again. It took me back to our first big night together, the night my boner turned to cold noodles. "Angela Burdine!" she repeated. To Starla, and anyone else with a brain, Angela was an even bigger star than Tracy Neuwirth. She actually did something besides suck in her cheekbones and throw back her hair. Angela sucked in her cheekbones, threw back her hair, and talked at the same time.

"And Lance Marano and Terence Floss," I added, involuntarily by now.

Fortunately, there are no uneasy silences in clubs—there's a constant, reliable din to drown any potential one out. But if we hadn't been in the club, the silent rift between Starla and me would have been deafening. I was touched that she wanted to talk to me. It was just sad that we couldn't think of anything to say. So we stood there and grimaced, while pretending to bop a little to Valerie Rapchuck's mix of seven Rick Astley songs, all of which were perfect for mixing with each other because they all sounded exactly alike. Valerie was doing it as a joke, but I was too busy grimacing to laugh. Tracy thought it was "mind-blowing" and was hiking up her dress and dancing like Zorba the Greek on steroids.

With great melancholy, the thought crossed my mind that Starla had been the high point of my life, but (except for the nuns) I was probably the low point of hers. I could see by the vacancy sign in her eyes that Delroy was right: I was a diversion on the way up that she might just want to drop now that her elevator had reached the penthouse. I wanted desperately for her to need me again, for anything—for a cheap thrill, for a meaningless pat on the back, for the seven bucks I'd just clawed. Deep down, I knew she never would, but I didn't have to face that just yet. Though it contradicted all the information in front of me, it wasn't hard to still pretend that she loved me as devotedly as I worshipped her—the great thing about a crush is that it lets you fantasize that the object of your desires is secretly returning your obsession with full reciprocity, "secretly" being the operative word.

I needed an excuse to see Starla again in less distracting circumstances. At one point in the mix, my mind snapped hard enough from Rick Ghastly torment for me to come up with a brainstorm. "Are you going to the benefit for I forget what disease at the Waldorf next week?" I asked Starla. "It's going to be pretty gala. Rachel Chaparal's a probable-show."

She looked interested. "No," she said. "I hear it's going to be star-studded. Tracy was going to take me, but she has to go away on a holiday." Victory.

"I'll take you," I beamed, pausing for effect. "I've got press tickets." Astley was starting to sound damned good.

"You do? You will? Oh, baby. Date," she said, offering me a firm handshake.

"Date," I said, shaking her hand so hard it almost fell off.

My big challenge now was getting tickets for this event. There *weren't* any press seats for it, but if I scraped that Favio money together, I could probably buy a pair, and Starla would never have to know any better. This was the first time in ages where I could be *her* entrée into something where the silverware would be properly placed. It would be worth every blood-stained penny.

A waitress brought Doric three vodka rocks and I saw him down them with more reckless abandon than Paul Newman swallowing raw eggs in *Cool Hand Luke*. Soon he'd be teaching maudlin show tunes to some hot new piece of trade. He and Randi had started the evening off so well, it's a shame they both had to resort to game playing, but I wasn't exactly going to matchmake for real when I had my own problems to iron out and dry-clean; that was just a mental game.

"Date," I said one more time, but Starla had moved over to the star corner, where she and Tracy were introducing themselves to Angela and Lance through ropes—narrow pieces of velvet that separated them from true celebrity. Starla tried to say hello to Terence, but he was just involuntarily grimacing while meticulously avoiding eye contact. I knew from all his press that the way to *his* heart was not to be overly friendly. It was to be as arrogant and full of yourself as he was. If you could convince him that you were an asshole of equal proportions, then he could respect you. Maybe by the end of the night, I could do something truly asinine that would make him my best friend for life.

"Are you all right?" I screamed over at Emil.

"Is Farrah Fawcett a good actress?" he said. That was a strange answer, but knowing Emil, I took it as a yes. He *looked* all right. His eyes were back in their sockets, and they were gazing fondly at the celebrity corner, a dose of fabulousness that was just the medicine Emil needed to come to. He didn't even seem bothered that no one was talking to him, not even to borrow a cigarette. As long as he had a ringside view of three famous people—any three famous people—he was the picture of health.

Finally, after introducing himself—"Thank you for coming to see my worldwide debut, ladies and dobermans. And now the first performance of many fucking international performances of the rock and roll sounds of . . . Spartacus"—Spartacus took to the stage with his eponymous band of marauders, hired hands who all wore shades and floppy hats, presumably so as not to be recognized, and who looked like their new religion was the assurance that this would be a one-shot disgrace. No one would ask for it again.

I hit a glance over at Terence, who looked on the threshold of nausea; he hadn't come to see this, and especially resented being thanked for it. Angela was intently communing with Lance and their drinks—kier royales, can you believe how hideous—as if nothing without a glass stem was happening at all, and Starla and Tracy were maintaining a safe distance from the herpes-ridden stage while keeping billboardlike, encouraging smiles plastered on their faces in their perennial roles as cheerleaders-in-spite-of-themselves. Delroy was right up there, stroking Spartacus's ego with a barrage of photo flashes someone would be bound to publish, even if just to trash the audacity of it all.

His opening song was, sure enough, "Born To Run," and it was done with the raspy, off-key eagerness of someone who'd spent his whole life lip-synching that song in front of a mirror and waiting for the moment when the star's car would run out of gas on some country road. In their Margo Channing dresses, Starla and Tracy should have been saying some bitchy line from *All About Eve,* but I'm sure the only Bette Davis movie they'd ever seen was *Jezebel.*

The song droned on—it must have been the twelve-inch version—and as Spartacus sweated and emoted with more and more desperation, the crowd's embarrassment level escalated and they started chattering loudly, increasingly treating the act as if it were a gnat in a faraway room. By the last chorus, the only one watching was Terence, maybe because Spartacus had made such an ass of himself that he had a whole new admiration for the guy. I said maybe. You couldn't tell by looking at Terence if he was enthralled or appalled—that's what a fine actor he is.

The song would have ended without anyone noticing, but Spartacus had a too-smart gimmick up his sleeve—canned applause that roared deafeningly through the club and forced everyone to attention. (Had he perchance gone cassette shopping with Emil's super?) It was a pretty brilliant ploy, giving Spartacus the reception he hoped for and wasn't going to take any chances on getting. Unfortunately, it backfired like shit hitting the world's biggest fan. When the applause is already taken care of, the live audience doesn't feel like it has to engage in it too. In the midst of this surrogate response, they stood there dumbstruck. Hell, they probably would have anyway.

"Thanks, guys, really appreciate it. You're blowin' my mind!" said Spartacus, as if this were Wembley and the applause for real. "I want to introduce the band now for you all." Introduce the band after the very first song? Another magnificent stroke. Maybe he sensed that the gig was coming to an early end and anything he did from here on was encore time. More likely, he wanted to get the intros out of the way and get back to his own ritualized self-glorification. In any case, the band members suddenly developed terrible posture, as if they had some spine-curving calcium deficiency, and hunched over obscenely as he called out their names. I crouched down to catch their grimacing faces—worth it.

They did get some feeble applause—this wasn't *their* fault—and quickly enough, Spartacus segged into a whiny-coyote version of "Stairway to Heaven," on which he slipped at one point and sang, "stair*case* to heaven." What next—"Honky Tonk Wom*en*" done with kazoos? Or maybe we could all hold up—or throw—our lighters while he sang

"Imagine" in pig latin. The funny thing is, no one bolted for the door. It was going to be one of those classic nights we could recount endlessly for cheap laughs. This kind of event is always much more amusing later, so you force yourself to endure it as it's happening, knowing the throb in your head will eventually pay off.

The only one who finally started to leave was Terence, who I guess wasn't that impressed after all. You could see the desperation in Spartacus's eyes as Terence walked toward the exit. Even though this guy was news to him, he'd seen the fuss everyone made over him all night and knew he must be Someone. As Terence got closer to the door Spartacus started singing faster and louder and whinier and more desperately until each word was shot out like a bullet through the skull. People were clutching their ears and pacing around in circles, as if compulsive movement alone would ease the pain. Delroy was running after Terence, anxious to get the photo he'd been too nice to snap all night. Oh, well—Terence Floss clutching his ears was not going to be a very hot photo anyway.

Spartacus was singing faster and louder, louder and faster, sweating watermelons. People were trying to make the ear-clutching look casual, like they all just happened to be cleaning out ear wax at once, but the nonchalant air was impossible to maintain. Things were getting to the point that if lethal weapons could be found, there would definitely have been a mass suicide in the next day's headlines. To distract from the pain, all eyes were turned toward Delroy and Terence, who by now had really snapped into cuckoo-ville. This was Terence's chance to prove he was an Actor, not just a silly little celebrity. They didn't write good rebel roles anymore, but in a nightclub at three in the morning, he could do a triple bill of *The Wild One, Rebel Without a Cause,* and *I Was a Fugitive from a Chain Gang* for a captive audience.

"I said no!" he screamed. "No, no, no!" As Spartacus kept singing, looking like an alarmed rabbit, Terence seized

Delroy's camera and flung it to the floor, where it smashed into hundreds of unsightly shards that added yet one more incongruous level to the decor. Terence stormed out the door just as Spartacus revved into his biggest finish yet—only the applause tape wasn't cued up properly this time, and there was dead silence in the room. The last time I'd heard silence here it was right before Starla's entrance at my party. As movie star exit music, it was much more terrifying.

Everyone stared at the shards in a hushed reverie of panic and confusion. Delroy was crying silently, the kind where your face moves but nothing comes out. I ran over and put my arm around him, not able to think of anything comforting to say. "I like your tie," I finally said, feebly. The club hadn't been so depressing since the "Did you hear about Garth?" night. Finally, one person—Tracy—broke out into uncontrollable laughter, and in no time the whole room was rolling with the reckless exhilaration and relief of guffaws that were clearing the air of tension like Wizard never could. Doric was laughing as he drunkenly escorted a Brazilian-looking boy, sure enough, out the door, making certain to inform everyone that they were going off on "an art mission." ("Play safe," I said vainly; ever since Doric had tested negative and started drinking, he'd deemed himself invulnerable.) Randi and her friends were laughing too, and it looked like she didn't care about anything anymore, only the anxious pursuit of a good time. Even Delroy started laugh-crying, then just outright laughing—it was quite an honor to have your camera destroyed by Terence Floss, after all. Spartacus didn't get to do another song. But the applause tape finally came on—thunderous.

I was starting to measure my life in terms of Momentous Phone Calls, and the next week I remember only as the one in which Vivien called, getting annoyed as I slammed the answering machine off during her speech and announced, "I'm here." The shrieking tone that rings out of the machine as you do this is enough to swear anyone off modern technology.

"Why do you screen calls?" she said, irritably. "That's so degrading."

"But I picked up for you," I said. "It's only really degrading for the people I don't pick up for. And they don't know I'm here not picking up, so they're not terribly degraded either. All in all, I find this an ethical and expedient process that hurts no one."

"Yeah, but now that I know you screen, it makes me wonder how many times I've left messages for you and you've been sitting right there, listening to every word and saying, 'No, she's not worth it.' "

"You've never left messages for me," I said.

"Yeah, but if I had . . ."

"Would you feel degraded?"

"A little," she said, lightening up her voice.

"Violated? Abused? Raped to the very core?"

"Yes," she exclaimed, vocally smiling harder. "Police—help! I've got a rapist on the line!"

"But it's all on the level. I have a license to violate souls: my magazine. That's what allows me—no, forces me—to run like the dickens from the human voice. If *you* had some of the loonies calling you that pester me night and day with their incessant psychobabble, you'd not only screen calls, you'd move into a high-security institution."

"Or Colette Joie's house," she laughed.

"This *is* Colette Joie's house," I joked. "This is Herve speaking. Who may I say is calling?"

"Never mind, I must have the wrong number—click," she giggled.

This was fun—the electric charge of my upcoming date with Starla was helping me enjoy Vivien more. And in more frivolous moments like these, she seemed less of a crusade and more of a flesh-and-blood organism. I knew AIDS was behind every joke—she was laughing only as a defense against her tension, the way I tittered nervously all the way through *Sorry Wrong Number.* But it was fun, anyway—a laugh is a laugh.

She wanted to take me to dinner at a fabulous new restaurant she claimed no one had heard about yet because—unlike everyone else in the world—they didn't want any press; it was all based on buzz so far. This sounded excitingly underexposed—the hyped places are flogged into a certain dazzle by necessity, but the ones that erupt spontaneously into fabulousness are the much more natural gemstones. Still, it was strange, and seemed to be the workings of the old Cha Cha, not the new, improved Vivien. Maybe she was regressing back to her glamour days as a result of the press injections she'd gotten lately. Press is like Lay's potato chips—betcha can't eat just one.

She said we had to go Thursday night at eight on the

dot—if you didn't show up on time, they gave your reservation to someone on a waiting list the length of the NYNEX Yellow Pages—which fit into my calendar just fine. The charity ball with Starla was Tuesday. Wednesday would be recuperation time. And Thursday would be my charity ball with Vivien. I swallowed my masculine pride and agreed to let her take me; the Waldorf tickets had erased pride, and money, from my being. Plus, I knew Vivien could afford it, being on a very generous trust fund that had allowed her to be a party girl back then and now a one-woman Geraldo Rivera Show. A trust fund is like marrying into money and not having to have sex with the person. My old school buddy Danilo Robespierre-Hague had always likened horrible things (like having to take incompletes) to being fucked without getting kissed, but trust funds are like being kissed without having to get fucked.

On Tuesday I picked up Starla at her new uptown digs, and the sumptuous lobby alone was intimidation enough to make me feel like a total schlep. The hideous but expensive fountain—made out of guilt, not gilt like the one at the Majestic Terrace—spelled out the reality: she wasn't slumming anymore.

I never got past the lobby, because Starla had decided that her place was too messy for me to come up—"a dustbin," she said, "the entire *Grapes of Wrath* movie." I think this was an act of kindness; she didn't want to rub her new grandeur in my already slobbering face. Not exactly wanting her new grandeur rubbed in my already slobbering face either, I obediently waited in the lobby as she took a full ten minutes—the final touch-up is the most crucial—to wend her way from her vanity mirror to public view.

It was worth the wait, despite the doorman drilling holes into me with his disapproving stares. She looked more glossy magazine–ready than ever. Her warm, autumnal brown hair cascaded all around her like Victoria Falls. Her makeup was stunning yet tasteful—a perfect walking ad for her products. And it was a new dress—black (of course), but simple enough to be shockingly effective. Starla didn't need fashion anymore—the less distraction from her raw materials the better.

The doorman gaped, as if he were committing her to memory for future fantasy reference. Then he sized *me* up and down one last time as if to say, What have you done to deserve this? To rub in my privileged status even deeper, I gave Starla a big kiss and made a three-act play out of my gentlemanly escort style out the door. I'm hers and you're not, I announced with my every self-satisfied swagger. Of course I wasn't either, but he didn't need to know that.

We oozed into the sleek, white limo Sylvia had let us have for the night, and the first thing out of Starla's mouth was, "This is the same car I rode around in with Tracy last time. I miss my Tracy." So my reunion date was going to be about Tracy. We were going to reminisce about Tracy, analyze Tracy, savor Tracy's every eyelash bat. That would take two minutes—then what?

"I love you," I said, foolishly. I knew the minute it came out of my mouth that it was the stupidest thing anyone had ever said at any time—stupider than Gary Hart urging the press to track him—but it was too late to take it back. Halfway through the "love," I wanted to make a retraction, but I couldn't think of anything to amend it to. I love a parade?

She swallowed hard and laughed, then pulled herself together and said, "I love you too" in the most encouraging tone possible. I knew she didn't mean it like I did by the way she patted me on the head as if I were a schnauzer who'd just retrieved a bone. *My* bone would never be retrieved—it belonged to Melissa Kravitz and Starla Rogers and all the other women who hadn't treated it with the respect it deserved and had psychically rendered it invisible so I could never use it again. Give me my bone back! I wanted to scream.

I made myself a tonic on the rocks, then saw that we were already at the Waldorf, so my big entrance was made glamorously guzzling a drink and throwing the glass back into the car. Starla had been in the middle of asking me what was new, but we dropped that evergreen of boredom and concentrated on the four or five photographers standing outside, waiting for some arrivals to pay their rent. They had a field day with Starla—she was just at that point where her photo had more than underground value, and might even be lucky enough to get into the "What's Not Hot" list soon. I felt like an overdressed accordion grinder's monkey standing there in my tux, being charitably included in the photos, but the lightning bolts of photo flashes were just as electrically charged as ever. Someday I'd know what it feels like to be photographed not out of pity.

I didn't mind the interruption in our conversation; there *wasn't* anything new, except for this date. In fact, whenever anyone else had asked me what was happening that week, the best I could come up with was, "I'm going out with Starla." What could be more important than that?

As we swept past the Grand Ballroom check-in rigama-role I handed them the tickets at Concorde speed so Starla couldn't see that they weren't press. Taormina had often told me, "Actually paying for a charity event is the ultimate sign of 'B.' " And sure enough, there she was at a table of people I knew had somehow weaseled their way into comps—Sean Valve, Jonathan Formento, Vogel Johns, Dovima, Mimsy and Daisy (so now they were on the charity circuit), and a couple I didn't know, who reeked of freebie. So there *were* comps—there always would be as long as these people existed, and these people would always exist. There's a certain smugness about the freebie people—they feel everything is owed to them—but they're my kind of people.

"My skin is sagging," said Taormina, on greeting me. She was pulling on her bony arms and trying to prove that gravity had finally caught up with her. "Look—it is leaving fucking skidmarks on the ground." If this was going to be the peak of the repartee, I was ready to join the Theater of the Deaf.

"The old team again," said Taormina's friend, who never introduced herself.

"The old team again?" I said.

"You and Starla," she explained, as if it was so obvious. Had the meeting of our two remarkable minds become so famous that even total strangers were trolling it around for cheap gossip? Great! I loved having people masticate over my private affairs, even if they were more made-up than Starla's face. We were legends—watch out, Liz and Dick. Eat your hearts out, Maury Povich and Connie Chung.

By now I was able to scan a room for celebs as skillfully as I could find my own name in print. The ballroom was a mess of pouff dresses and *lamé* handbags, but I did manage to penetrate the blur with my celebrity fog-o-vision and find Colette and Herve, ever so bored-looking, three tables away with a bevy of equally stultifying high-society types; Drindl, the singer on the brink of a big break and a big breakdown, with a guy who looked like a Spanish olive and who turned out to be the record mogul that had discovered, groomed, and schtupped her for stardom; and Angela Burdine and Lance Marano (God, when they were in town, they really worked it to death), looking like a couple who'd fallen off a deformed wedding cake. There were also too many conspicuously rich generic people to count, but reeking of bad taste as they were, there was something inherently exciting about them; it was expensive bad taste.

Everything about these charity events screams tedium. Everyone's in the same obscenely high income bracket; everyone's ancient and rigor-mortized, with polyester hair and teeth from a jar; and worst of all, your hands start hurting from all the clapping required over the endless, obligatory announcements, announcements from hell after which Spartacus's applause tape would be a godsend. But contrary to all logic, it was worthwhile, and maybe even fun, even if I had to pay to get there. Everyone has to pay in some way or another.

And certain tensions inevitably build up to give the tedium a run for its money. Once he took off his tux jacket, it turned out Lance was wearing a metal mesh top and fishnet stocking pants that looked like Eric Stoltz's face in *Mask*—definitely causing tension. The Colette contingent hardly cared that he was a rock star or even knew that any form of music had evolved since the decline of Patti Page. They just wished his outfit wasn't air-conditioned.

The other big frisson was the one between the two factions at any event like this—the ones who care deeply about the charity, and the ones who care deeply about a glittering night out. The latter group always emerges victorious, but not until the former one puts you through a draining presentation in which you learn much more than you ever wanted to know about what is (or more often, isn't) being done to combat the disease *du jour*. Mostly you care about how long it will take for the entrée to arrive.

I suddenly felt very guilty: I should be doing something for AIDS or, more specifically, for Garth—but then AIDS didn't have an event that night with a celeb of Rachel Chaparal's stature. I'd heard she was going to come, but I had no idea she was the fixture on which the whole event revolved, the Hoover sucking all these rich broads into her glittering, bitch-goddess nozzle. Rachel's airbrushed-with-a-blow-torch face was plastered on the programs, her name was hanging from the stage in monumental, Lurex-on-cardboard letters, and everyone was anticipating her arrival with unsightly drool they were trying to cover up with a feigned nonchalance. No one made eye contact; they were all too busy subtly looking for Rachel (or anyone else more interesting—party people are always in the market for a better deal). Daytime TV's grande dame, Rachel, thirty-nine (just like Jack Benny), was the quintessence of pricey tack.

Everything on her was always terribly lavish and yet terribly cheap. But who cared whether she was beauty or the beast— she was a four-time *Weekly World News* cover girl.

When the slimy prosciutto and melon is served as a de-appetizer, it's time to make the rounds. The trick at these things, I've learned, is to break the ice with a remark that has nothing to do with anything—not to be existential, just to be calculatedly weird in the way popularized by certain pseudo avant-garde stars. Taormina had the right idea with her sagging skin observation, it turned out. Drindl knew the game too. "Everyone's dying," she said, by way of hello. "Everyone around me—dropping like little, tiny flies land-ing inopportunely on one of those big zapping machines. It helps my singing, though. It gives me that pathos without which I can't create a tapestry out of a song's strands." Giorgio Donofrio, the record mogul, was fingering Drindl's thigh through her dress, and it offended Starla that this mar-ried man was still passing off what was basically a paid whore as a mere protégée. Once a Catholic schoolgirl, always a Catholic schoolgirl. Someday Starla would meet the guy with the right combination of morality and immorality to make her happy.

We didn't even eye Colette's table out of our peripheral vision; it wasn't there at all as far as our new boundaries were concerned. But it was amazing how many of the other richies knew Starla and were responding to her favorably, making a thin-lipped fuss over her as she twirled and giggled with a newfound reserve. She'd gone from larger-than-life to just life-size, as if some director had advised her, "Do everything you're doing, only half as big." It made her un-realness less intimidating and brought her down to a level cloistered people could relate to while still being enthralled.

As she hobnobbed with these extravagant ones I found my level at the comp table, with Sean Valve telling me he was having a big cast party for the movie of *Island of Glossed Souls,* but he couldn't invite me, and Vogel Johns informing me that next month *Limo* was going to start coming out twice as often. (Funny, *Manhattan on the Rocks* was coming out one one-hundredth as often as it used to. It was becoming as rare as the disease we were celebrating.) Jonathan Formento said something about how it felt like Miller time—pretty good on the calculatedly weird scale. Mimsy was whining about her nails and her complexion and her health club ("Working up a sweat gives me nothing but goddamned pustules.") and her overdrawn charge cards, and Dovima and Daisy didn't have anything to say—the most oblique remark of all.

Starla and I connected again, and everyone stood up and started applauding—it wasn't that big a deal. Oh, they were clapping for Rachel Chaparal's entrance, a grand one worthy of a special Emmy, or at the very least, a certificate from K mart. Followed by an all-male entourage of nine—clearly these guys would follow her anywhere—she swept in wearing a floral print pantsuit and matching turban that made her look like a human funeral home wreath. The shoulders were wide enough to stop up a dam; the feet clumped forward in the studious configuration actors are trained in, but as if done by a Mack truck. She was smiling broadly and clearly considered the whole room her personal runway, as she strutted, sashayed, and bulldozed her way toward the table, her entourage trailing her in single file as if they were carrying an imaginary forty-foot train. They'd probably carried hundreds more feet than that; Rachel had been married seven times.

"Everyone here is dressed like me," I saw her say. She liked that. Of the nine males, there were three young, attractive ones who looked like they could be potential hubby number eight. I couldn't believe I was just a few tables away from Rachel Chaparal and the future Mr. Chaparal; at least as I got more bored, jaded, annoyed, and fed up, the parties were getting better. This was one my mama would approve of. If I could snatch a piece of that turban, or just catch a waft of her scent—a frothy little perfume that could stun a moose—in a napkin, Mom would forgive me all my past sins and maybe even stop with the allergy pill routine.

Possessed by some kind of insane chutzpah, I strolled over to Rachel's table, though I didn't do it with quite the same flair as she had, and no one followed (not even Starla, who now had her own rules of working the room, and they no longer included me).

"Miss Chaparal," I said, interrupting the very grand monologue she was delivering to one of her three suitors.

"Yes," she said, looking as if she smelled something bad, maybe her own perfume.

"My name in Vincent DiBlasio, and I publish my own magazine. . . ." Pause. No recognition. Not even a fake "How wonderful." "And I just wanted you to know that I've loved you on *The Merriweathers* for years"—wrong thing to say—"and I think you're one of the few true Movie Stars left. Even though you're on TV, you exude the glamour and aura of a classic Hollywood movie star"—right thing to say—"and my mother loves you, too"—wrong thing to say—"but then so does practically everyone I know or talk to"—flawless thing to say—"because you're so wonderful." On the whole, I deserved a ten for lip-synch, ten for appearance, and zero for originality.

She paused for an eternity, cracked a Freddy Kruegerish smile, and said one word: "Yes."

But this wasn't a yes or no question. It wasn't a question at all. What did she mean? Yes, she is a fabulous star? Yes, she knows I worship her? Yes, my name is Vincent? Who cared? Rachel Chaparal talked to me. I floated off in a perfumey haze.

A while later I watched Angela and Lance waft over to Rachel—stars find each other like plankton—and after they all exchanged silly talk for a minute, Rachel started sizing Lance up and down as if he was potential husband material. She wasn't exactly undressing him with her eyes—he was already practically naked—she was sort of screwing him with her forehead, a variant on the "back me" facial language game I'd played that time with Colette. Angela quickly grabbed him by the elbow and dragged him away like she'd just shot a deer.

The paying homage process went on and on, as pouff-dressed ladies lined up to talk to Rachel and find out what new lesbian-incest-abortion drama was next—on the show, if not in her life. She was relentlessly pleasant, fulfilling her duties like a consummate professional; stars get paid lots of money to show up and care about these charities. This was just another acting job to her, and far less draining than having to act opposite Andrew Dane, her costar who, she'd told the tabloids, "had the personality of a placenta."

Starla was the next victim, and she went up to Rachel with such exuberance, Rachel acted as if she knew her. Or maybe Rachel did know her—after all, they were both starting to appear in the same trashy magazines, even if Starla was just front-of-the-book. They chirped and chatted, and all I could glean was that Rachel loved Starla's dress, and Starla couldn't wait for Rachel's upcoming-in-two-years nighttime special—she always did the little extra research that separates the pros from the pretenders. They talked endlessly and exchanged numbers—Rachel could become the new Tracy Neuwirth if Tracy (and Rachel) didn't watch out.

Back at our table, Starla and I had our first talk of the evening. "She's such a doll," she gushed.

"You two were certainly hitting it off. Are you going to become lovers?"

"Yeah, maybe after she marries everyone at that table she'll get around to me," she laughed.

"God, you were carrying on like best girlfriends. Was that the high point of your life so far?"

"Everything's the high point," she said, seriously. "Every moment is the high point because it's better than the one before it. Right now, this entrée is the high point.''

Everyone had started digging into the lamb dish that looked like a blood clot, and though Starla was only playing with it—rearranging it on her plate as if doing a beauty makeover—it was still terribly, terribly the high point. I got very depressed thinking about how Starla had segged so beautifully into this new milieu, and I was an outie every inch of the way, pond scum from Queens who belonged at bowling alleys and pizzerias and the Majestic Terrace, not the Waldorf. She'd joined the ranks of the people who can just be, without budging. I took it out on the lamb.

Rachel was escorted to the stage wings with her entire entourage, and as coffee was served we were treated to the scintillating dessert of boring people telling us boring things about this annoying disease. I would have preferred a crème brulée.

Someone told us a statistic that was better than last year's statistic, and we clapped. Someone else informed us of some promising new technology that might help victims of the disease in two centuries, and we clapped again. Our palms rosy red and aching, we now suffered from hand disease, and there was no cure for that either. We summoned one more round of applause to bring on Rachel and friends, who crowded the podium like people do on awards shows when some collaborative effort wins. She was like a traveling *St. Elsewhere*. Wouldn't it be great, I thought, to be so famous that you go everywhere, even onstage, with a plus-nine? They must be fun in the bathroom.

"Thank you." Rachel addressed the frothing crowd. "As you know, we are here for one reason and one reason alone—to combat lupus. Lupus is a dread disease, a chronic inflammatory disorder that takes its toll on the young and creatively vibrant—on the future of America." I'd never heard of a disease not referred to as "dread." And why is it always the young and creatively vibrant who are the only ones mourned? What about the old folks and the creatively bereft—the losers, assholes, and sociopaths, all of whom have just as much right to live?

As she carried on ("We in television land do care. I, Rachel Chaparal"—pause for effect—"care.") I sauntered near her table to survey what she had left behind. No one saw me; all eyes were on Rachel's hypnotic turban. And so I effortlessly slipped her monogrammed gold cigarette box into my pocket, the easiest haul I'd ever gotten in my life.

Rachel wound up her speech to the last slurps of caffeine, and everyone raced to the coat checkroom, where you got not only your coat but also a gift bag of scented kitchen magnets. It was raining outside, for only the ninth day in a row. Maybe that crackpot article I'd read recently was true, the one that said there was either no ozone left in the atmosphere, or too much of it, I forget which, so moisture can come pouring down without any interference. They predicted that it would rain at least once a day from now on and that we could all end up blowing water bubbles if they didn't start doing something about it, like building geodesic domes over cities or something. All the things they'd warned everyone about in the sixties were coming true—our indulgent life-style was robbing the air and the water of essentials, replacing them with waste and chemicals that really *were* wrecking not only our future but our present. And the constant rain wasn't going to wash any of it away, but just make us sopping wet on top of it. It wasn't nice to fool with Mother Nature, and now she was getting her revenge in a major way, via one environmental lightning bolt after another.

Chalking that ozone theory up as alarmist, I still started carrying an umbrella with me at all times. Polly Purebred's Hefty, accessorized with Diane Plewge's bubble glasses, was striking me more and more as the only sartorial answer. In the meantime, I would stop reading newspapers again.

I pretended not to see the car, just to give myself a few

more seconds to catch the departures. It was worth it—exits are the most fascinating rite of all because, on the thin line between social high behavior and reality-return, people are at their most vulnerable.

Mimsy was screeching about how her stockings were running and her nose was running and her nails were running, and there were no cabs so they'd all have to start running. Taormina was more bombed than Hiroshima and landed right splat in a puddle in the gutter, picking things out of the swamp and offering incisive commentary: "Seaweed!" she exclaimed, holding up what looked like a used tampon.

Drindl and Giorgio came out, and by now his hand was well inside her dress, fingering her labia in concentric circles—a real class act. She looked disgusted, but not so disgusted she wouldn't stand there and take it, bullets on *Billboard* charts no doubt racing through her head like sugarplums. As they hopped into their car she called out, "It's the rains of Ranchipur—the end of the world as we know it." The pathos never ends.

Black-clad Sean and Jonathan oozed out and very coolly didn't say a word, just walked cryptically around the block as if they were going somewhere exclusive that didn't even require transportation. They always had somewhere to go that nobody else knew about, or maybe just always walked cryptically around the block to make it look that way. Colette and Herve staggered out, talking about how they felt more bonded than ever now that they'd had an evening to catch up with one another's press—so it's an uptown disease too. They'd noticed me all evening, but suddenly looked me over as if they'd just made their first sighting.

"Keep away from my mother," Herve said, ominously. "You will be very sorry if you don't. I'll have you taken care of in no time." If he was going to deal in hackneyisms, I wished he'd go all the way: "You'll never work in this town again," or at least, "I'll have you destroyed with one phone call."

"Ooh," said Taormina, picking herself out of the gutter, "a fight. This is good." But they were gone, leaving everyone gasping as Starla looked confused.

"A long story," I told her. "Emil . . . well, never mind."

"*Chéri*, what happened?" she persisted. "I know Colette hates us, but—"

"Look," I explained, "every time Colette sees me, someone's throwing themselves on her and biting her ankles for some reason or other. So when I'm around, she gets that Pavlovian response and bolts—she doesn't want to be jumped."

"But you didn't do anything . . ."

"No. I've never been anything but disgustingly delightful with Colette. Believe me." If Starla thought I'd personally antagonized Colette in any way, she'd probably never talk to me again. Though her relationship with the Joies was at a standstill right now, Starla thought in the long term: she'd get them back.

"There's the car," she said, spotting it down the block, where I'd seen it a full ten minutes ago.

But as Rachel Chaparal and her nine dwarves came bustling out, we froze. Instead of single file, they were all around her now, like a nut cluster, and they were all talking at once, proffering explanations, excuses, and apologies *in re* the cigarette case, obviously hoping to God that she'd drop it so they could all move on with their lives. Two of them had dusty knees, as if they'd looked for the damned thing on all fours. Though there was little more they could humanly do, Rachel didn't look like she was going to let the subject go in this decade.

"That case was a gift from my fucking producer!" she said, getting even madder as a group of photographers caught her in all her totally unglam fury. Suddenly she was covering her face with the open handbag while searching through it with her other hand, a dexterous feat of confused prima donnaism. As intimate objects started falling out of the handbag and right through the hole in the ozone layer to the ground, her lackeys scurried to pick them up, not wanting a replay of the cigarette case tragedy. I felt very important, being the one who'd caused all this fuss, and it was a perverse pleasure I took in its being a secret shared only between me and myself.

"These fucking charity things!" fumed Rachel as they got into the biggest car I'd ever seen and sped off.

We got into our more modest luxury car, and the driver said, "Where to?" We ignored him; that gives you more time to think where to.

"What an event," Starla said. "A real treasure trove."

"The best so far—a night of a half-dozen stars," I said.

"You know *that's* right!" she beamed.

"The old team again." I held out my hand to swat her five, and she complied.

"The old team again," she echoed.

"Where to?" the driver repeated.

"Just drive around the block a hundred times," I suggested.

"Hey," said Starla, fixing her gaze on me like a vise. "I'm going to have to make an early evening of it. Big day tomorrow—Sylvia's introducing me to some new board members or something or other. But I do really, really, really, really"—one more, girl—"really appreciate you taking me tonight. It was the bestest, funnest, greatest time I've ever had."

I knew all that extraordinary exuberance meant it was totally over between Starla and me. We were back to square zero, relationshipwise. Tracy had taken over my role as the one she occasionally slipped and told growing-up horror stories to. I was another party pal to be psychotically perky with.

"And you got Rachel's number," I added. "Does she have a place in town?"

"No, she stays at a hotel," she said. She wouldn't tell me which one. What did she think I'd do—run over and barge into her room right then and there? I'd wait till tomorrow. Nah, I already had what I wanted—the shiny cigarette case.

"Goodbye," I said as Starla left—not "so long," as my mother had always instructed me. I took the car straight home, where I had to watch the rest of *The Naked Kiss,* Sam Fuller's film with Constance Towers as a sometimes-bald prostitute-nurse in love with a child molester. By the closing credits I was convinced that mine was the only life more polymorphously perverse than this character's.

I called my mother, who I knew would love being awakened for this.

"What's wrong?" she said, snapping back into consciousness with a jolt. "What happened?" Her first thoughts were always that some heinous, life-threatening disaster had occurred. Not only didn't she mind this prospect; I think she secretly thrived on it. Disaster gave her a chance to worry. It made her needed.

"Nothing happened," I said. "I just came from a charity ball with Rachel Chaparal."

"You're going out with Rachel Chaparal now?"

"No, I didn't go with her," I said, trying not to be annoyed. "But she was there, and I met her and talked to her."

"Oh, my God! What was she like? Like her character? Or even bitchier?"

"Mother, she was charming. We hit it off like two thieves. She is a total, total doll—everything you'd hope for and more. She said she's heard of my magazine. And—"

"And did you tell her I love her?"

"I'm getting to that. And I told her you love her, and—

this was the craziest thing, Ma—she reached into her hand-bag and pulled out this shimmery, gold cigarette case mono-grammed with her initials that she said she wants you to have. Because you sounded like such a devoted fan. Mother, that's much better than a stupid autographed pic-ture any day.''

"Oh!'' she was shrieking. "Oh! Oh! Oh! That must be the most famous cigarette case in the world. And the most expensive. And now it's mine. Your Aunt Jo Butch will be so jealous. Oh! Oh! Oh! Thank you, baby. Thank you, thank you, thank you! I love you, my baby!'' It was nice to hear some real appreciation after Starla's performance. "I've got to send her a thank-you note,'' she added. "I'll send it on a really nice mass card. And I'll put a 3-D Jesus in there.''

"Um, no,'' I stammered, "her last words to me were that you shouldn't bother sending her a thank-you note, in fact she'd *hate* it if you did. She never gets to see most of her mail, so it would be a total, total waste of time. 'But I'll know she appreciates it,' she said. 'I'll know.' Just like that she said it.''

"She knows everything,'' my mother beamed. "She's Rachel Chaparal.''

Call waiting beeped in, and of all people it was Garth, bringing me down with a mumbly speech that wouldn't have made much sense even if he wasn't dentalizing. He was calling from the hospital—they'd dragged him back—and must have been ringing every single victim on his list; no way was I the first. "I need some beef jerky,'' he said, angrily. "I absolutely need it, need it, require it, damnit.'' Not just any beef jerky, mind you, it had to be Slim Jims— six of them—from a very particular place at Twentieth and Third, taken out of their plastic wrappings and put in a cardboard shoe box. It was way past visiting hours, thank God, so I had an excuse not to go on a late-night beef by-product hunt. And having Mom on the other line was a good reason not to have to listen to him carry on about how he was going off to tour tropical countries ''where diarrhea is an Olympic event'' as soon as his Lotto ticket cleared. I clicked back to Mother, but she'd fallen asleep on the line. I pulled the phone out of the wall and joined her in slumberland.

14

My day of recuperation was spent renting movies and thinking about how, in the best of all possible worlds, I'd probably be working on the magazine. But I didn't need the rag anymore as my ticket to Tomahawk; once you're on those guest lists, they never take you off, even if you die. It's true that without the magazine I didn't have the rationale for being out anymore, but maybe just being there could be a rationale for itself.

Still, it was good to keep the *idea* of the magazine alive, to flog it as a pretense for living and partying. If the idea ever transmogrified into printed pages, all the better. My life became a procession of specters—of ideas—that I refused to cement into realness. Fuck it—this *wasn't* the best of all possible worlds.

The next day, I watched *The Oscar* again, a religious experience interrupted only by the calls that sporadically droned into my machine. Madam Tess Tosterone called to say that like Marnie, she has a psychotic fear of the color red. My mother called to say she was planning a big party centered on the cigarette case. Mary-Ellen called, only so I'd eventually call back and hear her message: "Dave, if this is you, I lost your number, please leave where we're having dinner tonight." (There was no Dave—he was one of many romantic phantoms she'd made up to impress people.) And Delroy left a long message saying that Garth was back in the hospital as if I didn't know, and it looked like this was going to be the last time. He had tuberculosis and three cancers and was a mere slip of a human being—blind, unable to breathe, and demented. "Not cute demented like all the party people we know who do and say silly things," he said. "But real, scary, horrifying demented." He started crying. "Oh, Vinnie, it's so sad." Elke Sommer, take me away.

Vivien swung around in a cab at twenty to eight, and we were off—the new old team again. She was in ripped jeans and an Adidas sweatshirt, and though she looked good in that Irish Spring commercial kind of way, I couldn't believe she had dressed so casually—all right, shittily—for what she said was so fab a restaurant. I hoped to God it wasn't one of those minimalist places like Ne Plus Ultra, where you have to practically shoot your animal of choice off a conveyor belt and torch it yourself.

"Bleecker and Broadway," she told the cabbie, and I screeched, "What? I thought the place was in Tribeca."

"Well," she grinned, "I changed my mind."

"Are we going there or not?"

"I found someplace better," she said, deviously. "Trust me."

"I hope you don't mean the Burger King on Fourth and Broadway," I said. "I don't feel like seeing Favio tonight."

"Neither do I, Vinnie," she laughed. "I wouldn't do that to us."

We pulled up in front of a big, ugly building that looked like a public school—dear God, don't make me go back *there*. It turned out it *was* a school that had ostensibly gone out of business and been converted into one of those cozy-dumpy-flannel-shirted community centers in which people discuss abortions over hot cocoa with nutmeg. It was covered with graffiti and didn't look like there was a fabulous restaurant in there by any stretch of the imagination. Maybe a bomb shelter or a pawnbrokers' convention.

"What the hell is this, a crack dealership?" I said. "I'm starving, and not really in the mood for a practical joke."

"There are donuts inside," she said, "and we can go out to eat afterward. Just come along with me, Vinnie. Do it for me."

She was probably bringing me in to take some test that involved racing around a big Skinner box in search of huge chunks of cheese. Or maybe she was going to make me volunteer for some character-building community service—not exactly what I had in mind when I prepared for a statusy night on the town. I'd rather eat some nouvelle shit than help troubled Hispanic teens over crullers.

As we walked into the building and headed toward the auditorium we were enveloped by bulletin boards carrying angry-looking notices with "Fight," "Help," and other monosyllabic words jumping off them. Closer to the auditorium's entrance, there were big signs, hand-painted in blood red saying "SCREAM for Life" and "SCREAM It Out." So karma had caught up with me, and I'd been trapped into an activist meeting. I always knew all the frivolity and carelessness and mooching off charity would eventually cost me some dues, and here it was, time to pay the piper. They were probably going to roast me in some AIDS-activist supremacy ritual.

"I'm sorry," Vivien said. "It's the only way I could get you here. We can have dinner somewhere on me afterward."

It was going to be on her anyway. But at my expense.

Vivien was greeted with a million enthusiastic hellos—she was an even bigger star here than on the party circuit. She introduced me to everyone as "a new member" and they all said, "Oh, a virgin. Welcome." I wasn't a virgin, but I wasn't exactly going to go into the Melissa Kravitz story first thing.

They handed me a SCREAM brochure, which gave a *Readers Digest* type rundown of the facts. I read it, to be polite, hoping against hope that there'd be a Danielle Steele excerpt on it. It said that New York, a city with more than half a million people infected with HIV, had only provided two clinics to deal with them. That as discrimination against people with AIDS soared, the mayor called for a complete defunding of the AIDS Anti-Discrimination Unit. That even the surgeon general has implied that the government's delay in dealing with the AIDS crisis was a direct result of ho-mophobia. That every AIDS death is akin to "genocide by our government," and that the time for polite acceptance is over; we have to fight back, to force our leaders into action, to SCREAM. I was used to that: "Give me my drink ticket!"

I looked around at the crowd of about 150 people and saw that no one there was wearing the smiley-face shirt that was helping to spread the "Don't worry, be happy" mes-sage throughout brain-dead America. Here, in their plaids and jeans and white tees, they worried. They seethed.

I noticed that Vivien wasn't the only woman in the bunch, and wasn't even the only straight woman (I could tell). "There are all kinds of people in SCREAM," Vivien told me. "Gay, straight, male, female, black, white, drag queens, little people. A lot of them have lost someone to AIDS. Some of them have AIDS themselves."

"There are people with AIDS in here?" I said, recoiling a little bit.

"Probably quite a few."

"But shouldn't they be—"

"PWAs—People with AIDS—don't just crawl up and die. They can lead productive lives, sometimes for a long time. And sick as some of them are, they want to spend their last energy fighting AIDS."

"You really are the fount, aren't you?" I said.

"I try."

"What did it for you?" I said, playing the reporter. "What made you join SCREAM?" I was miserable here, but wanted to make it as pleasant as possible by acting interested.

"I don't think it was anything in particular," she said, "just the accumulation of all the horrors. I mean, when Michael Bennett, Willi Smith, and Charles Ludlam—three of my idols—all died within the same year, it was definitely time to stop mourning and do something. I saw that no one was doing it for us, so we had to get off our own asses. And there was already this organization of people who felt the same way. They're not just mad—that's not good enough— they channel the anger into action.

"They really welcomed me here. They welcome everyone, except FBI agents and police—and even they're cool if they announce themselves. They're all really glad *you're* here."

Oh, yeah, right. Not one person recognized me from my pictures in *Fabulon,* and no one I mentioned my magazine to had even heard of it. These people were as isolated in their interests as the club people. They had their own AIDS celebrities, their own AIDS events, and their own AIDS rules. They didn't seem to know about anything else.

All the talk in the room centered on that one word, and it made me so uncomfortable I wanted to jump up and SCREAM any change-of-subject line: "What do y'all think of Heather Locklear's new hair?" or "This is an emergency: I need to find five people who like José Feliciano's 'Light My Fire' better than The Doors'. Don't ask why." I was desperate to go from AIDS to Zymurgy—from A to Z.

But I was forced to go along with the conversational flow, or at least listen in on it, thereby seeing every type of AIDS-fixation in action. I overheard one guy say he was in the group because, "I feel like if I fight AIDS, maybe I won't get it." Someone else was saying, "There are more cute guys here every week than in the bars, and I love it. I'm a safe-sex slut." (I walked away; safe or not, a slut is still a slut.) There was also a grotesquely fat guy named Slim who, Vivien later told me, eats as his only defense against potential bad health. His name used to be a literal one.

Vivien was talking to a man named Victor, who said his lover had died of AIDS six months ago, and he'd promised him on his deathbed he'd do something about it. It wasn't long before Victor, recognizing that I was a first-timer, seized me to drive home the point that AIDS activism was the new thing to do; it was hot, hip, happening, and hyped. He pointed to a table of clippings almost as plentiful as Star-la's—the magazines were starting to cover this group's every primal utterance, giving credence to what used to be considered the bratty whinings of the understandably oppressed. As I fingered through the articles I could see that in one year, the perception of SCREAM had gone from that of a low-budget self-indulgence to a major political force. The group just might be on the verge of filling the slot Angela Burdine left on the "What's Hot" list, and—I could just hear Favio saying this—it *was* the next big, fabulous thing. If anyone could do something for people like me who'd stepped in semen, they were the ones; I just didn't particularly feel like being there when they did it.

At least Diane Plewge wasn't there; I guess it wasn't *that* fabulous. And at least there was no one else there I knew who could be snickering to themselves that I'd shown up; clippings or no clippings, this was akin to Wendy's as far as being a desirable place to be seen. Just in case, I was prepared to address inquiries by saying, "Oh, Vivien dragged me here on the way to dinner." If anyone probed deeper, I'd say I was doing an article on the group. Research was the best excuse for being anywhere career-tapering.

The meeting began, and four people—"moderators," not

really leaders—took to the stage to conduct the discussions and votes (despite all the raw energy in the room, everything was neatly organized and democratic). Vivien alternated as one of these people, but tonight was not her night to do so, probably because she had to babysit me in the audience.

"Let's begin with a little bit of self-congratulations over the FDA, you guys," said a female moderator. The whole room burst into thunderous applause, and I clapped along with them, wondering why I was clapping for the FDA. Had they just signed on to do a miniseries? Vivien whispered that they had finally allowed some patients to import certain AIDS drugs from foreign countries, and SCREAM's protests had a lot to do with it. The applause didn't last that long. "What they gave us was a minor concession," whispered Vivien. "We want more." Why did people have to get drugs from as far away as France and Japan? I couldn't ask—this wasn't a school anymore.

I wondered if we'd each have to get up, as if at A.A., and say, "My name is so-and-so, and yes, I am an A.A.—an AIDS Activist." I was glad they didn't make "virgins" raise their hands and be publicly welcomed and deflowered, like they used to at *The Rocky Horror Picture Show*. I already felt like all attention was peripherally fixed on me anyway. I was experiencing the same malaise here as at Velveeta—I was an outie, a misfit all the way, but at least *there,* José was throwing bottles at me to make me feel at home.

The floor was opened up for people to shriek about homophobic remarks some politician may have made or to propose protests against those in power who are not doing the politically correct thing, and there wasn't anyone there (myself included) who didn't have *something* to bitch about. The safe-sex slut got up to complain that porno theaters where gay sex went on had been summarily closed down by the health department. He felt people should have the right to engage in public, casual sex if they wanted to, as long as they knew it had to be safe. A lot of SCREAMers agreed that the way to resolve this problem was to monitor the sex, not close the places down, but there was no real consensus. The subject was tabled, pending more concrete information—something I'd done in my mind long ago, baffled over why anyone would even want to have sex in *private*.

Vivien then got up with an amazing list of indignations—gripes she had that she wanted battled with loud SCREAM-ing fits. She said she'd found out that a camera crew from a cable channel, Channel 73, had refused to shoot a scheduled interview with a guy with AIDS. She knew of an emergency room doctor who wouldn't treat someone with AIDS. And she also proposed that core members of the group take "anger rides" to Albany and D.C. to SCREAM where it could really count. SCREAM had done enough jeering at individual bad guys. It was time they took on the whole, rotten organization that sets the tone for everyone else.

Breathlessly—boom, boom—these things were taken care of; with so many walking time bombs in the room, no one was going to dillydally. A protest was organized outside the Channel 73 offices, at which everyone would wear gloves and oxygen masks and chant, "Get away from me, Channel 73" and "You're infected with AIDS—Asshole Ignoramus Dum-dum Syndrome." They'd deal with the doctor by sending a petition to the hospital demanding his dismissal, and in no time someone was typing it up and getting ready to pass it around. And one of the moderators asked Vivien to go into the adjacent room and organize anyone who was interested in doing those two capital trips. She had two thousand dollars in the budget for both—enough for only one nice, new gown. She'd obviously have to repeat.

"See you in a bit," said Vivien, as she led about forty "angry riders" out. "Unless you want to come." Much as I wanted my babysitter, I didn't want to commit myself to any journey into fear. "I'll hang," I said. I could have made a go for the exit, but I'd never live *that* down.

As I looked around I noticed three guys sitting at a table

in the back of the room, ferociously stuffing and licking envelopes with an incredible sense of purpose. I took a flyer later and saw it was something about how it takes five to ten years for a new AIDS drug to be approved—oy, it was a brand-new attack on the FDA. Someone else was painting more signs with those monosyllabic words. It was like Santa's factory two weeks before Christmas, except here Christmas never came—there was always some other chore to do, some other verbal stink bomb to wrap.

The guy whose lover had died of AIDS got up and said, "Excuse me, but I suggested the Albany and Washington trips three weeks ago, and it never even came to a vote." Aha—so one of the elves was jealous. Well, maybe three weeks ago no one was ready for it yet. Or maybe he didn't phrase it persuasively enough—much as a group like this strives for a certain purity of ideas and clarity of purpose, people can't help but be tainted by personalities—I could see that already. Just like in any situation, the more forceful ones win out every time.

SCREAM was a jousting match of personalities, with subgroups within the group and different cliques within the subgroups. Each one wanted to do the most, and wanted the most credit for what they'd done. The tug-of-war was kind of exciting and elevated it from an us-versus-them situation to us-competing-with-us-versus-them. The competition was healthy, but I did find it amusing that people were fighting for status even here.

There were battles over everything. A lot of the SCREAM members, while wanting to make a statement, felt it should be done in a "reasonable" way. Well-dressed, unintimidating people—women, whenever possible—should lead the crusade in a tasteful manner, to get results with a minimum of feather ruffling. "But we *have* to ruffle feathers," someone else shouted, jumping out of his seat. "We can't just accept the status quo and march to our deaths. We have to shock people into action, wake them up with whatever abrasive processes we can think of. We have to stick hot, metal poles up their asses." He got a big round of applause—bigger than the FDA.

There was another debate over a proposed protest in which everyone would walk in circles outside Gracie Mansion carrying caskets that would represent all the dead and future dead. "Wait a minute, I have AIDS," one man said, "and that's a pretty heavy concept."

"We could make the caskets out of cardboard so they'd be lighter," said one of the moderators in all seriousness, and everyone cracked up.

Other issues came up in a rat-tat-tat of passion. One young, curly-haired guy suggested that as far as the group had come, they could go much further with a big, *People* magazine–ready name attached. Public awareness of AmFar had gone through the roof after Liz Taylor joined forces with them. If they could get their own Liz Taylor, he said, SCREAM would become a household acronym, with a lot more money to fuel their anger.

My mother was probably the only one who hadn't been won over by Liz Taylor's endorsement of AmFar; she still hadn't forgiven Liz for "breaking up" Debbie and Eddie's marriage. Maybe it was *Debbie* SCREAM should get; then the Mrs. DiBlasios of the world would be theirs.

I rummaged through my mental celeb file and realized I knew a lot of biggies who could help. Terence Floss had destroyed my friend's camera and could maybe pull the same stunt with network crews at a protest. Liza Minnelli had touched my hand eagerly and said, "Thank you," and could maybe get up in front of a heated mob and deliver the same heart-rending call to action. Best of all, I had Rachel Chaparal's cigarette case, around which I was sure entire rallies could be organized—this cigarette case cares! Forget it. The celebrity issue was shelved, the group deciding that if someone famous came along who really wanted to get involved, fine. Otherwise, it wasn't top priority—SCREAM was going to be in *People* anyway,

"How many of these babies are going to die?" someone behind me said, huskily. "My poor babies."

It was Taormina, who must have stumbled into the room in midmeeting under the influence of God knows what. She was the ultimate mystery woman, a walking camouflage—that is, when she was able to walk. No one knew her last name, where she was from, or what she did besides go out every night and drink herself to the ground. No one could even coax a good hangover remedy out of her. Her molasses-thick voice was laden with mystique, and her face was time-carved with experience, but we could never figure out what those experiences were. Was she a Russian spy? Or had she escaped from a prisoner-of-war camp forty years ago and been running ever since? Was she The Fugitive? What the hell was she doing at a SCREAM meeting? Did she think it was really A.A.?

"Of course I'm here," she said, reading my mind. "It's happening, isn't it?"—meaning either it was happening in the "hot, hyped" sense, or it was just happening—just there, like Everest. "What are *you* doing here?"

"Vivien dragged me on the way to dinner, and I'm writing an article." I'd forgotten that one good alibi was better than two shaky ones.

"Great idea," she cooed. "Don't forget to mention me—Ta-or-mi-na." Finally—the club sensibility meets the activist life-style, yet another bizarre combination platter served only in the ever changing café of New York.

"My poor babies," she repeated. "How many of these pretty, pretty boys will die?"

"Go to hell," someone turned around and snapped at her. "First of all, this is a meeting, not a social center. Second of all, save all your maudlin emotions for someone else. We're not here to sit around and boo-hoo."

"Testy!" said Taormina, not all that perturbed. "Didn't your parents ever tell you it's not polite to eavesdrop?"

Vivien came back with her posse, and not a second too soon. The fact that she was about to make a statement gave me the chance to shut Taormina up. "She looks incredible," gushed Taormina, as if at a fashion show. "Such a natural beauty. I remember when she—"

"Quiet," I said. "I've got to hear this. For my article."

Given the floor, Vivien laid out the plan for the trips. They'd be done when certain key governmental meetings were in session. And they'd rent big buses and bring along appropriate props (including effigies of the prez and the gov), dozens of banners, "and lots of vocal cords." With all the composure of a *Star Search* spokesmodel, she gave out her phone number and said that anyone who wanted to join either trip or contribute ideas should give her a call at any time. I felt like running up there drunkenly like James Mason in *A Star Is Born* and massacring her speech with self-serving slobber, which would at least have gotten me away from Taormina's heaving scrutiny and led to Vivien's ultimate proclamation of undying devotion ("Hello, everybody. This is Mrs.—Vinnie—DiBlasio"). But per usual, I chose to remain invisible.

"You don't have a pad and pen?" Taormina asked.

"Mental notes," I said, tapping my skull harder than I'd rapped on Emil's door.

The meeting ended the way it had begun—with everyone applauding themselves. This wasn't a gratuitous gesture of self-congratulation, it was much-needed positive reinforcement for their own uphill struggle. With all the ire and abuse they provoked, SCREAM had to constantly remind themselves that it was worth it. They *had* to show off their clippings on a table—not for all the Mary-Ellen reasons, but to reinforce their own strength among themselves.

After more goodbyes than at an Italian wedding, we got

out of there and into a generic Greek restaurant in the neighborhood, where we prepared to relax and eat moussaka with fat people—this was really my night for nonfabulous. "How many?" the maitre d' said, and we never got to answer, because a by-now-sandpaper voice behind us answered, "Three." It was Taormina, who'd followed us all the way from the meeting.

Vivien gave me a benevolent "get rid of her" look, but I knew it wasn't necessary. The second we sat down, I ordered several bottles of ouzo and plied Taormina with it until the poor thing crashed and burned on the table. She was a goner. Every now and then she'd crane up her head and mutter some inanity like the Dormouse in Wonderland, but soon enough she'd crash-land again and set us free.

So Vivien and I got to have our dinner after all. I wished it was at Zymurgy. I wished it was with Starla and Doric and hundreds of other people helping to distract me from panic. But Vivien and I got to have our dinner after all.

"Some meeting, huh?" she said.

"Some meeting. Should we order more ouzo? Why does that sound so obscene?"

"I signed you up on the way out, by the way."

"Signed me up for what?" Nobody has license with my name, short of anyone with a column or guest list who knows how to spell it right. "Signed me up for *what?*"

"I signed you up to be one of the people carrying caskets outside Gracie Mansion," she said. "It's the next big protest—photo opportunity!"

"Awwww, this is too much," I whined. "You know, you tricked me into going to the goddamned meeting, and now you're shystering me into holding a fucking casket. What next—I'm going to have to lie in the damned thing?"

"Relax," she said. "You're not committed to do anything. It just means you're down on the list in case you feel like it, OK?"

"I'm on the list. I've heard that before."

"I thought I was doing you a favor. Giving you a chance to help mankind, like the kids on those jeans commercials always talk about doing."

"What do you get, a percentage or something on every new recruit?"

"Yeah," she smiled. "It's just like Mary Kaye Cosmetics. For every casket you hold, I get a fabulous, pink car."

Suddenly Taormina was blearily lifting up her head and talking nonsense—"Ouzo, boozo, coozo, doozo, floozo . . ."—but soon enough she had another blackout and stuck her face in the bread. We left her there; Greek bread cushions any blow.

"So what's new with you and Starla?" she said. "Do you still have to lie to her when you go out with other girls?"

"Oh," I said, "I was being real stupid that time, like award-caliber stupid. There was never really that much between Starla and me. We don't report to each other in any major way. Reports of our love affair have been greatly exaggerated." This was the most honest I'd been since I admitted I was cheating in a history class sophomore year and had to take an F. It felt really exhilarating. The reason so many criminals ultimately confess is that it's a tremendous relief to let go of the lie and not have to pretend anymore; it's like being mentally unhandcuffed. But I still made sure to say my revelation in a way that made it clear there *could* have been something between Starla and me, and maybe still was; it's all in the intonation. I hoped Vivien didn't take my declaration of independence as a proposition. I had no one, and wanted no one; just my hot, alluring video machine, which I stuck it in nightly.

"Aha," said Vivien. "Well, what's *new* with Starla?"

All I knew about Starla was something Delroy had told me, but it was juicy enough for me to use to invoke a certain level of intimacy. "She's coming out with her own perfume soon—can you believe it?"

"No kidding," she said. "I read it in the papers two weeks ago."

"Oh," I said, reaching for that honesty again, "I guess that proves how tight I am with Starla. My big scoops have already made it to the dailies." Ozone stories or not, I had to start reading the papers again; I'd even lost touch with gossip.

Our food came and was so lemony it was like pure lemon juice reformed into the shape of souvlaki. The lemon juice killed the smell of the souvlaki. On the side were gobs of cucumber-yogurt dressing that killed the smell of the lemon. The whole thing was like a Rube Goldberg contraption of smell destroyers. At least, unlike Zymurgy, they used spices from after 450 B.C.

"So what about *your* love life?" I said. "You've managed to avoid being gossiped about somehow, which is a real talent in this town. Who wears the special condom in your world?" I felt like Baba Wawa interviewing Glenn Close, and like Baba, I was not going to let my subject go until she cried.

"Oh," she said, "no one . . . someone." I probed her with my eyes, silently trying to get her to say more. As someone who was kinda sorta in like with this girl, I had a right to know. "Someone I met a few years ago," she added. "Someone . . . a guy . . ."

"Drop it," I said, uncertainly. "I can see it's not your fave subject." This reverse-psychology tack sometimes got people to confess, but not Vivien.

"No, it's just that it's not the kind of thing I run around broadcasting. I spend so much time screaming about AIDS that to talk about my private life seems trivial. We're not living together or anything anyway. We're just there for each other in an open sort of way."

"No strings attached," I said.

"Yeah," she said. "Like you and Starla. No strings at all!"

269

"I want some strings, damnit," I laughed. The waiter came running over. "Did you say you want something?" he asked. "More cucumber sauce?"

"No, thanks," said Vivien. "He said 'strings.' "

"String beans?" said the waiter. I looked over at Taormina in the bread. "No, no, no. More bread, please," I said. A fresh batch of it would be nice, in lieu of pillows.

"I heard you know Heinz," I asked Vivien out of the blue, stammering it in a way that announced how clearly I knew it was a rotten choice of question. She brilliantly pretended not to hear, so I quickly substituted another question, to cover up my own crassness. "Do you miss your crazy years?" I asked, and though it didn't have the prurient value of the Heinz inquiry, I really did want to know. I mean, how could someone go cold turkey on so much fun and not become a basket case?

"No," she said, without hesitation. "I don't sit around missing them. Not that I regret them in any way. I learned a lot about myself and how to deal with people, and it was fine for who I was at the time. But it was a transitional period, a step on the way to where I am now."

"A Greek restaurant?" I laughed.

"No, you know," she said. "I'm on a higher plane now. More in touch. I have a wholer sense of who I am." Bang-bang-bang, three clichés you're out. "All the press I got at that time made me a little queasy, because it wasn't really about Vivien Dietrich the person, it was about Cha Cha—one, like, pie slice of my personality, the part that came alive at parties. It was a part I'd created, but it wasn't the whole me—there was this other person trying to develop but couldn't, because she was too busy trying to be fabulous. Now when I see my picture in the paper, I feel great because it's a picture of me really doing something."

"So you don't look back?"

"No way," she said. "I don't make any judgments about anyone else who still does it, but it's not for me anymore.

One thing I learned when I chanted was always to look to the future, to the next day. I kept that principle even after I stopped chanting."

"Why'd you stop?" I said. I had a college roommate who chanted at the top of his lungs day and night, and when I told him to shut his trap, he said he was chanting for me too. He was chanting for my happiness when the one thing that would have made me happy was his not chanting.

"Because," she said, "it was a pseudospiritual way of striving for material things, and I stopped wanting those. It seemed an incredible abortion of spirituality to pray every day for tax refunds and Porsches. Now I want change, and the way to get that is not by chanting."

"It's by screaming," I laughed.

"Screaming?" said Taormina, lifting her head out of the fresh bread I'd placed her in. "Who's screaming? My ears hurt—who's screaming? Shut them up."

"No one's screaming," said Vivien, patting her on her bread-crumb-speckled head. "Just the little demons inside your brain."

"Shall we get a check?" I said, anxious to flee before Taormina started throwing plates and people would mistake it for some quaint Greek custom, or worse yet, wouldn't. Besides, Vivien wasn't going to cry—ever.

15

A few weeks later I was awakened by some Cro-Magnon buzzing my buzzer even more relentlessly than I had at Emil's that time. This is cruel and unusual punishment— I'd rather wake up to chanting. If Favio were still here, he'd be all bright-eyed from an all-nighter and would have loved receiving guests at this hour—something to do in the desperate throes of a drug rattle. But Favio Didn't Live Here Anymore.

It was a guy in spandex bike shorts—messengers are the only ones who legally should be allowed to wear them— holding a monstrous bouquet of sunflowers the size of human heads surrounded by wispy, purple things that looked like microbes, they were so inconsequential next to those mutant sunflowers. Who on earth could have sent these blooms from Hades? They certainly weren't romantic, and were so extravagant they couldn't be business related either, not in *my* nickel-and-dime world. Aha—social.

"Hoping we're all still friends," said the card. "With love, Sandahl DeVol." I almost dropped them on the floor I was so combination amused-appalled. This woman was obviously not the queen of self-respect. She'd apparently mulled the Mise en Scène incident over in her brain all this time and decided that, rude or not, Emil and I were still valuable connections to have, or at least I was. *She* was apologizing to *me* for her having been so dishwater dull I'd publicly deserted her. That made me feel good about myself, and pretty shitty about Sandahl.

The phone was ringing—the phone always rings when you're dealing with a delivery. "Not home, not interested, and not to be trusted," sang out my outgoing phone message, causing the messenger to traipse away muttering, "You are one twisted mutherfucker." I ran over to the machine in time to hear Vivien say, "I know you're there, pick up. Vinnie, pick up. I know you're sitting there listening to me. . . . Oh, anyway, I just wanted to remind you of the casket thing today. It's at three in the afternoon outside Gracie. You're on the list."

This time I didn't pick up. I wanted to go to the protest, but I didn't. I wanted to hold the casket and make a statement, but I had so much else to do. I'd just rented a new release, *Bonjour Tristesse,* with Jean Seberg, and there were so many reasons why I had to see that—it was set on the Riviera; it had a brilliant title song; and I needed to consume anything with Jean Seberg, the woman who, in order to prove to her hometown that her baby wasn't black, supposedly had the miscarried fetus displayed in a glass case there. (Jean herself ended up dead, displayed in a car trunk.) Clearly, this was an unusual woman who begged to be scrutinized.

Bonjour Tristesse could probably wait. It was just that, possessed by a mortal fear of becoming an international nightclub laughingstock, I was in no rush to get to Gracie Mansion. This kind of thing may have been on the verge of being fabulous, but it was still a future flavor that only the truly compulsive had developed an affinity for yet. Doric went so far as to say that he refused to lift a finger to fight AIDS, because he was convinced the government was keeping a file on everyone who did, and someday they'd send them all to camps somewhere in Colorado along with the AIDS victims (his word).

I wasn't that bad. I mean, I'd sign a petition, or send money, if I had any, but the suggestion of hard, manual labor in person was pushing my good intentions well over the borderline. The peer pressure Vivien was applying to do it was a mere speck next to the unspoken constraining force of everyone else not to do it. It wouldn't endear me to Starla one bit. What was it really going to accomplish anyway?

Besides, there were two parties that night, and parties require a certain psychic preparation that simply can't be attained by walking around with a casket. One was my mother's gala affair for the cigarette case, which I'd allowed her to pick up from me on the condition that she clean up the apartment in the process (it was her condition—she begged for it). I wasn't planning to go to this party—I got flush with embarrassment just thinking about it—but I had to concentrate on sending them good vibes because I did, after all, want my mother to have a great time with this new, celebrity-fingerprinted toy. All the free time on my hands had suddenly gotten me believing in things like vibes.

The other big party was Sean Valve's movie wrap at a new place called Haute, and though Sean had made a point of not inviting me, I worked Delroy's nerves with every trick in the book until he agreed to take me along as his plus-one. I promised him all sorts of things to get him to comply, and now I was wishing I could remember what they were—my first- and second-born? Whatever, it was worth it to get into this one, and the look on Sean's face as I triumphantly sauntered in would be well worth bonus points.

I prepared for this do with extra-special care well into the evening hours. Though I was now reduced to dousing myself with those cologne flaps that you open up in magazines, I picked out the best one, not the cheap stuff. I conditioned my hair, yogurtized my skin, and even cleaned my nails, inspired by the glowing, if doomed, countenance of Miss Jean Seberg. As I put on the most expensive-looking outfit I owned—a black, velvety pantsuit that designer Jeremy Dyle had given to me in a fit of press worship—I had to blow a kiss at the mirror and pause to take it all in. Enthralled, I turned off the movie and put on my favorite old Bowie song—"Always Crashing in the Same Car"— shamelessly proceeding into a Ziegfeld-via-Pina-Bausch lip-synch production number for myself and a dysfunctional family of roaches that happened by in horror. At the height of my oozy, clean-nailed suavity, the phone rang, and I ran back to hear Vivien sounding excited all over again.

"Well," she beamed, "it was incredible. There were so many camera crews. So many people watching. And a huge turnout—over two hundred and forty of them were arrested—isn't that great? We really made our point in a big way. I know you're sitting there listening to this, but that's okay. I'd rather that than your *not* listening." Actually, I was only half-listening, anxious to finish up my song before the roaches started heckling. "Don't think I'm mad at you for not showing up," she went on. "I mean, I am a little disappointed you couldn't make it, but I'm sure you have a good reason—I was such a sneak about getting you to do it. The coffins got carried, don't worry—in fact, there were extra people. Imagine, a funeral with extra pallbearers. And there'll be plenty more chances. But, God, it was the best— a real event. Mister Mayor must be shitting." She kept on talking, but I had to run out and get Delroy, and besides, I'd gotten the gist of this monologue. If people could keep their messages down to two verbs and a noun, I think the world would be a better place.

Haute was one of those restaurants where all segments intersected, but only the most glittering stratum of each. The place was so shockingly unadorned it could make Ne Plus Ultra look like Mise en Scène, but people were still interested in sensory deprivation, and being new, it did have an intrinsic aura of excitement. New is a compensation for almost every conceptual flaw.

Haute was not designed for comfort. There were long wooden tables with purposely icy metal chairs; a very occasional bas-relief demonotonizing the stark, white walls; and nothing outstanding except for a huge deco clock that loudly ticked away, as if to say, Your time to social climb is running out—quicken your leaps. But, like every other exciting place I'd been to, this one wasn't about decor, service, or food—it was about the people. And what people—this was definitely what it looks like on top of the mountain.

All the stars of the movie were there—Stephanie Zane, Michael Groening, even Dale Stearns, who never goes out unless it's in her contract—and everyone else looked like they'd stepped out of the pages of *HG* by way of Favio's scrapbook, after being hand-painted by Richard Bernstein. There wasn't even a lot of downtown trash—none of the usual open-bar gate-crashers—and of the old gang, only the two most famous, Starla and Doric, were allowed (Delroy was there more as press than as a friend). This was living proof—Sean Valve could probably leave *Fabulon* now and never look back, just spend the rest of his life celebrating and being celebrated.

The only damper was that Delroy was being a menstrual cramp, sulking over the fact that Garth was irretrievably on the way out—that big clock on the wall was ticking his every last gasp. Much as I tried to convince Delroy that we should all be glad the guy would soon be out of his misery, that argument never seems to hold much water unless you're talking about a pet. Then again, Delroy's the one who kept his cat on a dialysis machine to the tune of a thousand dollars a week rather than have it given the injection of death that would have freed it.

And Delroy's the one who was so sympathetic to any mammal's demands that he let Mary-Ellen come along as his plus-two, telling her he'd try his best to sneak her in too (but if he couldn't, it was agreed that *she'd* have to crawl back home, not me).

They let her in; somehow the more exclusive the party, the looser they seem to be at the door, because the invitees are more major than usual and need to be pampered, even if they play havoc with the rules a little bit. Everyone was being alarmingly nice, even Sean; instead of pulling a "What the hell are you two doing here?" routine, he gave us a fairly warm (for him) hello, proving once again that success doesn't always have to create a Terence Floss; it can make someone a better person. Well, not really a better person; I knew this mood change had to be a temporary one stimulated by the fact that we happened to be at a party in honor of Sean Valve. Still, it was nice to see a half smile on his face, whether or not it was a mere hologram of real benevolence.

"My art sold really well," said Mary-Ellen, typically enough. I knew it didn't sell, because she wasn't forthcoming with any details about who'd bought it for how much, and this girl was not the type who'd be shy about reciting figures.

"Great," I said noncommittally and fantasized her being strapped to the second hand of the giant clock through eternity. I looked at Delroy, still sulking over Garth. This was a fun couple. "Relax," I said to him. "There's nothing anyone can do about it. Let's try to have a good time tonight."

"That's just what kills me," he said. "That there's nothing anyone can do about it."

"But we've known about Garth for a while," I said. "This point in time was inevitable—maybe it's for the best that we get it over with. Let it go. In any situation there's good and bad. For every Garth dying there's a Sean Valve going places. Tonight is Sean's night, and it's supposed to be about fun and success. Lighten up, for his sake. For my sake.'' It sounded terminally superficial, but if this was going to be a night out with the sulkers, I might as well have stayed home and listened to the rest of Vivien's phone message. If I had said any more, I'm sure it would have led to a cue for a Jerry Herman song.

"Don't be such a gloomy Gus," said a voice—Starla's voice. I had said that entire speech just for her, because I knew she'd overhear and agree wholeheartedly. Bam, it worked—I still had the magic. "Vinnie's right," she said. "Lighten up." We sounded like the kids from *River's Edge,* unable to summon much emotion about their friend's murder, but we looked better. "You look incredible," Starla gushed over me, the first time she'd commented on my appearance since her Ne Plus Ultra fete (so the yogurt worked too). She didn't look bad herself, especially glowing on the arm of her new celebrity friend—not Rachel Chaparal, who must have split town without returning her calls, but Lance Marano, who had obviously left Angela ("Not Hot") Burdine in the dust in favor of this tantalizing bundle of estrogen. So many queries raced through my mind: Were they really fucking? Had *she* snagged *him* or vice versa? How much press would she get for this? But I let it drop, knowing the answers could only hurt. Besides, they had already ambled on to schmooze with somebody else; I wasn't going to find out a single thing.

Revelatory moments of other famous folk were available to be absorbed anyway. The movie's stars—Stephanie, Michael, and Dale—were not gingerly perched in the roped-off Shangri-La usually reserved for those of boldface caliber; they were stomping around the room. In fact, Dale had already tied a few dozen on, so she was as far removed from the inscrutable diva her press had painted her as being as I was from a Dartmouth student. All her previous Greta Garbo career moves must have been engineered by some old, cigar-chomping troll who assumed a star had to be aloof, icy, and untouchable, a sacred cow. But thanks to Scotch lib, the real Dale was emerging, and she turned out to be a wild, undetoxifiable harpie who loved to jump spreadeagle onto men's waists and perform a slam-pogo while screaming lines from *Buckaroo Banzai*. That's just what she was doing with Sean, until Doric got wind of this and saw it as a chance to be brazenly heterosexual in public. He yanked her off Sean, stood her up like a mannequin, and wrapped her arms around his own neck as she complied in Gumby-like fashion. Joined together at the shoulder, they slow-danced to a fast song in a manner so eerie it will be remembered always. I'm sure she had no idea who he was, nor did she care, as long as he gave her a neck to hang onto. *He* would have impregnated her right there on the spot if everyone hadn't been watching—though with Doric, that was usually an incentive.

It was kind of creepy that Sean's avant-garde characters were being played by these major movie stars who reeked of Rodeo Drive skin clinics and pasta salads in hot tubs. It violated all the principles of everything the underground was supposedly based on, yet no one was too upset about it, least of all Mary-Ellen, who beamed, "The character Dale plays is based on me."

"An artist?" I said, nobly trying to keep up my end of the conversation.

"An architect," she said huffily, annoyed that I didn't know this latest development in her multimedia career. So her art had sold so well she could afford to become an architect. What a sick puppy.

Sean, intoxicated by so many things, came over and put his arm around me and said, "Pretty big deal, huh? Movie, movie, movie!" I got down on my knees, made the sign of the cross, and sang "Praise to Buddha" at him in all seriousness. I hoped he wouldn't notice I was mixing metaphors.

"I hated you for a long time," he said, "but now I can deal with you as someone with an intangible, but probable, reason for living." Sean hated everyone for six months, then liked them. The key was to ignore him for a while as if you were totally intimidated by his greatness, then throw him for a loop with the "Praise to Buddha" routine. "You know," he said, "I was going to invite you, because the list opened up a little bit, but I couldn't get ahold of your number."

"Really?" I said, almost exploding with joy. So I *had* been invited. I *did* belong here. This was the greatest news since Barbra Streisand got rid of her perm. I kissed Sean sloppily on both cheeks, in the shameless way perfected by Aunt Jo Butch, then realized I'd gone far too far and crossed the boundary of decorum. You're not supposed to get so familiar this soon. He schlumped away, wiping himself off with cocktail napkins and probably mentally etching me back onto the shit list.

"Delroy," I said, grabbing him deliriously. "Guess what? Sean said he was going to invite me anyway."

"But he didn't," quipped Delroy, bitterly. Leave it to a friend to put your triumphs into true perspective. What happened to the Pollyanna I used to love? Delroy truly needed some lightening-up dust. So did I.

Everyone in the room was coupling off, except for me, Delroy, and Mary-Ellen. I couldn't even work up a mental boner for my inevitable partner—myself—anymore. I guess I was experiencing the proverbial twenty-three-year itch. Without even the pseudodate Starla to lean on, the loneliness I'd been running from had caught up with me, and there were no distractions from panic—no love, success, or even witty conversation to take my mind off the absence of stimulus in my life. Having finally rented *Willy Wonka and the Chocolate Factory* (brilliant) and *War and Peace* (awful), it was time to leave the VCR behind and come alive with pleasure, like on those Newport ads. I was tired of looking into the fishbowl without swimming—I wanted some real action for a change. I still abhorred intimacy, but I finally felt like I might be ready to try it and find out why.

In a fit of hell-bent recklessness, I ordered baby's first drink: a vodka straight up. I figured cranberry juice or any other mixer would only complicate things. I downed it like medicine, making a point of not pausing to notice that it tasted even worse than medicine, maybe like kerosene or some kind of Windex-Plus mess. Calling up my sense memory skills once more, I pretended it was a delicious, syrupy lime rickey, and hell, the shit sure worked wonders for Dale, no matter how it tasted. The drink shot through my system like a race car, loosening my defenses to the point where I couldn't censor my thoughts anymore, so my mouth never stopped, and God knows what was coming out of it. Booze frees you to do and say whatever you want, and the great thing is, it's not until the next day that you realize what a fool you were. By then, you're supposed to apologize, but everyone else was so gone, they never remember what you said either.

My head was buzzing, my tongue was tingling, and I felt no pain as I wafted around the room like a badminton birdie, without a thought in my mind except to try to collect myself and savor this sensation—I'd learned from other popular vices (except sex) that the first time is invariably the best. Fortified with my new ammunition, I was way too unruly to find a mating partner—you're supposed to get loose, not totally bent out of shape—but I did get up the nerve to confront Starla. She was deep in a huddle with Lance, but how deep a huddle could it possibly have been?

"What was I?" I said, rambunctiously, interrupting them without compunction. It was a line from a movie, but I forget which one.

Starla looked taken aback, in a poised kind of way. Lance looked too blitzed even to care about what was going on—he was yet another glaring exception to the new sobriety.

"What were you?" Starla repeated. "You mean in a past life? Probably an Ethiopian king, I'd say, or maybe a Roman emperor. Wouldn't *you*, Lance?" Why is it that in past lives no one's ever a cotton picker or a Fuller Brush man?

"No. I mean what was I to you? Just another step on the ladder? Did you even like me?" Miniature Mount Rushmores of spittle were collecting at the sides of my mouth—it was not pretty.

"You're a friend," she said, reassuringly. "Don't be silly. You meant a lot to me—still do. Don't be insecure about yourself. You always do that. Buddy!" She held out her hand for a shake, power lunch-style. I would have had more respect for her if she'd slapped me with it and told me I was rat shit.

I never got to complete the handshake, thank God. Our tender moment was cut short by a news flash that had started close to the entrance and finally worked its way to us in a buzz: it was over for Garth—no more ticking, no more opportunistic infections, no more gossip vigil. He had died late that afternoon—toothless (the infections had hit his gums) and shaking uncontrollably under a dozen blankets. "It's over!" someone shrieked, with the tragic Greek delivery of an Irene Pappas.

Reactions ranged from hysteria to shock as the information was passed around—no one was sure where it came from, though no one doubted its veracity for a second. I hadn't seen so much horror in one place since I caught *The Tingler,* in "spine-chilling Percepto!" The room rumbled with a barnyard's worth of sobs, wails, and tsk-tsking—that clucking noise that makes nails scraping on a blackboard sound like chamber music by comparison.

But the funny thing was, after that got over with, the subject never came up again. Everyone had written Garth off long ago. No one, myself included, wanted his death to ruin this event, and a few seemed annoyed that it almost did. In a matter of minutes, I heard people return unaffected to their conversations about things like Orson Welles's caffeine addiction and Macintosh versus IBM, as if some all-powerful acting coach had snapped his fingers and said, "Change mood." I proceeded to ask Lance drunkenly whether he could tell the difference between Rosanna Arquette and Rebecca De Mornay, and was making no connection whatsoever, as he was preoccupied with trying to locate the source of a certain aroma only he seemed to notice. "Who cut the cheese?" he kept asking. "I'll bang the fucking skull into a pulp of whoever the wanker is who cut the fucking cheese."

The only one still doing the previous mood was Delroy, who was holding onto the mammoth second hand of the big clock, which actually lifted him a few feet off the ground as, oblivious, he wept. He'd still be rockin' around the clock if I hadn't pulled him off. I sent him home to do some silent mourning. I stayed for more vodkas and eventually trailed home alone and slept for sixteen hours.

If funerals were the parties of the eighties, then Garth's was one of the best parties of the decade. The dazzle! The turn-out! The festivity! They don't throw 'em like this anymore.

The service was held at St. Christopher's in the East Village, near where Garth used to live in a $175,000-a-studio co-op of the type that was increasingly common in this former wasteland of struggling artists and drug dealers. As upscale buildings shot up to gloss the East Village landscape, they displaced the artistic sorts that had made it so hot in the first place, burying alive a lot of tensions that would inevitably have to come back twice as alarmingly, à la *Poltergeist*. These tensions had already started to regurgitate— the neighborhood was fighting back like gangbusters—but so far there was no contest whatsoever.

David's Cookies had replaced art galleries. The Gap had risen up where an artsy, low-priced movie theater use to be. Hoity-toity people with money, and trust-fund kids from

Jersey, were sweeping in with very little regard for the street ambience, the park noise, the funk and grit of life on the edge. The hype around the East Village had threatened to kill it; tourists came in droves, and investors were their tour guides, allowing these styleless blank slates to slide in and transform it into their own personal playground of posh. I guess I was one of those people—I'd just convinced my parents to drum up every penny they had to get me a one-bedroom there.

As I waltzed up to the church in the awakening spring sun—alone—I encountered more interconnecting dramas than anyone ever did in those Irwin Allen disaster movies. A group of skinhead white supremacist neo-Nazis were putting up posters that showed an upside-down martini glass with a line through it, a symbol that apparently meant down with the rich, or maybe just down with martinis. I stood by in fascination as they seethed anger, even in the simple act of tossing the glue from a bucket onto the church facade and flinging the poster against it as if it were a bomb. "Die a slow, painful death, rich bastards," one of them was spitting out with a vehemence aimed at no one in particular. I'd never seen so much raw hate. It's saying a lot to admit it even made *my* stomach turn.

"Eat the rich," of course, isn't the skinheads' only party premise—they also openly despise many other specialty groups—but this was the theme they'd chosen to concentrate on here, where gentrification had given their nihilistic agenda a whole new rationale. The skinheads had timed their protest to coincide with Garth's memorial, knowing all their target sectors would be right there within spitting range. Though I thought that was kind of clever, it killed me that they were defacing St. Christopher's with poorly art-directed propaganda. Still, as I can barely button my shirt, am I really the right person to tell skinheads what they can and can't do? As part of Bush's kinder and gentler America, I could only stand by and not pass judgment.

Adding to the tense scene were the homeless people milling around—not the usual good-natured desperate bums, but unruly social rejects, all coming to a bitter broil under the new, headache-inducing sun. This belligerent army created by the city's negligence—people who are getting more and more combative because, as Pete Hamill said, they have absolutely nothing to lose—were rummaging through the overflowing trash cans and picking out the nastiest-looking bottles to aim at the neo-Nazi skinheads. I don't think there was any method to their madness, they just sensed that the skinheads were not the type that would give them generous donations if they *didn't* throw the bottles, so what the hell. It seemed to me that both camps should band together—a throbbing resentment for rich people is a big thing to have in common—but no way were these two gangs going to join hands on anything. Their resentments had different origins, textures, and results, and besides, the skinheads hated blacks too, even lower-class ones.

And so, the bottle-throwing event began. One bum kept flinging bottle after bottle with a revisionist sense of aim that could probably have him murdering an entire town over a game of darts. People were ducking and screaming, both amused and scared for their lives, but nobody moved totally out of the scene for fear of missing something. Another guy was rolling bottles as if he were bowling, racking up enough gutter balls to break every record since the beginning of recorded bowling time.

Unfortunately, the skinhead law is strongly predicated on bottle returns. They scoured the pavement for the ones that hadn't smashed into bits on impact and flung them right back ten times harder, until at least one bum was gushing blood from the head, and I thought for sure I was going to pass out and die right there to make for a double funeral. A few onlookers were alarmed, but if anything, this new development drew an even bigger crowd, hungry for some Christians-versus-the-lions-type entertainment. It was turning into a lynch mob that could take either group's side, depending on the whim of the moment, as long as they could stay in the fray. Even the bleeding bum was summarily wiping off his head with parking tickets he'd removed from cars so he could get back into the free-for-all.

Two priests, meanwhile, had gotten wind of the posters and were furiously shouting these bald maniacs down, telling them it was a sin to deface the house of the Lord—an argument that didn't carry much weight for them.

"Satan is our Lord," one of the baldies said, "and he don't live in no church."

"Or no fuckin' condo," another one screamed.

"Actually, yes he does," grinned the first one. Then they let out a hail of words the priests weren't even allowed to know, let alone hear, and chalked it up as another victory when these robed ones hung their heads in horror and finally skulked back into the church. The crowd roared, some in mortification, others in guiltless glee.

The skinheads, hoarse but never silent, then turned on *them*, screaming a litany of their favorite words at various well-appointed people on the street, some of whom, residents of Garth's building, were on their way into church. A couple of these richies responded with their own unpleasantries ("What's wrong? No talk shows to do today?"), but even the fiercest of them looked like he didn't want to get *too* involved in a fracas lest it upset his daywear.

"Rich faggot pig," barked a skinhead as I tried to get closer to the entrance, and I was kind of pleased that they'd pegged me as one of the rich. "Pig," echoed the bleeding homeless man, tossing a bottle my way and hitting my fly (it was only Evian—lightweight plastic. It would take a steel girder to get any results down there). Now the neo-Nazis and the homeless seemed to be joining together—just as I'd thought they should!—and soon, I was sure, the richies would be on their side too, all in a violent conspiracy against me. I wanted to run, but didn't want to move.

Things settled into some semblance of control as a couple of cops got the skinheads to try feebly to remove the posters and chill out, but this effort at law enforcement was done with kid gloves and lots of ginger. Past public debacles, like the Tompkins Square Park riot, had tied the cops' hands a bit, and they were so afraid of brutality charges, you wondered just how much you could get away with before they'd react. Murder, anyone?

I tried to hasten my entrance but couldn't avoid the sight of a group of angry marchers from the Mad Hatters, a SCREAM affinity group, appearing from around the corner and swarming toward the church—Christ! Did some avantgarde choreographer stage all this for a pre-BAM tryout? Leatherclad and sneering, they were holding the usual array of furious banners and effigies and intoning epithets not fit for family listening—stuff they'd just screamed, to buffo response, outside Bethune Hospital. They were undoubtedly protesting something to do with Garth's death—the invalidation of old Zymurgy drink tickets?—but I couldn't wait to find out. I had a party—I mean a memorial—to catch.

Alas, as I tried to enter the church, Victor—the SCREAM guy who'd told me how fabulous the group was at the meeting—grabbed me by the elbow and made for one more, giant interruption. He was a whole different person from the one who'd wryly showed me their clippings, and not just because he was wearing a "Mad" hat. He was screaming at me that Bethune had taken all mention of pneumonia off Garth's records, on his brother's urging. His face clenched into the wrath of a pit bull's, he was yelling, "What are you trying to hide, Bethune?" Coming right up into my face, he shouted at the top of his lungs, "Garth died of AIDS! Do you hear me—AIIIIIDDDDDSSSS!" What was he getting on *my* case for? I knew what Garth died of.

I untangled myself and pushed through the unruly crowds to the phone on the corner. I had to call my machine for messages—though I'd been out of the house for barely fifteen minutes, you just never know. Sure enough, there was a message from Mom: "Vinnie! *Vinnie!* I just saw on the TV about a building in your neighborhood that collapsed and people are dead like crazy. Was it yours? Dear God, was it yours? Pick up the phone, Vinnie. Answer me. Are you under piles of rubble and you can't get out? I told you that building didn't look solid. Whatever you do, keep breathing, keep sucking in air until help comes. Try to crawl to the phone and say something, just breathe heavy so I'll know you're alive. Vinnie? God in high heaven up above, save him!" I slammed down the phone and went to church.

Inside the small, postmodern temple of worship—the ultra-trendy kind where they probably used to hold Sunday folk masses and might someday even graduate to hip-hop—it was SRO with people who hadn't been up this early in years, and none of them seemed to have any clue that anything was going on outside. They were all dripping in the most tasteful black, with veils an appropriate excuse to camouflage their cracking, never-before-seen-in-daylight faces, and the mourning motif a chance to blot out the shattering noises from beyond the stained glass. As Spartacus delivered a touching memorial speech that unfortunately had nothing whatsoever to do with Garth—"He was a kind, gentle man, a poet, reticent to speak his opinions, caring only for others at any cost"—I scanned the room and spotted a Who's Who of everyone with any Garth connection, short of Colette Joie and Klaus Barbie. I silently ticked off the guest list. Doing it aloud might have been a little inapropos—but not *that* inapropos; this was like a disco/fashion show/memorial service, a gala reunion/event with a million times more posing than pathos. Still, I showed some respect and kept my mutterings to myself.

Starla was there, shockingly blond (did she think returning to her natural color would make her a more natural person?), with Lance, who looked pretty restless but whipped into submission by her masculine femininity. O'Dette came with a girl who couldn't have been old enough to be potty trained yet, and she was sniffing his cornrows up and down, then nibbling on them as if they were ropes of licorice. Taormina was there, looking black-widow spiderish in her lace veil and tulle-drenched dress, and, between her chain-smoking, was fidgeting in obvious desperation for a morning mimosa. (I had to nip my new taste for booze in the bud, and this was a living commercial for why.) Arianne and Marianne Ding showed up in their idea of toned-down outfits—matching green chiffon ensembles out of *Uncle Tom's Cabin* meets *Cat Women of the Moon,* via *Joanie Loves Chachi*—and next to them were the Dovima-Mimsy-Daisy trilogy, on the memorial circuit now and clearly thrilled for some new death to whine about. They were especially excited about this one, which was lending credence to their perennial complaint that Arianne/Marianne were taking over and making trashy fab again. "We'll have to change wardrobes one more time," moaned Mimsy. "I should have saved my last trashy wardrobe, not that I ever had one."

As usual, they had a point. Though Zymurgy had been cold clams for a while, it was Garth's death that put the last nail in its coffin. His brother, Marc—his only extant family—had flown in to seize control of the place and turn it into a sporting goods outlet (cleverly called Marc's). The last word was no more. Poor Spartacus would be reduced to selling bocci balls, if he was lucky enough to get a job there.

The Dings, meanwhile, had taken Spermicidal Foam from an every-other-night attraction to a nightly need; the urge for relentless, arm's-length decadence was now a 'round-the-clock obsession as the onset of the Bush administration sent the counterculture into a more panicky frenzy than ever. I couldn't believe the Dings would really be the ruling thing, instead of a novelty some other conservative tidal wave would eventually sweep into the murk. But who knew? My next move was uncertain—to climb, jump, about-face, or pace back and forth and wait. In the meantime, I could just sit still and note some more attendees.

Jonathan Formento and Sean Valve were with Valerie Rapchuck and a couple of Hollywood types, all looking like they'd just fallen through a hole in after-hours land and were stopping here on their way to some kind of clinic. Pat had swiveled in—still a woman (maybe after two more operations). Madame Tess Tosterone came as a man (a bigger fright you've never seen—it turns out it wasn't makeup; his head really *is* ten times too big for his body). Drindl and Giorgio Donofrio were there, and for once Drindl was probably safe from his advances—though if Giorgio did finger her, he could at least confess it shortly afterward. Sandahl, of course, had to be there—it was the only "hot" event even she could get into. Delroy was in the front row with Louis Vuitton bags under his eyes it would take a U-Haul to lift, though a camera was nowhere in sight. (No matter—Stanislaw, by now a converted paparazzo, had brought *his*, and was sneaking shots when no one was looking.) Doric was right behind him with goo-goo-eyed Mary-Ellen, who was wrapped in all her recent press taped together into what she called an "ink stole," and a boy who must have been O'Dette's girlfriend's cosmic twin. Vivien came with a bald, hulking guy in one of those tuxedo T-shirts you get at novelty stores—her mystery man, I brilliantly guessed. Even Emil was there, with, of all people, Marla Hotchner (the original Starla), and a few rows behind them there was, my God, Favio. Rounding out the cast list was José, dressed in what looked like a straitjacket and those see-through, vinyl hot pants, of all abominations. He was mysteriously positioning himself in the back of the church, maybe for a quick exit. The ultracaring Diane Plewge was nowhere to be seen. Neither was Vogel—rumor had it he'd "moved back to Ohio to spend time with his parents," which meant he'd developed AIDS. This news came the same week we heard that Horton Shreibel, the gossip columnist, had AIDS too, and barely merited a flinch. All this tragedy was becoming so surreal everyone was losing touch with the most basic emotional reflexes.

It was hard to concentrate on the proceedings, what with all the obligatory waving and schmoozing going on, but that was OK, because the proceedings were drifting further and further into the twilight zone. Marc was pontificating from the podium about how the death of Garth was the death of civility in New York as we knew it, and from here on in it would be a "barbaric catch-as-catch-can." (Funny, that's just what I'd thought Zymurgy was like.) One of the speakers slipped and revealed that Garth's real name was Gary Columbo (he was half Italian, half WASP—the half that doesn't believe in wakes), a trip-up that got the biggest rise of the day. Otherwise, the service was all about what *wasn't* said. For example—true to the protestors' warnings—none of the speakers mentioned AIDS. If someone, anyone, would just utter that magic expression, a duck would certainly plop down like on *You Bet Your Life* and they'd win a cash prize.

Communion was served, and at first only a handful of people got up to receive it—this was not the most popular free buffet in recent memory. But then, perversely enough, Starla and Lance joined the line, and suddenly dozens of people jumped out of their pews to join in too, for the thrill of having communion with a major rock star and his lovely perfume pasha. ("I received communion with Lance" became the brag line of the year.) Every possible religion and species turned up on that line—I'd never seen so much devotion.

I remained seated. As a good Catholic, I know you have to confess before you can receive the host. As a good party guest, you *also* have to confess before receiving the host.

"Your generation is so confused," said a voice behind me. It was the thinly veiled Taormina—I'd only sat in front

of her because, for very good reason, it was the only seat
left. I heard a bottle smash outside, but didn't flinch. "You
know everything," she continued, "and yet you know nothing. You don't even know what you want to fuck—oops,
penetrate." She made the sign of the cross and begged the
Lord's forgiveness, then ran to join the communion line to
be near Lance. Favio had just gotten off of it, and as he
twirled back into his seat, I did a listless wave at him just as
a test, the way you'd throw spaghetti against a wall to see if
it's ready. Amazingly, he didn't spit at me, but beamed and
said, "Did you get my message? A flush!" Oh, so that's
what that sound on my machine was. I'd assumed it was
either a bad connection or someone throwing up, but now
I remembered that when Favio was ready to make up with
someone, he called them and flushed his toilet bowl. It meant
let's get rid of the shit and move on. A touching gesture,
but I had nothing to be forgiven for. If anything, I should
be the one doing the flushing. And I had—I'd flushed Favio
out long ago. God, he was three scenes ago already.

"OK, let's be friends," I mouthed, benevolently.

"Of course we're friends," said Emil, thinking I was
talking to him. I hadn't run into him since that time at
Zymurgy. If people didn't keep dying, I'd never get to see
my pals anymore.

As the priest carried out some more verbal rituals (in
English, at least—this place *was* hip), waves of nostalgia and
Catholic guilt added to the pukey mixture of emptiness and
confusion already pickling my brain. I hadn't been to church
in years, unless you wanted to count the stop I'd made to
Limelight—a church converted into a disco—for a fetish ball,
replete with tit clamps and burnt genitalia. Being here amid
the churchly smells and sounds, experiencing the painstaking, lugubrious rite of bowed heads and clanking bells, took
me back to my childhood churchgoing days, when I lived
internally, before I had to turn myself inside out in order to
make it on the social circuit. Back then, every Sunday

brought an obligatory stop to this ordered world predicated on rules and reverences the willing could regularly escape to because they'd rehearsed a belief in it, much like the party people do every night. Freaked by such a public ceremony, my favorite fantasy was that I could sit in an enclosed booth, peering out at the mass through a one-way mirror that would effectively bottle my painful lack of interpersonal skills. Even beter, I wished I could stay home behind closed doors and perform my own celebration of belief in TV sitcoms and comic books rather than be scrutinized by the entire neighborhood in the name of fervor.

A murmuring voice stunned me back into the present with the gloomy portentousness it laced into every syllable. "He's over, over, over," it said ominously, somewhere in my row. It was Jonathan Formento talking to Sean Valve, and I craned my neck to catch the gist of it—some new gossip would bring me refreshingly up to date. I couldn't even gasp when it turned out they were talking about me— "Vinnie's so over, he could be an egg"—that's how taken aback I was. Over? *Moi?* Get real, people.

To distract myself, I went through the entire guest list in my mind again, this time texturing it by playing a guessing game of "What drug are they on?": "Starla—Evian, Lance—you name it, O'Dette—valium, Taormina—you name it . . ."

As the service ended, everyone did the sign of the cross, and there was the loudest roar of party talk I'd ever heard. It was such a relief to be able to unleash all the tidbits they'd been whispering or keeping to themselves; the verbal explosion was deafening. None of the talk was about Garth—he'd never be talked about again.

Rather than join in the hubbub, Starla and Lance raced out the door—this wasn't her crowd anymore—and I didn't even get a chance to say hello-goodbye. I told myself I wouldn't miss her—this pod person was as far removed from Starla as Starla had been from Chris. Though she looked as

293

stunning as ever, I don't think I'm tooting my own horn—well, not *just* tooting my own horn—by saying she didn't glow with him the way she had with me. She was doodoo, I told myself, the only way I could deal with the loss.

Everyone else loitered for a good twenty minutes to catch up, dish and trash, without any concern for the fact that we were in a house of worship. My guilt suddenly made me very noncommittal, and as people tried to get me to dissect this one's outfit or disavow that one's friendship—"OTR," they begged, "come on, off the record"—I could only smile beatifically and utter some reassuring proverb. My *on*-the-record remarks could always turn up in the magazine. (A funeral issue would be an interestingly ironic way to revive the rag.) Or I could just keep them to myself and woo everyone with positive energy. I could become Delroy, now that he didn't seem to be Delroy anymore.

"You look incredible, O'Dette," I said, not hedging any bets just in case *he* by some miracle became the new ruler again. "I'd love to have lunch with you sometime."

Amazingly, he answered me—failure had made him delightfully humble. "I dint do linch," he gurgled. "Ownless you wint to comb over and hilp groom miy digs zumtime."

"Sounds good," I said as he slid out with his love bunny. How sad that someone had to die to get O'Dette vulnerable enough to talk to me. Even sadder, I wanted to kick myself as I noticed Arianne/Marianne slipping out too, screaming and leading an entourage of seven they'd somehow picked up like lint. I should have been working *them*. Well, Vivien was still hanging. "I love you, Vivien," I said, and she kissed me on the forehead, not introducing me to her friend, who stood by spacey-eyed, as if he wasn't really there. I could tell by his too-serious demeanor that he was wearing that ridiculous tuxedo tee not as a joke at all; the guy just had no idea how to dress.

"Love—that's what matters, isn't it?" she said magisterially, making a go for it. If she ran up to the pulpit to deliver her usual sermon, she could save the day.

"What brought you here?" I wondered, seizing her at the exit and forcing some attention out of her. "You're not the funeral type." She just pointed at her male friend, shrugged cryptically, and sped off, the hulk trailing her like a shadow. "Oh, a date," I said swiftly, but she was gone.

Mary-Ellen was doing her mock-reverent act as she glumly commiserated with Garth's brother, though I later found out she was asking if he needed any help in designing the sporting-goods store. Finally, she traipsed out with Doric and the trade, and I repressed the urge to give her a kiss and say I love you, Mary-Ellen. In its favor, it would have been a fresh move—it definitely hadn't been done before. But on the minus side, I'd never stop regretting it. I worked on Fav . . . Charles instead.

"You look so healthy, Fav . . . Charles," I said. "Thanks for the royal flush."

"Wasn't this boring?" he exclaimed, looking terribly let down. "I don't know—I've been to so many better ones."

"I thought it was fair to middling," I said, "though the speeches were from Plan Nine. And Lance Marano going for communion was really a laugh and a half."

"Now *that* was cool," said Favio. There was an unbearable tension between us that was making us strain for super casualness; normally I'd never say things like "fair to middling" and "laugh and a half."

"There was a big riot outside," I informed him, "with bums and skinheads and stuff. It's probably still going on."

"Cool! I've seen all of that on 'Geraldo,' " he exclaimed, pulling a capsule out of his baggy, but fairly regulation, pants pocket. "Here's some Essence. It's the new Ex. Two dollars more, two dollars better. Be careful, though. Do too much and in ten years all your spinal fluid will evaporate and you'll totally gimp out."

After that, we ran out of conversation, and as I scanned for other observances worth recording, Favio lingered, waiting for Doric and company to invite him along on their margarita binge. Eventually, the Doric crew just flounced out in a self-contained, prealcoholic stupor, not stopping to take Favio, or any other excess baggage, along for the ride. Delroy was behind them, not even remotely aware that he was following anyone, just sailing out in a trance that was pulled along by the magnetic force of everyone else's memorial day drive. With his blank, unblinking eyes, he looked purpose free, not the Delroy who could make you sick to your stomach with optimism. Without his camera, he didn't even look like himself anymore. He seemed incomplete, edited, the Monarch notes for a human being. "Take care, you good guy," I said compassionately, but he was too far gone to hear. Favio just stood there, both listening in and looking for his next move.

"You know Marla, don't you?" said Emil, and I found myself fawning over this has-been, contrary to all intelligence and reason, telling her she was a legend in New York nightlife, and it was great to see she'd "matured so vividly." Emil, looking pretty pasty, said they had to leave and discuss some business venture—maybe an ashram for would-be models? Because of the cumulative embarrassments I had on file about him, I bet *my* life he'd never call me again. "You look great," I screamed as he limped out the door.

As people left, José leaned over and let them pick from between his teeth an invite to his new club, Ding Dong School—so *that's* why he'd positioned himself at the exit. Garth must have been rolling in his urn (he was cremated, not buried in the Zymurgy dollar bill casket).

"You look so thin. You probably have AIDS," José screeched at me, laughing uproariously at his own wit as I picked an invitation. That magic word. I couldn't get mad; it turned out that under his straitjacket, both his arms were in casts, no doubt as a result of a double whammy of karma.

Within minutes, Favio was following José to help him hand—and mouth—out some more invites around town, proving once again that when all else fails, indentured servitude can provide a long-delayed path back to fabulous.

A few skinheads had finally gained entrance into the church to wreak some havoc, a sign from God to leave. Outside, there were enough maniacs left to ensure a second act of flesh-crawling entertainment. As her boyfriend stood on the sidelines looking sweaty and uncomfortable, Vivien had joined the Mad Hatters, which was now jeering and taunting the homophobic skinheads with remarks like, *"You're* the plague, and there is no cure." The homeless were taking both sides, some yelling, "Burn in hell, homos," others saying, "Eat a bag of shit and die, baldies." Police were gathering around like birds, still not too anxious to lift a finger.

By now I might have been getting ready for my last finals and would have to know some bloody answers. Like, what was I going to do to make the magazine less of an anchor weight—just cut the damned thing loose and set it adrift? How could I work up the guts to get it up, in every feasible way, and stop blaming Melissa Kravitz for everything, from my fear of tongues to my utter revulsion for chocolate milkshakes? It would be nice to make something palpable out of the urge I had at Haute to actually start experiencing pleasure. But whom and what did I want? Once, I looked at a *People* magazine photo of Sly Stallone and Vanna White together and was disturbed to find them both vaguely appealing in their shimmery, robotic perfection. What did that signify? An illiteracy fetish?

Maybe these questions could be dealt with another semester, another day. And did any of this matter anyway, with macrophages waiting to explode in my body like viral grenades? What have you learned, Dorothy? Questions, damned questions. I popped an allergy pill, vowing to be true to my mother, at least.

I was stunned out of my reverie by Vivien's mystery hulk, who creeped up on me so unexpectedly, I almost jumped out of my skin. In his awesome hairlessness, he was kind of ominous-looking, but not a troll (or skinhead) at all. He looked more like Mr. Clean than Kojak—someone you'd welcome into your kitchen, though his jerky moves and highly distracting stammer made him more of a social outie than anyone in the Dukakis family. I thought Vivien could do better, but she could do a lot worse too—oh, God, couldn't I work up a firm opinion on anything? At least this guy had a cretinlike sincerity that's a very scarce commodity on the club scene. He even made eye contact.

"Y . . . y . . . you're not a b . . . b . . . bad guy," he finally said, after trying to launch a sentence for about five smashed bottles' worth of riot. "I'd love it if you re . . . re . . . reevaluated your life and d . . . did something." I stood there miserably as he tried to get out another utterance, but at long last he sputtered into defeat, and I grimaced in embarrassment.

Now it was my turn to think of something to say. "I feel like I'm being pushed off the edge of a cliff by a herd of rhinos," I grinned good-naturedly. "V . . . Vinnie," I added, holding out my hand and even stuttering a little; it's catching.

"I know. H . . . H . . . Heinz," he said, without any expression, and walked off to capture Vivien and leave. So that was the magnificent Heinz. A man of few words, but such words they were. "Vloolv," I never got to say to him. A bottle almost hit my head, and might have killed me right then and there. But almost only counts in horseshoes.